W9-CFV-970

Praise for Repairman Jack: The Early Years

"Fun reading."
—*Roundtable Reviews* on *Dark City*

"Sure to excite Wilson's legion of fans by shedding
more light on the background of their
favorite 'fix-it' man."
—*SirReadaLot* on *Dark City*

"If fans want to know how Repairman Jack
became the champion of the victimized,
they've got to pick up *Cold City*. It's a one-night
read that will keep the lights burning."
—*RT Book Reviews* (4½ stars)

"Refeshingly nimble . . . A breath of fresh air."
—*Booklist* on *Cold City*

"Guns blaze, fists fly, Jack plots, and bad guys get
what's coming to them. With a pulse-pounding pace,
this book reminds the reader about everything
they love about Repairman Jack."
—*Crimespree Magazine* on *Cold City*

ALSO BY F. PAUL WILSON

REPAIRMAN JACK NOVELS*

The Tomb
Legacies
Conspiracies
All the Rage
Hosts
The Haunted Air
Gateways
Crisscross
Infernal
Harbingers
Bloodline
By the Sword
Ground Zero
Fatal Error
The Dark at the End
Nightworld

THE TEEN TRILOGY*

Jack: Secret Histories
Jack: Secret Circles
Jack: Secret Vengeance

THE EARLY YEARS TRILOGY*

Cold City

THE ADVERSARY CYCLE*

The Keep
The Tomb
The Touch
Reborn
Reprisal
Nightworld

OTHER NOVELS

Healer
Wheels Within Wheels
An Enemy of the State
*Black Wind**
Dydeetown World
The Tery
*Sibs**
The Select
Virgin
Implant
Deep as the Marrow
Mirage
  (with Matthew J. Costello)
Nightkill (with Steven Spruill)
Masque
  (with Matthew J. Costello)
The Christmas Thingy
Sims
The Fifth Harmonic
Midnight Mass
The Proteus Cure
  (with Tracy L. Carbone)

SHORT FICTION

Soft and Others
*The Barrens and Others**
*Aftershock & Others**
*The Peabody-Ozymandias
  Traveling Circus &
  Oddity Emporium**
*Quick Fixes**
Sex Slaves of the Dragon Tong

EDITOR

Freak Show
Diagnosis: Terminal

* See "The Secret History of the World" (page 423).

F. PAUL WILSON

DARK CITY

A REPAIRMAN JACK NOVEL

THE EARLY YEARS TRILOGY: Book Two

TOR®

A TOM DOHERTY ASSOCIATES BOOK
NEW YORK

NOTE: If you purchased this book without a cover, you should be aware that this book is stolen property. It was reported as "unsold and destroyed" to the publisher, and neither the author nor the publisher has received any payment for this "stripped book."

This is a work of fiction. All of the characters, organizations, and events portrayed in this novel are either products of the author's imagination or are used fictitiously.

DARK CITY

Copyright © 2013 by F. Paul Wilson

All rights reserved.

Edited by David G. Hartwell

A Tor Book
Published by Tom Doherty Associates, LLC
175 Fifth Avenue
New York, NY 10010

www.tor-forge.com

Tor® is a registered trademark of Tom Doherty Associates, LLC.

ISBN 978-0-7653-6804-1

Tor books may be purchased for educational, business, or promotional use. For information on bulk purchases, please contact Macmillan Corporate and Premium Sales Department at 1-800-221-7945, extension 5442, or write specialmarkets@macmillan.com.

First Edition: October 2013
First Mass Market Edition: November 2014

Printed in the United States of America

0 9 8 7 6 5 4 3 2 1

To David Hartwell

Many years . . .

Many books . . .

Many edits . . .

Many thanks

ACKNOWLEDGMENTS

Thanks to the ususal crew for their efforts: my wife, Mary; David Hartwell, Marco Palmieri, and Becky Maines at the publisher; Steven Spruill; Elizabeth Monteleone; Dannielle Romeo; and my agent, Albert Zuckerman.

Special thanks to Tony Harrington for his input.

And a tip of the hat to Dennis N. Griffin and Andrew DiDonato for their wonderfully informative book, *Surviving the Mob: A Street Soldier's Life Inside the Gambino Crime Family*. An invaluable resource for a certain character in the trilogy.

—F. Paul Wilson
the Jersey Shore

SATURDAY

FEBRUARY 23, 1991

1. The van speeding down Seventh swerved toward him as he stepped off the curb. Would have ripped off a kneecap if he hadn't spotted it out of the corner of his eye and jumped back in time.

He'd come to West 23rd Street hunting lunch. Despite its grit and grime and unabashedly crass commercialism—or maybe because of it—Jack dug the big two-way cross street. Only a few blocks from his apartment, its mostly tiny storefronts offered a cross section of all the low-end merchandise available throughout the city, a mishmash of deep-discount, off-brand electronics, cheap luggage, Gucci knockoffs, the ever-present XXX peep shows, a dizzying selection of ethnic fast foods, plus an endless variety of VHS tapes, music cassettes, and CDs—all bootleg.

The humanity crowding the sidewalks was always varied, but on a Saturday at midday, despite the February cold, even more so. As a white guy in jeans and a denim jacket over a flannel shirt, Jack was barely noticeable among the yellow, black, and various shades of mocha, the saried Hindus, turbaned Sikhs, straights, gays, and unsures, socialists and socialites, bankers and bohos, tourists and transvestites, holies and harlots, felons and fashion victims, viragos and virgins, commies and capitalists, artistes and Aryans.

He was going to miss the bustling energy when he

moved uptown, but reminded himself it would remain just a few subway stops away.

Still, despite all the varied bright colors, the city had a dark feel. The recession was holding on, casting a pall that refused to lift, and everyone was feeling it.

Back in the day, his father used to come into the city now and then to visit Uncle Stu in his three-story brownstone a little ways downtown and toward Eighth Avenue. Sometimes he'd drag Jack along. Dad would always come away with samples of Uncle Stu's single-malt Scotches. Long gone was the Nedick's where they'd stop and grab hot dogs with the weird rolls and delicious pickle mustard. A McDonald's filled its shoes now, but as much as he liked Big Macs, he wasn't in burger mode at the moment. He eyed the line of chromed street carts along the curb. One offered Sabrett hot dogs—pass— while another offered mystery meat on a stick—pass again.

He paused near Seventh Avenue, before the redbrick and wrought-iron façade of the Chelsea Hotel. Across the street he spotted a gyro cart he'd visited in the past. The owner, Nick, had a vertical propane rotisserie that he used to cook the meat. He fresh-carved the slices and wrapped them in a pita with onions and a cucumber-yogurt sauce. Jack's mouth was already watering. Yeah, that would do nicely.

That was when he'd stepped off the curb. That was when the gray, unmarked commercial van damn near killed him.

It swerved to a screeching halt a half dozen feet away and he took a step toward it, ready to give the driver hell. But then the side panel slid back and three dark-skinned guys about his age erupted from within. Two wore beads and had scarf-wrapped heads, the third wore a backward trucker cap—typical streetwear, nothing special. Then Jack noticed that all three carried short, shiny machetes and looked out for blood. When Rico leaned out the front passenger window and screamed something in Spanish, Jack got the picture.

He turned and ran.

Last fall he'd been leading an uncomplicated life as a cash-paid landscaper/gardener, the lone gringo among Dominican immigrants in a five-man crew for Two Paisanos Landscaping. Rico, a member of that crew, came to view Jack as a rival for his leadership position. Pre-Jack, he'd been the boss's go-to guy. After Jack joined, Giovanni Pastorelli came to depend more and more on Jack because they shared English as a first language. The seething Rico began to ride Jack, most times via colorful Dominican insults that went beyond Jack's rudimentary Spanish, occasionally punctuated by a push or a bump. Jack realized the problem but didn't see what he could do about it, so he let it ride for months until the day Rico culminated a week of relentless heckling with a sucker punch to the jaw.

Jack still didn't remember much of what happened next. Apparently he flashed into berserker mode, launching a Hells Angels–style counterattack so vicious it left him in shock and a battered Rico coiled on the ground clutching a ruined knee.

The other Dominicans were Rico's buddies who used machetes to clear brush. The boss, Giovanni, fearing Jack would end up with one of those blades in his back, had fired him for his own safety.

It should have ended there. But for some reason it hadn't. Giovanni had mentioned a link to a machete-wielding street gang called DDP—Dominicans Don't Play—and told Jack he'd better get himself a gun. Jack had bought that gun but didn't have it on him now—he'd only stepped out to grab some lunch, for Christ's sake.

Jack raced west, putting some distance between himself

and his pursuers. He glanced over his shoulder and no-ticed the three *matóns* after him all wore baggy gangsta jeans halfway down their asses. That had to slow them down. He recognized the one in the trucker cap—Ramon—from Giovanni's landscaping crew, but the other two were strangers. DDP members? Why wasn't Rico, the guy with the biggest grudge, among them? Had he gone in another direction, trying to flank him?

Couldn't think about that now. Subway entrance ahead near Eighth Avenue. That van could be in motion, complicating things. Best to get off the street. A subter-ranean wind blew against his face as he scrambled down the white-tiled gullet into the token area. Train arriving. No time for a token and no transit cop in sight, so he waved to the attendant as he raced past the booths, hopped atop the turnstile, and leaped across. Good luck to his pursuers trying a turnstile hop in those saggy pants.

The fetid gale was stronger here, flowing up from the subway platforms one level below. A DOWNTOWN sign hung above a stairway to his left, UPTOWN over another to his right. He didn't care which direction he went, all he wanted was to go-go-go. The big question: Where was the train arriving—uptown or downtown side?

The wind began to die with the tortured *screeee* of train brakes.

Where-where-where?

The sound echoed from all directions, but seemed louder from the left. Without breaking stride he veered toward the DOWNTOWN sign. As he pelted down the stairs he saw the train pull to a stop below. An A train. Great. Get on that and he could take it all the way to Far Rockaway if he wished.

The loose weekend crowd on the platform gravitated toward the train as the doors slid back. Jack darted among the travelers, debating whether to take the train or climb the next set of stairs back up and crouch near the top while his pursuers boarded the train in search of him. Then he saw a rag-topped face peer over the railing.

No dummies, these *matóns*. And they moved fast despite their potato-sack jeans.

The guy on the steps let out a high-pitched howl as Jack raced by. The arriving passengers had left the train and hit the stairs by then. Jack reached the third set and faked going up a few steps, then leaped over the rail and through the subway doors just as they started to close.

The DDPer closest behind him didn't make it. He jabbed his machete through the crack, barely missing Jack. It had black symbols carved into its chromed surface. He tried to use it to pry open the doors, but the train had started moving and that wasn't going to happen. Ramon and the other DDPer came up behind their buddy and the trio made all sorts of gestures—shaking fists, pointing fingers—while shouting threats in Spanish. As they slid away, Jack refrained from any taunts, just stared and concentrated on catching his breath while the adrenaline buzz faded.

What would they have done with those machetes if they'd caught him? Decapitate him?

And why wasn't Rico with them? Because he *couldn't* be with them? Because Jack had screwed up his knee so bad he had to stay back in the truck?

Shit. Jack hadn't meant to hurt him like that. Well, yeah, he must have wanted to hurt him in the moment—wanted to kill him, in fact—but to think that he'd caused permanent damage to a guy just for acting like a dumbass . . . he didn't like that.

This rage percolating within . . . he was a little better at controlling it now. A little . . .

He pressed the side of his face against the window, expecting to see a receding cluster of *matóns* on the edge of the platform, and maybe hoping Rico would be with them. Instead he saw them running beside the train. They'd stuck their machetes in their belts and were climbing into the spaces between the cars behind his.

Crap! They weren't giving up.

Jack started weaving forward through the three-quarter-full car. Fourteenth Street was the next stop but the train was moving so slowly, he'd run out of train before then. As he opened the sliding door to move to the next car, he looked up. Blackness above. A soot-darkened tunnel ceiling. How much clearance? Two feet? Six? Subway surfers were doing it—at least that was what the papers said. Why couldn't he?

Well, he could climb up there, no problem. But could he survive? Stories abounded about some of those subway surfers having fatal encounters with low-hanging crossbeams.

He closed the door behind him and looked back through the car he'd just left. A DDPer was just opening the door at the rear end. Pretty clear nothing good was going to happen to Jack if he stayed at floor level. He had a feeling his only chance to come through this intact was up there.

He braced a foot on one of the side chains, then hauled himself up on the right handrail. He poked his head above the roof level and got a faceful of wind. Wan wash from caged bulbs set in the tunnel walls revealed the subway car's beveled roof, its smooth surface broken along the center by a series of low vents. Jack would have much preferred a flat roof—that curved surface made it too easy to slide off. Maybe he should rethink—

The door to the car he'd just left slid open. A quick glance showed the top of a scarf-wrapped head.

With no other choice, Jack scrambled up and started crawling along the filthy car roof. He heard a clang, felt a vibration near his trailing foot, and knew the *matón* had slashed at him with his machete. Jack increased his crawl speed, dragging himself along through the caked layers of soot and pigeon droppings—the A train ran aboveground for much of its outer-borough route—and didn't look back until he'd reached the first vent. The DDPer had just gained the roof and started crawling after him.

Shit.

Jack was half turned to face him when he felt a stinging impact just below his left shoulder. The guy had taken a wild, full-extension slash with his blade and connected. His dark eyes held a kind of crazy glee and he grinned through a wispy goatee as he raised his machete for another swing. But a passing crossbeam caught the blade and ripped it from his fingers, sending it flying with a ringing *clang*. That leveled the playing field.

"Now we're even, asshole!"

Jack felt the darkness rising. He resisted a mad urge to slide toward him, stick his thumbs in his eyes, and pop them from their sockets.

The strobing lights showed the guy's pained expression and Jack could tell by the way he tucked his left hand against his chest that the blow must have hurt—sprained his wrist no doubt.

"Hope you broke it!"

Furious, the DDPer raised his head and shouted something Jack didn't catch just as another crossbeam flashed by close above, tearing the scarf from his head. The glee left his eyes as his expression turned terrified. He did a reverse belly-scramble and slid back down between the cars.

Yeah, you gotta be bugfuck nuts to come up here.

Jack checked his arm. The denim jacket was sliced over his deltoid and blood seeped through. He'd barely felt it when it happened, but it hurt now. Damn, that blade must have been sharp.

He resumed his forward belly crawl along the roof, not sure if he should stop in the middle or try to make it to the next car. He paused midway, then kept moving, despite the pain in his left shoulder. If he could hop the gap to the next car . . .

Light ahead. The 14th Street station. The train started to brake, sliding Jack forward toward the gap. As it pulled into the station, he looked ahead and saw no crossbeams overhead. He took that as a signal to rise to a crouch and move. The deceleration pushed him to a higher speed than he intended, scaring him a little, but that turned into a good thing when he reached the gap just as a familiar face popped up for a look.

Ramon must have worked his way to the forward end of the car to cut Jack off should he try just what he was doing. His eyes went wide when he saw Jack charging him. He raised his machete but too late. Jack leaped the gap just as the train ground to a halt. Ramon lost his perch with the stop and, arms flailing, dropped to the inter-car platform.

But he wasn't down long. As the doors hissed open below, Ramon was crawling up to the roof behind Jack and giving chase.

Mind racing in search of a plan, Jack kept loping forward. Jump off to the platform? He glanced down and saw the debarking passengers weaving out among the new ones shuffling in. The car roof wasn't that far above the platform but a jump ran the risk of landing wrong—just a little off and his knee could twist or his ankle could go under, leaving him a sitting duck. Then he saw a DDPer, the one who'd lost his scarf and machete, watching him from the platform as he wrung his injured wrist.

That put a jump out of the question, so he hopped the gap to the next car.

Again, no sign of Rico. Because he wasn't able to get around?

Couldn't think about that now. Had to do *something*—and quick, because he was running out of train. Only two and a half more cars to go. He heard the doors below slide shut so he dropped to his knees and braced himself for the lurching start. Looking back he saw Ramon still on his feet and closing fast. He was trotting atop the car behind, grinning and brandishing his garden-variety black-steel machete. He hopped the gap between his car and Jack's—

—just as the train bucked forward. The sudden move made his leap fall short. His sneaker made toe contact with the car roof's rear edge, then slipped off. His expression turned from fierce grin to shock and fear as he dropped out of sight.

But not for long. Seconds later, as the train entered the tunnel, he was up again and coming Jack's way, though this time in a crawl instead of a run. The train picked up speed and the wind carried Ramon's trucker's cap away, but he didn't seem to mind. Jack continued his own crawl to the forwardmost vent duct on the roof and clung to it. He was counting on Ramon to keep coming. And he did.

Ramon and Rico and the rest of Giovanni's DR crew had been living in Brooklyn. Probably never rode the Eighth Avenue line down here. Didn't know that it made a sharp left turn to the east toward Sixth Avenue. Jack remembered many times needing a near-death grip on one of the poles inside to keep from bouncing off other passengers as it made that turn . . . just . . . about . . .

Now.

The train lurched left and Ramon began to slide right. Jack had his arms tight around the vent and stayed put. He could see Ramon's wide, terrified eyes as he dropped his machete—two down, one to go—and scratched at the filthy, sloping surface in a frantic search for purchase.

Fat chance, pal.

Jack watched his kicking legs go over the side, heard his terrified wail as his body followed, saw his clawed hands rake the roof all the way to the edge where they caught the lip, leaving Ramon clinging to the side of the train by his fingertips.

Jack fought the wild urge to slide over and kick at those fingertips, dumping Ramon off the train. He'd bang off the side wall, bounce against the train, get spun around and around until he either fell to the tracks where he'd end up ground meat, or get caught on the outside and be dragged into West 4th. Either way, he'd be eliminated as a threat.

But he held back, remembering how he'd let his rage take over with Rico. Look where that had put him.

Instead he imagined the view from inside the car: Ramon's panicked face pressed against the outside of a window, his prolonged scream drowned in the train noise. Would anyone look up and see? Maybe, maybe not. Would anyone pull the emergency stop cord? Again, maybe, maybe not, but leaning toward not. New Yorkers resented anyone or anything that slowed their subway ride. They might write him off as just another jerk working a variation on subway surfing. Might even *want* him to fall off.

The train straightened out, but Jack knew it wouldn't be long before it angled right to enter the West 4th Street station, a big nexus point at Sixth Avenue where a half dozen or more subway lines crossed.

The train pulled into the low-ceilinged station and Jack had to stay down if he wanted to keep his head. As it stopped and the doors opened, he peeked over the right edge of the roof and saw the two DDPers rush out and peel a shaken, weak-kneed Ramon off the side of the car.

Okay, no getting out that way.

To the left, over the wall, he heard a train approaching. The uptown tracks were over there.

He rose to standing between a pair of crossbeams and looked over. Another A train was pulling into the station. The beams ran above the wall. If he could get over there . . .

Ignoring the oily grime and rat turds, Jack took hold of the beam before him. His left hand, slick with blood dripping down his arm from his shoulder, slipped. He wiped it dry on his jacket, then hopped up onto the beam and began to crawl along on his hands and knees. He couldn't help but think of gymnasts he'd seen doing cartwheels and flips on something just about this wide. How the hell did they manage?

When he reached the wall he came to a vertical support that ran up into the dark. He had to rise to his feet and swing around it. A hairy maneuver, especially here. Falling off the far side would be a disaster—at best he'd lie crippled on the tracks; at worst he'd land on the third rail and get fried by six zillion volts.

He heard a shout behind him and a machine-gun rattle of Spanish. A look back showed one of the *matóns* on the car roof he'd just left. This guy still had his head scarf and machete. He hopped up on the same crossbeam and started crawling Jack's way.

Okay, no time for caution. That uptown A would be pulling out in seconds. Jack did a Wallenda along the next beam, arms out, one foot in front of the other. The train's brakes hissed as they released. It started rolling.

"No, dammit!"

Another vertical beam. Almost there. Jack swung recklessly around it and stepped on the horizontal on the far side. His sneaker landed on something squishy—a fresh rat turd?—and his foot slipped out from under him.

Oh, shit, he was falling.

At the last second he kicked out against the upright with his other foot, allowing him to belly flop onto the slowly moving roof of the uptown A. The air whooshed out of him on impact.

He gasped, struggling for a breath. Christ, that hurt.

Still fighting for air, he managed to turn onto his side and watch the DDPer go into a half crouch, ready to jump, then change his mind. As the train picked up speed, Jack waved, then rolled onto his back, temporarily wiped out.

2. After a brief rest to catch his breath and settle his nerves, Jack slid down between the cars before the train reached 14th. He'd planned to go inside and sit but, after looking down at himself—filthy, bloody, bedraggled, like a homeless guy who'd just ended a weeklong bender with a knife fight—he decided to ride the space between. He entered the car only after it pulled out of the 72nd Street station and avoided eye contact with anyone for the rest of his trip.

During the week the A train ran as an express most of the time, skipping from 59th Street all the way to 125th. But on weekends it ran as a local, allowing him to get off at 81st Street.

Back up on street level, he found a phone and called Abe.

"*Isher Sports.*"

"Hey, Abe, it's Jack."

"*You don't sound like Jack. Blechedich, you sound.*"

Jack didn't know what *blechedich* meant, but if it started with "blech," it probably meant something close to how he felt—which was pretty blech.

"Got a bit of a cut."

"*Oy vey. Stab cut or slice cut?*"

"A slice cut—upper arm."

"*A stitches-needing cut?*"

"You better believe it."

"*Okay, I know someone who can help. But cash only he takes.*"

Jack smiled. He'd figured he wouldn't have to tell Abe that he couldn't go to a hospital because of the identity issues and because the hospital might feel a need to report it.

"Yeah, well, I forgot to renew my Blue Cross anyway. He's a doctor?"

"*Sort of.*"

"What kind of 'sort of'? You're not sending me to a vet, are you?"

"*No-no-no. A regular MD he's got. It's a license he lacks.*"

"Swell."

"*I'll give you the address and call ahead to let him know you're coming.*"

"What's his name?"

"*Hargus.*"

3.   The guy who opened the door to the small, third-floor walk-up apartment had a wrinkled face despite his portly physique. Didn't seem old enough for all those wrinkles. The Wilford Brimley mustache was impressive, though.

He looked Jack up and down through wire-rim glasses, his gaze lingering on the bloody shoulder. "Jee-*zus!*" he said in a deep voice with a faint southern or southwest accent. "What in tarnation did Abe send me?"

"You're Doc Hargus?"

"One and the same."

"Sorry for the dirt. Didn't have time to shower."

"Well, that's a shame, 'cause you can't come in here like that. Get undressed."

"Where?"

"Right here."

Jack looked up and down the hall. "But—"

"You got skivvies on?"

"What?"

"You goin' commando?"

"No."

He was wearing boxers under the jeans.

"Well, then, strip down to your shorts and leave everything else here."

"But—"

The guy gave him a look. "Don't tell me you're worried about anyone stealing that mess."

Jack sighed. "Guess not."

As Hargus disappeared inside, Jack stripped and got his first look at the wound—a good two-and-a-half-inch gash across the belly of his deltoid. Removing the flannel shirt dislodged a clot and the blood flow graduated from an ooze to a steady trickle. Hargus reappeared with a wad of gauze squares.

"Slap these over it and come on in."

He closed the door behind them. He had a roll of tape spindled on his index finger and he used that to fix the gauze in place.

"Bathroom's over there. Wash up those hands real good before we do anything. Face too."

Jack complied—took three scrubs before they were presentable. When he stepped back into the narrow hall, he heard a voice call from the other end.

"Down here."

He followed it to an examination room where the doc had a suturing set laid out next to an open bottle of Pilsner Urquell. He lifted the bottle with a latex-gloved hand and took a swig as he gestured for Jack to sit next to him.

"Let's take a look at that."

He peeled off the blood-soaked gauze and peered at the wound. He took a pair of tweezers and probed around. Jack couldn't see what he was doing, but he could feel it—a creepy sensation but not terribly painful.

"What sort of blade did this?"

"Machete."

Doc's eyebrows lifted. "I'd've said something sharper, like a bowie knife or a box cutter."

"This wasn't your mother's machete. This was chromed and seriously honed."

"Well, you're lucky. It cut through the full thickness of your skin, through the subcutaneous fat—what little you've got—and just grazed the muscle."

"'Lucky' would be if he'd missed."

"The good news is, I won't have to do any subcutaneous suturing."

Jack wasn't sure why that was good, but good was good.

"And the bad news?"

"The bad news will be my bill."

"What's that gonna run?"

"Figure five hundred, give or take."

"Wow."

"Yeah, I don't have a great call for my services, but people who need me tend to need me real bad, so I charge up the wazoo. You good for it?"

Jack nodded. "Yeah, but I don't have much more than lunch money on me at the moment."

"Well, since Abe sent you, I'll assume you're good for it."

"You said 'give or take.' Give or take what?"

"I'll tell you the exact bill after I see how many sutures I have to put in to hold this thing together. Oh, and you'll need a tetanus booster too."

"Fire away."

He opened a small fridge stocked with vials of injectables and bottles of beer.

"Can you spare one of those?" Jack said, pointing to the green bottles. "You can add it to my bill."

Doc looked at him. "You old enough to drink?"

This again.

"Twenty-two last month."

"You don't look it."

"Can't help that."

"Nah, guess you can't. Probably pisses you off, doesn't it."

"Gotta say it does."

"Well, hang in there, because years from now you'll love it when the younger women make passes at you." He snorted. "A problem I never had."

He used a church key to pop the top and handed him the bottle.

"After all that dirt you were rolling around in—where the hell were you, anyway?"

Jack took a sip—*good* Pilsner—and tried to sound casual. "Top of an A train."

Doc stared at him. "No, really."

"Really. Long story."

"Well, with that kind of filth, I should put you on some antibiotic as well."

"You're the doc."

"That's the spirit. Defer to them's what knows whereof they speak." He hefted a syringe filled with clear fluid. "This is lidocaine to numb you up. Gonna burn like hellfire at first, but after that you won't feel a thing."

Jack tensed as the needle went in—not so bad—then the doc began injecting. He hadn't been kidding. Hellfire times two.

"It's okay to say 'ow' or wince," the doc said.

"No, it's not."

"Why not?"

"Because . . ." Why wasn't it? "Because it's just . . . not."

A smile lifted his mustache as he refilled the syringe for another dose. "Not manly?"

"Maybe that. But also pointless."

"Oh?"

"Do I want the pain to stop? Yes. Do I want you to stop injecting? No."

"Why not?"

"Because I want this gash closed and it will hurt more without the injections, right?"

"Right."

"There you go: Pointless."

"You always put that much thought into everything you do?"

"Try not to think. It's mostly automatic."

"Thinking's not bad."

"But overthinking's not good. I guess I'm an under-thinker. You know many overthinkers?"

"Plenty."

"Well, I'm making up for them."

"You've got an attitude, I'll hand you that."

"Not the first time I've heard that."

"I'll bet."

The pain faded. The doc clamped a curved needle trailing shiny blue thread between the jaws of some fancy, stainless steel mini-pliers.

"Looks like fishing line," Jack said.

"In a way, it is—just like nylon line, except it's sterile."

"Thanks for that. But your gloves aren't."

"How so?"

"Well, you've been holding that beer bottle."

"Not a problem. These aren't to protect you from me, they're to protect me from whatever's crawling around in your bloodstream."

"Nothing but blood."

"So you say, but I'll wear the gloves just the same."

Jack watched as he got to work, deftly piercing the skin and tying a knot to draw the edges together. Cutting the thread, then starting again. That injection had worked—didn't feel a thing.

"I figured you'd be putting in just one long thread."

"A continuous suture?" He shook his head. "Not good for what you've got here. Needs a mattress suture—individual ties. This is going to take a while. So why don't you tell me about how you wound up on the roof of a subway car."

"Okay, if you'll tell me something."

"Shoot."

"Abe said you don't have a license. How come?"

"Don't you think you should have asked me that before you let me shoot you up and start sewing?"

"I trust Abe."

Doc glanced up over his glasses. "Don't we all." He paused for a sip of his beer. "Opiates did me in. I started taking them for a herniated lumbar disk, then I started taking them because I liked the way they made me feel, then I was taking them because I couldn't imagine life without them. Stopped caring about my patients, stopped caring about my family. My marriage died and my practice dwindled. My only patients were fellow addicts. The dopers have an excellent grapevine and it got around real quick that I was an easy touch for oxycodone. Soon my practice was thriving again—as a prescription mill. Guy'd come in saying he has terrible back pain, I wouldn't examine him or anything, just scribble an Rx for whatever he wanted. He'd pay the fee and walk out with his precious little slip of paper."

"So basically you were selling prescriptions."

"Selling? I was flat-out pimping them. Some of those patients turned out to be DEA types who established a pattern and hauled me in. I got my license suspended a couple of times, made sham attempts to clean up. Finally the board rescinded it permanently. That was when I hit bottom. I finally cleaned up but they wouldn't let me back in. I'd fooled them a couple of times before and they weren't buying. So I'm reduced to this."

"You seem okay with it."

He shrugged. "I don't need a Mercedes or a big house. I'd prefer a better class of patients—no offense."

"None taken."

"I limit myself to a few beers a day, watch a lot of TV and videotapes. It ain't the high life, but it's my life."

Jeez, he thought. Sounds like me lately. Except the beer limit.

The doc said, "Now tell me the story of this wound here. And make it a good one."

Jack took another sip. "Well, it all started last fall . . ."

4. Tony and Vinny both got to their feet when Mama Amalia stopped by their table. Tony got a hug, then introduced Vinny, who got a gnarled handshake. Vinny had been here before—who hadn't?—but had never met her.

She wore widow's black and shuffled along. God knew how old she was. She'd been running her tiny Little Italy restaurant on Hester Street forever. The tourists visiting what was left of Little Italy and the few locals who weren't chinks ate in the main room at long tables covered with red-and-white checkered cloths. But she'd known Tony almost as long as she'd had the restaurant—called Amalia's, what else?—and so when he showed up, even for a late lunch like this, he got to eat in the little private room in back.

Vinny listened politely as they gabbed in Italian, then the mussels marinara arrived and she moved on.

Reseating himself, Tony "the Cannon" Campisi tucked

his napkin into his collar and stubbed out his cigarette. He was wire thin except for his deep barrel chest.

"Dig in."

He'd done all the ordering. Vinny would have preferred to order his own lunch—just on principle—but had no problem with what was coming. What wasn't to like about these mussels, linguine and clam sauce, and veal piccata with lemon and capers? Besides, if your capo wants to order for you, he orders for you, and you don't say nothing.

The waiter had brought a double order of the mussels in a big bowl, plus two smaller empty ones for the shells. They each dug in and began using their little two-tined shrimp forks to pluck the plump meats from their shells.

After a little small talk about how fucking cold it was but at least there wasn't a lot of snow and all that bullshit, Tony got down to the reason for inviting Vinny to lunch. Not that Vinny didn't know.

"Okay," Tony said. "You probably know what this is about."

"Yeah." Vinny's stomach turned sour. "Tommy."

Tony nodded. "I got all kinds a heat on me, Vinny. If John was out and about, it wouldn't be no problem. He'd tell me to handle it my way and I'd tell Tommy to get his own fucking junkyard."

Vinny raised his hands. "Everybody says the Chief's calling the shots from inside."

Back in December, when the feds raided the Ravenite Club—just around the corner from here on Mulberry Street—and hauled off Gotti and Sammy the Bull and others on a laundry list of charges, the family lost its boss and underboss in one shot. Not to worry, everyone said. The Chief right away set up a ruling panel—or like he called it, an "administration"—of four made guys to oversee the family business. That business ran to half a billion a year, so no one was taking this lightly.

"He is. But he's only calling them where the big picture's concerned. This piddly-ass shit—"

"Piddly to you, maybe."

"Look," Tony said. "You're a good soldier, and you're a smart guy. That junkyard shows you're thinking of the future, and you've shown me respect from the get-go. Don't think I ain't noticed."

The little speech seemed to wind him. He took a couple of deep breaths while he plucked his next mussel.

Vinny preferred to call it a salvage company—Preston Salvage—but he let the junkyard remark go. The idea was to have a way to show the taxman where your money was coming from. Tony had his appliance store in Ozone Park, Vinny had bought a little salvage yard in Canarsie. Aldo was related to Sammy the Nose but that didn't stop him from looking for his own situation. Tommy, though . . . Tommy "Ten Thumbs" Totaro was too fucking lazy to start his own front. The goddamn cokehead wanted in on Vinny's.

Vinny had been careful to give to Tony C a share of whatever came in. Vinny was a member of Tony's crew. As capo, Tony had a right to respect and Vinny had an obligation to show it. After all, he owed Tony for just about everything he had.

Back in the seventies, when he was nearing the end of his teens in the Flatlands, he started collecting a street tax from the pot sellers in his neighborhood. That part of Brooklyn was Gambino territory at the time, with Roy DeMeo's crew hanging at the Gemini Lounge, but none of the dealers was connected. Vinny was bigger than most of them and wasn't afraid to lay a little hurt on them as a convincer. He came from the Mangano wing of the family but his dad steered clear of all the rackets and stuff. Vinny couldn't claim direct connection with anyone currently in power, so he'd been on his own.

As time went by he teamed up with Aldo D'Amico to augment his shake-down money with smash-and-grab stuff like ripping radios out of luxury cars. Tony the Cannon was lower down the Gambino pecking order then. He didn't have the appliance store yet, but had a little social club off Avenue J where his small crew would hang out. Tommy Totaro, a couple of years older and a connected Gambino, was already in with them. Vinny and Aldo would bring the radios there and deliver them to Tony in the back room. He was paying between one-fifty and two for a digital Becker. Vinny and Aldo were so regular with their merchandise that Tony told them to hang around and call his club home. Maybe he'd have some work for them.

That was how it began. Tony brought him in, showed him the ropes, gave him work. Tony's crew grew as he worked his way into other rackets. Vinny helped Tony run his craps and card games, his numbers, and his pony parlors.

Somewhere along the line he picked up the name Vinny Donuts. He wasn't crazy about it. He liked zeppole and, with a last name like Donato paired with a big round waist, what else were they gonna call him? For a while he gave up the zeppole, but the name stuck, so finally he said, What the fuck, and went back to munching.

In the eighties, when Tony opened a used car lot, Vinny and Aldo helped him stock it. A sweet deal. He'd pay them up to five hundred apiece for any car they could steal, then change the VIN and put it on his lot. Sometimes he'd send them out on what he called "custom orders." If a guy told Tony he was in the market for a white-on-red '82 Cutlass Supreme, Vinny and Aldo would go out and find one, usually by the next day.

Tommy had already become Tony's go-to guy in the crew—that was before he developed a taste for the nose candy. Before long Tony added Vinny and Aldo to his right hand.

Yeah, he owed Tony.

He looked at him. "The salvage business ain't exactly minting money as it is. With Tommy there . . ."

"I know, I know. But he's been whining that he doesn't have nothin', and how he's senior to you, and being a Gotti cousin he got in the ears of Junior and Peter—"

"They should tell him to get off his ass and find his own thing."

"Hey, easy on the silverware."

Vinny looked down at his hand and noticed his shrimp fork was bent almost to a right angle. He straightened it out.

"Hey, look," Tony said, "you got a right to be upset. But don't think of it as doing something for Tommy, think of it as doing something for me. It gets the association off my back and you pick up a few debts—I'll owe you, and the Gottis'll owe you. That ain't such a bad thing."

" 'Owes' will probably be the only thing I'll have left by the time Tommy's through."

Tony leaned forward and gestured with his fork. "Look. I'll make sure the association sends some extra cleaning your way."

That would help. A business like Vinny's was always good for laundering cash.

"And there's a coupla chop shops in your area who can slip you their leftovers after they've stripped what they want."

That would help too . . .

"All fine and good, but I'll still be in business with Fredo."

Tony looked puzzled, then his eyes lit. "Oh, the *God-father* guy."

"Yeah, the loser brother."

Vinny didn't know a single guy in any of the families who didn't love those films, especially the first one. His own father hadn't been connected, but he'd taken Vinny to *The Godfather* shortly before he dropped dead. Vinny still remembered him ranting as they drove home after. *Looks great, huh. But they didn't show you the whores and the junkies and the guys who get the crap beat out of them for being late on their payments.*

Eventually Vinny wound up being one of the guys who administered those beatings.

"Yeah, well, unlike the movie, Tommy ain't John's brother," Tony said. "When the Chief gets out, if Tommy don't clean up his act, he could wind up just like Fredo."

Vinny nodded agreement, but he wasn't so sure. Gotti getting out was a "when" as far as Tony was concerned, but more like an "if" for Vinny. Word was the feds had hours and hours of tape from their bugs in the Ravenite Club, and that this time something was gonna stick to the Teflon Don. Then again, John Gotti had a knack for getting to a jury.

His stomach churned at the thought of the Chief landing a life sentence. Vinny would be stuck with Tommy Ten Thumbs forever.

"You're a smart guy, Vinny. You'll figure it out."

Here was the second time Tony had called him "smart." That wasn't necessarily a good thing. All the "family" and "omerta" and the rest of the stuff in the films was just bullshit. Guys would rat out their mothers if they thought it could help them beat a rap, and sometimes even put a couple into the back of a friend's head when ordered to. And if a boss thought you were too smart, he might think you had an eye on his spot. Uneasy lies the head that wears the crown and all that. A boss might want to eliminate a guy who might be too smart for his own good.

Was everything Tony just said bullshit? Was he putting Tommy in with Vinny to keep an eye on him?

5.   "Hey, Julio," Jack called. "Need a hand?"

The Spot had closed early tonight. Yeah, the place was a bar and this was Saturday night, but business sucked. The recession contributed, of course, but The Spot had been going downhill for a while, especially after Harry Detrick, who'd owned a ninety percent share, had let his ex-wife fern it up. Julio had the other ten but that left him no say. The locals' attitude seemed to be, *Been there, done that, don't feel like doing it again,* and so they moved on to other spots. As for tourists, it simply didn't look that inviting from the outside. Even Lou and Barney had paid up and gone home tonight.

Should there come a great apocalypse, destroying most of the watering holes in the five boroughs, The Spot would still have a tough time making Zagat's Top One Hundred Taverns in NYC. The small bar that occupied the end of the room nearest the door had bottles racked against the de rigueur mirrored wall behind it. Square tables were scattered about the rest of the space. Usually the place was dim, lit only by beer signs and the bulbs in sconces along the wall. Now the overheads were on for cleanup, revealing the tacky, peeling wallpaper and flaking hammered-tin ceiling.

Julio glanced up from where he was wiping down one of the tables. He was short and muscular with wavy black hair and a thin mustache.

"Nah, you been cut, meng."

"That was my left arm. I'm right-handed."

The shoulder was bothering him some, but no biggie.

Since he'd first discovered it last year, The Spot had become Jack's favorite hang. That was why he'd stopped by after spending the bulk of the afternoon in search of a new apartment.

After Doc Hargus had finished his stitch job, Jack had dressed in the hall and headed for home. Trouble was, Rico and his DDP goons could still be patrolling his neighborhood. They didn't know Jack's address—only Abe knew that—but they'd spotted him on West 21st last fall and chased him before he'd lost them. That must have been why they were on 23rd today: They figured he lived somewhere in Chelsea. Technically he lived in the Flower District, which was part of Chelsea. But if they were still cruising the area they might spot him again.

And so he'd ditched his sliced, bloody, filthy jacket, substituting a hoodie and big, hip-hop shades. Hood up and pulled way forward, he'd taken the D downtown to the 34th Street stop and quick-walked home from there. After a shower and a set of fresh clothes, he got back into disguise—this time with his Ruger .357 Magnum tucked in the small of his back—and went in search of a real estate agent to show him some apartments in a less hostile neighborhood.

The latest apartment he'd seen—he'd decided it was too small—had been here on the Upper West Side, so he'd naturally gravitated to The Spot for shelter from the February chill. Regular though he was, he'd never been here at closing time.

"Give me a rag and I'll help you out," Jack said.

Julio shrugged. "They in the back."

As he was searching the curtained-off back room behind the bar, he heard the front door open. When Julio's surprised "Darren!" filtered back, he stepped up to the curtain and peered around the edge in time to see a guy about Jack's age walk in. Well, *walked* wasn't quite right. He was on crutches.

"Hey, Julio."

Darren . . . wasn't that the name of Harry Detrick's kid? This guy seemed the right age. He had a thick neck and huge shoulders and upper arms; looked like he worked out a lot—a *lot*.

One peek at how the left leg of Darren's warm-up pants was pinned up to his knee was all Jack needed to answer a lot of the questions that had been bugging Julio and him.

"*¡Mierda!*" Julio said. "What—?"

Darren said, "Accident," but offered nothing more. His tone and expression were bland but his eyes held a bitter blaze.

He had a right to pop into The Spot whenever he damn well pleased: His father's will had left him ninety percent ownership.

Jack decided he'd be a fifth wheel out there, so he stayed put.

"But how, meng?"

Darren shrugged. "Friendly fire."

What? Last they'd heard, Darren was in the army and had been shipped over to Saudi Arabia for Desert Shield. Everyone knew war with Iraq was coming but it hadn't started yet. At least it hadn't made it to the news yet.

A middle-aged woman in a pants suit came in behind him. "Some asshole got careless with a machine gun and shot his leg off." She wasn't holding back: Her bitter expression matched her tone.

Jack had seen her before—Nita, Darren's mom, Harry's ex. She used to come in and water the ferns in the windows, but three months ago, somewhere around Thanksgiving, she seemed to drop off the earth. Now Jack had a pretty good idea why.

"We were on maneuvers," Darren said. "One lousy fifty-cal round in the worst possible spot. They couldn't save it."

"You could have been *killed,*" Nita said.

You poor bastard, Jack thought. You get sent over there to fight for some other country's oil fields and you lose a leg before the fighting begins. What the fuck is wrong with this picture?

"Anyway," Darren said, "I know you've been wanting to talk to me, but I've been kinda busy rehabing down at Walter Reed."

Julio shook his head in dismay and gestured to the nearest chair. "Don't even think about it, meng. Sit down." He looked at Nita. "You shoulda told me."

"I didn't think. I was down there with him."

She walked in but came to a sharp halt when she saw the dead ferns.

"You didn't water them."

"I kept thinking you'd show up. Sorry."

Jack hid a smile. He knew Julio wasn't the least bit sorry. He hated those ferns.

"Hey, Ma, don't worry about the ferns. You can always get new ones."

Jack caught Julio's quick eye roll.

"You wanted to talk?" Darren said.

"Yeah." Julio glanced at the place where Darren's lower left leg used to be. "But—"

"No. Go ahead. Shoot."

"Darren!" Nita said. "Must you?"

"Sorry, Ma."

Julio took a deep breath. "I wish you'd wouldn't sell to Zalesky. Anybody but."

"Why?"

"He used to be married to my sister Rosa. We got bad blood."

Jack managed a grim smile. *Bad blood* barely touched it.

Neil Zalesky, affectionately known in these parts as *hijo de puta,* had gotten a little too rough with Rosa once too often during their marriage, so she dumped him. Zalesky couldn't let go. Jack didn't know if it was some obsessive attraction or whether he simply hated the idea of being rejected by any woman. Whatever it was, Zalesky had started an ongoing campaign of harassment—juvenile stuff like sneaking in while she was out and peeing on her bed, or worse. Despite numerous restraining orders, he'd kept it up. No physical harm done, but knowing he was getting into her home whenever he felt like it was freaking Rosa.

Julio had reached the breaking point. His proposed solution was to take the Louisville Slugger he kept behind the bar and apply it repeatedly to the hijo de puta's skull until he'd reduced it to the consistency of rice pudding. To keep Julio from landing on Death Row, Jack had followed Zalesky to Rosa's one night. Unseen, he had orchestrated a nasty fall that resulted in multiple fractures. While Zalesky was in the hospital, Jack had invaded his apartment and robbed him of all his hidden cash, every last dollar.

Zalesky blamed Julio, of course, and had decided buying The Spot was the best revenge.

"Oh." Darren glanced at his mother. "I didn't know."

Nita stepped forward. "We've had no other offers, Julio. In case you didn't know, there's a recession going on."

"I know it." He gestured around at the empty bar. "Believe me, I know like crazy."

"Well, you can appreciate how lucky we feel we got any offer."

Jack fought an urge to step out there and say something. He'd offered to loan Julio the down payment, but the stubborn bastard wouldn't take it. Some Puerto Rican macho thing.

"Listen," Julio said. "Lemme take over the place and run it. I buy you out slow, a little bit at a time, but in the end I'll see you wind up with more than that *puta* will give you. You know I'm good for it."

Darren shrugged. "I got no doubt about that, Julio. Dad always said you were the only reason the place kept running. I don't want to sell it, but . . ."

"We'd both like to keep it in the family," Nita said, "and you're like family, Julio. It's been what?—a dozen years now."

Jack had heard the story a number of times. When his dad died, Harry—Darren's father—was beneficiary of the old guy's life insurance policy. After paying the funeral expenses, he took what was left over and bought The Spot. This was right after the city almost went broke and property values were in the dumps, so he was able to buy it for cash at a bargain-basement price.

"Thirteen," Julio said.

She nodded. "Things were great until that bum started gambling—"

"Ma," Darren said. "Do we have to?"

She got all teary. "Sorry, honey. It's just . . ."

Darren looked at Julio. "Thing is, I know the place'll be worth more once the economy comes back, but I need the money now." He tapped his left thigh. "The army's fitting me with a new leg and I want to get a new start somewhere else. A new life, you know? Somewhere warm, someplace far away from here, where nobody knows the old me."

Jack understood that perfectly. *Been there, done that.*

After a long pause, "How long before . . . ?" Julio didn't seem to be able to bring himself to say it.

"The sale?" Darren said. "I spoke to Zalesky last night.

I've been out of contact with him too. He says he's got the down payment ready and waiting, and can have the mortgage commitment in a couple of weeks. Sorry, man."

Julio said nothing but Jack could sense what he was feeling. Really, what could he say to this kid who'd been so senselessly, wastefully maimed for life, who wanted to cash out and start all over?

6.   Jack waited till Darren and Nita were well gone before stepping through the curtain.

"My offer still stands."

Julio looked at him and shook his head. "We been over this too many times, meng."

Jack ignored him. "Look, I've got the down payment cash sitting in my apartment getting moldy. It's yours, interest free, and you pay me back when you can."

"No."

They both knew Julio had no credit history and no bank was going to give him a mortgage based on his declared income. Harry had been paying him under the table with whatever he hadn't lost on the ponies.

"How about trying to get a mortgage by putting the business up for collateral?"

Julio slipped behind the bar and hefted the baseball bat he kept there. "How about the hijo de puta get, oh, I dunno, brain damaged? Like so bad he can't add two and two? Nobody give him a mortgage then."

They'd been over this a million times too.

"Yeah, and who do you think will be suspect *numero uno*, eh?"

Before Julio could answer, the door opened again. Jack expected to see Darren or Nita reappear, but Julio yelled, "We closed!" without looking.

"Not for me."

Jack recognized the big guy in the dark blue suit: Vincent Donato. Known in various circles as Vinny Donuts or Vinny the Donut. He was empty-handed tonight, but sometimes he showed up on his weekly visits munching on one of his trademark pastries. Probably already had dessert. Jack wondered what his mother called him. Vincenzo, maybe?

Vinny did collections for a Gambino crew. Harry Detrick had been into them for big losses on the ponies before his sudden death from stepping in front of a bus. Since Darren had been out of reach in Saudi Arabia at the time, the shylocks came to Harry's partner, Julio. If Julio didn't keep up Harry's payments, they threatened to go after Nita.

All this happened just around the time Jack had liberated about fifteen grand from Zalesky. So they'd been using that to pay Harry's vigorish to the Gambinos. Julio had had no qualms about taking that money.

"You're late this week," Julio said. "I thought you forgot about me."

"In your dreams. You got the money? And don't give me no shit about 'later.' Later is now."

Julio put down the bat and placed the envelope on the bar. "Lemme ask you something. If your guy Gotti goes down for the count, you gonna stop comin' around?"

Vinny's piggy face twisted in a sneer as he snatched up the envelope and pocketed it. "In your dreams, spic."

As the mobster turned and walked out, Julio's face darkened. He was reaching for the bat again when Jack gripped his arm. Julio snatched his arm away but left the bat where it was.

"We gonna have to do something about that guy," Julio said when the door closed behind him. "And soon. Zalesky's cash won't last forever."

No lie there.

He added, "I still don't know why we didn't just pay him off totally with the puta's money. I mean, right away. We'd have had plenty left over. Now . . ."

"Because I need to keep tabs on him. This keeps him coming around."

He wasn't ready yet to let Julio in on his plans.

Julio shrugged. "Okay. You call the shots on that one."

"You know," Jack said, "with Gotti still in jail, you'd think these animals would be at each other's throats, but it's all business as usual."

The Gambino family seemed to have taken Gotti's arrest in stride. Multiple murder and racketeering charges, yet the ones who came here to collect acted like nothing had happened.

"That's 'cause he's the 'Teflon Don.' The feds can't make nothin' stick to that guy."

"So they say. We'll worry about the Donut later. First priority is keeping this place out of Zalesky's grubby hands."

Julio tapped the bat. "I told you—"

"I've got a better way."

"Oh, yeah? Right off the top of your head you got a plan?"

"Not exactly. I've had months to work on it, because I was afraid this day would come."

In truth, when they couldn't get in touch with Darren and hadn't heard any more about the sale, Jack had begun to hope that either the kid had changed his mind about selling the place, or Zalesky had backed out of the buy. No such luck. From what Darren had just said, Zalesky was still intent on owning The Spot. Yeah, Julio held a ten percent stake, but that meant he had a right to only ten percent of the profits. Easy enough for Zalesky to kick him out on the street and see to it the books never showed a profit.

But Jack had a compiled a load of research and was ready to make his move against the guy. He agreed with Julio that Zalesky had to go, but not Julio's way.

Jack's way.

SUNDAY

1. Well, I learned something today, Jack thought as he emptied his revolver at the target. Gloves and handguns don't go together. At least not these gloves.

A wasted night, and now a wasted morning. He'd spent much of last night in the Pelham section of the Bronx at a sports bar called The Main Event, nursing beers and waiting for Zalesky to show. He hadn't.

That had surprised him. From Jack's previous reconnoiters, The Main Event appeared to be his hang, and on a Saturday night, even in the post–Super Bowl doldrums, the sports world still had basketball—NBA games and pre–March Madness college ball.

Maybe Zalesky wasn't a b-ball fan. Or maybe, like Jack, he was a fan of an out-of-town team. Because apparently "sports" here meant New York teams only. Last night he'd suffered through a Knicks win over the Washington Bullets that even Patrick Ewing couldn't make interesting.

His disinterest left him able to whine at every opportunity to the bartender—whose name was Joe, of all things—about how his cheap-ass grandmother wouldn't come across with the money he needed for a surefire investment opportunity. The old bitch was loaded but wouldn't invest a goddamn dime in her own grandson.

He'd been hoping Zalesky would overhear, but you can't overhear if you're not there.

Today, as they said, was another day.

And today involved some shooting.

This morning he'd put a fresh bandage and some Bacitracin ointment on his shoulder wound. It looked angry and he was glad he was on an antibiotic. He'd popped a couple of Advil for the pain. Doc Hargus had refused to give him anything stronger—"Don't keep any of that shit around," he'd said—and the Advil did just fine.

He'd donned the hoodie disguise and made his way without incident to where he garaged his Harley; then he'd driven to Doc Hargus's place to pay him the five hundred fifty he owed him for the patch job. The doc told him to come back in a week for suture removal.

After that it was straight out to the Calverton range near the eastern end of the Long Island Expressway. He didn't like helmets but had worn one today to keep his face from freezing and flaking off like old paint. He tried to come out here twice a month to improve his aim and familiarity with the Ruger—chambered for the .357 Magnum, but he shot the cheaper .38 specials for practice.

He'd tried a half dozen rounds today while wearing his driving gloves. A big no-go. Not only did they ruin his feel for the trigger, and thus his aim, but made it damn near impossible to reload. Today he'd adopted a one-handed stance to disturb his left shoulder as little as possible. But the soreness in his right deltoid from the tetanus shot wasn't helping either.

Christ, he felt like a whiny old man.

He was pulling off his gloves when he noted a bearded guy—a young Arab—approaching from his right.

"I have seen you," he said in a thick accent.

"Yeah, well, I guess so, 'cause I don't see how you could miss since you're looking right at me."

Jack checked him out. Thin, bearded, one of those

bigger skullcaps holding down unruly black hair. He was wearing a red leather jacket and jeans instead of robes, but all in all a cookie-cutter Arab. The beards did it—worn pretty much the same length and always black. Made them all look the same.

"Yes. You drive truck to Diab."

Did he mean the Mummy?—that was what Bertel had called his Egyptian customer. Jack had made cigarette runs to the Mummy's Jersey City drop, but if he'd ever heard the guy's real name, he'd long forgotten it.

Whatever, he didn't see any good reason to admit he'd been there, especially to a guy he didn't recognize.

"Never heard of Diab and never saw you before in my life."

The Arab bared his teeth. "You lie!"

Jack didn't see much point in answering.

The guy added, "You spy!"

"'You lie!' 'You spy!' So you're what, the Arab Doctor Seuss? Hey, I got one for you: You nuts! No buts!" Not a good morning for this kind of crap. He could feel his frayed temper looking for a target. "Get lost, asshole."

"Why are you here?"

"To play tiddlywinks, what else?" Jack said as he continued reloading the Ruger.

The guy looked confused. "You FBI? You CIA?"

Jack spat. "Not hardly."

"What is your name?"

"Tell me yours first."

"No!"

Jack shrugged. "I guess we have nothing to say to each other."

The Arab clenched his teeth. "Very well. I am Kadir Allawi. Who are you?"

"I am no one."

"You owe me your name!"

"Get. Lost."

The guy raised his hands as if to grab Jack's hoodie but held back.

"You tell me!"

Looking into the guy's eyes, Jack flipped the cylinder closed and hefted the Ruger. He cocked the hammer—not at all necessary, but it made such a nice ratchety sound.

"You really want to start something with a guy holding a loaded gun?"

Kadir—if that was his real name—hesitated, then screeched through his clenched teeth and stomped away. He joined a crew of similar bearded types—Saudis, Palestinians, Egyptians, who knew?

Probably time to go. Jack emptied the Ruger at the target, then packed it away. He'd be riding back to the city on an unregistered motorcycle with a bogus license carrying an unregistered firearm. If he got stopped and searched, having that firearm loaded would only complicate matters.

He looked over at the Arab and his three friends staring his way.

He almost wished they'd start something, give him human targets. He'd had to run from trouble yesterday. He was in the mood to take it to someone today.

Yeah, definitely time to go.

2.   Kadir Allawi seethed as he watched the American stow his pistol in a pouch at the rear of his motorcycle.

"Do you really think he followed us out here?" said Mahmoud in Arabic. He stood over six feet and kept his red hair hidden under a knit cap.

Kadir had no doubt. Why else would he be here?

"He used to deliver cigarettes to Tachus's uncle across the river. I saw him there many times, I am sure of it."

"That doesn't mean he's spying," said Ghali.

Kadir shook his head. "I saw him right here, at this very range, last year. He was shooting with the one who supplies the cigarettes." He paused as he made a connection. "Not long before Sayyid's arrest."

He didn't know why he'd said that. Sayyid had been captured after shooting that Arab-hating Rabbi Kahane. An unforeseeable set of circumstances had foiled his escape.

"Still . . ." said Ghali.

"I saw him many times, I tell you, and he saw me. Yet he denied it to my face. He's spying on us."

"Why?" said Ramiz. "He can't know what's coming."

"We know that the FBI has been watching the refugee center, trying to trace contributions. They know we are followers of Sheikh Omar. Anyone who has been paying attention knows what is coming." He held up the 9mm semiautomatic they'd been taking turns shooting. "Especially now that he's seen us practicing with this."

Ghali and Ramiz still looked dubious, but Mahmoud seemed convinced, and he was the only one of their number who had true combat experience—with the mujahideen in Afghanistan. Usually when they came out here they'd fire Mahmoud's AK-47, but this time was different. They needed to become comfortable with the pistol.

"Maybe we should turn the tables and follow him," Mahmoud said.

Kadir turned as the motorcycle revved. "No. I have a better idea. Let's go. I'll drive."

He didn't have a license, but he very much wanted to be behind the wheel right now.

As Kadir led the way to their beat-up van, he wondered at the change that had come over him in the past few months. But then again, a lot had happened to him. He'd been a part of the plot to kill the Jew Kahane, for which his friend El Sayyid Nosair now awaited trial;

he'd been the sole survivor of what could only be described as a massacre of Tachus and others who had been
his only friends in this cursed land. But without a doubt
what accounted most for his changes were the teachings
of Sheikh Omar Abdel-Rahman, the blind cleric whose
visions of worldwide jihad had infused Kadir with holy
purpose.

Sheikh Omar's fury flared in many righteous directions.
He wanted to topple the secularist Mubarak from his pedestal in Egypt and install an imam in his place. Was that a
mad dream? No. Not for Sheikh Omar. Just as his *fatwa*
had led to the death of the traitor Anwar Sadat, so too
could his holy influence topple Mubarak. Sheikh Omar
also raged against the Saudi monarchy for allowing U.S.
troops to trod the holy land where Mecca lay, and for
allowing them to start launching missiles into Kuwait last
month.

American bootprints might not mar the soil of Kadir's
homeland of Palestine, but they supplied Israel with arms
and money, helping it suppress his people.

He needed to strike back at America, and why not right
now—at this American who was spying on them? A small
gesture, but he could consider it a starting point.

They piled into the van and took off after the liar.

"I'll shoot him," Mahmoud said from the passenger
seat.

Kadir didn't care for that idea. "I don't think we want
it to look like an assassination, do you?"

Mahmoud shrugged. "You're probably right."

"And we want to save that pistol for something more
important."

If they used the pistol now, Kadir worried about the
FBI matching this shooting to the one they had planned
for later.

"What else?"

Kadir smiled. "A traffic accident."

This section of the road between the shooting range and the expressway was deserted at the moment. Perfect. He gunned the engine and picked up speed. The rider was holding to the limit so Kadir gained on him quickly.

When he caught up, he simply rammed his rear wheel.

The motorcycle swerved onto the shoulder, out of control. It tipped and sent the rider tumbling into the ditch along the side of the road.

"He might still be alive," Mahmoud said. "Should we finish him?"

"Yes."

But as Kadir braked, Ghali pounded on the rear of the front seat.

"Someone's coming!"

Kadir looked in the mirror and saw a dark pickup truck heading their way.

"Get us away from here!" Mahmoud cried.

Kadir understood and hit the gas. Mahmoud had been questioned numerous times by the police and the FBI about a connection to the Kahane killing. He could not afford any further involvement in the American legal system.

As they sped away, he watched the pickup slow by the overturned cycle. Kadir routinely splattered mud on the van's license plate to make reading it difficult. He prayed to Allah that the truck driver didn't get a good look.

"That's what he gets for lying to me," Kadir said.

Mahmoud was looking at him. "I just had a thought. Maybe he didn't lie."

"Why do you say that?"

"When did you last see him?"

Kadir shrugged. "Around the time Sayyid was arrested."

Mahmoud smiled. "You didn't have your beard then."

True. Kadir had not been a righteous follower of the

prophet then. Now he was, and to cut the beard was *haraam*.

"Do you think he's dead?" Ramiz said, staring out the rear window.

Mahmoud grunted. "If not, he's had a bad scare. And if he is—one less infidel to deal with when we bring jihad to these shores."

Kadir smiled and nodded along with his faithful companions.

3.   "Well, look who it is," said a familiar voice.

Jack realized his helmet must have come off because his face was buried in dead grass. Slowly, carefully, and with no little pain from his low back and pelvis, Jack rolled over to find Dane Bertel looking down at him. Bertel . . . same as ever with his weathered face and the gray hair sticking out in all directions.

Bertel shook his head. "I oughta leave you here."

"What happened?"

He remembered cruising along, his Discman playing *The Traveling Wilburys Vol. 3*, and all of a sudden flying through the air.

"Vanload of Mohammedans whacked you off the road from behind."

Mohammedans . . . Bertel's archaic term for Muslims and Arabs. He'd also called them *oil-mongering, hummus-slurping, camel-humping bastards*. And Jack had a pretty good idea which Mohammedans might have done it. He raised his right arm for a hand up.

"Sure it wasn't you?"

Bertel didn't offer his hand. "Don't think it wouldn't have crossed my mind."

"You still pissed at me?"

Bertel seemed to think about that. "Yeah, a little. But not that pissed."

Jack used to drive for him, running unlabeled cigarettes from NC to NJ, delivering them to the Mummy. But things got complicated and finally too hairy for Jack. They hadn't parted on the best terms—Bertel felt like Jack had left him hanging.

He gripped Jack's hand but didn't pull. "Sure nothing's broken?"

His back and shoulder hurt like hell, but he didn't think anything was broken. He'd rolled off the embankment and, though the ground was hard, he hadn't slammed into a tree or a big rock. Much as he hated the helmet, it had probably spared him a concussion or worse before it came loose. The leather jacket was scraped almost all the way through. He didn't want to think what his skin would look like if he'd been wearing only a sweatshirt.

"One way to find out."

Pain shot through his lower spine as he let Bertel help him to his feet, but it didn't last long. He staggered around in a circle. His left hip hurt but everything seemed to work. He waved his arms and was rewarded with a jolt of pain down his left.

Shit! His sliced shoulder.

He pulled off his jacket, then began unbuttoning his shirt.

"What the hell are you doing?"

"Gotta check on something."

When the shirt was loose enough, he pulled it off his left shoulder and checked the bandage. A little blood seepage. He lifted it for a peek—all the sutures seemed intact.

Bertel was leaning close. "That's a nasty one. How'd you get it?"

"Long story."

"Okay, then let me try another question: How'd you get on the wrong side of those swarthy bastards?"

"One of them says he works for your Mummy friend, said he'd seen me at the Jersey City drop and thought I was spying on him."

Bertel smiled. "Are you?"

"Yeah, right." Jack began walking up the incline toward the road. "If I ever saw him before, I don't remember. But when I told him so he got all pissed."

"Pissed enough to try to kill you?"

"Looks that way." Then he saw his Harley. "My bike! Look at my bike!"

"That's not rideable," Bertel said.

"No shit."

His fury blossomed, ready to explode. If he could get his hands on that bastard—

"We'll put her in the back of the truck."

Jack bottled the rage and looked at Bertel. Why was he being so accommodating?

"Thanks. That'd be great."

After much grunting and groaning, with Jack guarding his left shoulder, they slid it into the rear of Bertel's F-150.

"Guess I'm lucky you came along when you did," Jack said once they were in the cab and rolling toward the LIE. "On your way to the range?"

Bertel nodded. "I was headed out there when I saw them ram you. I didn't know it was you, what with the helmet and all, but I swung around and came back. They were stopping—to finish you off, maybe?—but kept going when they spotted me coming."

"Finish me off? Why would they—?"

Bertel shrugged. "That wasn't a little love tap on your fender. You took a break-your-neck tumble there. That's why they call them 'donorcycles,' kid."

"You sound like my sister."

Kate had said the same thing when he'd bought the Harley.

"Yeah? She work in an ER or something?"

Jack caught himself before he could say she just got out of a pediatric residency. Was Bertel trolling for information?

"Something."

Bertel grinned. "Still as clammed up as ever."

Jack glanced through the rear window at his Harley. Maybe it was time to rethink this whole motorcycle thing. He realized he was shaking inside. He hadn't seen it coming. He could have been killed. Or worse, broken his neck and ended up a quadriplegic.

"Donorcycle or not, why would they think I'm spying on them? I get paranoia—I mean, I'm more paranoid than the average guy, but that's a real stretch."

"Not if you're up to no good," Bertel said.

Jack looked at him but Bertel's gaze was fixed on the road ahead. "And they're not?"

"You ever hear of Abdel-Rahman?"

"What's that? A kind of noodle?"

"Jesus! Sheikh Omar Abdel-Rahman. He's this radical Mohammaden who preaches worldwide jihad—that's holy war—and he won't be satisfied until we're all Mohammedans. For the past month he's been frothing at the mouth about this whole Desert Storm thing. Those guys in the van are all his followers. And his followers tend to be the kind who blow up embassies and set off car bombs in shopping centers."

"Terrorists?"

"No, professional babysitters. Of *course,* terrorists. That tall one with the red hair—Mahmoud Abouhalima—he's Omar's sometime chauffeur and is one bad actor. He was involved in killing that rabbi last fall."

"Kahane?"

Bertel glanced at him. "Good for you. Most people have already forgotten about that." His eyes narrowed. "Oh, wait. Didn't you tell me you were at the East Side Marriott the night it went down?"

"Yeah. Following Tony."

Bertel looked back at the road. "Yeah. Tony."

Tony Zahler had been Bertel's right-hand man on the North Carolina end of his cigarette running operation. He and Jack had blundered into a human-trafficking operation last fall. Jack had been forced to drive one of two trucks loaded with prepubescent girls from the Outer Banks to Staten Island, while Tony was kept behind as insurance. If everything went smoothly, Tony would go free. If Jack screwed up, he'd die. Jack did as he was told but a pair of masked gunmen had busted up the sale. Tony was found in the Outer Banks house with his brains splattered all over a wall.

When Bertel had demanded to know why Tony was dead and Jack still alive, he'd told Bertel the story—leaving out the gunmen's identities. He'd also told him about an incident a week or so before that—about spotting Tony dressed as an Orthodox Jew and following him to the Marriott the night Kahane was killed.

Bertel shook his head. "Still haven't figured that one out."

Neither he nor Bertel had been able to come up with an explanation.

"Probably go to our graves not knowing. Only Tony knows and he's not talking."

Bertel sighed. "Anyway, the Kahane hit had jihad written all over it but nobody wants to see that. The cops can place Abouhalima and his cab at the hotel, but no one can pin anything on him. The one who works for the Mummy is named Kadir. He, along with a bunch of other formerly innocuous Mohammedans, have been radicalized into jihadist drones by Abdel-Rahman—known to his minions as the beloved Sheikh Omar."

"You think they're planning some terrorism?"

"Right now, only among themselves. Sheikh Omar is trying to take over the local mosques. He's especially interested in the Al-Kifah Afghan Refugee Center in Brooklyn—downstairs from the Al-Farooq Mosque. A ton of money flows through the Afghan relief charity there and he wants to tap into that stream for his own ends."

"Which are?"

"Toppling Mubarak tops his list."

Jack's expression must have given away that he hadn't a clue who Mubarak was.

"Oh, for Christ sake, Jack, you have no idea what I'm talking about, do you."

"Well, hell, I can barely keep up with what's going on in New York, let alone the world."

"Mubarak's president of Egypt and Sheikh Omar hates him. Wants to use that relief money to fund a move against him. He's started a nasty campaign to get rid of the current honcho at the relief center—a guy named Shalabi who wants to keep all that money going to Afghanistan."

"And you know all this . . . how? You sound like the spy I'm supposed to be."

Bertel shrugged. "Me and Riaz Diab—the Mummy—we talk now and then. He's Egyptian, Sheikh Omar's Egyptian, Shalabi too. He's kinda friends with Shalabi and says the guy's afraid for his life. So afraid he's already sent his wife back to Egypt, and he's getting set to split too."

"So why wasn't this Sheikh Noodle out at the firing range too?"

Bertel laughed. "He's the last guy you want to see out

there. He's blind. But his stooges look like they're gearing up to do his dirty work."

"Which is?"

"Kill Shalabi."

"But if he's leaving . . ."

"If he's alive, even in Egypt, he can always cause them trouble by influencing where the donations go, maybe even come back to New York. If he's dead . . ."

Jack leaned back. "Well, I hope Shalabi's packin' when they find him, and he blows the sons-a-bitches away."

"That won't happen. He's not the type. But however it goes down, Sheikh Omar is going to be in charge of the Al-Kifah Afghan Refugee Center and its cash flow very soon."

"And this matters how?"

Bertel shook his head. "I don't know. But sometimes events that seem far removed from anything that'll ever affect you can sneak around later and bite you on the ass."

"Maybe *their* asses'll get bitten."

Bertel glanced at him again. "You thinking about extracting a little vengeance for this accident?"

Jack shook his head. Yeah, in an ideal world, he'd love a chance at some payback against the guys who bumped him off the road. But this wasn't that world. If yesterday was any example, overreacting could start a chain reaction that escalated and reescalated. He already had Rico and the DDP out for his blood. He didn't need another feud in his life.

"Nah. What's in that for me? A little revenge, a little salve for my hurt pride? Not worth the risk. I'm gonna let it go."

"See? That's why I wanted you driving for me. You've got perspective. You want to come back?"

"Nope."

"Why not?"

"Perspective."

Bertel didn't look too pleased with the answer.

Too bad. Going back with Bertel meant making drops at the Mummy's place. Jack didn't intend to have anything more to do with the Arab world—now or in the future.

Besides, he had to solve the Zalesky problem before Julio did it his way. Last night had been a bust. Today had to be better.

4. Jack's incessant whining finally paid off.

He'd arrived at The Main Event early today—early meaning shortly after noon but in time to grab a rubbery bar pie for lunch as the Knicks started to play the Heat. He'd ensconced himself on the same barstool as yesterday and began pestering Joe with the same rant about his rich grandmother who wouldn't back him on a surefire investment.

Nobody seemed terribly interested in the game. Maybe because after bombing the hell out of the occupying Iraqis for the past month, the U.S. had rolled armored divisions into Kuwait last night, turning the air war into a ground war.

Desert Storm was rolling. Rah-rah-rah.

Zalesky hadn't shown yet, but Jack kept up his complaints until two raggedy, bearded, long-haired guys wearing camo boonie hats stumbled in. The kind of guys—Vietnam burnouts, maybe—who make most people avoid eye contact.

The blond one banged on the bar three times in synch with his announcement: "We want *beer*, we want *food*, and we want the *war*!"

Behind the bar, Joe wisely turned off the Knicks-Heat

game and switched on CNN. Nobody objected. Certainly not Jack.

Had a war ever before been captured live on TV as it happened? Fascinated, he watched the tanks rolling through the desert. He almost forgot to continue his whine. If Zalesky was going to show, he hoped he didn't wait too much longer. Jack was on the clock—had to leave soon so he'd have time to get cleaned up for his dinner date with Cristin.

He'd been combing through issues of *Popular Science* in prep for his scheme, looking for an angle, a way-out investment that had a patina of credibility. He'd glommed onto an article about the glowing future of fiber-optic cable. He'd read it and reread it, learning enough to be both wildly enthusiastic and totally boring on the subject.

At around two o'clock he was maybe halfway into a rerun of his spiel about its applications in the telecommunications field—Joe's eyes were literally glazing over—when Jack recognized a handsome thirty-something guy with dark, slicked-back hair breeze through the door. Zalesky had arrived.

He zeroed in on a couple of locals seated at a table near the big rear-projection TV in the corner and dropped into a chair. Looked a lot better than he had last time Jack had seen him—back in November when he'd shown up at The Spot to threaten Julio about buying the place. Today he was walking without a limp and his arm seemed fine, though he did appear to have put on a few pounds—the result of inactivity after his injuries, maybe? Still pretty trim, though. Apparently no permanent damage from that fall.

Too bad.

Joe walked off, deserting Jack in mid-sentence, and made a beeline for the table. Jack watched in the mirror as Joe made a show of taking orders, but along the way he leaned over and whispered something to Zalesky. Zalesky leaned his chair back and stole a glance at Jack, then nodded and patted Joe on the arm. Did Zalesky pay referral fees?

Joe returned and busied himself with refilling the burn-outs' beers until Zalesky approached and leaned against the bar a few feet away. Jack concentrated on Desert Storm on the TV.

5.   *Kid at the bar's got a rich grandmother . . .*

Joe's whispered words had propelled Neil across the room.

His fall off Rosa's building had kept him out of the game too long. He'd broken his left shoulder, cracked a few ribs, and bruised his hip bone. Everything had taken forever to heal—man, he couldn't believe he'd fallen last fucking November and the shoulder *still* wasn't right. Might never be without surgery.

Somehow Julio had been behind it. Oh, yeah, people swore he was in The Spot all that night, but Neil knew the rope hadn't come untied by itself. Whatever, no more climbing down walls—Rosa's or anybody else's—for him. That left getting to her through her beloved little brother. And kicking his ass out of the bar he part-owned was going to be *so* sweet.

He'd been digging into his savings to get by. And now that he was healed up—sort of—business was off. Not so bad—he was used to ups and downs and knew things would pick up. But then that kid, Darren Detrick, had called, saying he was ready to sell his father's bar.

That put the pressure on. Neil was always on the hunt for a fresh mark, but right now he especially needed a score. The chances of this one panning out were low but he couldn't afford to leave any stone unturned. If he was going to buy The Spot out from under that fucker Julio, he'd need a big down payment. He had almost fifty Gs in his safe deposit box, but he'd need more.

He shook his head. Sometimes you can be too fucking smart for your own good. To pacify the tax man, he filed annual 1040s and declared just enough income to put him above the poverty line. All well and good until he wanted to buy something like The Spot. His declared income wasn't enough to qualify him for a heavy mortgage, so he had to produce some major scratch up front.

And he was goddamn well gonna produce it.

He checked out the kid from the corner of his eye. Brown hair, brown eyes, flannel shirt, worn jeans, work boots. Looked harmless enough, and anything but rich. Probably a waste of his time but . . .

"Gimme a Bud Light, will ya, Joe?"

"Sure thing, Neil."

Neil winced at how staged that sounded. The kid rubbed a hand across his mouth, almost as if he was hiding a smile.

As Joe twisted off the cap and slid the bottle down the bar, he pointed to the kid. "You two should meet. Neil's our go-to guy for investments."

Neil put on a self-deprecating smile and stuck out his hand. "Hardly. Neil Zalesky."

"Lonnie Beuchner," the kid said, shaking his hand with a wimpy grip.

Neil hated guys who couldn't give you a firm handshake. And *Lonnie Beuchner*? What kind of fucked-up name was that? Bet all the kids had called him "Peuchner" in grammar school. Probably high school too.

Joe said, "Lonnie's trying to get his grandmother to invest in this great idea he has but she's stiffing him."

Easy, Joe. No need to lay it on with a trowel.

Neil grinned and raised his eyebrows. "Investing? You hardly look old enough to drink."

Lonnie looked offended. "Hey, listen—"

"Only kidding, guy." Neil gave him a comradely slap on the back. "What's this investment?"

Lonnie launched into this yawner of a spiel about fiber-optic cable and its future in telecommunications. Neil interrupted before he dozed off.

"Hey, that sounds great."

Lonnie leaned forward with almost messianic intensity. "It's life-changing, Neil. A guaranteed fortune-maker. Bill Gates had the Big Idea for Microsoft and quit college to pursue it. That's what I want to do: drop out and start my own fiber-optic company."

Neil wanted to laugh in his face. Bill Gates . . . right. You drop out of college, kid, and guess what you'll be— a fucking college dropout.

He needed to steer this conversation around to the really important topic: Grandma. Lonnie could shove fiber-optic cable up his nose till it came out his ass, and Neil wouldn't care. That wasn't why he'd come over to the bar.

"But you can't do that without money."

"Yeah," Lonnie said, the fire fading. Then he brightened. "Hey, you wanna invest—?"

Neil shrugged. "Maybe. But your grandmother knows you better than I do, and if she doesn't have faith in you . . ."

"She's just shortsighted. If she could only see how fiber optics—"

Not again.

"Your grandmother's got enough to fund you?"

"In spades."

Neil would have loved to ask how much, but that wasn't the way to get these things done.

"But she's not parting with any."

"Bingo. She's totally cheap. The bitch."

Neil raised his hands in a peacemaking gesture. No

one should talk about their grandmother like that. But it did offer a perfect opportunity to find out if anyone else was in the picture.

"Now hold on. Maybe your grandfather won't let her."

"Grandfather? He's long gone."

Excellent.

"Somebody else in the household putting in a discouraging word, maybe?"

"Nah. I'm the only other one in the household now, but I'm back off to school tomorrow."

More good news.

"Where's that?"

"UNC."

"Good school." Good and far away. "*Great* b-ball team."

"You a Tarheels fan?"

"I'm a fan of winning teams, and your guys are winners with a capital *W*." Turning the talk back to Grandma . . . "So, you're leaving your grandmother all alone?"

He made a face. "Just the way she likes it. My mom thinks she should have a live-in but Nonna won't hear of it. Too cheap."

Now we're talking.

"Well, then, let's give the lady the benefit of the doubt. Maybe her money's tied up in annuities or stocks that she can't sell right now. Let's face it, the market's for shit these days."

"You kidding? She's old-country Italian. She'd have the money stuffed in a mattress if it would fit. It's all in cash in bank accounts, doing nothing."

Neil resisted rubbing his hands together. This sounded good—*real* good. Maybe this little detour to the bar wouldn't be a waste of time after all.

He gave his head a sad shake. "Such a waste. Money

should be put to work, not left to molder in bank vaults."

"You're telling me? Fiber optics, man—fiber optics is the way to go!"

As casually as he could, Neil said, "Which bank, by the way?"

"Chase."

He gave a sage nod to hide his glee. "A good, solid institution."

Never hurt to state the obvious. And it never hurt to have a couple of contacts inside a bank. Contacts who, for a modest fee, would ferret out the details of his nonna's finances. Just one vital piece of info was missing. But how to get it?

As he considered his options, he lifted his Bud toward his lips—but stopped halfway as a sour note sounded in his brain.

"Hey, wait a minute. Did you say she was 'old-country Italian'? But your name is—"

"Beuchner. Yeah, my mother married a German, much to Nonna's eternal dismay. But let me ask you: Can you get much more Guinea than Michelina Filardo?"

Neil laughed—not because it was funny, but because he'd just been handed the last, most important piece of info on a mark—what he'd been fishing for since he'd stepped up to the bar.

Asking for a name was always the hardest part because the first response on the other side tended to be, *Who wants to know and why?* But now he had all he needed: the name of a rich old widow and where she kept her money.

"No, that'd be pretty hard."

He just had to hope that Michelina Filardo was public-spirited enough to catch a thief. Neil was reasonably sure the world-famous Zalesky charm was up to the rest.

6. As usual, they met in Roman Trejador's suite. And, since he hopped from hotel to hotel about the city, this was not the same suite as the last.

When Nasser al-Thani arrived he found Ernst Drexler already there, his glossy black hair swept straight back from a widow's peak that pointed down to his aquiline nose. The Austrian was dressed in his ever-present, ever-tacky white three-piece suit; his black rhinoceros-hide walking stick leaned against a nearby wall.

Trejador lounged on the couch. Fiftyish, urbane, Spanish by birth with dark good looks, his rough childhood had contributed to his skills as an actuator, making him the first choice of the High Council of the Ancient Septimus Fraternal Order when it needed a problem solved. He was resplendent in his Sulka silk-and-satin smoking jacket, even tackier than Drexler's suit—practically an antique.

Nasser wore a simple gray thobe.

"Greetings, Nasser," Trejador said with no accent, raising his martini. "Spring water on the bar."

Although alcohol was legal in his native Qatar, Nasser had never developed a taste for it. Even during his Oxford years among prodigious beer quaffers, he'd never been tempted.

Drexler sat in a straight-back chair next to an end table. He poured a little beer from a green bottle into a short glass, then checked his watch. "You're almost late," he said with a faintly German accent.

Without responding, Nasser poured himself a glass of Evian. He'd grown to dislike Ernst Drexler over the past few months. Trejador referred to him—behind his back, of course—as "Ernst the Lesser" to distinguish him from his late father, a legend in the annals of the Order.

Trejador said, "We anxiously await your assessment of the local Muslim situation."

"And by 'we,'" Drexler added, "he means more than we two. The High Council grows impatient. It wants the money returned."

Nasser peeked into the bedroom as he passed the half-open doorway, hoping for a glimpse of one of Trejador's whores, but it appeared empty. Too bad. The women he hired were unfailingly young and attractive. Especially a semi-regular named Danaë he'd seen on a number of occasions.

"I know it's been a long wait," he said as he seated himself opposite the other two. "But we can't set a trap for the hijackers without the help of the jihadists, and they've been embroiled in an interfactional turf war."

"While the thieves squander the Order's money," Drexler said.

Nasser did not acknowledge the testy remark. "The problem has been that we have no stick to prod the jihadists into action, nor do we have a carrot. On the first go-round, they needed money. The prospect of a couple of million to fund their holy cause made them easy to manipulate."

The plan had been so simple. The Order's goal was to foster chaos. The jihadists' goal was to scour Russians and Americans and all non-Muslims from the Mideast, topple all the secularist regimes, replace them with *sharia* theocracies, bring holy war to America, then wipe Israel off the map—preferably, though not necessarily, in that order. The massive, inescapable chaos that would accompany those goals was just what the Order wanted. But the jihadists had needed money.

Enter the Order last fall, via Nasser al-Thani, with an offer they could not refuse: Nasser would front them three million U.S. to purchase a truckload of young Caribbean and Central American girls. They would auction off the girls at prices guaranteed to double the money. They would repay Nasser the principal plus one million interest. The remaining two million was theirs to keep.

Of course the more suspicious among them questioned why Nasser didn't do this himself. He explained that, even though slavery was accepted in the Muslim world, as a distant relative of the Qatar royal family, he could not dirty his hands with trade in children. Earning a thirty-three-percent profit on a short-term loan was incentive enough for him. The situation was win-win all around.

All went swimmingly until the slavemongers and the Arabs met at the exchange point on Staten Island. Gunmen ambushed the Arabs, cold-bloodedly killing everyone in sight, and made off with the cash and the girls. Neither had been seen nor heard from since.

The High Council had fronted the money and wanted it back. But more than that, it wanted to make a statement about interfering with the business of the Ancient Septimus Fraternal Order.

Trejador's eyebrows lifted. "Our grimy little jihadists don't need money? Did they win the lottery?"

Nasser smiled. "No, but in a way, they expect to."

Drexler leaned forward. "How, pray tell?"

"They're poised to take over the Al-Kifah Refugee Center right across the river in Brooklyn. The Afghan relief charity it runs funnels donations from other Muslim centers all over America, amounting to about one hundred thousand a month, give or take a few."

"They why did they need our money?" Drexler said.

"The jihadists we were dealing with had no say in the center's funds. Then, as now, under Mustafa Shalabi, all the Al-Kifah money goes where it's supposed to—to help the hordes of Afghans trying to recover from the pounding they took from the Russians. But Sheikh Omar Abdel-Rahman wants that money to fund his worldwide jihad, to start overthrowing people like Mubarak of

Egypt and Saddam Hussein in Iraq. He looks harmless but he's an Islamic Hitler. A fiery speaker who can rile up the Muslim masses. He was behind the assassination of Anwar Sadat."

"Pure chaos," Drexler said. "Isn't this exactly what we want?"

"In the long term, yes. But in the short term, if they get their hands on the Al-Kifah account, they'll have no financial interest in working with us. And isn't it our goal to have a voice in the timing and placement of the terror they cause?"

"It is." Trejador sipped his martini, then nodded toward Nasser. "You called this meeting, so I assume you have a plan?"

"Sheikh Omar's followers are planning a coup—undoubtedly violent. Shalabi knows this. He's readying to flee the country, but before he goes I'm betting he'll empty the Al-Kifah account to keep it out of Sheikh Omar's hands."

Drexler snorted. "I hope you're not about to suggest we offer this Shalabi protection."

"On the contrary. I propose we strike first."

7. "It's wine o'clock," Cristin said. "And I'm free-ee-ee-eezing."

She made a show of shivering despite her fur-lined trench coat.

Jack glanced at his watch. Only five o'clock but the sun had sunk out of sight behind the Manhattan skyline just visible across the river. And yeah, the wind did blow cold out here in this car lot.

He'd decided the Harley had to go. He was too exposed, too easy to spot, too vulnerable on the thing. Wheels weren't a necessity in the city—pretty much a luxury, in fact—but growing up in rural New Jersey had embedded a mind-set that required a car be immediately available at all times. When he'd mentioned to Cristin that he wanted to check out what was for sale, she'd volunteered to come along.

"Let me take a quick look through these and then we'll find a nice warm bar."

She smiled as she scanned the rows of used cars. She'd been letting her dark hair grow out a little, and the wind whipping along Queens Boulevard swirled it into her face.

"Used car lots in February. You sure know how to show a girl a good time."

"Hey, you said you wanted to come along."

"I may have been having a small stroke at the time."

"No, it's because Sunday is our day and you wanted to spend every second you could with me."

Sunday nights—and sometimes afternoons too—with Cristin. She'd been his high school girlfriend's best friend. Shortly after running into each other here in the city, they'd fallen into a routine of dinner out followed by un-inhibited no-strings sex at her apartment. Every Sunday since early November except for Christmas when she'd gone back to Jersey for the long weekend. The no-strings part was crucial to Cristin.

"Oh, right. I forgot. But just to be on the safe side, can we stop by a hospital for a quick CAT scan before we have that drink? Just in case?"

"One of those Irish coffees you like will warm you up and heal your brain."

"I'm not so sure. Just hurry up and check out these junkers, will you? If my coochie freezes, you'll be out of luck tonight."

Jack laughed and gave her a quick kiss. "No way. That's too hot to freeze—or even reach room temperature."

She grinned. "Better believe it."

He hurried toward the cars as fast as his aching hip would allow.

"Hey, what's with the limp?" Cristin said.

He'd been able to hide it till now, but the cold was stiffening it.

"Little accident with the Harley this morning." He hadn't mentioned his sliced shoulder either. Sooner or later he'd have to.

"Ohhhh."

He looked at her. "You sound disappointed."

"Here I thought you were limping because you were glad to see me."

He laughed again. "*Always* glad to see you."

He moved among the cars. This used lot in Jamaica was the third—and now last, obviously—they'd visited. The other two had been fenced in and locked up. This one had no fence, so he could browse.

He wove among the Toyotas and Hondas and Fords and Chevies and whatevers but nothing appealed to him. Yeah, they'd all do, but something was missing . . .

The showroom was closed, which was why Jack had wanted to come out on a Sunday. He was not yet ready for a pushy salesman. But then, who ever was? But as he passed the showroom window he stopped. A little convertible, black on white, sat angled to the right. A hand-written placard had been inserted into the front license plate holder.

1963
Corvair

The car had been old before he was born, but somehow it called to him. He turned and waved to Cristin.

"Take a look at this!"

She angled through the lot and stopped at his side, slipping her arm through his.

"Look at what?"

"The Corvair."

"Isn't that the one that was 'unsafe at any speed'?"

"So someone said."

"And didn't you tell me you wanted something safer than the Harley?"

"You know me—Live-on-the-edge Jack."

She laughed. He liked that sound. "Really? Since when?"

"Hey, I'm just looking."

She tugged on his arm. "You've done enough looking. Time for alky-hall and then food and then more alky-hall and then lots of fucking."

"In that order?"

"Can you think of a better one?"

They began walking back toward the street.

"Mmm . . . no. Whose turn to pick?"

"Mine. And I'm in the mood for Chinese tonight. But *good* Chinese."

"Chinatown?"

"Yes!"

"You got it."

When they reached the sidewalk he took one last look at the Corvair in the window—and could almost swear it was staring back.

8. Kadir jumped at the sound of the knock on his door. Closing his Qur'an, he rose and padded across the room.

Someone at his door? This could not be good. He knew almost no one in Jersey City—certainly no one well enough to feel they could visit him unannounced.

He stopped halfway to look out the window. The street outside was empty—no idling car, no sign of anyone watching. Jersey City tended to be quiet on a Sunday night.

He approached the door and gave a quick, cautious look through the peephole, then pulled away. A young woman in a dark *khimar* stood in the hall. She knocked again.

"Kadir, are you home?"

He peeked again, taking a closer look. Most of her face was visible and looked familiar, reminding him of—

"Hadya?" He pulled the door open and stared at the woman. A battered suitcase sat next to her on the floor. "Hadya, is that you?" he said in Arabic.

She smiled. "Yes, of course it's me. But why are you so surprised?"

"Why wouldn't I be?"

"But didn't you get my letter?"

"What letter?"

He pulled her inside and shut the door. A hallway in a foreign land was no place to be talking to his younger sister.

She looked confused now. "I wrote you a letter to tell you I was coming."

"I never received it."

Her hand flew to her mouth. "Oh, no! I thought you'd be expecting me."

Kadir was baffled. "But why are you here? Did something happen—?"

"No-no. Mother and father are fine—still struggling to make ends meet, but healthy. I came because Uncle Ferran said I could work in his bakery."

Their mother's brother owned a bakery on Kennedy Boulevard. Kadir had worked there when he first came over, until he learned how to run a cigarette stamping machine for Riaz Diab. The Ramallah Bakery was very successful and Kadir knew his uncle was expanding . . . but Hadya?

"You came all the way to America to work in a bakery?"

"As did you. There is nothing back home, Kadir. Nothing."

"It is hard work, and you must rise long before the sun."

She smiled. "I am not afraid of hard work or long hours. I am glad for *any* work and *any* hours. There is no work in Jordan, Kadir. And you know how Uncle Ferran likes to hire family."

True. Uncle Ferran had no children of his own, while Kadir and Hadya were two of nine. Kadir had been born shortly after the Six-Day War in Israeli-occupied Palestine, Hadya three years later. They grew up under the Zionists. His father finally moved the family to Jordan where he went to work in a clothing store. But as for Father's children . . . no work, no future. Kadir blamed Israel . . . and the Americans who made Israel possible.

And worse, when the PLO supported the Iraqi invasion of Kuwait last year, the Kuwaiti government expelled every Palestinian it could find—nearly half a million people. Most of them flooded into Jordan.

How terrible things must be back home for Father to allow one of his daughters to travel alone to America.

"But I had no idea you were coming."

Fear flitted across her features. "You'll let me stay, won't you? At least until I can find a place of my own."

He forced a smile and embraced her. "Of course, of course. You're my sister."

Would this complicate his comings and goings? He didn't know how Hadya would feel about jihad in America.

"Oh, thank you, Kadir. For a moment I thought—"

"My home is your home. I just wish I had known. I would have prepared the bedroom for you."

"Do not trouble yourself. I will sleep on the couch."

"I will not hear of it. The bedroom is yours." He stepped back. "Let me look at you."

She was clothed with proper modesty in accordance with al-hijab—a khimar over a dark *abaya*, leaving only her hands and face exposed. His little sister had grown into an observant Muslim woman.

She might prove very useful.

9. Cristin covered her mouth as she laughed around a mouthful of beef and broccoli in garlic sauce. "I can't believe you're such a klutz."

Jack didn't look up. He was concentrating on manipulating the tips of his chopsticks around a shrimp in the heap of fried rice on his plate.

"I grew up in a meat-and-potatoes house in the hinterlands, better known as Middle of Nowhere, New Jersey."

"So did I."

"No. You grew up in Tabernacle, a bustling metropolis compared to Johnson."

"Okay, so we had a pizza place, but never Chinese takeout."

Jack had trapped the shrimp. Now to get it to his mouth.

"And don't forget—you've had four years in the city to practice. I haven't been here a year yet."

Into his mouth—success. But jeez that was a helluva lot of work for a single shrimp.

They'd settled on a little restaurant on Elizabeth Street. The neon sign over the front window was in Chinese and they were the only Caucasians in the place. Cristin had assured him that this was a good sign. He'd come to enjoy Chinese food at college, but had eaten it with a fork. This place hadn't offered any utensils beyond chopsticks, and Jack was determined to conquer them.

Leaning back, he took a swig from his Tsingtao and watched Cristin manipulate her sticks like she'd been using them all her life.

Sundays with Cristin. Jack had become used to the ritual but lately had found himself feeling a little restless with it. He didn't want to want more but . . . he wanted more. Not more *than* Cristin—more *of* Cristin.

But her party-planner job kept her tied up all week. And forget holidays. He would've loved to have spent New Year's Eve with her, but no way. Her biggest night of the year—parties up the wazoo.

He said, "*The Doors* opens Friday. Want to go see it?"

"Sure. I love their music."

He wasn't a particular fan, though he liked "Roadhouse Blues" a lot. He'd much rather catch *The Silence of the Lambs,* but figured *The Doors* was more up her alley.

"I know."

"How do you know?"

"You've got all their CDs on your shelf."

"'Light My Fire' is like the story of my life." She smiled. "Besides, it'll make for a warmer Sunday afternoon than car hunting."

"I meant opening day."

Her smile widened. "What? You've got the hots for Val Kilmer?"

Perfect opening: "No. Just for you. Enough to want to see you twice in one week."

Her smile faded as she shook her head. "No can do. Got a big corporate party Friday night."

"How about during the day?"

Another head shake. "Meetings."

"How about Saturday then?"

She sighed and reached into her pocketbook. She emerged with a business card and handed it to him.

"See that?"

He looked at the card: bright red with *CELEBRATIONS* across the middle in lemon-yellow script. "Events" ran below it in smaller block print. An 800 number was tucked in the lower left corner.

"'Events,' huh? What happened to 'parties'?"

"Memo from on high: We're no longer 'party-planners,' we're now 'event-planners.' Because while a party can be an event, an event is not necessarily a party. And events tend to be more profitable."

He looked again. "Your name's not on it."

She shrugged. "The company has them printed up. All the planners get the same card. But that's not the point." She took the card back and held it up between them. "The point is, I make very good money with these folks. I'm socking away a ton. But Celebrations isn't the only party—sorry, event-planning service in town. Loads of competition out there, and so to do the job right, I've got to be available. I've been building a very tony client base—CEOs, state senators and assemblymen, deputy mayors, city council members—and that's important, because I work on commission. The more elaborate and expensive the party, the more I take home."

"I know, I know. It's just—"

She made a show of looking over her shoulder. "Is that a string I feel attaching to me?"

Cristin had a thing about no strings. Jack was no fan of them either, but sometimes she took it to extremes. Not once had he slept over. He was looking for a new apartment—he'd never asked her to his current place because it was such a dump—but he was sure if she came on a Sunday, she'd leave before morning.

"No. Just me looking for a little flexibility."

"I could work seven days a week at this job, but Sundays tend to be slow, so that's my day off. The rest of the week—I'm booked."

"I get it."

She popped a sauce-laden broccoli floret into her mouth. "We set ground rules when we started, right?"

Well, *she* had. But yeah, he'd gone along.

"Right."

"Aren't things good between us, you know, as friends with benefits?"

"Better than good. Great."

"Then can we agree not to ruin it with strings?"

"You got it. *The Doors* next Sunday?"

She smiled. "It's a date."

10.   Maybe the MSG in their food had some sort of aphrodisiacal effect on Cristin. Or maybe she was simply Cristin being Cristin. Whatever the cause, as soon as the apartment door closed behind her she practically attacked Jack, yanking at his belt buckle. Before he realized what was happening, his jeans dropped to the floor along with the Ruger in its SOB holster. It landed with a loud *thunk*.

"What the—?" she said.

"Just my wallet."

He kissed her, hoping to distract her. But her curiosity wasn't about to be turned.

"Then your wallet must be filled with gold coins, because—holy crap!" She'd twisted and craned her neck to see around him. "Is that a *gun*?"

"Um, yeah."

Well, standing there with his jeans around his ankles, and the Ruger's grip and hammer protruding from the nylon holster, what else could he say? He waited for some horrified response, but instead she dropped to her knees for a closer look.

"Oh, coooool!"

Cool?

She looked up at him. "When did you start carrying this?"

"Um, today."

Sort of true. After their first few Sundays together, when he'd had a couple of close calls trying to hide it from her, he'd stopped carrying when they were together. But after yesterday's narrow escape, he'd decided he needed to be armed at all times.

"Why?"

He decided he may as well tell her the truth, but he made it sound like a question: "Would you believe I've got a bunch of Dominicans mad at me?"

"Monks?"

Was she kidding? Then she winked and he knew.

"What did you do to make this necessary?" She patted the holster. "Steal their Frangelico recipe?"

"Long story. A bunch of them almost caught me yesterday, so I decided I needed to keep an equalizer handy."

"Can I see it?"

"It's right there."

"Will you take it out for me?"

"The pistol?"

She slapped him on the leg. "We'll get to that later. First . . ."

"Okay." He winced as he squatted next to her and reached for it. "You can—"

"Oh, my God!" She was staring at the large bruise on his thigh. "Did those monks do that?"

"No. That's from my Harley yesterday."

"No wonder you've been limping."

He pulled the Ruger free of the holster. Its nickel finish gleamed.

"Take it. Just keep your finger away from the trigger."

"Heavy!" she said, then handed it back to him. "Okay. Time for you to shoot me."

"What?"

She laughed and slid her hand up his thigh. "With your *other* gun, silly."

They resumed undressing each other but that came to another halt when Cristin spotted the bandage on his arm.

"What?" she said, running her fingers over it.

"Those monks."

"The Dominicans?"

"Well, they did run the Inquisition. Accused me of heresy."

"No, really."

He didn't want to get into it.

"Just a disagreement. It'll all work out."

"You're sure?"

Not in the least, he thought. But he said, "Absolutely." He put his arms around her. "Now where were we?"

11. They'd caught their breath now and lay entangled under the sheets—Jack on his back and Cristin snuggled next to him. Neither spoke. Neither felt the need.

After a while she kissed his cheek and said, "Whatcha thinkin', my battered Lincoln?"

He'd been thinking about their dinner conversation and how he still wished they could have more than one night a week together. No point in bringing it up again.

"Thinking about that Corvair."

Not entirely untrue. Flashes of its front end kept popping into his head.

"Oh, *reeeeally*? In *my* bed?"

"It's stuck in my head. You know, like part of a song

gets stuck in your brain and keeps repeating and repeat-ing? That car's doing something like that."

"Then there's only one thing to do."

"What?"

He figured she'd say *Buy it*. But this was Cristin Ott.

"I'm gonna have to fuck it out of your brain."

He laughed. "I'd like to see you try."

She succeeded, but the effect was only temporary.

MONDAY

1. "Pie?" Abe said, looking scandalized. "You brought pie for breakfast?"

Jack had wanted to try something different. He'd stopped in a mom-and-pop called Costin's that carried a little bit of everything. It served hot coffee but had no seating. A convenience store that looked like it had been around since long before anyone dreamed up the term. Some of the dusty items on the shelves looked like they'd been there since it opened.

But the boxed pies looked fresh so he'd picked up a peach and brought it to the Isher Sports Shop.

"You might not have ever had pie for breakfast," Jack said, "but you've heard of eating fruit for breakfast, right?"

"Of course."

"And I know you've eaten pastry for breakfast."

Abe waggled a hand. "Once, maybe. Okay, twice."

Jack pointed to the pie. "Well, the filling is fruit and the crust is pastry."

Abe's gaze shifted to the pie, then to Jack—his wide-eyed expression made it obvious he was experiencing an ecstatic epiphany—then back to the pie.

"I think maybe you're onto something."

He reached under the counter and produced a knife more suited to skinning rhinos than cutting a pie. He sliced across the diameter, then made a similar cut at a ninety-degree angle. He pried up the quarter nearest him and took a big bite from the pointed end.

He rolled his eyes as he swallowed. "A *balmalocha* of breakfast, he is. Vast vistas of possibilities open before me."

"This balmalocha," Jack said. "It's something I want to be?"

Christ, I'm starting to sound like him.

Abe nodded. "Sort of like a maven."

Jack knew maven. He pulled out a quarter of the pie and went to work on it. As good as it looked. Abe finished his first piece and attacked a second.

"Crumbs," Abe said around a mouthful of pie.

"What?"

He swallowed. "A crumb topping, like on Entenmann's crumb donuts, and this would be perfect."

Jack thought the pie was pretty damn near perfect as it was.

Abe brushed off his hands on his shirtfront, smearing a bit of peach filling across the breast pocket, and then placed a plain cardboard box, a little smaller than the pie, on the scarred counter.

Jack nodded toward it. "What's that?"

"What you asked for."

"Which is . . . ?"

"*Nu?* You got Alzheimer's already?"

"Not that I know of."

"Didn't you call me yesterday and tell me you wanted to 'bug' someone's car?"

"Oh, right."

As soon as Jack had left Julio's on Saturday, he'd called Abe to see if he could help him out.

Last fall, Jack and Julio had trailed Zalesky and one of the old ladies he was scamming. They watched him pick her up at her house and drop her off at a bank with a briefcase. After she returned, he put that briefcase—

presumably full of cash from the bank—in the trunk. They waited for nearly an hour, then he dropped her off home with the briefcase.

Neither had been able to figure out how he was working his scam. Easy enough for Jack to put eyes on him, but he needed ears too. He couldn't get a line on how to counter Zalesky without hearing his sales patter.

Jack pulled the box closer. "So soon? You work fast."

"Fast, shmast. All a matter of knowing who to call."

Jack lifted the lid and found a tangle of wires coiled around a couple of black metal boxes the size of cigarette packs.

"Looks complicated."

"Not to worry." He pointed to one of the boxes. "This one with the little antenna is the transmitter. Its wire attaches it to this tiny electret microphone. This other box is the receiver. Its wire attaches to an earplug so you can listen. Range is supposed to be one hundred meters—"

"What's that in feet?"

"A little over three hundred."

Jack pictured a football field. "Nice."

"The operative word is 'supposed.' My friend says you shouldn't count on the full one hundred. If you want to be sure you don't miss anything, stay within half that."

Jack thought that was still pretty doable, but saw potential problems.

"Battery life?"

"Long. It's voice activated. Doesn't draw power until there's something to transmit."

"Cool. Does this guy do installation?"

Abe shook his head. "This guy? Like a hermit he lives. Barely leaves his basement."

Jack had figured custom installation was a long shot anyway. "Well, I sure as hell don't know anything about electronics. How do I get it into his car?"

Jack couldn't see any way to plant it on Zalesky himself,

and since driving his marks around in his car seemed to be part of the scam . . .

"You know already how to break into a locked car, yes?"

"Well, yeah."

"So all you've got to do is sneak into his car, put the little microphone where it can pick up voices, and then hide the transmitter."

Jack laughed. "Is that all?"

"What else? Simple already."

"Yeah. Simple." Like who will bell the cat?

Zalesky drove a late model Dodge Dynasty. Jack knew nothing about the model's interior, or its trunk. How was he going to hide that bug inside Zalesky's car with no one the wiser?

And then an idea.

"Got a phone book?"

Abe reached under the counter and produced a battered copy of the Yellow Pages. It occurred to Jack that he seemed to have one of just about everything down there.

"What for?"

"Gonna start calling car rental places."

If he could get his hands on a Dynasty for a dry run at installing the bug, this might work.

2.   Vinny glided past a row of warehouses in Canarsie and turned into his salvage yard on Preston Court. He hadn't wanted his own name on the business, so he'd left the original: Preston Salvage.

His fists tightened on the steering wheel when he recognized one of the cars in the lot. Tommy's cherry red Nissan 300ZX.

Okay. Be cool. This may work out.

If Tommy's being here brought in the extra business—over and under the table—that Tony had promised, the financial end might come out okay. But money wasn't the only consideration here. Preston Salvage was Vinny's baby, something to call his own. He'd hunted around, he'd done the legwork, found it, made a deal for it. Now he had to share it with Tommy Ten Thumbs Totaro. He didn't like sharing. Never had. Never would.

The forced calm shattered as soon as he stepped into the office and found Tommy in *his* chair . . . behind *his* desk . . . going through *his* papers with the short fat sausage fingers that had earned him his nickname. Only mid–late thirties or so, he had his head down and Vinny could see a bald spot growing within his wavy, sandy hair.

He looked up and smiled. "Howdy, pardner."

"That's my chair," Vinny said.

"Yeah, well, there's another one right over there."

"And that's my desk."

"Well, there's only one desk, and I needed to get acquainted with your operation here."

Good thing he wasn't carrying at the moment or Vinny figured he might have already popped Tommy a couple of times by now.

Tommy shuffled the papers. "I was going through your expenses here and I noticed bills from a marina out in Jamaica Bay." He grinned. "You got yourself a party boat you never told me about?"

Vinny unclenched his teeth. "It ain't a party boat. It belongs to the company."

"The company's got a boat?" Tommy's smile broadened. "I didn't get to go through all the assets yet. That means *we've* got a party boat."

Vinny could almost see the fantasies dancing in Tommy's head: a bag of blow, a couple of pros, and sailing off to sea for an all-night party.

"I don't think—"

"What's it called?"

"*Daisy Two.*"

Tommy made a face. "What kinda name is that?"

"The kinda name it came with."

"That's one fucked-up name for a party boat. I mean, Vinny, that's gotta go. I don't wanna be out there drivin' Miss *Daisy.* I want a muff magnet. We'll name it *Tommy's Torpedo* or something along that nature."

Much as Vinny would have loved to let Tommy brag to his buddies about his new boat and then get an ugly surprise when he brought a couple of broads down to the dock to show it off, he figured he'd rather crush his dreams now. So he went over to the corkboard on the wall, unpinned a photo of *Daisy II,* and tossed it on the desk.

"That look like a torpedo to you?"

Tommy snatched it up and grimaced. "You're kidding, right?"

"That's *Daisy Two.*"

"No fucking way! That's some kinda fishing boat!"

"You got it. A small trawler, to be exact."

"Since when do we fucking sell fish?"

Vinny noted the "we" and it felt like a bitch slap, but he kept his cool.

"Sometimes we feed the fishes."

Tommy gave him a few seconds of blank stare, then the light dawned. He grinned. "Oh, yeah. One of the sidelines. You use the car crusher for that, right?"

"Of course."

"Lemme see it in action."

Vinny wanted to tell him to fuck off, but knew he was stuck with the prick.

"Why not?"

He led Tommy out into the yard and around the small mountain of tires toward the rear lot.

Tommy pointed to the tires. "Whatta y'do with these?"

"They're mostly a pain in the ass. We got a baler. We sell 'em by the ton, but not for much. A lot get ground up and used for padding in playgrounds or put into asphalt."

Around the rear, the E-Z Crusher had center stage—two huge twenty-by-eight-foot steel plates like a big open mouth, waiting to be fed. He looked around for Zeke, who usually worked the crusher, but didn't see him. He noticed the flatbed was missing, which meant he was probably out on a pickup.

No problem.

Vinny hopped up on the front-end loader. The engine was still warm, so it started right up. He worked the levers to get her rolling and wheeled her over to one of the stripped junkers. Looked like an old Mitsubishi. He got the forks under it, guided it across the yard, and dropped it into the E-Z Crusher's twenty-foot bed. Then he started up the crusher and stood back to let it do its thing.

Vinny never tired of watching the heavy upper steel plate slowly pancake a car. It occurred to him that he wouldn't mind seeing it do a similar number on Tommy Ten Thumbs.

Maybe someday.

3. "I do believe I should be charging you," Melinda said as Neil Zalesky seated himself opposite her.

He raised his eyebrows. He didn't like the sound of that. "Really? What makes you say so?"

She smiled. "Did a little research."

Neil watched her light a cigarette. Though not a beauty by any stretch, Melinda Costanza wasn't bad looking. She and Neil had had a little fling while he was married to Rosa but it ended when she found someone else who was unattached. Since she'd been the one to break it off, and since Neil hadn't been terribly torn up at the news she was leaving him—although he'd pretended otherwise—they'd remained friends. Mostly that was his doing because of where she worked: Chase Manhattan's main branch in Manhattan.

Occasionally he'd buy her lunch at this little midtown pub near her office—on him, for old times' sake—and occasionally at those lunches he'd ask her for information on a certain Chase customer. She'd look up the account and provide details as to how much was on deposit. This morning he'd broken tradition and called her, asking her up front to find out what she could about a certain Michelina Filardo. He needed a score real quick-like and wanted to know if he had a live one in Filardo.

"What sort of research?" he said.

"I checked back on the other accounts you've asked me about and a fair number of them withdrew princely sums shortly after your inquiry."

Neil's turn to smile. "Pure coincidence."

"Really? I'm not so sure."

"You said, 'a number of them.' I could see you being suspicious if *all* the accounts had 'princely' withdrawals, but that's not the case."

Truth was, some of the marks weren't the least bit civic-minded and turned out to be dead ends.

"Still, I found enough of them to be considered a trend."

Where was she going with this?

"Any complaints, allegations, or investigations?"

"No."

He shrugged. "Like I said: Pure coincidence."

She shook her head. "You can be real smooth, Neil. I've seen you in action—I mean, I've been on the receiving end."

Yeah, he thought. Didn't take me long to talk you right out of those black lace panties you like so much, did it?

He feigned shock. "You can't think—"

She waved her cigarette. "Don't worry. I'm not the whistle-blowing type. I think it's kind of cool, actually."

Neil pushed back a grin—had to keep playing this straight—because it was oh so true: The wimmins loves the bad boys.

"Really, Melinda, I'm just doing background checks for clients to see if these potential investors have the assets to participate in certain financial instruments."

He hoped that made sense. He was winging it here.

Her smile widened. "Uh-huh." Reaching down, she pulled a manila envelope out of her shoulder bag and slid it across the table. "Michelina Filardo."

Neil resisted opening it. "Thank you, Melinda. You're the best." He knew the address and phone number would be in there, but he had to ask. "Where's she live?"

"Carroll Gardens."

He frowned. "Don't think I've ever been there."

"It's on the other side of the BQE from Red Hook. Old Italian neighborhood. She owns a brownstone clear on Clinton Street. No other holdings listed, but that doesn't mean they don't exist."

"And the account?"

"Checking and savings. Turns out she's fairly comfortable. Twice widowed. And she's the only name on the account. She makes regular deposits and no withdrawals. Ain't computers just ducky?"

"No withdrawals?"

She shrugged. "Usually means she's got an income-producing investment somewhere."

That didn't jibe with what the grandson said about her wanting to keep it under a mattress, but no biggie. She could own a house somewhere she was renting out.

The important part was no other name on the account. That meant no one hanging over the old broad's shoulder to spot a big withdrawal and start asking questions.

"My client will be glad to know."

"Your client. Right." She pointed her cigarette at him. "I'll be watching this account, Neil baby. And if I see a big withdrawal, I'll want a piece."

Neil was tempted to tell her to shove her cut but he had no other contact at Chase with Melinda's access to the bank's computer system. He'd have to give her something, but only if the Filardo broad came through. In the meantime, he'd avoid admitting anything.

"You offend me, my dear," he said with a shocked expression.

"I'll be even more offended if I don't get my cut. Now buy me some lunch. I'm starved."

"Yes, Melinda dear."

4. Jack ordered the open-face steak sandwich and a draft pint of Smithwick's Pale Ale, then he adjusted his little disposable camera where it sat on the table and took a shot of Zalesky and his lady friend. He couldn't use a flash but the light in here was pretty good. He took a couple more for insurance.

He'd begun watching Zalesky's place from the bookstore early this morning. He'd followed him to midtown on the subway and then to this Irish pub where he met the lady in the dark blue business getup.

He studied them out of the corner of his eye. To quote the Isley Brothers, "Who's That Lady?" Had Zalesky taken the bait and did this gal have anything to do with Michelina Filardo? Or was she just an acquaintance? The two seemed comfortable with each other. Jack was no expert in body language but he didn't look like a guy making a move.

Still, Jack took the pictures because he might have to get in touch with this lady at some point.

Jack finished off his meal with a Pepsi rather than another Smithwick's, good as it was. He had a martial arts class later this afternoon and needed to be sharp.

When Zalesky and his lady friend finished, he got a couple more shots of her. They walked out to the sidewalk where they parted with a quick hug and an air kiss—two more shots. Jack noticed Zalesky carrying a manila envelope he hadn't arrived with. Much as he would have loved to learn what was in it, he tailed the woman . . . all the way to a Chase branch.

He followed her in and stayed just long enough to establish that she worked there.

Michelina Filardo banked at Chase.

He smiled as he exited to the street. Looked like Zalesky had taken the bait.

5.   With his sweatshirt hood pulled forward and his Ruger stuck in his belt, Jack dropped off his camera at a one-hour photo place, then headed for the Ishii dojo for the two o'clock *bo* class.

He'd heard purists sneeringly refer to the dojo as "the *Blackbelt Theater* dojo." That was because the guy who ran it, Ishii Masaru, was more of a marketer and a streetfighter than a devotee of a certain school of martial arts. He taught use of the bo staff, *tonfa, yawara* sticks, *nunchaku*, plus various karate techniques. No edged or pointed weapons. He emphasized defense, but *aggressive* defense—the kind of defense that would leave an attacker unconscious, or at the very least battered into helplessness and wishing very much he had picked on someone else. His approach was informal: A *gi* was not required, but Ishii-san did insist on everyone removing his shoes.

His dojo occupied the second-floor of a former slaughterhouse on far West 12th Street in the Meatpacking District. About nine or ten guys were practicing at the moment. Jack liked to come early in the day because the classes tended to be smaller than later on. Ishii-san, a squat little man, maybe fifty years old, was at the door. Jack gave the sensei a half bow upon entering.

"I think I'll just watch today."

"Because?" Ishii-san had come over as a teenager and spoke with only a hint of an accent.

Jack pointed to his left shoulder. "Bad cut. Don't want to mess up the stitches."

He nodded. "One can learn through the eyes, but better through the hands and feet."

"Absolutely."

The old Yogi-ism, *You can observe a lot by watching*, flashed through his brain but he decided not to share.

"An accident?"

Jack figured if he could tell anyone, he could tell his sensei.

"A machete." When Ishii-san frowned, Jack added, "A type of sword."

His eyebrows lifted. "So? How many?"

"Three."

"Ah. You were alone?"

"Very."

"And how did you defend yourself?"

Jack shrugged. "I ran like hell."

"Yes!" he said with a grin. "Against overwhelming odds, with no one else to defend, that is the wisest course."

Jack sat cross-legged on a mat while Ishii-san handed out pool cues to the class. This was what Jack loved about the guy and kept him coming back. His philosophy was, *You are not going to find yourself defending your life or your family or your girlfriend with a perfectly balanced bo; you will have to make do with whatever is at hand.*

Jack noticed three guys in the class he hadn't seen before. They were built like gym rats, with massive pecs and biceps, and seemed to be friends. By the way they handled the cues—like baseball bats—he gathered they were newbies.

Just as the class started, Preston Loeb rushed in. Maybe glided in would be a better term. He stood six-one with a slim build and long black hair, tied today in some sort of topknot. He was already in his gi—damned if it didn't look custom tailored—and had a large Gucci bag slung over his shoulder. Normally he had a delicately handsome face, but today it lay hidden under a mass of white makeup accented with colored streaks and crimson lips.

Ishii-san stared at him in shock. "Kabuki?"

"Yes!" Preston said in his lilting voice, kicking off his shoes as he dropped his bag against a wall. "We're rehearsing *Yoshitsune Senbon Zakura*."

"My favorite."

"Really? I'll make sure you get a ticket. Sorry, but we were running through the *chūnori* scene and I didn't have time to get out of makeup."

Ishii-san was studying Preston's makeup. "Who do you play?"

Preston struck a vamp pose and fluttered his eyelashes. "Shizuka, of course—Yoshitsune's mistress."

Preston was a couple of years older than Jack and had been attending the dojo long before him. The regulars were all used to his flamboyant behavior. But the three newbies looked flabbergasted.

"What the fuck?" said the biggest of the three.

Preston turned to him. "What? Surprised to find a faggot in a dojo?"

The guy's mouth worked. Preston got off on shocking straights, and most people had never heard a gay refer to himself as a faggot.

"Yeah . . . no."

"Hellooo-ooo! It's gay S-and-M-ville, bubby—the Meatpacking District, and I'm packin' meat. If you come here, you must be looking for us, because, just like Visa"—his arms shot out in an all-encompassing gesture—"we're everywhere you want to be!"

The guy reddened. "Fuck you."

Preston threw his hands up in mock praise. "Hallelujah! That can be arranged, sweetie." He fluttered his lashes again. "Pitcher or catcher?"

The guy had at least fifty pounds of solid muscle on Preston and looked like he was ready to charge.

"Everybody quiet," Ishii-san said. "Everybody quiet. We begin lesson."

As the class took up their cues and faced their sensei, Preston sauntered past Jack on his way to grab a cue.

He smiled and winked. "That'll give him something to think about. Not joining us, sweetie?"

"Hey, Pres. No, looks like I'm on the DL this week."

"What? Sprain your back again trying to blow yourself?"

"Yeah, just can't seem to get it right. I think I need lessons."

This was an ongoing thing between them.

Pres winked. "Any time, sweet cheeks."

Jack shook his head as Preston moved on. That guy's mouth was going to get him in trouble someday. But Jack could understand his attitude. Pres considered Chelsea and the Meatpacking District his home turf and he wasn't going to back down from any gay-bashing attitude. If you came here, you didn't challenge his being gay, you had to represent why you *weren't*.

Jack liked living in Chelsea, but Rico and his DDP buddies knew he was here, so he had to move on.

6. After leaving the dojo, Jack spent the rest of the afternoon canvassing the car agencies for a Dodge Dynasty to rent. Nobody had one. He finally tracked down a used car lot in Queens that also did rentals. It didn't have a Dynasty available but had a Chrysler New Yorker. The owner/salesman he spoke to swore that the New Yorker was pretty much the exact same car as the Dynasty except for some extra trim and a higher price tag. So Jack rented it for a day.

As he was driving away from the lot he couldn't help swinging onto Queens Boulevard and down to the last lot he and Cristin had visited. He stopped outside the showroom for another quick look at the '63 Corvair and it looked even better. He didn't go in because he wasn't sure he could risk buying and registering it under his phony "Jeff Cusic" identity. He'd have to think on that.

He drove the New Yorker to the nearest supermarket and parked in an empty, out-of-the-way corner of the lot. He popped the locks and got to work.

That time back in November when he and Julio had followed Zalesky, the hijo de puta had put his old lady mark in the backseat. So Jack figured that was the place he wanted his mic.

He made a close inspection of the Chrysler's rear cushions and found a spot in the folds, down near one of the seat-belt receptacles, where the tiny mic could pick up conversation but be damn near invisible unless you were looking for it. He then crawled into the trunk and discovered a place where he could tape the transmitter out of sight. Through trial and error, he found a spot that would allow him to push the mic between the rear cushions.

Yeah, he could bug Zalesky's car—*if* the auto dealer hadn't been exaggerating too much about the similarities between Dodge Dynasties and Chrysler New Yorkers. Otherwise he'd just wasted a perfectly good afternoon.

TUESDAY

I. "Watch for it," Jack said as he crouched in Zalesky's cramped trunk. "I'm pushing it through."

The backseat's padding muffled Julio's reply from within the car. "Go-go-go! Let's get this done, meng."

Zalesky lived over an Italian bakery in a mixed commercial-residential neighborhood along Crosby Street in the Pelham Bay section of the Bronx. But he tended to park his car around the corner on Roberts Avenue. Jack and Julio had trained up from Manhattan and spotted him in The Main Event. They located his car, then waited until shortly after midnight when he left the bar and strolled back to his apartment.

Figuring he was in for the night, they made a beeline for the car where Jack picked the lock on the passenger door. Once inside, all he had to do was pull the trunk release lever and they were in business.

Turned out the used-car guy had been right on the money: the Dynasty and the New Yorker were like two peas from the same pod. Jack found the chosen spot for the mic in the rear cushions down near a seat-belt receptacle, and used an awl to poke a hole through the fabric and the padding behind it. He left the tool in the hole while Julio took his place and Jack went around to the trunk. They left the courtesy lights on—not only did they provide illumination in the interior and the trunk, but made Julio and him appear to have nothing to hide. Just two guys trying to fix something in their car.

"Okay. Here it comes."

He had a length of monofilament fishing line tied to the mic. He wrapped the other end around the tip of a thick, heavy-duty flathead screwdriver and, using the awl as a guide, pushed it through the hole.

"Got it?"

"Yeah," Julio said.

Jack withdrew the screwdriver, leaving the fishing line trailing through the hole.

"Okay, unwrap the string and pull the mic through— but slowly and *gently*."

As Julio took up the slack from the other side, Jack guided the mic to the hole and pushed it through until he heard from Julio.

"Got it."

He pushed it a little farther, then hurried around to the rear seat. He adjusted the position of the mic in the cushion folds by the receptacle. Damn, that looked good. As good as invisible. Now to make sure it still worked.

He hustled back to the trunk and turned on the transmitter. Then he used the duct tape he'd brought along to fix it high and out of sight under the rear window deck. He tucked the wire into the edges of the trunk space to hide it.

"Okay," he told Julio. "Start talking—you know, normal conversation tones."

Jack hopped out of the trunk and began walking away. As he moved he turned on the receiver and put its earpiece in his ear. Julio's voice came through loud and clear. Half a block away he could still understand what he was saying.

He hurried back to the car.

"It's working. Let's get out of here."

He took one last look in the trunk and saw no sign

that anything had been tampered with. He sat in the rear seat and looked around. No sign of the mic.

My work here is done, he thought.

Now it became a simple matter of waiting and watching.

2. Stakeout duty.

Reggie shifted from one butt-buggering spot on the old Volvo's passenger seat to another. This was cop stuff. Or private-dick stuff. He wasn't either but he'd been stuck doing it for days.

Once again he found himself paired with Kris Szeto, Eastern Eurotrash from Romania or Yugoslavia or Bulgaria or one of those places. Wherever he came from, he had a thick accent of some sort and was heavy into black leather. His hair was as dark as his jacket, but shinier. Like vinyl. Reggie wondered if he dyed it. Maybe he rubbed some of that dye on his jaw, because he always looked like he needed a shave, even when he didn't have any stubble.

At least he wasn't a raghead. This watch duty was that Arab al-Thani's idea; and Szeto's boss, Drexler of the white suit, was going along with it. When Drexler said, "Jump," Szeto said, "Which cliff?" Drexler had told Reggie to tag along. Reggie didn't *have* to obey. Unlike Szeto, he wasn't part of their mysterious organization, which wasn't something you joined like the Elks or the Moose Lodge—you had to be *asked*. And nobody was asking Reggie.

But even though he wasn't a member, he owed Drexler and his gang. He flexed his knees . . . yeah, he owed them that. After that son of a bitch Lonnie—not his real name, Reggie was sure—busted his kneecaps, Drexler arranged for an orthopedist to fix them. And the guy did a good job. They hurt most of the time, especially in this goddamn cold weather, but at least he could stand and walk on them.

Drexler kept him around, housing him in some big old building on the Lower East Side like some sort of pet, but Reggie didn't mind. He didn't have nothing else going at the moment. He figured he could pretty much count on some ongoing support because he was the only one alive who knew what Lonnie looked like. And, thanks to a little fiction Reggie had concocted, Drexler believed Lonnie was in on the ambush that had cost his organization three million simoleons.

Lonnie . . . Reggie was pretty sure he didn't know shit about the hijackers, because he'd been just as scared and shocked as Reggie when the shooting started. He wouldn't even have been there if Reggie hadn't dragooned him into driving the second truck. But Drexler didn't need to know any of that.

Through the weeks and months, Reggie had become interested in the Order. Its public face was some sort of social/business/political networking group, but Reggie had gathered that it went a hell of a lot deeper than that. First off, no one knew how old it was—or those who did weren't talking. Reggie had gone so far as to visit the New York Public Library to look it up and had got nowhere. When he'd complained at the desk that they had almost no information on the Order, he'd been referred to the "restricted" section.

The old guy in charge of the restricted stacks said a few exposés of the Ancient Septimus Fraternal Order had been published over the years but the books tended to disappear from the shelves. The most recent, *Septimus Secrets* by an obscure scholar named Max Soltys, came out twenty years ago from a small press. It claimed that the Order stretched back to prehistory and throughout the ages had included many of history's movers and shakers as members. Soltys died in a boating accident shortly after publication; the small press was bought out and soon went out of business. Copies of the book were no longer for sale anywhere. The last copy was stolen years ago from these restricted stacks.

Coincidence? Conspiracy? Reggie had no way of finding out. But he did know he wanted in.

So when Drexler told him to ride shotgun with Szeto while he watched for a certain Egyptian—some guy named Shalabi or Wasabi or Kemosabe or whatever—no way Reggie was going to say no. Trouble was, the raghead lived in someplace called Sea Gate on the ass end of Coney Island. A gated community, no less. And they were all sorts of serious about the gated bit. Szeto had tried to get in—"Just to look around, is so beautiful"— and the guard kicked his butt back outside the gate. They went looking for another way in but the entire end of the island was fenced off—the fence even ran down the beach, almost to the water. Sure, you could walk around the fence, but who wanted to do that? And you'd only get kicked out by the Sea Gate PD. Yeah, the dinky little place had its own police force.

That was the bad part about Sea Gate. The good part was how it was surrounded on three sides by water. So if you wanted to drive anywhere, you pretty much had to come down Neptune Avenue. Which was where they'd been sitting, just east of West 37th Street, spending their twelve-hour shifts drinking coffee, eating sandwiches, and starting up the car every so often so they wouldn't freeze their asses off.

"So," Reggie said after a sip of his third cup of bitter coffee, "let me ask you about this 'Order' of yours."

Szeto wasn't much of a talker. They'd tried listening to music but Szeto couldn't stand the stuff on the radio, and the tape he'd played for Reggie had sounded like heavy machinery with bad gears. Reggie had lasted half a song before threatening to throw it out the window. They'd settled on silence but it was getting to Reggie.

Szeto stiffened at the question. "Order? What is Order?"

"The Ancient Septimus Fraternal Order."

He did a slow turn toward Reggie. "How you know about this?"

"Your boss, Drexler. He's got me staying in this old place downtown and it's got this big seal inside, and under it is 'Ancient Septimus Fraternal Order.' I never heard of it before."

He neglected to mention trying to delve into the group's history.

"Is group that helps members make, you know, connections. Business, government, that sort of thing."

"Yeah? What business are you interested in?"

"Me? I am security."

"Really? Why does a fraternity need security?"

"Are rules."

"And you make sure people follow the rules?"

Szeto nodded. "Someone must. Rules are necessary. But if no one enforce rules, what good are rules?"

Well, he had a point. But Reggie realized he had learned exactly zilch from the guy. He was about to press him when he spotted a black Mercedes sedan come through the Sea Gate gate and roll their way along Neptune. They'd been told to watch for just that kind of car.

"Hey, ain't that him?"

He grabbed the clipboard from between them and found the license plate number. Yep. It matched.

"Is him," Szeto said.

Without needing to be told, he was already turning the ignition key. The guy driving the Mercedes matched the description of Mustafa Shalabi. Well, as best Reggie could tell. They all looked alike to him.

Drexler and al-Thani wanted to be notified immediately if he was headed for the airport. Reggie had practically memorized the New York City map while killing time waiting for Shalabi to show, and now, as they followed, he realized Shalabi was cruising past the connection to the Belt Parkway that would have taken him to JFK. Looked like he had a local destination.

Shalabi stayed on Neptune Avenue all the way east through Coney Island and into Brighton Beach where half the signs were in Russian. He parked on the street; Reggie and Szeto stopped half a block past him and watched as he entered a door under a sign that read *Odessa Travel Agency*.

"Okay. This is interesting."

Al-Thani and Drexler had said they didn't want Shalabi leaving the country, at least not until they had a chance to talk to him. Reggie hadn't a clue what they wanted from the raghead, and didn't really care. But if he was hitting a travel agency, that could mean he'd soon be hitting an airport.

Twenty minutes later he was back out the door and heading for his car. They followed it back to the Sea Gate entrance.

"We must call," Szeto said.

"First let's find out when he's leaving."

"How to do that?"

"We ask at the travel agency."

"What if they do not tell?"

Reggie smacked a fist into a palm. "I'm sure we can persuade them."

Szeto grinned. "Is good plan. I like you, Reggie."

Wish I could say the same about you, Reggie thought.

They drove back. At first the woman at Odessa Travel refused to give them any information. That lasted about twenty seconds—right up until Reggie walked behind the counter and gave her shoulder a painful squeeze.

"When and where—*now!*"

She winced and said, "Tomorrow! Lufthansa to Frankfurt!"

Reggie looked at Szeto. "Where's Frankfurt?"

Szeto gave him a you-must-be-kidding look. "Germany."

The woman said, "From there he goes to Kabul."

Where the fuck was Kabul? He looked at Szeto again.

"Afghanistan," he said.

"Don't gimme that pissant look. You come from over there. If I said 'Topeka,' you wouldn't have a fucking idea where—"

"Kansas."

Shit.

"Well, give yourself a fucking geography merit badge." Reggie released the woman's shoulder and grabbed the handset off the desk phone. "You don't mind if I make a call, do you, sweetie? Don't worry. It's local." She shook her head. "Good."

He pulled the number from a pocket and punched it in. He recognized al-Thani's voice on the other end.

"He's getting ready to move. Heading to Frankfurt tomorrow, then to Kabul." Reggie made it sound as if he knew exactly where those places were.

"Good work. Keep watch in case he moves early. We will contact you."

"How?"

They didn't have a car phone.

"We will join you after dark."

And then he hung up.

After dark? Shit. He'd been hoping to get a break from this bird-dog detail. Looked like the whole rest of the day was going to be more of the same.

He looked at the travel agent, then scanned her desk. He saw a photo of a little boy and a girl at a park tacked to a corkboard. He popped it off and showed it to her.

"Your kids?"

She swallowed and nodded.

"Cute," he said, folding it. "You want them to stay that way, you won't tell anybody we were here."

Another swallow, another nod.

He shoved the photo into his pocket and walked out. People with kids were so *easy*.

The big question now: What did Drexler and al-Thani have planned for this Shalabi after dark?

3. Neil waited until midmorning to place the call. Didn't want to make it too early because a lot of these old broads slept late. Didn't want to wait until noon because a lot of them went out to lunch.

"*Allo?*" Definitely an old lady's voice.

"Is this Mrs. Michelina Filardo?"

"*Yes. Who's a-calling?*" she said with a prominent Italian accent. "*If you gonna ask me for money, you can a-just go to hell. I—*"

Feisty old bag.

"No-no. Nothing like that, Mrs. Filardo. My name is Nathan Munden and I'm with the New York State Banking Department."

"*Oh, no, you don't! You think I'm a-born yesterday? Next you be wanting my a-Social Security number!*"

"Please, Mrs. Filardo. I already know your Social Security number. And this isn't a scam. There's nothing wrong with your account. We simply need your help with a problem at your bank branch. Can I come over and speak to you about it?"

"*I'm a-no sure . . .*"

"I've got a badge and an official identification card, if that will make you more comfortable."

He'd found it best not to mention right off that his card identified him as a member of the Banking Department's fraud investigation unit. At least not over the phone. The word "fraud" tended to get old folks worked up, and he could better finesse her in person.

"*Badge? You gonna arrest me?*"

He forced a laugh. "No-no-no! None of this involves you and you don't have to be involved if you don't want to, but I'm hoping you'll be a good citizen and help us catch a thief."

"*Someone a-steal from me?*"

"No." Didn't the old girl listen? "As I told you, this does *not* involve your account. I repeat: This does *not* involve your account. I can explain everything better in person. May I come over?"

"*Now?*"

"Before lunch or after lunch, whichever is more convenient."

He didn't want to give her too long. The longer the lag, the greater the chance she'd blab to someone.

"*You come now. I'm a-wanna hear this.*"

She bit! He pumped a fist. Now he had to move in close and set the hook. Once that was done, all he had to do was reel her in.

"Excellent. I can be there in half an hour."

"*This better not be a-bullshit. I can smell a-bullshit a mile away.*"

"None of that stuff, I assure you, Mrs. Filardo. This is the real deal. See you soon."

Christ! he thought as he hung up. This old broad was a bitch on wheels. No surprise she wouldn't front her grandson's business, harebrained or not. Still, she was going to let him through the door. That was the biggest hurdle. Once he sat her down and exposed her to the full intensity of the magical Zalesky charm, she'd be putty in his hands.

4. Jack sat in his usual spot by the window of the used bookstore/coffee shop and pretended to read while keeping an eye on Zalesky's place across the street. He'd decided to extend the rental on the Chrysler New Yorker— the only functioning wheels he had at the moment—and had left it parked down the street.

Around quarter to eleven, a guy stepped out of the doorway next to the Italian bakery: Zalesky, wearing a fedora and dressed in a dark suit with a white shirt and a red-and-blue-striped tie.

Right away Jack was up and moving. This was not going-to-the-sports-bar attire. This was the same outfit he'd worn when Jack and Julio had tailed him to a meeting with another of his marks.

Jack followed him just far enough to make sure he was heading for his car, then doubled back to the Chrysler. He started rolling toward the Bruckner. If Zalesky was heading for the Filardo place, Jack didn't need to follow. He knew the address. If he had another destination in mind, it didn't concern Jack.

Jack let Zalesky pass him on the Bruckner and then trailed him south to the Brooklyn-Queens Expressway. As they crawled along, he crept to within one car length of Zalesky's Dodge. On the off chance the hijo de puta was talking to himself, he turned on his receiver. Instead of Zalesky, he heard a scratchy voice talking about the Knicks. Zalesky was listening to WFAN.

Okay, the good news was the hidden microphone was working beautifully. The bad news was the radio was activating the transmitter, and that would shorten the battery life. Well, Zalesky didn't seem to use the car much. Jack could only keep his fingers crossed.

The slow traffic left plenty of time to take in the ugliness of the Twin Towers of the World Trade Center to his right across the East River, dominating and ruining the skyline of Manhattan's lower end; on the left they passed Brooklyn Heights, Cobble Hill, and then finally Carroll Gardens where Zalesky made his exit.

No question: He'd made contact with Michelina Filardo.

Yes!

5. Neil stepped out of his car and glanced up and down the tree-lined street. Probably nice and shady when the leaves were out. He turned his attention to the house—a neat three-story brownstone with wrought-iron railings. Living in a place like this wouldn't be hard to take. Not hard at all.

He glanced down as he took the ten steps up to the front door. Looked like it had a basement apartment, or a least room for one. According to the printout Melinda had given him, Michelina Filardo was sixty-one years old. The grandson had said she lived alone. He had a feeling he was going to have to bring his A game with this broad. She knew enough not to fund her grandson's half-ass scheme about fiber optics or whatever bullshit he'd been spouting back at the Event. Would she swallow Neil's line?

Of course she would.

A little lady looking older than sixty-one opened the inner door. Her grandson hadn't been kidding: Michelina Filardo was old-country Italian, right down to the widow's black and graying hair pulled back into a bun.

"Hi, Mrs. Filardo. I'm Nathan Munden with the New York State Banking Department. I called you a short while ago."

"I remember. I'm a-no *stupida*. Show me you badge."

"Yes, ma'am."

No problem. He had impressive ID, and had added a little something extra, just for her. He pulled out his badge, his ID card in its leather folder, and his calling card. Both the latter said he was a member of the State Banking Department's fraud investigation unit.

She opened the glass storm door a couple of inches and he passed them all through.

As she was inspecting them he said, "Turn over my card."

She did so, stared at it a moment, then looked up at him. "What's this?"

He gave her his sincerest smile. "Your Social Security number. On the phone you seemed worried that I was going to try to trick you out of it. I just wrote that there so you'd know I'm not trying to trick you—I already have it."

"How you get it?"

It had been included on the printout Melinda had provided, but she didn't need to know that.

He shrugged. "State Banking Department, remember? We tend to know these things."

Well, that was the clincher. She pushed open the door. True to his gentlemanly civil servant image, he removed his hat as he stepped through.

In!

She was staring at his card again, the front now.

"What's a-this 'fraud'?"

"I investigate people trying to cheat the banks, and someone's doing just that not ten blocks from here at your Chase branch."

"No!"

"Yes! They're using the computer system to shift funds to a private offshore account when one of the depositors makes a large cash withdrawal. They think they're getting away with it, but we're on to them."

"Then a-you should arrest them!"

"We will. Oh, believe me, we will. But the trouble is, we don't know who is doing it. We know it's happening but we can't identify the hacker—that's the term for someone who illegally enters a computer system. We do know he or she is operating out of the branch at Hamilton and Summit, but we don't know who."

"What you want a-from me?"

"We need a regular depositor at the branch to make a large withdrawal while we're watching the computers. We'll know which terminal was used to run the hack and when we find out who was at that terminal at the time, we'll swoop in and nab him."

Her eyes narrowed. "And why you a-come to me?"

"Because you're a longtime depositor. Who would expect you of being an undercover agent working with the Banking Department's fraud investigation unit?"

Now her eyes widened. "Me? Undercover?"

That word got them every time. Well, almost every time. The ones who had a sense of civic duty were the best marks for this game, which was why Neil favored the old ones—the older the better. Anywhere in the seventh decade was good.

Forget about trying the "civic duty" hook on anyone much younger: *You're from the Banking Department? Fix your own problems, asshole.*

But these old folks were a different breed. If the mark was male, World War Two or Korea vets were the easiest. They'd fought for their country in wartime and were more likely to be willing to help out the government. For the women, anyone who'd lived through the Depression and had seen banks fail had feelings for their fellow depositors, even if savings were insured these days.

But then add "undercover" and that usually clinched it. He'd seen it in their eyes time and time again: *I'm going to be an undercover agent for the government . . . me.*

"Yes, but don't worry. There's no danger to you or

your money. This is strictly white-collar crime. No guns, no violence, this person is stealing simply by fooling the bank's computers."

"They steal a-my money?"

"Yours and your neighbors'."

"I don't understand."

"It's very complicated, and I'm not sure I understand it completely myself. But we know it's happening. And your end is very simple. This Saturday I'll pick you up and drive you the ten blocks to your local branch where—"

"Why on Saturday?"

Neil hid a smile because he knew then he had her. He had already stopped asking *if* she was going to do it and switched to *when* they were going to do it, and she was still on board.

"Because our crook"—no accident in using *our*—"only does his dirty work on Saturdays when the bank's computer centers are understaffed. However, we'll make sure they're fully staffed when we know our undercover agent Michelina Filardo is on the job and setting the trap."

He was laying it on thick, he knew, but he sensed this lady needed an extra dose of the Zalesky charm and silver tongue to get her fired up and all gung-ho to trap this thief.

He waited for some sort of positive response, but she was holding back. Okay, time to hit her with one of his closers—again, playing it as if her participation was all settled and done, with only the details remaining.

"Now, one thing we need to be very clear on: You cannot mention this to anyone—*anyone*. And there's a very good reason for that. You know and I know that most people are *blabbermouths*. Am I right? I bet you can think of a couple of your neighbors right off who, if you told them how you're going to help the government catch a thief on Saturday, they'd be right down at the bank yakking about it. Am I right? Am I right?"

She was nodding now. "Mrs. Naccari. What a *boccalone*!"

Neil had no idea what that meant, but was pretty sure Mrs. Naccari couldn't be trusted with a secret.

"Right. And I'm sure you know plenty more like her. Remember: loose lips sink ships, and telling the wrong person will sink our chances of nailing this creep who's stealing honest, working folks' hard-earned money."

She kept nodding. Good. Her head was going in the right direction. Up and down was good.

"So, I'll pick you up after lunch on Saturday, say around one thirty or so, and we'll drive down to the branch to make your withdrawal."

"How much?"

"The withdrawal? I think twenty thousand will do it."

She gasped. "What? No! That's a-too much!"

He shrugged. "We need a sizable amount to tempt the creep. And don't worry: It won't be out of the bank vault more than an hour or so. You take it out, the computer boys identify the creep, and we redeposit it. Easy as pie. No one will know that you helped us catch a thief."

She was shaking her head. "Twenty thousand . . ."

"But what you need to do is notify the bank ahead of time that you're going to make the withdrawal and to have the cash ready for you."

He always had the marks set up the withdrawal a couple of days ahead of time. It avoided so many hassles, especially suspicions about a possible hostage situation. The withdrawal wasn't coming out of the blue. This was no emergency. It all had been arranged days in advance. The cash would be waiting.

"I know this is a lot to throw at you at once, so here's what I'll do: I'll come back tomorrow afternoon and walk you through arranging the withdrawal."

She still looked uncertain about the amount. Time to back off and give her breathing room.

"You have a lovely home, by the way."

"I have lived here many years."

Probably bought it for a song too. From the look of the place and the size of her account, she could afford to lose twenty grand—twice that—and not squawk.

"Well, I'll be going now. I'll stop back tomorrow afternoon." He shook her hand. "You're a good citizen, Mrs. Filardo. The country could use more people like you."

And then he was out the door and sailing toward his car. He'd set the hook but couldn't be sure how well. This old broad was a tough one. But he'd have her ready to reel in after tomorrow's visit.

6. Jack watched Zalesky stroll out of the Filardo house with a definite bounce to his step. Whatever had gone down in there must have gone his way. Jack wished he knew what. Too bad he hadn't been able to wire Zalesky himself. As it was, he'd simply have to assume that the game was on and continue to keep an eye on him.

Jack turned on his receiver on the remote chance that the guy would talk to himself as his drove. No such luck. Only Madonna's "Justify My Love" pulsed through the earpiece.

Damn.

7. Nasser al-Thani cursed the moon as he hurried through the sand with the others. Why tonight, of all nights, did it have to be full and glaring down at them like a spotlight?

The moon wasn't the only problem. The frigid wind

off Gravesend Bay blasted through his thin coat as he fought off another wave of nausea. In the past he had targeted certain people for death, even helped plan their demise, but never before had he personally participated in the act of murder. His gut churned at the prospect, but he saw no way out. Drexler had put him in charge of the mission and he had no choice but to prove his mettle.

He had no choice about the timing either. Mustafa Shalabi had a ticket for an outbound plane tomorrow morning. They had to confront him tonight or they would miss him. And they had to reach him ahead of Sheikh Omar's thugs, who might also have learned of Shalabi's travel plans.

He let Drexler's man, Szeto, lead them down the beach to the end of the Sea Gate fence. Szeto and the newcomer, Reggie, had scouted the route earlier. The American's mobility was somewhat limited due to his reconstructed knees, and so he brought up the rear. The three of them rounded the fence, putting them officially in Sea Gate, then headed back up the dunes.

Nasser found a shadowed spot near the end of Ocean-view Avenue, shielded from the near-day-bright moon-light, and gathered the other two close. The only good thing about the cold weather was that it kept everyone indoors. If this were summer, they would have been no-ticed by now.

"We split up here and meet again outside the house in ten minutes." He checked the glowing dial on his watch. "No later than eleven forty-five."

They'd had to leave the car on Polar Street, on the other side of the fence. That meant walking to Shalabi's house. Sea Gate was such an insulated community, it wouldn't do at all to have a group of three strangers walking along its streets. But three isolated individuals, strolling different routes, that was another story. They all knew the address and had mapped out the separate routes they were to follow.

Reggie left first, since he moved the slowest. Then Szeto. Nasser waited half a minute, then set out on his own route—up Oceanview and turning left on Highland Avenue. Sea Gate had its own police department—tiny, but a presence nonetheless. He kept an eye out for a patrol car as he walked, but encountered none. He stepped behind a tree trunk as a car rumbled by—no use in being spotted, even by a disinterested party—but did not see another for the rest of his walk.

When he found Shalabi's house, he was relieved to see the Mercedes still parked outside. Worst-case scenario had been the Egyptian leaving while they were walking here. Szeto was already crouching in the shrubbery on the shadowed side when Nasser arrived. Reggie showed up about a minute later.

"I already check back door," Szeto whispered. "Is locked."

The front door will undoubtedly be the same, Nasser thought.

Shalabi was running scared. In a gated community like this, one might grow careless and leave doors unlocked, but not when you feared for your life.

Szeto shrugged off his backpack and removed a short, heavy pry bar. Used properly, it would allow them to break in and subdue Shalabi with a minimum of fuss.

Used properly . . .

Szeto had assured him he was experienced with its use, and the three of them had discussed the best way to proceed.

"Let's not waste any more time, shall we?" Nasser said.

The trio moved to the rear entrance. Reggie eased open the storm door and held it. Two panes of glass allowed a look inside, revealing a small, dark utility room lit by light filtering from the kitchen beyond; a washer and dryer lined the wall to the left.

Shalabi could be anywhere in the house. They could not allow him time to call 911, so Szeto had suggested a way to bring him to them. Obviously he'd done this before.

Nasser watched as Szeto forced the pry bar's flat tip between the door and the frame, right below the knob. When he had a firm, two-handed grip on it, he nodded. Nasser gave the door three sharp knocks.

They waited. A silhouette appeared in the doorway to the kitchen. Light filled the utility room.

Shalabi.

"Now!" Nasser whispered.

He gave the door a hard kick as Szeto yanked back on the pry bar. Shalabi was halfway to the door when it sprang open with a shower of splinters. His mouth formed an elongated O within his beard as he began backpedaling. But Szeto, the pry bar raised above his head, was already charging. He smashed it across Shalabi's skull once, twice, and the man went down without a sound.

Nasser motioned Reggie inside and caught the storm door as it swung closed. He pushed the broken door shut behind them and stood over the fallen Shalabi, facedown on the floor, bleeding but still breathing.

"What do we do now?" Reggie said.

"Drag him into a hallway so you won't be visible through a window."

"Then what?"

"Mister Drexler says he wants his death to look like someone has made an example of him, to send his allies a message—a warning. I'll leave the particulars up to you."

Reggie smiled as he pulled out a knife and flicked open a four-inch blade. He looked at Szeto. "I guess that means we improvise."

"I do not understand this 'improvise.' "

"It means we have a little fun."

Szeto grinned. "Ah yes. I understand fun."

As they began dragging Shalabi deeper into the house, Nasser moved away.

"Leaving the party?" Reggie said.

"He's only part of the reason we're here. I'll take care of the rest."

He wanted no part in mutilating an unconscious man. Shalabi had shipped his family off to Cairo. By all rights he should be alone in the house, but without being able to keep the place under direct surveillance, that was only an assumption right now.

Nasser moved quickly through the first floor. Only one dirty plate in the kitchen sink: a good sign. He checked every room and closet. All empty. He found the master bedroom on the second floor. Two suitcases lay on the queen-size bed: one open, partially packed with clothes, the other closed. He unzipped it and raised the top.

Cash. He rifled through the banded stacks and guessed it totaled close to two hundred thousand dollars. As suspected, Shalabi had no doubt cleaned out the Al-Kifah Refugee Center's bank account and was personally going to take it to Afghanistan before his blind rival could get his grubby hands on it.

Well, now it belonged to the Order, leaving Sheikh Omar Abdel-Rahman empty-handed. Without their anticipated windfall, he and his followers would be cash strapped and willing to listen to another get-rich-quick proposal by the man from Qatar.

Nasser stuffed the money into the empty backpack he'd brought along, and left a parting taunt for whoever might come later. Then he returned to the first floor. As he reached the bottom of the stairs, he heard two muffled reports. Then Szeto and Reggie reappeared, the former unscrewing a suppressor from his pistol and the latter wiping his knife on a towel.

"Clubbed, stabbed, and shot," Reggie said with a grin. "I believe that sends a message—in spades."

Szeto said, "You wish to see?"

Nasser forced a smile. "I trust you."

"So other than sending this message, what have we accomplished here?" Reggie said.

Nasser gave him a stern look. "You ask too many questions."

Reggie folded the knife and held up his empty hand. "Just asking."

"What I will tell you is that what has happened here tonight may lead to allowing you a little personal time with the man who broke your knees."

"That fucker, Lonnie?"

"If that is indeed his name." Nasser doubted it.

Reggie's grin was fierce as he flicked the knife open again. "Oh, I am so there."

"Enough chatter. We leave by the routes we came and meet back at the car."

Nasser watched them go, then began turning out the lights. If Shalabi's friends and associates assumed he was fleeing the country, it might be days, perhaps weeks before anyone discovered his body. Not that it mattered. The first step had been taken along the road to trapping the hijackers who had stolen the Order's millions and eventually reclaiming what was left.

He would be sure to make an example of them to send another sort of message: Do not interfere in the Order's business.

WEDNESDAY

1. "The door!" Mahmoud said in harsh, whispered Arabic. "It's broken!"

"No!"

Kadir could not believe it. He stepped closer to Shalabi's back door and, sure enough, the frame was splintered near the lock.

They'd waited until three A.M., when the moon was sinking in the western sky, then cut a hole in a section of the Sea Gate fence and slipped through. The low, bright moon cast long shadows, and Kadir and Mahmoud had kept to those as they'd slunk through the streets toward this darkened house.

This was the last thing Kadir had expected. Sheikh Omar had chosen them to remove Shalabi, had even issued a fatwa, saying, "We should not allow ourselves to be manipulated by his deviousness," and declaring that Shalabi was "no longer a Muslim." Jihad demanded his permanent removal.

The plan was to subdue him, bind him, and put him in the trunk of his own car. Before closing the lid, they would tie a plastic bag over his head. Then they would drive him out of Sea Gate to a grave they had already dug in a deserted stretch of sand out near the end of Ocean Parkway. By the time they reached Gilgo Beach, he would already be dead. All they would need to do then was drop him into the hole and fill it in. Mustafa Shalabi would never be seen or heard from again. They would leave his car parked at the airport and everyone would assume he'd fled the country with the refugee center's funds.

A perfect plan.

Kadir had never killed before, but he was ready for it. Never had he felt himself so filled with rage. Just yesterday U.S. forces had sent the Iraqi Republican Guard fleeing from Kuwait with their collective tails between their legs, then massacred them on the Highway of Death. Kadir was hardly a supporter of Saddam Hussein and his secular regime, but Saddam was an Arab, and humiliating him before the world was to humiliate all Arabs everywhere. Jihad against America, led by Sheikh Omar, was the only response, and Kadir was ready to vent his rage on whoever stood in the way. Mustafa Shalabi was one such person.

He peered into the dark, silent house. Had someone else—another of Sheikh Omar's followers, perhaps—got here first? That seemed unlikely. Who else could know? Mahmoud, a friend of Shalabi, had used his cab to drive the traitor's wife, Zanib, to the airport for her flight to Cairo. Mahmoud had overheard him tell her that he would be following in a day or two. No one else knew of his planned departure.

Kadir touched the door and it swung inward.

"He sleeps upstairs," Mahmoud whispered. "Quickly."

Flicking on his pencil flashlight, he slipped past Kadir and entered the house. As Kadir followed, he caught a reflected glint of light from the floor as they entered the kitchen. He turned on his own flashlight and saw a small puddle of thick red fluid.

"Mahmoud! Blood!"

Mahmoud turned and his flash beam joined Kadir's on the floor.

Air hissed between his teeth. "Upstairs!"

He turned and ran. Kadir followed. They found the bedroom empty with two open suitcases on the bed, one full of clothes, the other empty.

No, not completely empty. As Kadir aimed his flash beam, he saw a piece of paper. A note?

He snatched it up for a closer look, then groaned when he recognized what it was.

"What's wrong?" Mahmoud said.

He handed him the half of a hundred-dollar bill.

Mahmoud growled as he crumpled it in his hand. "Some gutless swine is laughing at us!"

"But who?"

"Not one of our people."

"Someone from the refugee center, then?"

Mahmoud tugged on his red beard. "Perhaps. Perhaps someone else knew he had emptied the account."

Kadir sat on the bed. The money had been the other reason for their presence here tonight.

They'd failed on both counts. How were they going to face Sheikh Omar?

Mahmoud tugged his arm. "Come. We can't stay here."

He rose and followed Mahmoud down the stairs. As they reached the first floor and started through the living room, Mahmoud stopped.

"We should make sure he's gone. He could be hiding."

The dark rectangle of a hallway beckoned from his right. He stepped toward it and his foot slipped; he went down, landing on one knee. As something wet soaked through his pants leg, he braced himself against the wall and his flashlight lit up a body lying in a pool of blood. Kadir cried out in shock and scrabbled back to his feet.

Mahmoud came up behind him. "Mustafa," he whispered, his voice suddenly hoarse.

Kadir's gorge rose. Shalabi was barely recognizable. His clothes were saturated in blood from his slit throat, and he'd been severely battered.

"Who . . . who did this?"

Kadir admitted to himself that he was relieved he wouldn't have to kill Shalabi, even though he was a traitor to jihad.

After a pause, Mahmoud said, "We did."

"What?"

"That is what we have to tell the imam."

"Lie?"

To their spiritual leader?

"We cannot let him think we failed him."

"But we were supposed to hide his body so no one would know."

"Well, we cannot do that now. Look at all that blood. It's everywhere. We cannot possibly clean it up and leave no trace."

He was right . . . soaking through the carpet, splattering the walls . . .

Mahmoud added, "We need say only that Shalabi is dead. We will say there was no money in the house. Both are truths."

Yes . . . yes they were. Kadir could live with that. But . . .

"What do we say when he asks us where the money is?"

"Another truth: We do not know."

True, they didn't.

"But who would do this? Who would strike such a blow against jihad?"

Mahmoud spat. "Only the vilest snake."

Kadir couldn't see one of Shalabi's followers doing this to him. It had to be someone else.

"The FBI perhaps?"

"Perhaps. They may have wiretaps on the phones at the refugee center. They could have done this in an attempt to shock and silence Sheikh Omar. When we take over the center, we shall ensure the removal of any surveillance. And our leader will make fools of the FBI when he brings jihad to America."

Kadir imagined an explosion in the base of one of the Trade Towers, saw it tipping into the second, and both going down in plumes of smoke and rubble.

"I pray to Allah to make it so."

"Allāhu Akbar."

"Allāhu Akbar."

Leaving Mustafa Shalabi where he lay, they fled the house and Sea Gate.

2. Kadir stepped into his dark apartment and closed the door behind him. He yawned as he turned on the light. He felt jittery and a little depressed about Shalabi's death. Certainly he had deserved to die, but not in such a manner. The FBI was ruthless, yes, but to mutilate him so—

"Kadir?"

He cried out and spun at the sound of his name, then pressed a hand over his galloping heart as he recognized his sister.

"Hadya! You frightened me!"

She had been here less than three days and he wasn't yet used to having someone else in the apartment. She stood in the bedroom doorway dressed in an ankle-length abaya; a blue scarf dangled from her hand. Her dark hair was parted in the middle and fell to perhaps an inch below her ears.

"I'm sorry. I've been worried about you. You didn't come home last night, and when I arose and found no sign of you on the couch, I didn't know what to think."

He wasn't used to anyone questioning his movements either, and had not thought to prepare a cover story, so he turned the conversation toward her.

"What are you doing up so early?"

"I'm going to work."

Oh, yes. The bakery. Uncle Ferran fired up his bread ovens well before dawn. He'd wasted no time putting her to work. Every new hire, family or not, started on the early shift.

"Of course. You'd better get going, then. But be careful out on the street. Do you want me to walk you over?"

She smiled as she began wrapping her scarf around her head. "I met a woman from the bakery. Her name is Jala and she lives in the building next door. She's going to meet me out front and we'll walk over together. It's only three blocks and the streetlights—Kadir! Your leg!"

He looked down and saw the bloodstain over his left knee from when he'd slipped in Shalabi's blood.

"It's—it's nothing. I cut my knee."

She bent toward him. "Let me—"

"It's nothing, Hadya." He backed away. "I'll take care of it."

"But—"

"Go. You'll be late for work. You don't want Uncle Ferran to think you are lazy."

With obvious reluctance she tightened the scarf and hurried out.

When she was gone, he dropped onto the couch and leaned back, closing his eyes with a sigh.

Hadya meant well, but she asked too many questions.

3.   "Do you think today is too soon to approach our little jihadists with the new deal?" Nasser said.

After catching up on his sleep and changing into a thobe, he'd brought Shalabi's cash to Roman Trejador's suite. Drexler had joined them for lunch. The remnants of a sandwich platter lay scattered around the table.

Trejador glanced at Drexler. "What do you think, Ernst?"

The request surprised Nasser—Drexler, too, from his expression. The two had been at odds for months over the stolen money. What was Trejador up to? Disarming him? Or using an available resource? Ernst Drexler had gained a reputation as a very capable actuator—a position Nasser envied.

"Well . . ." He cleared his throat. "I believe they'll be reeling in shock for a while—good work, by the way," he added with a glance at Nasser.

Aren't we all so collegial today, Nasser thought with a nod of acceptance.

"Undoubtedly," Trejador said, "but they won't feel any repercussions until Shalabi's corpse is discovered. The brutality of his passing should create a backlash, causing a drop-off in donations to the center, leaving our friends with severely diminished prospects of collecting the funds they need."

Nasser remembered thinking last night that it could be a long time before the body was found.

"Then perhaps we shall have to speed discovery," he said. "I'll put on a thick Egyptian accent, call one of his neighbors, and say he's answering his phone and I'm worried about him."

Trejador nodded. "That should set things in motion."

Since he had the floor, Nasser decided to press his case. "Might I also suggest that I go to the Al-Farooq Mosque this afternoon and ask for Shalabi? He will not be available, of course."

"Why deal with the mosque when we have access to the sole survivor of the robbery?" Drexler said.

"Kadir Allawi? He is my ultimate target, but I wish to appear ignorant of the infighting over the mosque and the refugee center. I cannot ask for Tachus, because he was gunned down by the men we are after. That will leave me with no one but Kadir. And Kadir will put me in touch with the jihadists."

Trejador was nodding. "Yes, I think an indirect approach is best. Sheikh Omar's jihadists supplied most of the men who were killed by the hijackers. They will want revenge. Your motive will be clear to them: You want your money back."

"I can offer them financial incentive as well." He pointed to the cash-stuffed backpack. "Say, two hundred thousand dollars?"

Even Drexler smiled. "Pay them with what would have been their own money had they gotten to Shalabi first? I *like* it."

"I do too," Trejador said. "Go to Brooklyn today. Then call one of Shalabi's neighbors tomorrow. Tighten the financial screws and they'll do exactly what we want."

Nasser leaned back, satisfied. He was beginning to be accepted as an equal with these two. They liked his plan for trapping the hijackers—a reverse on the Trojan horse ploy—because it risked no further investment from the Order. If his scheme worked, it would result in return of the Order's stolen millions.

And the next step after that, he hoped, would be appointment as the Order's newest actuator.

A knock on the door. As the junior member of the group, Nasser instinctively rose to answer, but Trejador waved him back.

"I'll get that."

He sauntered to the door and opened it, admitting a young, attractive brunette Nasser immediately recognized. He'd met this one before, even remembered her name: Danaë.

One of Trejador's whores—he was notorious for them. The High Council disapproved, but he explained that he was too involved in the Order's business to spare time for an ongoing relationship. Therefore he rented his women—they arrived, earned their fee, and left. A business transaction, no more, no less. But apparently he had recurring favorites, and this Danaë appeared to be one of them.

He escorted her down the short hallway to the bedroom. On the way, she made eye contact with Nasser and winked. She remembered him too.

Drexler leaned close and whispered, "I don't like this. She has seen us. I don't like harlots knowing my face. He is too reckless, too careless about who he consorts with. It's going to backfire on him—on all of us—someday."

Nasser didn't know about that, and was spared the need for a reply by Trejador's return from the bedroom.

Drexler rose. "The meeting is adjourned."

"Is it?" Trejador said with a smile and raised eyebrows.

"I'm certainly not discussing the Order's business with an outsider around."

"As you wish."

Nasser nodded a good-bye and headed for the door. Instead of thinking about his visit to the mosque, his head was filled with visions of Danaë. He liked that she recognized him, and her wink set his loins astir. He imagined her without her clothes, her legs coiled around him.

Someday, when he was chief actuator, he'd make a point of being reckless and careless too, and have his own Danaë.

4.   Jack bottled his frustration as he watched Zalesky leave the Filardo house alone—again. His second visit in as many days. What had gone down in there? Jack knew no more about the workings of Zalesky's scam than when he'd started.

Patience, patience, patience.

When he and Julio had followed the hijo de puta last fall, Zalesky had driven his old lady mark to a bank—her bank, Jack assumed—on a Saturday. Why a Saturday? Had it simply happened to work out that way, or because banks closed early on Saturdays? If that was part of his method, then Jack had to figure on waiting another couple of days before Zalesky zeroed in for the kill.

He followed Zalesky out of Carroll Gardens back to the BQE. He watched him go up the northbound ramp, then dropped him. He wasn't interested in whatever else the guy did, only in his relationship with Mrs. Filardo.

On impulse, he headed for Queens and that used car dealership in Jamaica he and Cristin had visited on Sunday.

The showroom was open, so this time he went in. He ambled over to the '63 Corvair convertible. He ran his fingers over the glossy white of the vented rear hood—that was where they placed the engine in these babies. The black top was down and hidden under a snap-on cover behind the rear seat.

"'The poor man's Porsche,'" said a voice behind him.

It belonged to a chubby guy in a white shirt who could have been related to Abe—except for the comb-over.

"Sorry?"

"That was what they used to call the Corvair, because both had rear-mounted engines."

"It looks new."

He grinned. "Yeah, she's in cherry condition. Interested?"

"I've got a friend who might be. He likes to tinker with old cars."

"Well, this one needs no tinkering. She's got barely ten thousand miles on her, and the original air-cooled,

two-point-four liter, aluminum flat-six engine *purrs*.
Even has the famous two-speed Powerglide automatic
transmission lever."

Remembering Cristin's question as soon as she saw
it, Jack said, "Okay, I gotta ask—"

"*Unsafe at Any Speed,* right?" The salesman grimaced.
"Everybody asks about that."

Ralph Nader's book had damned the Corvair's handling so thoroughly that it had had to cease production.

"Well?"

"A trumped-up hatchet job," the guy said with real
vehemence. "Nader made his consumerist bones on a lie.
The NHTSA did tests later that completely vindicated
the Corvair, but by then it was too late. The model was
deader than the Edsel."

The handling issue didn't matter much to Jack. Not
like he intended to take it on cross-country trips. And he
figured if he could handle a Harley, he could handle a
Corvair. But on to the most important question.

"What's the damage?"

"I can let you drive it out of here for ninety-nine
ninety-nine."

Ten grand?

"For a thirty-year-old car?"

"Twenty-eight. A *classic* car that's been garaged for
most of those years. Check out that finish—it's the original."

Jack had to admit it looked good.

"Want to take it for a ride?"

Did he ever, but he wanted to keep up the "friend"
barrier.

"I'll tell my friend the price and see if he wants to
take a look."

As Jack turned to go, the salesman said, "I can let it go
for nine even, but that's rock bottom."

Jack waved. "I'll tell him." Then he turned back to the

salesman. He couldn't resist. "Maybe I'd better take that test drive. I mean, just to let my friend know it still works."

The salesman grinned. "Let me go get the keys and we'll back it out the rear doors."

Jack didn't know why, but he wanted this car. He knew it was stupid to buy a vehicle nearing the end of its third decade, and yet, something about it called to him. The simplicity of its lines, maybe. He couldn't say. He figured sometimes you just *want* something and this was one of those times.

But if it drove any way less than perfectly, he'd take an immediate pass. He was no mechanic. Looking under the hood was like looking at a space shuttle cockpit—he had no idea what anything did, and didn't care to learn.

While he waited, he ran over possible purchase scenarios, and then had a brainstorm: Why not put up the money and let Julio buy and register the car under his name?

If he'd do it.

5.   Kadir had been listening to Sheikh Omar speak in the mosque when Mahmoud pulled him away.

"The man from Qatar is back," he said in Arabic. "Asking for Shalabi."

Kadir's mouth went dry. He'd had no sleep since sneaking out of Sea Gate early this morning and his back ached from sleeping on his couch after the unaccustomed labor of digging Shalabi's unused grave yesterday.

"Why now? Why today? Do you think he knows?"

"How could he? No, he says he has a plan to regain the money that was stolen when Tachus and the others were killed."

That was all well and good, but why had Mahmoud come to him?

"What can I do?"

"It seems he knows you. And if he can't talk to Shalabi, he wants to talk to you." He gave Kadir a hard look. "How does he know you?"

"He . . . he knows Riaz Diab, and Diab had me introduce him to Tachus." Poor Tachus . . . gunned down like a dog. "He also came to my apartment shortly after the attack, asking if I'd seen anything that would help them track down the killers."

"And?"

"I told them what I'd seen: two men in masks with machine guns killing everyone in sight. I had no more to offer. I still don't." He glanced down the stairs toward the refugee center. "Is he alone?"

"Yes. Why do you ask?"

"No reason."

Kadir remembered the man hadn't been alone that time when he'd visited his apartment. He'd been accompanied by a strange man in a white suit who had unsettled Kadir.

He looked at Mahmoud. "What did you tell him about Shalabi?"

"As little as possible: that he hasn't come in yet today and nothing more. Same as I would under any circumstances. He has no need for an explanation."

They went downstairs and found the man from Qatar waiting alone in the office of the refugee center.

"Kadir," said the man in English. "I am glad to see you are well. Since Mister Shalabi is not available, I will speak to you."

"What about?"

"I wish the return of my investment."

The flat statement rattled Kadir. "I . . . I do not have it. I had nothing to do with—"

The man from Qatar raised his hand. "I know. The only way I can see to retrieve it is to lure the thieves from hiding. For this I will need the help of you and your friends and Mister Shalabi's contacts."

Mahmoud leaned forward. "Why should we help you?"

The man gave him a scathing look. "First off, the Qur'an says that when you accept something into your hands for safekeeping, you bear the responsibility of keeping it safe. When you fail to do that, you must make restitution."

Kadir began to sweat. This man couldn't expect *him* to come up with three million dollars!

He and Mahmoud both began talking at once but the man silenced them with a tolerant smile and another raised hand.

"Do not trouble yourself. I placed the funds in Tachus's care, and Tachus was killed along with the others. But I expect you"—he pointed to Kadir—"and you"—then to Mahmoud—"as his friends to assist me. For my part, I will regain my stolen funds. For your part, you will bring retribution to those who killed Tachus and all with him—some of whom I'm sure were also your friends."

"What sort of retribution?" Mahmoud said.

"That will be left to you. After my associates and I extract the whereabouts of the stolen funds, we will hand the killers over to you for final disposition."

. . . my associates . . .

That could only mean the man in the white suit and others like him.

"If you have associates," Kadir said, "why do you need us?"

"Because we need a leak."

"I do not understand."

"In order to trap them, we must lure them out, and

we can't lure them out unless our plans are leaked to them."

"I still don't—"

"Tachus's plans were leaked and the leak came from your side."

Mahmoud bristled. "How can you know that?"

"Because *my* side did not know where the transaction would take place. I left that entirely up to Tachus. So that leaves *your* side."

Kadir remembered that night, all the bloody, punctured bodies strewn about . . .

He said, "The one who leaked the location might have been among the dead."

"Possibly. But I sense these killers have numerous sources of information. If you have your people send out word that an auction will be held, the killers will hear about it and—we hope—make another attack. But this time we will be waiting for them."

Kadir glanced at Mahmoud. Their eyes met, then Mahmoud shook his head.

"As much as Tachus's blood and the blood of our friends cry out for vengeance," he said in Arabic, "we cannot participate in this. We have higher concerns."

He meant the imam's worldwide jihad, of course.

Kadir nodded in agreement. "We cannot be turned from our holy course."

The man from Qatar replied in Arabic. "I know your holy course, and I support and applaud it. But any cause, no matter how holy, requires funding. I will pay a bounty of one hundred thousand U.S. dollars on each of the heads of the killer thieves, to be used for your holy cause, should you aid us in their capture."

Two hundred thousand dollars . . .

"That is very generous," Mahmoud said, "but we are well funded. And even if we were to help, that is not a decision we could make."

"I see."

The man from Qatar stood there, looking very disappointed. Finally he sighed and pulled a wallet from within his thobe. He removed two cards and handed one each to Kadir and Mahmoud.

"Here is my number. If your leaders decide this is of benefit to the holy cause, call me."

Saying no more, he walked out.

When he was gone, Kadir turned to Mahmoud. "That is a lot of money to turn down."

Mahmoud shrugged. "Helping him would jeopardize jihad. Besides, with the refugee fund now at Sheikh Omar's disposal, we have guaranteed worldwide jihad a steady flow of cash, with no risk at all."

"But Tachus—"

"As much as my blood boils to avenge Tachus, we cannot risk it. What if this man's plan backfires? What if we are killed? Or what if we are caught by the FBI and plans for jihad in America are exposed." He shook his head. "No, no. Too risky. Jihad comes first."

Kadir could not argue with that.

6.   Jack needed new videos but was uneasy about getting cornered by DDPers in his usual local video store. He headed up Ninth Avenue to midtown where most of the shops specialized exclusively in XXX fare, but managed to find one that limited its porn to a curtained-off section in the rear.

He immediately recognized the tall guy in dreadlocks. How could he forget him? Nothing special about his dreads, his height, his milk chocolate skin, but the big, black, Aaron Neville–class mole in the center of his forehead was unforgettable.

"Hey," Jack said. "Eighth Street Playhouse, right?"

The guy gave him a puzzled look. "Uh, yeah. I go there."

"You must go there a lot, 'cause every time I'm there, so are you."

He smiled. "Don't recognize you, but you must like old movies."

"Love 'em."

The West Village theater was a revival house that became famous for running *The Rocky Horror Picture Show* every Friday night for fifteen years. Jack had never been a *Rocky Horror* fan, but he liked the older films the place brought back to the big screen.

"Well, you came to the right place."

"Yours?"

He shook his head. "I wish. But they let me do some of the ordering, and I've stocked in a lot of oldies but goodies. What do you like?"

"Usually SF, horror, weird."

"Got plenty of that."

"But I'm in kind of a dark mood lately."

His face lit. "Let me take you to the noir section."

"You sell wine too?"

"No, just—" He paused midstep as he came out from behind the counter, then grinned. "You had me there for a moment. Good one."

"I'm here all week."

Jack wasn't a wine drinker, but his uncle Stu, besides being a Scotch lover, used to extol the virtues of Oregon pinot noir until everyone's eyes glazed over.

He led Jack down a narrow aisle. "I've started a little rating system here, so if you come in and I'm not around, you can still find the good stuff by looking for my tag on the back of the box."

He pulled out a copy of *The Wild Bunch*.

"One of my faves," Jack said.

"Well, sure. I mean, what's not to like? But look here."

He flipped the box and pointed to a little Magic Marker circle with a black dot in the center. "That's my tag—that's the Milkdud seal of approval."

"Milkdud?"

"Yeah. Me."

Jack glanced at that big old mole looking down at him like a third eye and the light dawned: It did resemble a certain brand of chocolate-covered caramel.

"Oh. Got it."

He shoved the tape back into its slot. "Let's hit the noir bar." Farther down the aisle he stopped at another section. "The classics are *Double Indemnity*—"

"Seen it."

"*The Killers.*"

"Seen it."

"*Touch of Evil.*"

"Seen it—didn't care much for it."

"That means you missed stuff and need to see it again."

Jack shrugged. "Too many I haven't seen once."

"Good point. Okay, why don't we set you a theme—say, 1950."

"The year? That's a theme?"

"Why not?" He began pulling tapes out of the rack—looked like he could have done it with his eyes closed. When he'd extracted three he handed them to Jack. "All released in 1950."

Jack found himself holding *Sunset Boulevard*, *All About Eve,* and *In a Lonely Place*. He'd seen the first two, but had never heard of the third. It did have Bogart, though.

"Really? All made the same year?"

Milkdud shrugged. "Don't know about made, but released the same year. Watch 'em back to back."

Well, why not?

"Will do. But I've got a problem: No credit card."

Milkdud thought about that. "It's against store policy, but if I can't trust a fellow regular at Eighth Street, who can I trust?"

They shook hands.

"I think this is going to be the start of a beautiful friendship," Jack said.

7. Kadir found his sister waiting on the couch when he returned home.

"You should be asleep," he said.

"I couldn't sleep. I'm too worried."

"What about?"

"About you." Hadya held up the dark green twill work pants he'd worn to Sea Gate. "I went to the laundromat today and brought these along to clean."

A dark splotch remained over the left knee area, but it was no longer red.

"Th-thank you."

"But Kadir," she said. "There is no hole in the fabric. How could you cut your knee enough to bleed that much without breaking through the cloth?"

Sudden fury bloomed within him. "How dare you question me in my own home. I bring you in, give you food and shelter, and you interrogate me?"

She stiffened and lowered her eyes. "I'm sorry."

"You have no idea what is going on in the world! You have no idea what I am doing to change it." He snatched his pants from her hands. "I have been doing God's work and don't you dare question me!"

She looked up at him, tears in her eyes. "Yes, Kadir. I am very sorry."

Her tears doused his anger. Hadya was younger and Father had no doubt kept her sheltered. Lines were being drawn in the sand of the world and she had no idea

where they were. She needed to be educated, and he
knew just the man to do it.

He went to the shelf where he kept his Qur'an and
took down his portable tape player. As he hit the rewind
button, he turned to her.

"I want you to listen to Sheikh Omar. He is a wise
and holy man who has opened my eyes and been a
source of great inspiration."

When the tape stopped rewinding, he handed her the
player and the lightweight headphones that came with it.

"Listen and learn."

She could not help but be moved by the imam's words.
Soon she would understand, soon she would join his following.

THURSDAY

1. "Well, what do you think?" Jack said, pointing through the window into the showroom.

He'd dragged Julio out to Jamaica before The Spot opened to see the Corvair. Julio seemed less than impressed.

"Looks like a white frog, meng."

"It's got a sweet ride."

The test drive yesterday had been fun. He liked the way it handled. Despite the age of its engine, the car still had good pickup. He preferred front-wheel drive but the weight of the engine sitting over the rear wheels gave them extra traction. Best of all, with the top down he still had some of that motorcycle feel of riding in the open.

Julio shook his head. "But it's *white*. Like vanilla."

"I won't ask you to drive it, or even ride in it."

"Yeah, but you want me to *own* it."

"Only on paper."

"What if people find out?"

"No problem. It'll all be legal."

"That's not what I mean. People find out I own a car like that, they'll take away my Newyorican badge."

"Your what?"

"You can't be a PR and own a car like that. It ain't allowed. They'll send me back to San Juan for retraining."

"Ha. Ha. Very funny. I've got the cash right here in my pocket. You gonna do this for me or not?"

"Course I'm gonna do it. But you just can't tell nobody."

"My lips are sealed." Jack shook his head. "Newyorican badge. Sheesh."

Laughing, they headed inside to do the deal.

2.   "A pretty sweet deal," Tommy Ten Thumbs said. "It's given me some ideas."

They'd been watching a couple of the yard's workers feed the chassis of stripped cars—two, sometimes three at a time—into the crusher where they got pancaked.

The chassis came from various chop shops here and there around Brooklyn and the Bronx. Stolen cars were much more valuable in pieces—as someone once said, the whole was much less valuable than the sum of its parts. Once all those valuable parts had been stripped away, you couldn't leave the naked chassis lying around. Something had to be done with them, because should the cops raid a chop shop, they were evidence against it.

That was where Vinny came in. The chassis arrived at night and by the next afternoon Vinny had reduced them to unrecognizable tangles of steel. He sold the tangles for scrap, which would eventually end up in foundries that melted it back into new steel, some of which would find its way into new car chassis.

Before he dropped out of high school, Vinny remembered a biology teacher going on and on about "the miraculous cycle of life"—how deer ate plants and wolves ate deer, and then when wolves died their bodies rotted to fertilize plants which deer came and ate, and on and on. Vinny figured he was part of the miraculous cycle of cars.

And besides, recycling was the new buzzword. Vinny was just pitching in and being a good citizen.

But now Tommy had "ideas." He hadn't asked what they were. He knew he'd hear about them sooner than he wanted. And sure enough . . .

"So I been thinking," Tommy said, "we get to dip our beaks by disposing of the frames, right? But the real money's in the parts. You know what I'm saying? Somebody else is eating all the meat and we're getting the bones. That seem right to you?"

Vinny didn't look at him—kept his gaze fixed on the crusher. "Seems perfect to me."

"You mean you like them getting all the gravy?"

Now he turned to him. "Look. I bought this to have a legit business. So that if the tax man ever comes and asks me where I got the money to buy my house, I point to this place. It's a cover, Tommy. Just like Tony C's got his appliance store."

"Yeah, but Tony's big-time. You're just small-time."

"Ain't always gonna be that way."

Tommy's eyes narrowed. "You planning on making a move?"

Whoa. What was this? Asking about a plot against Tony C? Tommy's look said if something was in the works, he wanted in, but that could just be an act. Was Tony C suspicious? Again, the question: Was that why Tommy was here?

"A move? On Tony? You fucking crazy? Don't let me hear you say anything like that again, y'hear me? First off, I ain't stupid. And second, I owe that guy everything. But I don't plan on being Tony C's collection boy and shuttle driver the rest of my life, either. You?"

"No fuckin' way."

No secret Tommy wanted his own crew. So did Vinny one day. With Gotti inside—calling the shots still, but inside was inside—things might shift around, loosen up.

They might get their crews sooner than if the Chief was still outside.

"So I make myself useful here. People can clean some of their cash through my place, and they can dispose of stuff that might get them in trouble if they're caught with it. I'm making extra out of sight, but more important, I'm making connections. And meanwhile I got a completely legit side to the business that makes real money."

"But not a lot. And that's where my idea comes in. I can get a couple of chop guys in here. We bring in cars and strip 'em ourselves. Parts are worth a fuckin' fortune."

Christ, this guy was stupid. Vinny tried to explain it in language he'd understand.

"Tommy, the shylocking we're in is completely illegit, right?"

"Right."

"The pony parlor and games we help Tony run are the same, right?"

"Right."

"That means if the wrong people look into them, we can be in trouble, right?"

"Right."

"And what do we do if somebody tries to connect us with that shit?"

"We back off and say, 'Hey, no, that ain't us.'"

"Right. But this salvage business here, it's in my name, *this* is me. I can't back off it. So if we put a chop shop here, and the heat comes down, I'm a goner. They'll have me dead to rights and I'll wind up in a cell in Rikers next to the Chief."

Tommy laughed. "Never happen. You're in Tony's crew and Tony the Cannon's too protected."

"Nobody's too protected."

"Hey, you ain't makin' sense, Vinny. We got chop-shop leftovers comin' in here. You can go down for them."

"No, I can't." He ticked off the points on his fingers. "Number one, the VINs are gone. Number two, they come in at night. Number three, they get crushed the next morning. Number four, they're sold and outta here by that same afternoon. I keep nothin' layin' around. Nothin'! Can't do that with a chop shop, Tommy."

Vinny turned and walked away. Fucking idiot.

"Hey, Vinny!" he called after him. "We're talking big money here."

Yeah. More to suck up your nose. The guy was nothing but trouble.

3. Kadir was beginning to fear that Sheikh Omar had gone insane.

He usually spoke from his chair but tonight he was standing and waving his arms as he screamed out his hatred for the USA and all things American. He was infuriated by the humiliating defeat of Iraq's Republican Guard—destroyed so completely that President Bush had called a cease-fire today after a mere one hundred hours of fighting. A one-hundred-hour war! Unthinkable! So incensed was the imam that he quite literally foamed at the mouth, soaking his white beard with spittle.

He had no sympathy for Saddam Hussein either, calling him a traitor to Islam who heaped shame upon the Arab world.

Kadir felt the same, almost ashamed to show his face on the street, knowing that the Americans he passed would be laughing behind his back.

The mosque was crowded—the Iraqi defeat had brought Muslims from all nationalities to pray—and all had been listening raptly at first. But now Kadir noticed ripples running through the crowd of worshippers as one leaned toward another and whispered, and then that one learned toward yet another. Had another tragedy befallen the Mideast?

He saw Mahmoud gesturing to him from the side, his expression grim. Something was definitely wrong.

He rose and hurried over. One thing good about having a blind cleric for a spiritual leader was that he could not tell when you had to leave in the middle of one of his teachings.

"What's wrong?" he whispered when he reached his side.

Mahmoud cocked his head toward the door. "Downstairs."

When they reached the outer office of the refugee center, he closed the door behind them and leaned close.

"They've found Shalabi."

So soon? Kadir had hoped for a week, perhaps even a month, Allah willing.

"How? Who?"

"A neighbor went to check on him and found the door broken. He went inside and found him, then called the police. Word of the condition of the body has leaked."

This was bad, very bad.

"Should we have moved the body?"

"It would have made no difference. We couldn't hide all the evidence. Even without a body, it would be obvious he had been killed. Either way, suspicion would be falling on Sheikh Omar."

Of course it would. Their falling-out had been very public, at least to the Muslim community. Especially after Sheikh Omar had issued that fatwa against him.

"Well," Kadir said, "perhaps the police can suspect he was behind it, but how can they blame a blind man?"

"They cannot."

Kadir shook his head. "He will be angry at us, won't he."

"Yes, but not for long. Shalabi is out of the way and the refugee fund belongs to jihad."

Kadir hoped he saw it that way. He didn't want Sheikh Omar to issue a fatwa against *him*.

4. Jack smiled as he watched the closing credits of *All About Eve*. He'd seen it before, but only on TV with commercial breaks every fifteen minutes or so. He hadn't appreciated how dark and cynical it was, but that all came through loud and clear in a viewing uninterrupted by detergent and antacid ads. He was also impressed by the symmetry of its what-goes-around-comes-around ending.

He liked symmetry. Life or reality rarely presented it, offering mostly chaos instead. Symmetry had to be imposed by humans—through religion, through fiction. The most satisfying stories always seemed to impose a level of symmetry on reality.

Tomorrow night's entry in the 1950 film festival: *In a Lonely Place*.

Which was pretty much where Jack was now. He wished he had Cristin to watch it with him.

5. Kadir came home and found his sister sitting on the couch, listening to Sheikh Omar's tape. Her expression was troubled.

"What is wrong?"

"I have finished the tape."

"And? Are you not enlightened? Filled with holy purpose?"

"I wish to hear more."

Kadir fairly leaped to the shelf to fetch her another. The great imam was working his magic upon her. Soon she would be as devoted to Sheikh Omar as her brother.

FRIDAY

1. Kadir was shaking as Ali Mohamed escorted him and Mahmoud from Sheikh Omar's office. He glanced at Mahmoud, who had paled up to the roots of his red hair.

Sheikh Omar had been furious. Not the screaming fury he'd shown against America last night. Today his fury had been cold and quiet, directed at the two of them, demanding to know why they hadn't told him that Shalabi had been dead when they arrived. When they tried to answer, he wouldn't listen, saying if they had told him, and he'd known the condition of the body, he would have had them report it to the police.

Everything would be different now if they had, he told them. He could have announced that he had sent the two of them on a mission of reconciliation only to discover to their horror that the poor man had been slaughtered like an animal.

But as it was, everyone thought Sheikh Omar was behind the brutality. Important donors were calling in, one after the other, to announce that they were cutting off their support. The river of donations that had been flowing into the Al-Kifah coffers was quickly dwindling to a trickle.

Sheikh Omar might have excoriated them for hours longer had he not found it necessary to prepare for

Salaat-ul-Jumma, the Friday Prayer. He declared them traitors to jihad and dismissed them from his presence.

"You two had better find a way to make this right," Ali Mohamed said.

He matched Mahmoud in height but was far more massive.

Kadir could barely think. Sheikh Omar wanted nothing to do with him. It took all his resolve to keep from bursting into tears.

Then he remembered the card the man from Qatar had given him . . .

He glanced at Mahmoud. "Maybe there is a way . . ."

Mahmoud offered a puzzled look.

Ali Mohamed said, "You had better find it quickly."

"Remember when Shalabi helped us arrange for the auction of certain items last fall?"

Ali nodded. "I oversaw some of those arrangements."

Kadir had heard that, and was relieved to have it confirmed.

"Could you oversee such arrangements again?"

"I could. You are expecting another shipment?"

"We could arrange it."

He caught a sharp look from Mahmoud who opened his mouth—

Kadir pushed on before he could speak. "It will have nowhere near the potential profit of the last, but it could net us two hundred thousand—all of which would go to jihad."

Ali Mohamed's eyebrows lifted. "Such a sum would also go a long way toward bringing you back into Sheikh Omar's good graces. But you must be quick about it. Jihad calls me to duty in the Sudan."

"We will begin to make arrangements immediately."

"Good. After prayer I will begin contacting the buyers, tell them to be ready. Boys or girls?"

The question took Kadir by surprise.

"Both," he blurted.

Ali smiled. "Excellent. That will bring a good response."

Kadir tugged on Mahmoud's arm and they fled to the street.

"What were you thinking in there?" Mahmoud said as they walked against the cold wind blowing down Atlantic Avenue.

"Do you see any other choice? We have to work with the man from Qatar."

"I see that now, but you didn't tell Ali it is going to be a decoy operation."

"I thought it best not to. He might not want to make the arrangements. And besides, how do I explain to him, as the man told us, that the leak came from our end? Much simpler to let him think that we will be offering real merchandise for auction. Those he contacts will think the same. Remember, if those two gunmen are not lured into the trap, we get nothing."

Mahmoud stared at him a moment, then clapped him on the shoulder. "Kadir, I think I may have been underestimating you."

Everyone, from his father, exiled from Palestine and working in a clothing store in Jordan, on down through his brothers, and his sister Hadya, and then just about everyone he had met in this godless country, had been underestimating him. Well, no more.

"Come. We need to find a phone."

"We'll be late for prayer."

"This is jihad, this is God's work. He will understand."

2.   Roman Trejador watched al-Thani smile as he put down the phone.

"Good news, I take it?"

The Qatari nodded. "Excellent news. The jihadists are on board—practically begging to proceed."

"So soon?" Drexler said, sipping coffee. "The body was discovered less than twenty-four hours ago."

Roman too had to admit his surprise at how quickly they'd responded.

Al-Thani said, "The brutality of Shalabi's murder is the key. It had just the effect I expected it would."

Nasser al-Thani was proving quite an asset. Roman had invited him and Drexler to formulate preliminary plans for the trap. Now it seemed they would have to come up with hard details and logistics instead, and soon.

Drexler frowned. "Just what effect is that?"

"Well, Shalabi was definitely on the move, and he was going to take all the refugee fund's cash with him. Sheikh Omar's crew had to do something. Simply making him disappear would have been the best. They could have pocketed the cash for jihad and smeared Shalabi's name as an embezzler. Even leaving it to look like a simple robbery-murder would have worked. Some suspicion would have fallen on Sheikh Omar, but nothing serious. But the condition of his body has caused ripples far and wide."

"How do you know this?" Roman said.

"Ever since I called Shalabi's neighbor with my concerns about his well-being, I have kept tabs on the Islamic communities for reaction. It came almost immediately. I heard from my father of all people—he's in Dohar and even he had heard about it. Everyone is shocked and many regular donors are withholding support. Our young friend Kadir sounded near panic."

"And thanks to your work, they've turned to us," Roman said. "As a result, we can have some say in what they do, and make sure it doesn't work against the Order's purposes."

"That is why this is so perfect. The Order will be the

silent partner in this enterprise. After it is done, and after we pay the jihadists the bounty, I will have a close bond with them. And if in the process we get back most of the Order's money—"

Drexler held up a finger. "*When* we get it back."

Al-Thani nodded. "Yes, of course. *When* we get it back, we will be able to fund jihadist chaos right here in America, tailoring it to the Order's needs."

Roman turned to Drexler. "I fear I'm not quite so sanguine about your 'when.' The plan depends on a number of factors we cannot control."

"Such as?"

"The targets themselves. The two hijackers. First off, they must *hear* of the auction."

"I believe we can rely on that," al-Thani said. "Kadir told me that the same person who oversaw setting up the auctions last time is already at work, contacting the same people. If the gunmen are keeping their ear to the ground, as the expression goes, they will hear."

"Fine," Roman said. "But can we count on them to *act*? They have three million tax-free dollars in their pockets."

"Well, they also have thirty little girls. Or at least they had."

"Yes, whatever do you suppose they did with them?"

"What do we care?" Drexler said. "The only thing that matters is that those two killers—whoever they are— have an *agenda*, and if they think more children are going to be put up for sale, they will move heaven and Earth to stop it."

Roman smiled at him. "You are so sure of that. Why?"

"Because the hijackers did not simply kill those Arabs waiting to take delivery of the children, they genitally mutilated them."

"I continue to think you're overstating the importance of those wounds."

"Not in the least. The survivor, Kadir, had mentioned it when I interrogated him. To confirm that, I had one of our brothers in the medical examiner's office procure copies of the autopsy reports for me. Kadir had not been exaggerating. Every single corpse received multiple post-mortem bullet wounds to the pubic region from an automatic weapon, literally obliterating the genitals."

"I saw the reports as well," al-Thani said.

Roman shrugged. "I'm not calling the mutilations into question, simply wondering about the conclusions being drawn."

Drexler leaned forward and held up his index finger. "If the gunmen had been there simply for the money, would they have made the extra effort to do that? I doubt it. They didn't have time for games or mischief. That was pure rage. Those mutilations were also a warning to anyone else planning to sell children."

"I'll concede that."

"Good." He held up a second finger. "When Reggie and the other driver—the one he calls Lonnie—fled the scene with a truckload of the girls, why did the killers give chase? They already had the money."

Roman figured he'd answer Drexler's question with one of his own. "Why didn't they kill Reggie and Lonnie when they caught up to them?"

Drexler lost a little of his steam. "That remains unclear. Reggie was unconscious at the time and can't tell us. We do know that someone broke his knees."

"But left him with his manhood. Explain that."

"I cannot—at least not until we catch them. Maybe they'd spent their rage on the others. But do you have an explanation as to why they took the girls with them instead of simply leaving them there? That would have been the expedient thing to do."

No argument there.

"Why do you think?"

"Because expediency has no part in what they do. I believe they planned to return them to their families."

Al-Thani shook his head, looking baffled. "That would mean we are hunting murderous altruists." He shook his head again. "Somehow . . ."

"Not altruists!" Drexler said, banging a fist on his thigh. "Men with an agenda, a cause, a *mission*! They do not wish to do *good*. Their aim is to do *harm* to people who harm children. Those are two different things."

"What if they suspect a trap?" Roman said.

Drexler gave a nonchalant shrug. "No matter. They will *have* to react. Their agenda will not allow them to ignore rumors of a child auction."

"But then they will come prepared for a fight," Roman said.

"And so will we. They numbered two last time."

Al-Thani said, "What of that driver . . . Lonnie? Do you think he'll show up?"

Back to Lonnie again . . . questions kept circling around him. Roman was pretty sure he knew the answer to that, but let Drexler take it.

"The mysterious Lonnie remains a question mark," Drexler said.

Al-Thani added, "He could have been working with them. That could be why they let him live."

Roman was tiring of the conversation. They'd been over this many times before.

"They also let Reggie live," he said.

"Yes, but they broke his knees. Not long after the attack, an apparently intact Lonnie was back to smuggling cigarettes to Riaz Diab. That is not the action of someone who just earned a share in three million dollars."

Roman remembered how Drexler had set out to capture Lonnie and find out what he knew. The plan had ended in disaster for the two operatives sent to round him up. After that, Lonnie dropped out of sight—so completely, he might as well have fallen off the face of the earth.

Al-Thani said, "If they suspect a trap, and still come, they will bring backup."

Drexler shrugged. "Perhaps, but not much. I see their mission as a sort of shared psychosis. I see them as very secretive. They cannot involve others to any great degree. They will not arrive with an army." He smiled. "But we will."

Roman said, "I hope to be as sure when the time comes."

"We hold all the cards. We will know the truck's destination, they won't. We can have our forces positioned in advance, while our prey will have to improvise."

"What if they decide to hijack the truck en route?"

"Only we will know the route in advance. The drivers won't be told until they pick up the truck. But a mere hijacking does not fit with their mission. They wish to punish the traffickers."

Roman said, "We have to find someone to play the middleman, to act as the Judas goat and lead them to the killing ground. Reggie seems the obvious choice."

Al-Thani smiled. "Perhaps. He made the delivery before. His presence behind the wheel might lend an extra layer of credibility."

"But what of the ambush?" Drexler said. "Operatives from the Order would be—"

"We have already lost two good operatives," Roman said with a pointed look at Drexler. "I don't think the High Council would wish to risk more."

Al-Thani said, "All I have to do is go to the Al-Kifah Refugee Center and say it's for the cause of jihad and the entire mosque will volunteer."

"But we must be careful," Roman said. "We walk a

high wire here. Some of those Muslims lost friends in the original massacre. We can't allow emotions to rule. Cool heads must prevail because we want these men *alive*. We must stress that to everyone we involve in the trap. *Alive*. Dead men can't tell us where they've stashed the Order's millions. Hammer that home: They are no good to us dead."

Drexler smiled. "But long before we and the jihadists are through with them, they will wish they were."

3. "Enough already with the fresh air," Abe said, holding down his black fedora against the wind. "Put the top up."

Jack glanced at him as they drove along one of the Central Park traverses. He'd talked Abe into going for a spin in the Corvair. Naturally he'd put the top down.

"You're kidding, right?"

He looked at Jack with a poor excuse for a glare. "Does this *punim* look to you like it's kidding? Up-up-up!"

"But the purpose of a convertible is to give you access to fresh air while you drive."

"Not on the first of March. That's *meshuggeneh*! What, you think I've got polar bear blood in my veins?"

The traverse didn't offer much of a shoulder, so Jack waited until they had to stop at a red light at Fifth Avenue. He jumped out and pulled up the top.

"What? You do this by hand?"

"On this baby, yeah. The top's so light, you don't need power assist."

As it dropped onto the top of the windshield frame, Jack hopped back inside and locked down the two latches.

"There. Comfy now?"

But Abe was looking past him. "You carrying?"

Oh, shit. DDP?

"Yeah. Why?" Jack turned and his heart picked up pace when he saw a grizzled cop walking toward them. Not beating as fast as it might have were he looking at a guy with a machete, but still . . . "Uh-oh."

"Where is it?"

"Under the seat." He looked down—no sign of the Ruger—then back to the approaching cop. "What did I do?"

"I have no idea."

But the cop's weathered face broke into a smile as he reached them. "Sweet ride," he said, admiring the Corvair. "I had a red one when I was a kid. Can't believe these things are still on the road."

"Want a ride?" Jack said, jerking a thumb toward the narrow backseat. "Bring back old times?"

The cop's face took on a wistful look. "Used to call mine Sarah. Got laid for the first time in a backseat just like that. Named the car after her." He shook his head. "But my back would never forgive me for getting in there. You got a name for this one?"

That hadn't occurred to Jack, but a name leaped immediately to mind.

"Yeah. Ralph."

He frowned. "Ralph. You gay or something?"

"Last time I checked, no. It's *Ralph* . . . you know, as in *Nader*?"

The cop's stare turned blank. A car honked behind them. The light had turned green. He slapped the top.

"Better get moving. Enjoy it, kid, whatever its name."

Jack moved the dashboard lever to "D" and waved as he took off. *Kid* . . . He'd turned twenty-two last month. When would people stop calling him "kid"?

Abe stared at him, his tone dripping scorn. "'Want a

ride?' he says. 'Want a *ride*?' Are you *farblonjet* in the head already?"

"I knew he couldn't take me up on it."

"What if he was off duty and said, 'Sure, can you drive me home?' And Mister Schlemiel the chauffeur here with an unregistered Magnum under his seat has no choice but to do so."

"But he didn't, so let's enjoy the ride."

"Under the seat is a bad place for a gun unless you've got a holster there. You've got a holster?"

"Not there."

"Well, then, it could slip out any second—you accelerate too fast it slides to the back; you stop too hard it's between your feet."

"Well, sitting is too damn uncomfortable with that big bulky thing sticking in my back. I think I need something smaller."

Cristin's discovery of the Ruger Sunday night had got him thinking smaller and less clunky; something he could hide better.

"Not for nothing is it called a 'Magnum.' You want smaller, I can get you smaller. How much smaller?"

"Something that's a comfortable fit in back."

"We might have to change the caliber. And to go compact, we'll probably have to go semiautomatic." Abe shook his head. "Oy."

"I know you prefer revolvers, but—"

"Me? I should prefer? It won't be me carrying a jam waiting to happen."

Jack ignored the comment. According to Bertel, Abe had never evolved from the revolver.

"Oh, and maybe a backup—something real small, in case I don't want any bulk but don't want to go naked."

"Naked?"

"You know—unarmed."

"A concealed backup, you mean."

"Yeah. Teeny-weeny. Like for an ankle holster."

"Next time you come by I'll take you shopping downstairs."

Jack could hardly wait.

SATURDAY

1. Jack had been settled in his usual spot by the window of the Pelham bookstore/coffee shop since noon. He'd already followed Zalesky to Mrs. Filardo's home twice this week. Neither time had he left with the old woman. When Jack and Julio had followed him last fall, he'd picked up his mark and driven her to a bank on a Saturday. Jack had a feeling today would be one of those Saturdays.

Of course, Zalesky could have struck out with Mrs. Filardo, and that would be a major bummer. Jack would have invested a lot of time and research, all for nothing. He couldn't see how he'd ever be able to work a setup like this again. If Zalesky had indeed struck out, the only solution left would be to let Julio work him over with his baseball bat, like he'd wanted to from the very start.

Time dragged. And then, a little before two, the man appeared in his suit and hat, looking like a card-carrying member of officialdom.

Jack closed the book he'd been pretending to read and headed outside to his own ride. He'd decided against using the Corvair to tail Zalesky. He'd held on to the rental Chrysler and brought that along instead.

He followed Zalesky along the same old route down to Carroll Gardens and watched him stroll into the Filardo house. Moments later he emerged with an old lady on his arm. Jack had never seen Michelina Filardo, but this had to be her: widow's black dress with bunned hair, the whole old-country Italian package.

Neil shook his head as he helped the yammering crone into the backseat of his sedan. Such a sweet-looking old lady on the outside. But inside . . . her grandson hadn't been kidding: Michelina Filardo was a bitch on wheels.

He hid a smile as he slammed her door and walked around the rear to the driver's side. Bitch though she be, she hadn't stood a chance against the Zalesky charm and silver tongue. He'd fired her up and she was all gung-ho to trap this bank creep who was stealing honest working folks' money.

"You drive a-careful now," she said in her thick accent as he slipped behind the wheel. "No quick starts and a-stops, jerking my head back and a-forth. I got artheritis, you know."

Arthur-itis?

"The valise for the money is there on the seat beside you," he said.

" 'At's a briefcase, not a valise."

There's a difference? Whatever.

"Yes, ma'am."

Neil eased into traffic and headed for the old lady's Chase branch. A ride short on distance but long on *Watch-out-for-that-truck* and *Don't-hit-that-old-man* warnings and orders to "Stop" long before he reached a red light or a stop sign. It seemed like ages before he pulled to a halt before the bank.

"All right," he said, hiding his relief as he turned in his seat. "We're here. We made it."

"Just barely. Who a-you think you are—Parnelli Jones?"

Parnelli Jones? Who the fuck was Parnelli Jones? Anyone else, he might have asked, but this broad? He let it ride.

"As we discussed, all you have to do is go in, identify yourself, and let them pack the money in the valise."

"I'm a-tell you it's a briefcase, not a valise," she said, pulling it onto her lap. "And I'm a-still don't see why we have to do this on a Saturday."

"Because," he said, trying not to scream that he'd *explained this a dozen times al-fucking-ready,* "our crook only does this on Saturdays when the bank's computer centers are understaffed."

"And they'll have the money for me? I'm a-no have to wait while they count it out?"

"That was why we made the call on Wednesday, remember? So they'd have it all ready to go when you arrived."

Before she could say anything else, he hopped out and hurried around to her door. He helped her out and started her toward the bank.

She stopped and turned to him. "Any teller?"

"Yes." How many times had he told her that? "The crook isn't a teller. It's someone in the back."

The withdrawal had been arranged in advance. Unless somebody inside had screwed up, the money should be waiting.

"And remember," he reminded her for what was also at least the dozenth time as she turned away, "it's nobody's business why you're making the withdrawal. Somebody asks, you say nothing."

"So you a-tell me," she said with an annoyed look. "Many times. I'm a-no *boccalone,* you know."

Neil smiled through gritted teeth and returned to the driver's seat where he sat there with the motor running, drumming his fingers on the steering wheel.

· · ·

Jack watched the old lady disappear inside the bank. What a difference it made to be able to listen in on what was being said. When he and Julio had followed Zalesky, they could do little more than guess at what was going down in the car.

Now he understood the reason for Zalesky's return trip to the Filardo home on Wednesday. Pretty slick having her call up the bank and give them a heads-up that she was coming in. The guy was either pretty smart or he'd learned the hard way.

Jack had to hand it to him, though: He had a great talent for patter. Still, he had his hands full with that tough old lady. Dealing with her was no walk in the park—well, maybe Central Park at two A.M.

Neil sat and waited, and sweated a little. Just a little. This hustle had two points where it could go south. Here was the first: getting the money out of the bank and into the car. The second was getting the mark out of the car and back into her home without tipping the scam.

He watched the dashboard clock second hand do its tick-tick-tick thing. Though it seemed much longer, it took her only twelve minutes to make the round trip. As he saw her step through the bank entrance, he hopped out and opened the passenger door for her.

"No problems, I assume?"

"Well," she said as she eased herself onto the back-seat, "the manager or whoever she was, she ask a-me many questions but I tell her to a-mind her business."

Neil hid a grin. *You may be a bitch, but you're* my *bitch.*

Once he was back behind the wheel, he swerved into traffic and got rolling.

"*Madrone!*" she called from the backseat. "You try to a-kill me?"

Don't tempt me . . .

"Sorry. I just wanted to get away from the bank as fast as possible, just in case the wrong person saw me and recognized me as an investigator."

He drove a couple of blocks and parked in a lot adjoining Coffey Park. They could idle and wait here. He turned in the seat to face her.

"Now, as we discussed, I want you to make sure all the money's there."

She'd placed the briefcase on the seat beside her. Her arthritic fingers popped the latches and she pushed up the lid. Neil craned his neck and saw two banded stacks of hundred-dollar bills.

She ran her hands over the stacks. "All here."

"Twenty thousand. You're sure?"

"I'm a-sure. I can count."

"Okay," he said, digging the key out of his jacket pocket. "As we discussed, I want you to close it and lock it and hold on to the key."

She took the key and did just that. Then he placed a typed sheet of legal-size paper on the briefcase and handed her a pen.

"Now, sign this, stating you've checked the money and personally locked the briefcase."

"Why you put me to all this a-trouble?"

"It's not my doing, believe me. I know it's a pain, and I'm sorry. But as I told you, this all comes from the legal department. We have to establish a chain of custody to build a case against this perpetrator."

Lawyers were always a good excuse for muddied waters and useless paperwork. Give the mark a legal-looking document to sign and suddenly everything was legit. The chain-of-custody was more legal bullshit that allowed a sweet opportunity to make the switch.

After she signed, he folded the sheet, then grabbed a roll of yellow tape from where it sat on the front seat.

He tore off two pieces and stuck one over each lock on the case.

"What for is that?"

"Just another precaution. Those damn lawyers. Oops." He gave her a contrite look. "Sorry about the bad language."

"I'm a-hear worse in my day, lemme tell you."

He took the opportunity to lift the briefcase from the seat. She grabbed for it but he was too quick for her.

"Ay, where you think you go with my money?"

"We've been over this before, Mrs. Filardo. As part of the chain of custody, the money's got to be locked up and out of reach of both of us."

"All well and good for you," she said, "but 'at's a-*my* money."

"It's not going far. Just the trunk."

He got out, popped the lid, and placed the briefcase within. Below the floorboard, hidden in the empty spare tire well, sat an identical case, tape and all, waiting for the switch.

When he slipped behind the steering wheel again, he said, "Now the hard part: waiting." He held up his car phone. "After three I'll call in and we'll see if our plan worked."

"I'm a-no see how those phones work without a wire," she said.

"Think of it as a type of walkie-talkie."

She leaned forward. "And another thing I'm a-no see is how me taking my money out helps this thief a-steal from a-the bank."

Time to repeat his computer bullshit. Computers were like magic to most people. They could do things the average person couldn't begin to understand—Neil counted himself among those—but he at least knew they had their limits. People from this old broad's generation, however, thought they were capable of anything.

"It's all done with computers, Mrs. Filardo. I had to take a course in computer science to understand it myself. But his scam only works with large withdrawals, and he only targets long-established accounts. We started new accounts to lure him in but he didn't bite. That's why we needed the help of a good citizen like you."

"But I'm a-still don't see . . ."

Would she never ever shut up? Trapped in the car with a complaining motor mouth. He'd make that call ASAP.

. . . we needed the help of a good citizen like you . . .

Jack shook his head. Talk about laying it on with a trowel . . . but it seemed to be working.

Twenty large . . . nice score.

He'd found a spot on Franklin Street in front of a row of stores where he had a view of Zalesky's Dodge. He turned off the car and removed the earpiece as Mrs. Filardo prattled on. Man, that lady could talk. She never shut up.

Jack had watched Zalesky put the briefcase—taped locks and all—in the trunk, same as last fall. But he knew a lot more now than he had then. That night in November when he'd put Zalesky in the hospital, he'd used the opportunity to raid the guy's apartment. In a closet he'd found another briefcase with what looked like banded stacks of twenties. But instead of a hundred twenties, each stack contained only two—one on top and one on the bottom. The rest were singles. What should have been two thousand dollars was actually only $138.

So, Zalesky had to have a duplicate of that briefcase

hidden in the trunk, with phonied-up stacks of cash—hundreds instead of twenties top and bottom this time. All he had to do was make the switch. Simple.

And yet . . .

Jack had been listening to Mrs. Filardo and she didn't strike him as a dummy. Was she really going to fall for this? He didn't see how.

He reinserted the earplug and her voice came through loud and clear. If Zalesky followed the same schedule as last time, he'd only have to wait until a little after three. That was going to seem like forever.

"Patience, patience," he muttered. "It's gonna be worth it."

The big question was, when to make his move? That would depend on what happened next.

The old broad was still yakking about computers and how she didn't understand this and didn't understand that when 3:05 finally—*finally!*—rolled around. Her constant chatter had him debating whether to end it here. She was so damn suspicious, he figured he might well have to walk away empty-handed. But he couldn't do that. He had no other prospects ready. He had to make this work.

He held up a hand to shush her.

"Time to call in."

He punched in his own number and began talking to his answering machine.

Hopeful expression: "It's me—Nate. Did he make his move?" Change to the puzzled face: "What? Why not?" Now to disappointment. "Really. That's too bad. Well, we tried. Yeah, I'll tell her."

He ended the call and heaved a deep sigh.

"No go," he said. "He didn't make his move."

"Why not?" the old lady said.

"They don't think it was enough money. Twenty thousand . . . I'm sure you think that's a lot, and I know *I* sure think that's a lot, but apparently our crook feels more comfortable with a larger amount."

She clucked. "Oh, 'at's a-too bad. And I'm a-wasted all this time."

It's all about you, ain't it, lady.

"The team at the fraud division asked me to thank you for your cooperation."

"Well, 'at's all a-fine and good, but where's a-my money?"

Oh, you bitch . . .

"The money?" He hesitated, staring at her, watching the distrust grow in her eyes . . . just the way it was supposed to. "Oh, right. Sure. I'll get it for you right now."

He got out, opened the trunk, and retrieved the original case. No switcheroo. At least not this time. And who knew if there'd be a next time? Especially with this bitch. But he was pretty sure he could make it happen.

He opened the rear door and placed the case on the rear seat.

"Here we go, ma'am."

He stripped off the tape, then pushed it toward her. She looked at him, confusion warring with suspicion across her features.

He pointed to the case. "Want me open it for you?"

She shook her head. "No-no. I can do."

She still held the key. Her hands shook a little as she keyed the latches and popped them open. Quickly she lifted the lid and stared at the two stacks for a few heartbeats. Then she picked up one, then the other, and fanned through them.

All there, lady—all two hundred C-notes.

She looked up at him, naked relief in her eyes.

"What?" he said, looking offended. "You don't trust me?"

"Well, I'm admit I was a-having second thoughts about this. I was a-having the feeling you thought you were dealing with a *donnicciola*."

"Pardon?"

"A silly old woman. You know what they a-say about no fool like an old fool."

As he got back behind the wheel, he figured the time had come for a little stroking.

"You're no fool, Mrs. Filardo. Someone as brave and public-spirited as you is a long, long way from a fool."

He put the car in gear and headed back to her place. Along the way he loosed some deep, sad sighs.

"Ay, what's a-wrong?" she finally said.

"Nothing. Just that . . . well, nabbing this guy would have meant a promotion. And with a baby on the way, the raise would have come in handy."

"Aw . . . a *bambino*."

"Yeah, our first."

As he pulled to a stop before her place, he turned and said, "Do you think . . . ?" and then let it taper off. "Never mind."

"What?"

"Well, do you think you might be willing to try this again . . . with a bigger amount?"

She cocked her head. "How much a-bigger?"

He took a breath. "Fifty thousand."

Her eyes widened until he thought they'd pop out of her head. "Fifty—!" She blurted something that ended with "—*ricco sfondato?*"

"Sorry?"

"How much a-money you think I have?"

"The department knows exactly how much you have."

Well into six figures.

She relaxed a little. "Yes, I'm a-suppose they do."

"You redeposit that twenty thousand there on Monday, and then next Saturday we do exactly the same procedure—but with *fifty* thousand. The big difference will be that I don't think he'll be able to resist a withdrawal of that size. He'll make his move, and we'll catch him in the act, and that will be that. He goes to jail, your money goes back into your account, and I get a promotion. The good folks win, the bad guy loses, and all's right with the world. What do you say?"

"I'm a-have to think about it."

"Of course you do. It's a big decision. I'll call you Monday. Just remember: tell no one about this. You'd be surprised how word gets around."

After walking her to her door, he returned to the car and sat for a moment behind the wheel. Usually he could tell about a mark, but this old battle-ax . . . he didn't know which way she'd go.

He crossed his fingers. He needed that cash.

Jack popped out the earpiece and stared after the Dodge as it drove away. Had to hand it to the guy: He was a major creep, but a creep with major *cojones*. He'd had the old lady's money in his trunk but had passed on it, opting instead for a chance to more than double his take.

Jack remembered Julio saying how Zalesky had bragged about using a "fake-out." Maybe this was part of his play: Take the lady's money, get her fearful that she's been taken for a fool, then give it back to her, every cent. All of a sudden the tables are turned one-eighty, suspicion morphs to relief and maybe even a little guilt, leaving the mark feeling bad about doubting the man. Next time he asks for her help, she'll jump at the chance.

And what an actor. The promotion, the baby . . . a real tear-jerker scenario.

The fake-out was necessary for a big payday. Jack had

ripped a goodly sum off Zalesky. For revenge, he'd made an offer on The Spot. But an offer was only hot air. Darren wanted to seal the deal, and to see that through, Zalesky was going to have to come up with a sizable down payment. And for that he needed a big payday.

So it wasn't over yet. Jack was pretty sure Zalesky could talk the lady into another try. Which meant the two of them would have to replay this whole procedure next Saturday. Well, Jack would be here too.

And that was when he'd nail him.

2. "What's this?" Jack said, peering at the contents of a glass-topped display case.

He'd been down here in Abe's basement weapon shop before but hadn't made his way into this back corner.

"I should sell only for self-protection? I sometimes sell to collectors too."

"These look *old*."

Abe shrugged. "Not so old."

"Well, I didn't mean older than *you*."

"A comedian he's become. I'm saying not Civil War old, but old. I collect early twentieth century."

"*Your* collection?"

He nodded. "It's always changing. I buy, I sell, I trade for things I like."

Jack pointed through the glass at an odd pistol. "What's this baby? Looks like a Luger on a starvation diet."

"Such good eye you've got for a novice. That's one of my favorites: a Bergmann 'Mars' from 1903. A recoil-operated semiauto designed by Louis Schmeisser. The first to use a 9mm round, invented by Bergmann. But it was nine by twenty-three, not the nine-by-nineteen parabellum the Luger used."

Jack moved on to a boxy pistol with a long, tapered barrel. It had a red "9" carved into the rounded grip. A strip of rounds jutted from the breech.

"Another favorite," Abe said. "A Mauser C96 broom-handle model from the First World War. This one was chambered for the 9mm parabellum, hence the 'nine' on the grip."

"Is that how it fired—with the rounds sticking up from the top?"

"That's a stripper clip. They didn't use magazines to insert in the handle in those days. Instead they top-loaded the rounds through the receiver, pushing them down into the handle. The strip that holds them is then thrown away or saved to reuse another day."

Jack glanced at him. "But you're going to sell me something that loads with a clip, right?"

"'Clip'? What's this 'clip' you're talking about?"

Was he kidding?

"You know—the thing you load with bullets and shove into the handle."

"A *magazine* you're talking. Not a clip. Don't ever call a magazine a clip."

"Why not?"

"Just . . . don't."

"What the big deal?"

"It's like calling a bagel a kreplach."

"That's a big help."

"They're *different*. Don't do it."

"Okay, okay." Sheesh.

"Now, about your new main carry," Abe said, wandering toward the pistol area. "I've been giving that some thought and I think I have just the thing for you."

Jack followed to where Abe took a flat box off a shelf and handed it to him. Jack lifted the top. A small semiautomatic pistol with a flat black finish lay inside. Near the muzzle end of the slide was a large G with a small-lettered

"LOCK" in its belly. After that a "19," then "AUSTRIA," and finally "9x19." That pretty much said it all.

"A Glock 19?"

Abe nodded. "This model is fairly new. The company introduced it just a few years ago as a compact version of the standard Glock 17. It's considerably lighter and smaller than your Ruger, and will stop your kvetching about how it feels in the small of your back."

Jack lifted it from the box and hefted it: definitely smaller and lighter.

"I love it."

"Just be aware that semis have a lot more working parts than a revolver, so for something going wrong you've got a higher risk."

"Like jamming."

"Exactly."

"How often does that happen with a Glock?"

Abe had a pained look as he spoke. "Hardly ever. Almost never."

"'Almost never' is good enough for me." He replaced the pistol in the box and closed the lid. "Sold. Now, what about a teeny-weeny backup."

"On that I've been thinking too. How teeny-weeny?"

"Ideally, palmable but still packing a wallop."

"I think I know just the thing." He stepped over to a pile of newspapers. "I spotted one in here."

As Abe began thumbing through a tabloid, Jack saw *Shotgun News* on the front page.

"That looks like the new issue."

"You have?"

"Yeah."

"Well then . . ." He found the page he wanted and folded it back. Handing it to Jack, he pointed to an ad with a photo. "You can study this at home."

Jack checked out the ad. It showed what looked like

a compact semiautomatic, chrome finish with black grips.

He read the header aloud: "'Semmerling LM4. World's smallest .45 ACP.'" He looked up. "Sounds good."

"Not so fast. A few things you should know. It looks like a semiauto but in reality it's got manual repeating double action."

Jack ran that through his brain as he studied the photo. "You mean I have to work the slide by hand?"

"Yes—but forward rather than backward to eject the shell. That means: fire, work the slide, fire again, work the slide, and so on."

Jack frowned. "Not too crazy about that."

"The slide can be worked with the thumb. With a little practice you should be able to get off a shot a second."

"How many does it hold?"

"Four plus one."

Jack shook his head. "Only five? I'm not exactly Annie Oakley on the target range."

"But they're forty-five caliber. Don't forget, this is for backup. If you use it, most likely it'll be at close range. If you manage just one torso hit close in with a forty-five ACP Hydra-Shok, you're not going to need another."

"Can't argue with that."

"Another drawback you've got: If you take both the Glock, which is nine-millimeter, and the Semmerling, which is forty-five, you're going to have to stock in two types of ammo. Some mavens recommend your main carry and your backup should be chambered for the same round."

Jack shrugged. "I don't see that as a problem." He tapped the tabloid. "I take it you don't have one of these hanging around?"

"Like hen's teeth to come by. Only maybe six hundred LM-fours ever made. Every time one comes in, a collector buys it. But I can check around and see if one's available."

Jack looked back at the photo—grainy, poorly lit—but something called to him. Like the Corvair. He shook his head. Inanimate objects were talking to him now.

"Do that. I think I may—"

The phone rang. Jack could hear its upstairs counterpart echoing down the steps.

Abe grabbed it and said, "Isher." After listening a few seconds he put his hand over the mouthpiece and whispered, "One of the brothers."

Brothers? The Mikulskis?

Jack had got himself trapped in a sex-trafficking operation last year that involved two truckloads of prepubescent girls. It had been broken up—decisively—by two masked men with machine pistols. They'd been ready to eliminate Jack just like the others but Abe had vouched for him. The brothers, who'd identified themselves to Jack only as Deacon Blue and the Reverend Mr. Black, had cut him in on the three million they'd removed from the dead traffickers. Abe had told Jack later that they were known as the Mikulski brothers, but wasn't sure that was their real name.

Jack nodded: Yeah, he'd take the call.

"You're psychic, maybe?" Abe said into the phone. "He's right here." He handed the receiver to Jack.

"Who's this?" Jack said.

"Deacon Blue."

"Hey, what's up?"

"Spend all your money yet?"

"Working on it."

"We're hearing whispers about another deal like the one we interrupted last fall."

"Yeah?"

"This one sounds a little smaller. Interested?"

"You did pretty well all by yourselves last time."

"We might need your help this trip. You said to call you if that came to be the case. We're calling. Want to talk?"

He hesitated. "How soon do you think it's going down?"

"Sounds like next week."

The only thing Jack had going next week was the Zalesky scam. He had to be around for that next Saturday, otherwise he was free. But did he want to get involved with these guys? He'd seen them at work—remorseless, methodical killers. But he'd also seen their other side. And he sort of owed them.

"Okay. Let's talk. When and where?"

"How about we pick you up in front of Abe's around ten A.M. tomorrow. We'll go for a little ride."

"See you then."

He handed the phone back to Abe and then pointed to the box with the Glock 19. "Can you giftwrap that for me? And some appropriate ammo too?"

"Of course. I've got a soccer shinguard box that should hold everything. What are you going to do with the Ruger?"

"Good question."

"I can give you something in trade. Always a market for Magnums."

Jack found himself unsure. "I don't know. My first gun . . . I feel I should keep it. You know, like Uncle Scrooge kept his first dime?"

"I don't know from your uncle, but we're talking a weapon here, one you're not supposed to own in this city. The more of those you have, the greater the chance of getting found out. Remember the KISS rule: Keep It Simple, Schmuck."

Jack figured he was probably right, but still wasn't sure.

"Let me get back to you on that after I've tried out the Glock."

"Not a problem." He put his hands on his hips. "New car, new weapon . . . what next?"

"New apartment."

SUNDAY

I. At 10 A.M. sharp, a battered 1985 Lincoln Mark VII pulled into the curb in front of Abe's. Some kind of heavy-duty engine that didn't sound like the original equipment grumbled and rumbled under the hood. The tinted window slid down to reveal Deacon Blue behind the wheel. His brown hair was shorter than when Jack had last seen him. Dark aviator shades hid his eyes.

"Hopinski."

Jack walked around to the other side of the low-slung sedan and pulled open the door. The passenger seat was empty. The Reverend Mr. Black—blond hair and similar shades—lounged in the rear seat. Both wore fatigue jackets and jeans.

Black raised a hand. "Hey, you."

"Hey, guys."

The car began rolling before Jack closed the door.

"Before we do anything else," Blue said, "we need a name for you."

From behind him, Black said, "Yeah. It gets old saying 'you' all the time. And we know it isn't Archie. You wanna go with 'Jeff'?"

Jack stiffened. *Jeffrey Cusic* was the name on his phony ID he'd got from Ernie, supposedly the best money could buy.

"You guys been doing some research?"

"We're good at it. Got another name you prefer?"

He trusted these two. They'd taken his back one time when he hadn't asked. Turned out he hadn't needed them, but they'd been there just in case.

"How about Jack?"

"Jack what?"

"Just 'Jack' will do. And what do I call you guys— Mikulski light and Mikulski dark?"

"Black and Blue'll do," Black said.

"All right. Where are we going?"

"Just motorvatin'," Blue said as he turned onto West 79th. "Sunday morning's the only time driving's any fun in this town."

He had a point. Traffic was almost nonexistent. They cruised up a ramp onto the Henry Hudson Parkway. The Hudson River glittered under a pristine winter sky and Jack caught a glimpse of the boat basin before they headed downtown. They had the road pretty much to themselves.

"How are those little girls?" Jack said.

Blue shrugged. "We checked with . . . our affiliate a while ago. She'd never had to handle that many kids at once before, but she got it done. Those who hadn't been actually sold by their parents have been returned home. The others went to relatives here in the States."

"You're sure about your affiliate?"

Blue nodded. "Oh, yeah. She's devoted. She's got a network, and even diplomatic connections. She can make things happen."

He thought about a certain little girl among the twenty-eight who'd been rescued.

"Remember Bonita?"

"Yeah," Black said from the back. "The one who didn't want to let you go."

"Right. Any idea where she wound up?"

"Nope. We don't get personally involved. We get them out of trouble and our affiliate gets them back home.

I'm sure she's fine—all the girls wound up with a share of the loot we grabbed from the slavers."

The road sloped down to sea level around 57th Street and they continued downtown past dilapidated piers.

"What's going on this time?"

Blue said, "Word's slipping around that a mixed shipment of young stuff is coming in. A dozen or so. Another Arab deal. The same guy as last time—Ali Mohamed—is putting out the word. He's not saying when or where the auction's gonna be held, just letting the pervs know so they can have their cash ready."

"Auction . . ." Jack shook his head. "Last time it was supposed to be held in the Hamptons. Think it'll be the same place this go-round?"

Blue shook his head. "I'd be *real* surprised—especially after the way things turned out."

"That," Black added, "and the fact that the guy who took point on the arrangements back then is now with Allah. Last time, everything led back to an Afghan refugee center in Brooklyn, and this looks like it's following the same pattern."

"The Al-Kifah, or something like that?"

"Yeah. Exactly. But how the hell do *you* know about it?"

"Guy I know thinks it's full of Muslim crazies."

"He's right. The same crazies who tried to strike gold on the kiddie trade last time."

Jack sensed an alarm go off somewhere in the base of his brain.

"Hey, guys, do either of you get the feeling this could be—?"

"—a trap?" Black said. He laughed. "Ya think?"

"Yeah," Blue said, "don't look suspicious at all, do it."

"So why are we even discussing it?"

"On the off chance that it might *not* be bogus. Or it

might be a trap involving real kids. They might be thinking that if we try to break up the sale like last time, they'll be ready and jump all over us. That way they end up with us *and* a shipment of kids. If we *don't* show up, they sell the kids as planned and make off with their dough."

"Win-win," Black said. "For them."

Blue said, "That's why we called you. We need an extra set of eyes to keep tabs on all the players. You game?"

The totality of the situation began to dawn on him. A year ago he had still been in school, trying to deal with his mother's death and the revenge he'd taken on her killer. He'd finally dropped out of his old life to start a new one that made more sense. Since then he'd wound up killing a second man and crippling a third.

This morning he'd got up and showered. Normally he'd have wandered down to 23rd Street and grabbed an Egg McMuffin and coffee—even though McDonald's coffee sucked—but his newly developed aversion to machetes forced him to choose another route. So he'd trained uptown, grabbed a coffee and a cheese Danish at a deli, and waited outside the Isher Sports Shop, which wouldn't open until noon.

And now here he was on an easygoing drive with two of the stoniest stone killers the world had never heard of. And they were asking him for help to set up more killings.

Just another Sunday morning in the big city, right?

Did this new life make any more sense than the old one?

He wasn't sure. But he didn't have a third alternative to choose from at the moment.

"What's it going to involve?"

Black said, "We keep an eye on certain Usenet newsgroups and—"

"Usenet?"

"Computer stuff. I think I told you about that. It's how the pervs stay in touch these days."

Jack shook his head. "High-tech pedophiles. What's wrong with this picture?"

"Yeah. A lot of one-handed typing going on. But just 'cause they're pervs doesn't mean they're stupid. The Internet's much safer than the U.S. mail. We've wormed our way into a local BBS slime hole where they trade pictures and info. The location of the auction will pop up there in code."

"You know the code?"

Blue's expression was bleak. "We convinced someone to tell us."

Jack decided not to ask for details.

Black leaned forward, thrusting his head between the two front bucket seats. "Even though we can find out when the auction's going to happen through the perv boards, we won't be able to know when and where the pickup and delivery will take place—at least not directly. As far as the *when* goes, we can assume the deal will go down right before the auction, most likely the same night. The middlemen won't want to keep the kids any longer than they have to."

"Yeah," Blue said. "The longer they have them, the greater the chance of getting caught with them."

The cheese Danish curdled in Jack's stomach as he remembered the way one of the traffickers last year had referred to a couple of the girls dying en route.

"And don't forget 'spoilage,' " he said.

No one spoke for a moment. The Mikulskis knew what it meant.

"Anyway," Blue said, "when we get an idea of when the auction's going down, that's when we step up watch on that refugee center."

It all sounded so loose and disorganized. Jack found himself uncomfortable with it.

"How are we going to know who to watch for? I figured you two for the types who'd have more of a plan going in."

"Last time," Black said, "we learned where the auction was going down and traced the Hamptons rental back to this guy Tachus Diab, who spent a lot of time at the refugee center and the mosque connected to it. So we watched him. And when he rented a big limo, we followed. When he led us to a bunch of ragheads and a rental truck big enough to hold a coupla dozen kids, we knew the deal was going down."

Blue said, "It's not like they were unarmed last time. They'd come prepared, ready for a possible double-cross from their supplier. But they hadn't been prepared for us. They had no idea what hit them."

Black said, "Trap or not, this time they *will* be prepared. And they're playing cagey. They're keeping the location under wraps, no doubt till the last minute. But we do know it's an Arab deal. So, until we learn more, all we've got is that refugee center."

"Which sort of changed hands, recently," Blue said. "Somebody made hamburger out of the former head honcho there, and now the blind Santa Claus is calling the shots."

The blind Santa Claus . . . that had to be the sheikh guy Bertel had been talking about.

"How does that affect us?"

Black ran his fingers back through his unruly blond hair. "It doesn't. Apparently they need money all the time, and if running children as sex slaves adds to their coffers, they're all for it."

"Money for what?"

"Blow up American embassies overseas, I guess."

Blue smiled as they passed through the shadows of the Trade Towers. "In that case, I mean, if you look at it like that, I guess you could say it's your patriotic duty to lend us a hand."

Jack looked past Blue at Lower Manhattan flowing by to their left. "Could they be planning on blowing up something here?"

"Only a matter of time," Black said, his expression grim. "Only a matter of time."

Jack leaned back. He thought about the Muslim crazies out at the Calverton range who'd run him off the road. Bertel had said they were involved with the Al-Kifah center. Would those sons of bitches also be involved in the slave trade? Good chance. He owed them a little hurt.

"I'm in," he said. "When do you need me?"

"You got a phone?"

Jack did now. His Jeff Cusic identity had been good enough to convince NYNEX to let him have a phone line. He recited the number and Black wrote it down.

"Got an answering machine?"

"I do." Though he didn't know why. Only Cristin ever called him, and only rarely.

He handed Jack a slip of paper. "That's our mobile phone number. Don't use it unless it's an emergency."

"You mean if I want a beer or two and don't feel like drinking alone—"

Blue laughed as he steered them around Battery Park at the lower tip of Manhattan, and headed back uptown. "Don't even think about it."

"You carrying?" Black said.

Jack nodded.

"That same Ruger you had last year?"

"Picked up a Glock 19 yesterday."

"Know how to use it?"

"I will by this afternoon."

"We might want you to carry more firepower."

"Like those machine pistols you used on Staten Island?"

Black smiled. "Our darling HK MP5s. Yeah, there's no arguing with them."

Jack shook his head. "Too wild for me. I'll be better with something I'm more used to, and comfortable with."

Blue sighed. "He's probably right." He glanced at Jack. "But have extra magazines—lots of them."

As they tooled up the FDR, the brothers floated possible scenarios. One thing was certain: The Arabs would choose a deserted area.

"Think they'll try the Jersey Pine Barrens?" Jack said. A long-shot wish—he'd grown up on the edge of the Barrens and would feel right at home there. "That's about as remote and deserted as can be."

Blue shook his head. "There's a bunch of Arabs living in north Jersey, but only a few in Jersey City are players. The real players live in Brooklyn. They won't do Staten Island again—trap or not, that's way too obvious. I'm betting down by one of the Long Island beaches—they're deserted this time of year—or maybe the Pine Barrens out by Manorville."

Black said, "Manorville's kind of far out—unless the auction's in the Hamptons again. If it's closer in, I'd go for someplace like Gilgo Beach or some other godforsaken stretch of sand."

Jack thought back to his stay on the Outer Banks when the girls had been shipped in on a trawler.

"What if they bring them in by sea?"

"Really risky with all the Coast Guard around here—we're talking *the* major port in the Northeast. That last shipment came in on the Outer Banks where surveillance is stretched thin. No, I think they'll be wheeling into the city from the south, probably by the route you took."

Jack considered the manpower necessary to monitor every rental truck heading north toward New York City. Mind-boggling.

They turned off the FDR on East 79th Street, zipped

crosstown to the park and straight through it. The Mark VII stopped in front of Abe's shop, exactly where it had picked him up.

As Jack got out, Black eased out behind him from the back and took over the passenger seat.

"You're in?"

Jack nodded. He would have felt a lot more comfortable with a more definite plan, but helping out would even up a few debts, positive and negative. Yeah, he could be another set of eyes for them. And if it came down to doing more than that to keep a bunch of kids from being sold as sex slaves, he'd go the distance if necessary.

"Call me when you need me."

He slapped the car roof. They tooted as they drove off. Jack watched them go, wondering what he'd just got himself into.

2.   "I love the bay window," Cristin said, looking out on the street below.

After splitting with the Mikulskis, he'd driven the Corvair out to the Calverton range to break in his Glock—and decided he loved it. Lightweight, smooth action, and accurate as all hell. Best of all, he hadn't seen any of those Arabs out there. Might have done something stupid if he had.

Then he drove back to town, picked up Cristin, and took her along on his ongoing apartment hunt.

"Oh, yes," Margaret the agent said. "You can do wonderful window treatments here."

Margaret was showing them a third-story apartment in a brownstone in the West Eighties, just walking distance from The Spot. Jack had discreetly nixed anything on 82nd Street—the location of the 20th Precinct—and this was the third place they'd seen today. She'd been playing to Cristin on the assumption that she would be the lady of the house and therefore have a big say in the decision. In truth, Jack had brought her along because she seemed to have a good eye for this sort of thing. But mostly because he liked being with her.

He came up behind her in the angular bay window, slipped his arms around her waist, and rested his chin on her shoulder as he checked out the street below. He liked the trees sprouting from their fenced-off squares of earth in the sidewalks, liked the look of the other brownstones across the street.

"I kinda dig this place," he whispered.

"If you had a place like this," she whispered back, "I'd even come and visit." She smiled. "Or visit and come."

Cristin, Cristin, Cristin.

Well, she'd seen his current place in the Flower District from outside and had declined a look inside. Not that he'd pushed. He was kind of ashamed of it. Spruced up it might qualify as a dump. But he'd had to conserve every penny when he'd first come to the city and that place had been cheap as hell.

Another thing he liked about this apartment was the alley that ran alongside it, allowing for windows in the two bedrooms. So what if they faced a blank brick wall? At least they had some sort of natural light coming in, and he could open them for extra air.

Plus, Rico and his crazy fellow Dominicans had pegged him as a Flower District dweller. The Upper West Side was a world away from there.

He tightened his grip around her. "Think you'd ever like the window enough to come and stay?"

She turned and stared at him with wide eyes. "Did you just ask me to move in with you?"

"Not without a lot of thought and much trepidation."

Not true. The words had popped out of his mouth on their own, but were no less sincere because of that.

She continued to stare. "Are we talking a relationship? Attachment? *Strings?*"

Uh-oh. The *S* word.

"I'm just saying—"

"The rule was—*is*—that we're friends and that's all. We're friends who fuck each other's brains out, but we're still just friends. Right?"

"Right. But—"

"No buts, Jack. The whole idea is that either of us can walk away from the sex part and the two of us will still remain friends. Right?"

"Right." He bit back another *but*.

"You're not falling in love or anything like that, are you?"

Well, maybe a little, he thought.

He wasn't sure. Did he want to be with her every moment of the day and sleep by her side every night? No. He needed his space just as she needed hers.

Did he spend every waking moment thinking about her? No. He had a life. Well, sort of.

But he cared about her, thought about her, missed her often when they were apart, wished he could call her and share certain things when they popped into his head. When did all that cross the line into love?

He shook his head and said, "No. But I'm heavy into *like*."

She smiled. "That's quite mutual. I don't think I've lasted this long with any one guy before. But please don't tell me you're starting to feel possessive, because that's, like, *poiiiiison.*"

He imagined her with another guy and didn't like it. Didn't like it *at all*. Was that what she'd consider possessive? He decided to turn the tables on her.

"Let's try something. Close your eyes."

She did.

"Now," he said, "imagine me with another woman."

"Doing what? Walking down the street or fucking?"

"Not walking down the street. Picture that and tell me how you feel."

"What's she look like?"

"What difference does it make?"

"Just tell me: more like Roseanne Barr or more like Claudia Schiffer?"

No contest.

"Claudia Schiffer, of course. How does that make you feel?"

Her smile broadened. "It makes me feel like making it a threesome!"

Jack had to laugh. "You're impossible!"

She opened her eyes. "You think I'm kidding?"

Cristin, Cristin, Cristin. She'd told him about a couple of her lesbian affairs, one with his ex-girlfriend from high school, of all people.

"Anybody else, maybe. But not you."

"Well, if you'd said Pamela Anderson . . ." She waggled her hand. "Eh. A little too obvious for my taste. But Claudia Schiffer is *hot*. How'd you manage to hook up with her?"

"I didn't say I—"

From somewhere behind them, Margaret cleared her throat. He'd forgotten all about her.

"Any questions about the apartment?" she said, looking a little bit flustered.

"I like it," Jack said. "But I've got to tell you, I don't have much of a credit record."

"Are we talking *bad* credit?" she said.

"I guess we're talking none at all."

Margaret said, "I'll talk to the owners. Usually that can be resolved with a higher security deposit."

"Talk to them."

Something about this place . . .

3. Kadir noticed Hadya take off her headphones out of the corner of his eye. He put down his Qur'an. Uncle Ferran closed the bakery early on Sunday and the two of them had spent a quiet afternoon and evening.

"Well, what do you think?"

This was the third of Sheikh Omar's tapes she had listened to and he was anxious to hear how he had inspired her.

She frowned. "He is so angry."

"Of course he is angry. Look how the Western world treats Islam, how it supports Israel against our homeland. How could he *not* be angry? What righteous Muslim would not share that anger?"

"Perhaps anger was not the right word. He is so full of . . ." She hesitated and looked away.

"What?"

"You will be angry."

"No, I won't." What could she be thinking? "I promise."

"Your Sheikh Omar is full of hate."

"Hate for America, of course. Look at what the Great Satan has done just this past week: slaughtered Muslim soldiers in Kuwait and Iraq. Plus they supply the arms that allow Israel to keep its boot on the necks of our people."

"But he hates Muslims too. He hated Sadat, he hates Mubarak, he hates Saddam Hussein, he hates the Saudi princes—"

"Because they allow American soldiers to tread the holy ground that is home to Mecca."

Her eyes took on a pleading look. "But hate is not our way, Kadir. Allah has said through the Prophet—"

Kadir shot to his feet. "Do not *dare* tell me what the Prophet says! I know! I have studied at the feet of Sheikh Omar!"

"The Prophet does not teach us to hate," she said defiantly.

"But he teaches jihad! And that is what Sheikh Omar teaches. One world, one faith—Islam!"

She rose and faced him. "What has happened to you, Kadir? You were not like this when you left."

"No. I am older and wiser and more experienced. He has opened my eyes."

She walked past him. "He has poisoned you. I am going to bed."

Kadir stared at the bedroom door after she closed it behind her. Was she blind? How could she not see?

4. As soon as the door to her apartment door closed behind her, Cristin pressed her hand against the small of Jack's back.

"Is that a gun or are you just—no, that's a gun. Can I see it again?"

"Different gun this time."

He pulled out the Glock, removed the magazine, and ejected the round in the chamber.

"Why'd you do that?" she said, taking it from him.

Cristin was unpredictable. She might pull the trigger—just for the hell of it.

"It's got no safety lever. Safer this way."

She turned it over in her hands, running her fingers over the black matte finish.

"I liked the shiny one better. This one's kind of . . . ugly."

"But easier to tote around."

She smiled up at him. "You always carry one when you're with me?"

"I do."

"Why?"

"To protect you."

"Ohhhh, noooo." She handed it to him. "When you're with me, *you're* the one who needs protecting."

Yeah, he thought, but not from you.

"Dinner put me in a tequila mood. Care for a snort?"

His night to pick the restaurant and he'd chosen a Tex-Mex place called the Coyote Bar & Grille.

"Don't mind if I do. I'll accept only Cuervo."

"You got it."

As she swayed toward her liquor cabinet—which held only Cuervo Gold anyway—he looked for a place to stow the Glock. A low, Oriental-style chest sat against the hallway wall opposite the door. He pulled open the top drawer and saw a small beaded tote bag. The zipper was undone and he couldn't help see the contents . . . oblong objects that looked like—

Dildos.

He was still staring when she returned with the shot glasses.

"Hey, I saw in the *Times* today that Penn and Teller have a new show opening in a few weeks. We really should—" She stopped, followed his gaze, and laughed. "You found my toys!"

"I guess I shouldn't be surprised. But . . ."

"Different sizes, one's battery operated, and there's even a strap-on in there. Hey, if you want me to I can put it on and—"

He dropped the Glock into the drawer and slammed it shut.

"No way. Don't even finish that thought."

She handed him a shooter. "Well, feel free to borrow one to use on me should you ever run out of steam."

"With you? Impossible."

She clinked her glass against his. "*That's* what I like to hear!"

5. "You know," Cristin said as they lay together after exhausting each other, "I don't want to lose this."

"Lose what?"

"You and me. We're too good together."

No argument there. She seemed to know instinctively how to bring him to peaks of pleasure, and she'd taught him how to do the same for her.

"Why would that happen?"

"Because I think you're getting involved."

"Of course I'm involved. We're both involved."

"I mean *involved* involved. You know, where we have to think about each other. I want you to go about your business during the week without wondering what I'm doing at any given moment, and I want to go about mine without wondering if you're wondering about me. Because if I know you are, that's going to work on my head."

He figured it best to tell her what she wanted to hear. "Okay. I don't wonder about you during the week."

She raised her head. "You don't? Why the hell not?"

"What? Wait—"

She laughed. "You're *waaaay* too easy."

He stared at the ceiling. "Women."

She nudged him. "Hey! Don't lump me with the herd. You've never known anyone like me, and you'll never know another."

"No argument there."

"But you know where I'm coming from, don't you?"

"Yes, I do."

"Do you really? Sunday is *ours*. But the rest of the week is *yours*. And the rest of the week is *mine*. Separately. We went into this saying neither of us wanted strings. That's why it's worked."

Jack still didn't want strings—at least not any that weren't of his own choosing. But he'd come to the point where he wouldn't mind a few between Cristin and him. But she wanted no ties to anything.

So he'd do it her way.

"Okay. You're right, you're right, you're right. No strings."

She nuzzled his throat. "Repeat after me: *Noooo* strings."

"*Noooo* strings."

The alternative to *noooo* strings was *noooo* Cristin, and that was not something he wanted to think about.

MONDAY

1. After training to Doc Hargus's to have his sutures removed—"You heal up good, kid" and "No charge for removal" had been pretty much the extent of their conversation—Jack donned his hoodie-cum-shades ensemble and trotted over to 10th Avenue, then walked down to the Meatpacking District. Overhead loomed the long-deserted tracks of the defunct New York Central High Line, scheduled for demolition . . . soon. Not a whole helluva lot going on down at street level either. Pre-noon was a little early for the locals, so Jack had the sidewalks mostly to himself.

Hundreds of slaughterhouses and meatpacking plants had given the area its name. But the industry had moved elsewhere, and as the packers moved out, the place became a haven for pushers, gays, and transsexuals. BDSM clubs like the infamous Mineshaft dotted the area until the AIDS epidemic shut them down. The gays, transsexuals, and druggies stayed, but as the meat industry continued moving away, rents in the big brick buildings fell. Ishii-san had taken advantage of that.

Word was out that the sensei was conducting a noon class in yawara technique and Jack didn't want to miss it. Yawara were thick, short shafts of sturdy wood with enough girth to fit comfortably in the palm and long enough to leave an inch or so protruding from each end of a closed fist. Very nearly a concealed weapon, and Jack found that attractive. At various times he'd heard them referred to as *kubotan,* sometimes *koga.* He needed to learn more, which was why he was heading for the dojo.

Up on the second floor he found a good two dozen students, the steroidal trio from last week among them. Not many sensei in the city taught *yawarajutsu,* so no one wanted to miss this class.

Ever the entrepreneur, Ishii-san had stubby little yawara arranged on a table for sale, along with key-ring kubotans and hard plastic kogas. Jack found a wooden yawara with slightly flared ends that fit comfortably in his hand and bought it.

To begin, Ishii-san had them all sit cross-legged on the floor while he explained the history of the yawara. He'd just started in about how it developed from the Buddhist Kongou when Preston showed up—again in full kabuki makeup but this time wearing a salmon kimono.

"A thousand apologies, sensei," he said, bowing. "We're having another dress rehearsal but I rushed out because I didn't want to miss this."

Ishii-san acknowledged the apology with a little bow of his own. "You have stick?"

Preston reached inside his backpack and produced a ribbed stick that looked like polished redwood.

"Of course."

As Pres kicked off his sandals Jack noticed he was wearing white, split-toe socks. Ishii-san waited until he'd arranged himself and his kimono at the edge of the group, then resumed his talk. After a brief history lesson, he reviewed the human body's pressure points, most of which were sitting ducks for someone even minimally skilled in yawarajutsu.

Then Ishii-san clapped his hands and had everyone line up to practice the moves. Pres stripped off his kimono to reveal a tight mauve T-shirt and even tighter

black bike shorts. Then he made sure to position himself
next to the gym rat who'd had a beef with his makeup
last week; Preston had easily won the ensuing verbal altercation. Jack hoped today would be quieter. Yawara
were cool and he didn't want the class disrupted.

"Ooh, you look so big and strong," Pres murmured to
his pumped-up neighbor. "So much sinew."

The bigger guy turned red and Jack knew this was not
going to turn out well. Not well at all . . .

2.   Vinny's stomach went sour when he recognized
Tommy's car in the Preston Salvage lot—parked in Vinny's own fucking reserved spot, of course. But the car
beside Tommy's was a stranger.

He pulled his Vic in beside the unknown and got out.
He started for the office but stopped when he thought he
heard Tommy's voice through the side door of the garage.
Tommy? In the garage? He might get his stubby fingers
dirty.

Curious, he walked over for a look and found Tommy
and two strangers standing around a white 1988 Accord Integra hatchback. Immediately he knew what was
up. The tool chest and the acetylene torch setup standing by the front bumper confirmed it.

Honda had a policy of not changing its parts much
over the years, so they were interchangeable up and
down the Accord family line. Integras were always top
targets for chop shops. This car was worth tons more in
pieces than whole, and those pieces could be sold off in
minutes.

He felt his blood begin to heat up.

"Ay, Vinny," Tommy said. "Wasn't expecting you till
later."

Vinny pointed to the car and the equipment and

played dumb. "What's all this?" he said with a heroic effort not to talk through his teeth.

"Found it sitting on a street in Bensonhurst last night and couldn't resist. Andy Manganaro lent me a couple of his guys to take it apart."

"We already had this discussion."

Tommy smiled. "Yeah, I know, but it was just sittin' there. How could I pass it up? It's worth a small fortune in pieces. Andy's already got buyers for the parts. We're talking an easy coupla thou here."

"Yeah?"

"Yeah. And then we cut off the VIN, stick the frame in the crusher, and sell it for scrap."

Vinny glanced around. He needed something to swing. A tire iron, maybe, even a baseball bat. Then he spotted the long-handle fire ax on the wall. Perfect.

"What I say about this kind of activity here?"

"Hey, Vinny, lighten up, okay. We'll be outta here before the day is done."

Tommy was probably right, meaning the risk was small, but Vinny had said no chopping here and that meant no chopping. He grabbed the ax and moved toward the car.

"This day is done right now."

"Hey, what—?"

Vinny imagined Tommy's face in the center of the hood as he raised the ax and sank the blade into his nose.

Tommy started for him. "What the fuck?"

Vinny spun and jabbed a finger at his face. "Don't even think about it."

He then went around the car, driving the ax blade into all four fenders, both doors, and twice into the roof panel.

When he finished, the car was worth shit.

Resting the ax on his shoulder, he turned to the two terrified choppers.

"Pack up your shit. One of you drives this out of here and leaves it on some street, I don't care where. The other follows in the car you came in and I don't ever see your ugly mugs again. I do and you end up like this car. Got it?"

They glanced at Tommy, who was staring in shock at the ruined Integra, then nodded and got packing.

Vinny, too, stared at the Integra. Maybe he was also a little shocked by what he'd done, but he had to admit it had felt damn fucking good. Suddenly the world seemed a brighter place.

Keeping a grip on the ax, he headed for the door.

"You can't do this, Vinny! You can't do this shit to me!"

Vinny stopped and turned to him. "Hey, you know what? I think I just did. And so now what you gonna do, go crying to Tony? Or Junior? Tell you what, Tommy. You want a chop shop, you go start one. But none of that shit here."

With that he stepped through the door and slammed it behind him.

Damn, that felt good.

3.   To Jack's relief the yawara class, although not entirely incident free, ended without Preston getting his nose punched to the back of his skull. Some pushing and shoving had gone down, though. Every time Preston got too close, the steroidal guy—whose name turned out to be Troy—would shove him away. Pres never shoved back, never offered the least resistance, just smiled and sidled closer.

Troy's two equally pumped-up buddies kept egging him on to flatten the faggot; Jack noticed a normally quiet guy he'd seen in other classes join the pack. He wondered why Pres was being so passive. It made him look weak and defenseless, an easy mark. And Jack knew he was anything but. He'd seen him in action.

Ishii-san didn't merely hold classes here. He gave personal instruction and members were allowed to come in whenever the dojo was open to practice on the equipment. Jack had been around for a couple of Preston's workouts and he'd been impressed. The guy was lightning fast.

As soon as the class was over he slipped back into his kimono, grabbed his backpack, and headed for the door.

"Rehearsal calls," he said as he hurried out the door in his clacking sandals.

Jack noticed the three gym rats and their new hanger-on following in a pack. That prompted him to tag along too.

An odd little parade heading along West 12th toward Tenth Avenue: a male geisha in the lead, followed by four guys in their twenties, followed in turn by a lone male.

Led by Troy, the four increased their speed so that they caught up to Preston as he was passing a wide, recessed delivery bay between two abandoned warehouses. They shoved him in and followed.

Jack sped up and arrived to see Pres facing the three gym rats as they blocked the dead-end recess. The hanger-on, in true hanger-on fashion, hung back.

"All right, Tinkerbell," Troy said. "You had your fun. Now we get ours."

Preston smiled as he dropped his backpack. His hands crossed and disappeared into the wide sleeves of his kimono.

"Girl, I bet it took you the whole class to come up with that line. No, wait. Probably the whole *week*."

He removed his hands from his sleeves but only one of them was empty. He held a nunchaku with two ribbed handles of heavy-duty wood . . . painted pink.

The three rats and the hanger-on burst out laughing.

"Oh, shit, you gotta be kidding!" said one.

"Looky-looky," said another. "Nunchuk Barbie!"

Even Jack couldn't suppress a smile. Pres did look totally ridiculous: red-streaked whiteface, a kimono, and pink nunchaku. But Jack was smiling for another reason. The nunchaku meant he wouldn't have to get involved here. He'd seen Pres work out with them.

These guys had no idea what they were asking for.

"They aren't Barbie," Preston said as he struck a pose. "They're Hello Kitty, bitch."

Jack moved up beside the hanger-on.

"You're better off back here."

The guy looked at him. "No fucking way, man." He unsheathed a tanto with an eight-inch blade. "If he's got—"

Jack grabbed his arm. "You know how the sensei feels about blades."

"This ain't no dojo."

Jack's right hand was in his jacket pocket, wrapped around his yawara stick. As the hanger-on moved forward, Jack pulled it out and rammed it down on the space just above his right collarbone. The tanto dropped from nerveless fingers and clattered to the pavement as the pain buckled the guy's knees. He wouldn't be doing much with that arm for a while.

Clutching his shoulder he looked up at Jack with an agony-contorted expression. "What the fuck?"

"You'll thank me later. Trust me."

The rats had made their move on Preston, charging as one, and he was responding. The nunchaku handles were pink blurs as they whizzed through the air, clacking against skulls. Troy went for a body tackle but Pres spun away and jabbed one of the handles yawara style into his right kidney as he passed. With a groan, Troy dropped to his hands and knees. He'd be peeing blood for a week.

Pres danced among the other two, wreaking havoc on their heads. As one threw a punch, Pres locked the nunchaku chain around the exposed wrist and used the assailant's momentum to swing him around and slam him facefirst into a wall.

Two down.

He advanced on the third, battering his head and breaking fingers when he tried to block the sticks. As he went down, Troy staggered to his feet again but one of the flying handles flattened his nose with a spray of blood. He fell like a tree, down for keeps.

It seemed to be over almost as soon as it had started. Four men had been standing at the beginning, now three were out cold and the fourth was retrieving his backpack. He slung the nunchaku over his shoulder and walked toward Jack. As he approached he looked down and spotted the tanto.

"Really?" he said, staring at the guy. "Really?"

As the hanger-on, still clutching his shoulder, cringed away, Pres turned to Jack. "You?"

"Didn't see any need to add a blade to the equation. Plus I wanted to try out my new yawara."

He shrugged. "I could have handled him, but I appreciate the thought. How about I buy you lunch?"

"I thought you had rehearsal."

"Fuck rehearsal. I know my part backwards, and we've got another full dress tomorrow. So, lunch?"

Jack grinned. "You asking me on a date?"

"If that's the way you want to see it," he said with an exaggerated flutter of his eyelashes.

"How about Dutch?"

"Even better. I'm a little short—in the money department, that is, not where it counts."

"That would be the yawara department?"

"No, my dick, dumbass."

Jack shook his head. "Is this an example of the lunch-time conversation I can expect?"

"You make a great straight man."

"In more ways than one. Where we going?"

"The Empire?"

"Sounds good. And it's on my way."

As they turned to leave, Jack leaned over the hanger-on. "You're welcome."

The guy looked over at the still forms of the three rats, then gave a silent nod.

4.   At Tenth and 22nd, the Empire Diner was a long way from the Empire State Building. Then again, maybe not. A chromed miniature of the skyscraper graced the outer corner of the flat roof.

Preston's getup didn't raise a single eyebrow. But then, this was Chelsea.

They took a booth by the window. Tenth Avenue traffic passed in relative silence beyond the glass as they both ordered beers—Jack a Bass, Pres a Beck's Light.

He raised a painted eyebrow at Jack. "Usually I order something frothy with fruit and an umbrella."

Jack deadpanned. "Frothy and fruity? *You?*"

"I'm a walking contradiction."

Jack would have liked the meat loaf and mashed potatoes but they didn't start serving that until five P.M. He settled for an Empire bleu cheese steakburger. Preston ordered something called "New York Meets Hong Kong" which turned out to be stir-fried vegetables over rice with sautéed tofu.

"You a vegetarian?"

"Nothing ethical or anything like that. I've no aversion to gobbling meat."

Jack felt obliged to do an eye roll. Pres seemed to be searching for Jack's buttons. Jack wondered if he had any. He didn't care how people got their jollies, but he did find the constant stream of innuendo wearing. In fact, he was pretty sure Pres would make innuendo out of the word "innuendo" if given the opportunity.

"Okay, seriously." He ran his hands down the front of his kimono. "Veggies help preserve my slim, girlish figure."

"Which is why those guys thought you were such easy prey."

"Exactly."

"You gotta admit, you kind of goaded them into it."

This time he raised both eyebrows. "*Kind* of?"

"Okay, deliberately and with malice aforethought. Why?"

"Because they had 'gay basher' written all over them. I figured they should get bashed by a gay before they tried bashing one. Now they'll think twice."

"Oh, more than twice, I'd say."

"Thanks for not helping out."

That stung. "Hey, listen—"

Preston's expression flashed concern and his hand darted across the table to cover Jack's hand—but only for a second.

"No sarcasm intended, Jack. I mean it: Thanks for letting the faggot handle it on his own."

Jack shrugged. "I've seen you practice with those sticks. I knew who'd be walking away and who wouldn't. But why pink?"

A sly smile. "Why not? It fits my persona. Just another prop in my performance."

"The play?"

He laughed. "No! My life! All life is a performance."

"Yours, maybe."

"Oh. You think yours isn't?"

Jack tightened inside. "What do you know of my life?"

"Nothing. That's why I asked you to lunch."

"I don't get it."

He pointed around the diner. "Look at the costumes on the performers. The twinks with the perfect haircuts and well-trimmed mustaches and too-neat clothes; the leather daddies in their biker jackets, too-tight jeans, and engineer boots; the Goths with their black clothes and their kohl and their piercings; the bears with their sleeveless flannel and exposed hirsuteness."

"Don't forget the weird guy in the kabuki makeup."

"Him too!"

"You gonna leave that on all day?"

"Might. I like Japanese theater—a precursor to modern drag, you know, with males playing female parts. Now, about these people—"

"You do that makeup yourself?"

"Interrupt me once more and I will scratch your eyes out. But no, I live with the makeup artist. Desiderio is a genius, by the way. Back to these people here—they're all fringeys, all flying their particular freak flag so they can recognize each other."

"Fringeys, huh? Is there a manual on this?"

"Absolutely. *Preston Loeb's Field Guide to Fringey Flora and Fauna*. But you must have lost yours."

"What?"

Pres leaned forward. "Look. Like most gays I have excellent gaydar. You don't cause the slightest blip, by the way. Not like that basher, Troy."

Jack laughed. "What? Troy isn't gay!"

"Please, Jack, he who yells 'faggot' the loudest is typically a flamer himself. I'm telling you, if that boy was any further in the closet he could see Narnia. But, in addition to gaydar, I also have excellent fringe-dar, and it howls every time I see you."

Jack wasn't exactly following.

"Sorry."

"Don't be. It means you're one of us." He made a sweeping gesture across the room. "You're a fringey. Trouble is, you hide your freak flag."

"I never knew I had one."

"Oh, but you do. You've got the biggest, hairiest freak flag of them all. I just wish I knew what it looked like. But you've buried it. You've buried it so deep even you don't know what it looks like."

"Maybe I don't really have one."

Pres was shaking his head. "Oh, no. You do. You're the fringeyest guy in this room, Jack, but only two people know it—me and you."

"Make that one: you."

"You're in denial."

"No, I—"

"That's your performance, Jack. You play the norm when you're anything but." His eyes lit. "Hey! I see a movie franchise. *The Invisible Fringey! The Fringey Walks Among Us! The Fringey Strikes Back! . . .*"

Jack leaned back and let Pres riff on movie titles while he pondered the whole question.

Freak? Fringe dweller? Me? Nah!

Then again, he'd killed two people in the past year. He guessed that would tend to put someone on the fringe of society. But he didn't think Pres was talking about that.

What *was* he talking about, then?

5.   When Kadir returned home from the Al-Kifah center, he was surprised to find Hadya sitting on his couch, listening to a tape. She had a yellow pad on her lap and was taking notes.

He wanted to shout his joy to Allah but restrained himself. He did not want to reveal how he was gloating inside. He had known she would submit. No one but a lifelong infidel could resist the mighty imam's teachings.

She quickly pulled off the headphones and lay her pad aside.

"How are you, brother?" she said in Arabic. "How was your day?"

"It has been good, but I must ask you to continue your listening to the imam in the bedroom so that I may rest."

"You're not feeling well?"

"No-no, I'm fine. It's just that I won't be home tonight and need to nap now so that I'll be fresh later."

Her brow furrowed with concern. "Why won't you be home?"

"That is not your concern."

"Another errand for Sheikh Omar?"

Something about the way she said "errand" irked him—as if he was some sort of errand boy. He was on an errand for no one tonight. Sheikh Omar knew of the plan, but the plan was Kadir's. Well, his and the man from Qatar's.

"Hadya, you are a guest here. It is not your place to question my comings and goings."

She lowered her head in acknowledgment. "May I ask you a question on another matter, then?"

"Of course. A question about the imam's teachings?"

"No. At the bakery today they were talking about the brutal murder of one of Sheikh Omar's enemies."

Kadir's insides tightened. "Yes. A terrible thing."

"People think Sheikh Omar is responsible."

"Lies!" he shouted.

Hadya flinched back. "But they say he issued a fatwa—"

"That is true, but this is all a plot by the FBI to discredit him in the eyes of the faithful! Why do you vex me with this nonsense?"

"Because . . ."

"Because why?"

"Because although his body was discovered on Thursday, they say he was murdered sometime between Tuesday night and Wednesday morning."

A wave of cold swept over Kadir. He had a feeling where this was going.

"So?"

"Wednesday morning you came home with blood on your pants. Please tell me that didn't come from the murdered man."

Kadir resisted a sudden urge to throttle her. Keeping his voice low, he said, "How could you think such a thing of me?"

She shrugged. "I do not think. I am asking. You are devoted to Sheikh Omar, who declared that Mister Shalabi was no longer a Muslim. You came home after the time of his death with pants that were bloody but not torn. I can't help but have questions."

Kadir bottled his scream of rage. He had to put a stop to this line of thinking here and now.

He grabbed his Qur'an from the shelf and held it before him. Closing his eyes he said, "I swear by Allah that I did not in any way harm Mustafa Shalabi. Nor do I know the identity of whoever did him harm." He opened his eyes and stared at her. "Now do you believe?"

She looked genuinely contrite. "Of course. I know your righteousness. You would never swear a false oath in the name of Allah. I am sorry I thought . . ." She shook her head. "It's just . . ." She seemed to run out of words.

Time to act the big brother.

"I forgive you. You are new to this strange land. It is all overwhelming. I was overwhelmed too at first, but I came to see that I was here for a holy purpose." He pointed to the tape player. "Go back to the tape. Continue your education in jihad, your enlightenment as to our true purpose here."

She looked away and reached for the player. "Yes . . . my education." She rose. "I will leave you to your nap and listen in the bedroom."

When the door closed behind her, he held up his Qur'an and gave silent thanks to God that his sister was listening to the wisdom of the imam. He also prayed that tomorrow's endeavor would have a successful end.

TUESDAY

1. For some reason, Jack had thought it would be a good while before the Mikulskis called, but his phone rang just two days after their scenic ride. He was pretty sure it wasn't Abe or Cristin, so that left the brothers.

"*Jack.*" Black's voice. "*Word's out: the auction goes down two A.M. tomorrow.*"

Jack glanced at his clock radio. "That's like fourteen hours. Where?"

"*Amityville.*"

"Sheesh. A new horror."

"*Yeah. Worse than any fucking poltergeist. I'm parked on Atlantic Avenue near Fourth, with a clean view of that refugee center we talked about. Been watching for about three hours now. We're gonna need an extra body, so if you still want in, drive on over here and relieve me.*"

Jack wasn't sure what he wanted. He wanted the sale of children stopped, for sure, but kind of wished the Mikulskis could handle it on their own. Despite all his string cutting, he felt bonded to the two murderous brothers. On the other hand, he'd made an offer on the apartment yesterday and the real estate agent had just called back: The landlord was okay with a no-credit-record tenant if he put down extra security. Jack was scheduled to meet with her in an hour.

Priorities, priorities . . . the apartment could wait. Those kids couldn't.

"I'm still in. What should I bring?"

"You'll want your heat along because we don't know where this'll take us. No worry about food—couple of places with takeout here, but you might want a bottle to pee in."

"I don't know Brooklyn that well."

"Fastest route is the Manhattan Bridge onto Flatbush Avenue, make a right onto Atlantic. Look for the Mark Seven on your right. I'll give you my spot."

"I'm on my way."

2. "You are sure you can drive?" Mr. Drexler said as the Mercedes pulled into a Hertz lot on Coney Island Avenue in Flatbush.

Reggie sat in the backseat. The robed Arab, al-Thani, had the wheel, while the man in white commanded the front passenger spot.

Reggie flexed his knees. "Good as ever."

Not true. They were stiff and they hurt all the time, but he didn't want to be left out of this operation.

First off, he had a personal stake. The setup was a trap for the two guys who had broken up the biggest deal of his life. If he'd been able to wholesale those girls as planned, he'd have been pretty much set for life. Well, maybe not his whole life, but he was pushing forty and his cut would have covered a damn good fucking part of the time he had left.

But even worse, his suppliers—the people who'd delivered the girls to him—never got their cut. Well, in a way they did—a big cut of the *zero* Reggie collected. As a result, he couldn't go back to his old contacts because his name was shit with them. That made the second reason all important.

He wanted—no, he *needed*—to prove himself useful to these people, this organization. Whoever they were, they had money, they had connections, they had *power*. He'd heard about groups like this, but he'd always written them off as crackpot bullshit. But he had a growing feeling that these guys were the real deal. He knew that because they didn't refer to themselves by some bullshit name like the Illuminati or the New World Order or anything like that. He'd heard them mention "the Order," but never anything more specific. When your organization was so powerful that you didn't have to mention its name, that was saying something.

He smiled at that: Not saying spoke loads louder than saying.

So he needed to be an important part of this sting. He could drive—his knees were plenty good enough for that, especially since he'd be driving automatic transmission all the way.

"But you walk with a limp," the long-robed al-Thani said.

"I kept up with you in Sea Gate, didn't I?"

"Not quite."

"All right, I'll admit I ain't as quick as I used to be. But who is? The thing is, you know I'm game. I proved that last week. And I can do this route standing on my head."

"Sitting in the driver's seat will be quite enough," Mr. Drexler said.

The guy in the white suit seemed to be the head honcho here. Al-Thani answered to him, and to a third guy Reggie had never seen, referred to sometimes as "Roman" or "Trayadoor" or something like that.

Mr. Drexler added, "I hope that the possibility of

being reunited with your old acquaintance Lonnie has not caused you to overstate your abilities."

"Not even a tiny bit, Mister D. I'm good to go. I swear."

No lie there. No chance in hell that Lonnie would show up at this shindig. Reggie had led these two on about Lonnie being involved in the heist, and how Reggie could finger Lonnie and Lonnie could finger the two guys who'd killed everybody in sight and taken off with the girls and the money. That line of bullshit had worked to give him some value to their "Order." But after tonight, after they'd got their hands on the two shooters, Reggie would lose that value. And so he had to find other ways to make himself useful.

Mr. Drexler looked at al-Thani. "I still prefer Szeto."

Szeto, always fucking Szeto.

Al-Thani's lips twisted. "Let's think about that. Szeto is not a citizen, does not have a valid license, and has never driven the route. This man is American by birth, has a legitimate license, and he's experienced with this sort of thing. By all criteria, he's the better choice."

Reggie had yet to meet an Arab he liked, but he could have kissed this one—given him a little tongue, even.

"Very well," Mr. Drexler said, turning to Reggie. "A young Palestinian named Kadir—you've ridden with him before—will be along for the trip."

Reggie remembered him from the time Mr. Drexler had tried to capture Lonnie. What a royal fuckup that turned out to be. Kadir didn't say much, which was fine with Reggie.

Al-Thani said, "All right. Go inside. Arrange a one-way rental to Arlington, Virginia. Pick up Kadir at the refugee center, and head south. He'll have the name and address of who you are to meet. Your contact will turn the truck over to you and you will drive it to the address Kadir will give you. He will have maps for both ends so there will be no confusion. Any questions?"

Oh, yeah. Reggie had plenty. He wanted to ask why the big charade? Why not just put out the word that another multimillion-dollar deal was going down and wait for these assholes to show up?

Instead he said, "How do we contact you?"

Al-Thani handed him a slip of paper. "I will keep my mobile phone with me at all times. That is my number. Memorize it."

Reggie studied it. A 212 area code. He committed the other seven digits to memory and handed it back.

"I ought to have one of those phones too. We always carried one when we made a run."

"If you were transporting real cargo, I would agree. But exits and rest stops are plentiful along your route. Each has a gas station of some sort. You will have no trouble contacting us should the need arise."

Reggie nodded. He got the message: If anything went wrong, al-Thani didn't want anyone—cop or hijacker—finding a phone that had been used to call his number.

Like Reggie gave a shit. He'd rather have a phone along. But this wasn't his operation and he didn't want to make waves of any sort. Not even ripples. He'd be a good soldier and do just as he was told in the hope that maybe they'd let him join up.

Because right now his future was a black hole and this bunch was his only hope.

3. Atlantic Avenue sported two lanes each way and wide, busy sidewalks. Jack arrived around two. When he showed up, Black pulled out of his space and let him take it. Then he double-parked and eased himself into the Corvair's passenger seat where he pointed out the place Jack was to watch.

"Watch for what?"

Black shrugged. "To tell you the truth, I don't know. My bro and I are heading out on the island to scope out the Amityville place, get the lay of the land, find a vantage point so we can see who's coming and going. Basically sniff around and see what kind of stink it gives off."

Jack stared at the entrance. The sign over the double doors had green Arabic squiggles above *MASJID AL-FAROOQ* in red. At six stories, the building was by far the tallest on the block. The second and third levels showed floor-to-ceiling windows. A steady flow of Arab types passed in and out of the doorway.

This was the place Bertel had gone on about. Wheels within wheels . . .

"Busy place for a refugee center."

"Al-Kifah takes up just a tiny part of the first floor. Upstairs is a mosque and Islamic center. I don't pretend to know what else goes on in there."

Jack felt at sea. "I still don't get what I'm looking for."

Black turned in his bucket seat to face him. "Figure it this way: If the jihadists are expecting a real shipment of kids, they're gonna have to pay for them. The money—and it's got to be cash—is gonna have to come from Al-Kifah. I don't have a photo of any face you should look for, but if you see heavy-duty wheels roll up, and see an Arab with a satchel surrounded by a bunch of wary-looking guys come out that door and pile into it, you get on that phone to us."

"And then what?"

"You don't let it out of your sight. We'll all keep in contact and one or both of us—depending on what the Amityville scene looks like—will catch up with you as backup."

"What if they've got the money stashed somewhere else?"

He shrugged again. "Then we're shit out of luck on

this end and we'll have to concentrate on Amityville. These are the only contact points we know. That's the hand we've been dealt. We'll play it the best we can."

Fine, but Jack wasn't even sure what game they were playing.

Black handed Jack a mobile phone. "Plug this into your lighter socket. The number's programmed in just in case you lose it. You see something, call right away. Probably best if you call in every hour or so no matter what, just so we know everything's cool on this end."

"How long do I hang out here?"

Black reached for the door handle. "Well, if nothing's shaking here by one A.M., I think you can pack it in."

"One A.M.?" Jack glanced at the dashboard clock. "That's like eleven hours."

"Yeah, a long time on your ass," he said, getting out. "Stay as long as you want or can. We appreciate the help."

He slammed the door, jumped into the Mark VII, and roared off.

Stay as long as you want or can . . .

Shit.

Soon as he'd heard those words Jack knew he'd be here for the duration.

He restarted the Corvair's engine and turned on the heater. Another downside of a convertible top in winter, besides not being able to put it down without freezing, was lack of insulation. The heat seeped out through the fabric like it was netting.

So he sat and watched the sun slip behind the mosque, which meant he'd be restarting the car even more often. He checked the dashboard clock again. Just three now. He'd been sitting here for only an hour but it seemed like half a day.

As he warmed his hands over the heating vents, he saw a blue Ford Taurus pull into the curb before the mosque and stop beside the fire hydrant. The driver's door opened and a skinny guy with a mullet haircut got out and limped around to the sidewalk.

"Holy shit!"

Reggie. Jack would know that face and that haircut anywhere.

He reached for the phone but hesitated before hitting the speed dial. He was going to have to hear an I-told-you-so from whichever Mikulski answered.

Oh, well . . .

He pressed the button and Blue answered.

"You'll never guess who just showed up," he said.

"Don't keep me in suspense."

"Reggie of the broken knees."

"Told you so! Didn't I tell you that guy would be back to bite you on the ass?"

The brothers had warned him about letting Reggie live, but the man had been unconscious at the time and Jack simply hadn't been able to kill him. He'd settled for breaking his knees with a tire iron. He must have got them fixed up because he was walking pretty well. But how had he connected with the Arabs?

"Yeah, he's back, but I don't see this as a bite on the ass. This is more like a bit of luck."

"Yeah? How so?"

"Reggie's experienced in hauling . . ." How secure was a mobile phone transmission? Best to play it safe. "You know what."

"We do know. And I see what you mean. You think . . . ?"

"Yeah. This could be the real deal."

"He driving a truck?"

"No."

"He could be heading out to meet it. Follow him. Keep us informed."

"Will do."

"This just got more interesting."

"It did."

"Hey, Jack."

"What?"

"Thanks."

The line went dead. Jack put the phone aside and watched the Taurus.

A couple of minutes later, Reggie reappeared with a young Arab in tow. Jack leaned forward for a better look and smiled. The paranoid jerk from the firing range who'd thought Jack was following him.

Guess what, shmuck: You were wrong then, but you're right now.

Reggie hung a U-turn from his parking space and headed west. Jack pulled out and followed.

This was getting better and betterer.

4.   "Hey, Camel Boy," Reggie said as he cruised the lower end of the New Jersey Turnpike. "Did they tell you the change in plans?"

"What?" the Arab said.

"We really *are* picking up a load of kids."

"What? But I was told—"

"You were told bullshit. A dozen kids will be in the back of that truck. That means a big payday for you guys."

Kadir's eyes lit. "Sheikh Omar will be so pleased."

Reggie had no idea who Sheikh Omar was but he obviously was important to Camel Boy. Reggie didn't know why he was lying to Kadir. Just bored and felt like messing with his head, he guessed.

He glanced in the rearview and saw that same car.

"I think we're being followed."

If he'd been driving with Moose he probably would

have said *We got a tail,* but this twitchy Arab with the bad English probably would have checked his ass.

Camel Boy did exactly what Reggie expected him to do: Turned around in his seat and stared out the rear window.

"Where? Who?"

"I don't know who, but I know where—about two cars behind us—and I know what—that little white convertible with the black top."

He would have mentioned it was a Corvair but Kadir wouldn't have any idea what that was.

He'd taken Third Avenue to the Gowanus and then across the Verrazano. He'd first noticed the car on the Staten Island Expressway and remembered his uncle had had a Corvair when he was a kid. He'd noticed it again on the Goethals Bridge, and now here he was in south Jersey near the end of the turnpike and the car was still behind him.

Maybe it was his imagination. If you were headed from Brooklyn or Staten Island to, say, Wilmington or Baltimore or DC, this was pretty much the only route you could take. So yeah, he could be wrong, but he didn't think so. He'd slowed down and speeded up and always the damn Corvair stayed two or three cars back, right behind him. On the other hand, what kind of an idiot trailed somebody in a thirty-year-old car that was so easy to spot?

He ran through his options and settled on a couple: Get off the turnpike and see if the Corvair followed. But he'd just passed Exit Two and Exit One was a ways off. Then he spotted a sign saying the Clara Barton Rest Stop was coming up. He could pull in there and see if the Corvair did the same.

But why bother? Al-Thani and Mr. Drexler had indicated that they hoped he'd be followed. That was the whole point of the charade: Make it look as real as possible.

He wondered if he should check in with them. He had al-Thani's number but he'd got the impression it was for emergency use only.

He decided this wasn't an emergency, so he drove past the service center. To his surprise, the Corvair turned into it and disappeared.

"Well, I'll be damned," he said. "I guess I was wrong."

5. "Goddamn idiot!" Jack said, pounding the steering wheel as he headed for the gas lanes.

He was used to his Harley going forever on a tank of gas and he hadn't expected this kind of trip. He'd figured he might have to follow someone out to Long Island at most, not all the way down the goddamn New Jersey Turnpike and beyond.

As a result, he hadn't gassed up earlier and his engine was running on fumes now.

He pulled up next to a pump and looked around for an attendant. In any other state he'd hop out and fill up himself. But not good old NJ. No self-service here.

He spotted someone approaching in his sideview mirror and rolled down his window.

"Fill it with regular."

"No time for that," said a startlingly familiar voice.

Jack looked up and saw Dane Bertel leaning on his car.

"What? What are—?"

"No time to waste. Pull over there and park, then get in my truck."

Jack couldn't think, couldn't form a complete sentence.

"I . . . I—"

"Stop yammering and move it or you'll lose him."

Still no sign of an attendant, so Jack pulled around the pumps and into the indicated space. He removed the plastic shopping bag from under the front seat and slipped the mobile phone in with his Glock and the extra magazines. By the time he was out and locking the car, a dark Ford F-150 pickup had pulled up behind him—the same one Bertel had been driving last Sunday. He hopped into the passenger seat. The tires chirped as Bertel got them moving.

"I don't get it," Jack said.

"What's to get?"

"Why are you following me?"

"So I can find out why you're following them." He looked at Jack as they accelerated back onto the turnpike. "Why *are* you following them?"

Jack hadn't expected that. "Whoa. Let's just rewind here a little. Who says I'm following anyone?"

"Let's not play games, Jack. Answer my question."

"No-no. You're the guy who comes up and says get in my truck or we're gonna lose them. I can just as easily say, 'Lose who?' "

"But you didn't. You got in the truck."

"Touché. But that doesn't change things: You first."

Bertel shrugged. "Not much to say."

"You're FBI, right?"

He laughed. "No way!"

"CIA, then."

He shook his head. "I'm self-employed. You know that."

"No. I don't know that. I know what you *seem* to be, but when you come right down to it, I don't know a damn thing about you."

"Well, you know I'm not exactly a law-abiding citizen."

"Neither are some CIA folks, from what I read."

"I'm not CIA, FBI, NSA, DoD, or any other acronym."

"Then why are you following them?"

"Told you: I'm not following them. I'm following you."

"Bullshit."

"No. Really. It's true."

"Why?" He couldn't imagine why anyone would follow him.

"Because you're so damn easy to follow in that old white convertible."

Jack fought a furious urge to pull out the Glock and shove it in his face. He kept his hands in his lap and willed his voice toward calm.

"Would you please make sense? Please?"

Bertel glanced at him, then sighed. "I've been keeping an eye on that building for a while now."

Jack leaned back. Bertel had gone on about Al-Kifah last week, and had seemed to know a lot about it. Not a big stretch to believe he'd been watching it. Finally Jack was getting somewhere.

"You've really got it in for that place."

"Well, why not? The Al-Kifah Afghan Refugee Center is run by a bunch of bad actors since its founder, Mustafa Shalabi, moved on to be with Allah."

Jack had seen a piece in the paper about finding his mutilated body.

"I remember you saying they were out to get him. And I guess they did."

"Did they ever. Shalabi used to refer to Al-Kifah as the 'Jihad Center.'"

He pulled into the left lane and accelerated.

"Holy war instead of just helping refugees?"

"Right. Because basically Shalabi was waging holy war against the Russian Army in Afghanistan."

Jack had never been much interested in foreign affairs, but he picked up tidbits here and there via osmosis from the radio.

"Didn't they kick the Russians' butts?"

"Yeah. With the help of U.S. Stinger missiles. The Russian army withdrew two years ago but left a puppet government and millions of displaced Afghans. So the refugee charity was necessary. But now that this crazy blind Mohammedan has taken over, the donations are going to go toward killing infidels."

"Such as . . . ?"

Bertel made a broad sweep with his arm. "Look around you."

"Americans?"

"You got it."

"But why? Didn't we help them—?"

"Doesn't matter. Mohammedans can't give gratitude to infidels. It all goes to Allah."

"You mean they'll start sending suicide bombers here?"

"They don't have to *send* them—they're right here, in that mosque. And why not? They blow up embassies and barracks over there. Why not Macy's or Times Square on New Year's Eve here? 'Jihad' pretty much gives Mohammedans the green light to do anything they damn well please in the name of Allah. And it ain't terror if you ain't killing civilians."

Jack stared at him. "You *are* CIA."

He shook his head. "We gonna go through this again?"

"You know too much. And don't give me any of this stuff about 'me and the Mummy talk now and then.' You're tuned in. So if you're not FBI or CIA, then you're *ex*-FBI or CIA."

His expression darkened. "I'll tell you what I am, Jack. I'm someone nobody will listen to. I'm a lone voice

crying in the halls that jihad is coming to America and
no one wants to hear it. Everyone thinks I'm crazy. But
remember this, Jack—remember who said it and where
you heard it: When a Mohammedan does blow up a
bunch of innocent Americans here in the U.S., he will be
connected, directly or indirectly, to the Al-Kifah Afghan
Refugee Center."

The truck cab fell silent as they sped along, the speedometer wavering in the seventies. Jack didn't know what
to say. He'd always associated suicide bombers with the
Middle East—blowing up Tel Aviv coffee shops. He
couldn't see that happening here.

He remembered as a kid watching the footage from
Beirut where the U.S. Marine barracks had been pancaked by a suicide bomber, just like the American em-
bassy before it. Something like three hundred Marines
dead and a group called Islamic Jihad taking credit. But
that was long ago and far away.

"But what's in it for them? I can see it happening in
Israel—I mean, the Arab world wants Israel gone. But
we're way over here."

"No, Jack. We're over there. We just demolished Iraq's
entire army in a hundred hours. And where were we
based? Saudi Arabia. And where's Mecca? Same answer."

"So what?"

"Infidel troops using their Holy Land as a base to
launch attacks against fellow Arabs. It's pushed Sheikh
Omar to the edge of madness. And there's one Saudi
over there named Osama bin Laden who started a well-
funded jihad group two or three years ago called al-
Qaeda. He's so crazy mad and so rabidly anti-American
that the Saudi government is banishing him to the Sudan. Want to take a guess where he has ties in the U.S.?"

"The refugee center?"

"Bull's-eye! He and Sheikh Omar are natural-born

allies. They—" He pointed ahead, toward the neighboring lane. "That looks like your friends."

A blue Taurus with New York plates. As they got closer, Jack recognized the number—he'd memorized it. He wondered if he'd have been able to catch up with them if Bertel hadn't come along.

"They're not my friends."

"Then why are you following them?"

Should he tell him? Yeah, why not? Bertel knew half the story already. Jack had had to tell him something last fall—give some explanation as to why he was quitting his smuggling operation. He'd been making good money running cigarettes from North Carolina to Jersey City, but that whole little-girls-for-sale episode had soured the idea of smuggling anything.

"Answer me one more question: Why were you following me?"

"I told you: I've been watching that building when I can, more so since Shalabi's murder. I'm driving by this afternoon and I see this nifty Corvair convertible. Imagine my surprise when I see you behind the wheel. You don't see me because you're focused on the door to the Al-Kifah center. So I park down the other end of the street. I see a car pull up and a white guy picks up Kadir Allawi. I figure you're watching because you've got a hard-on for the guys who ran you off the road. But I've got to say I'm curious about Kadir driving with a white guy—his contacts are purely Mohammedan. Then I see you start to follow them. I figure I'll follow you just to keep you from doing something stupid. But it turns out to be the trip that never ends."

"If I'd had any idea it would be like this, I'd have started with a full tank."

"Just as well. I'm sure they made you as a tail."

"Like hell. I always stayed two or three cars back."

Bertel laughed. "In a vintage convertible? You kidding me? You might do okay at night, but with the sun still up? Forget about it." He pointed again at the Taurus. "That's the kind of wheels you should have if you're tailing someone. Bestselling car in the country. A zillion of them on the road. So many, they're damn near invisible. Same with this baby." He patted the dashboard. "The F-150 pickup's the bestselling truck in the *world*."

Maybe buying Ralph hadn't been such a good idea. Then again, he didn't plan on making a career out of bird-dogging people.

Bertel eased into the right lane, three cars behind the Taurus—only two southbound lanes down this end of the turnpike.

"Okay, now," Bertel said. "Your turn."

Jack paused, wondering how to begin. He decided to come in from left field.

"You ever think of Tony?"

"What's Tony got to do with you following these two yahoos?"

"Plenty. Do you?"

"What? Think of Tony? Yeah. He was the best manager I ever had down there."

"Okay. The white guy you saw picking up what's-his-name—"

"Kadir Allawi."

"Whatever. Name's Reggie. He's the one who left word to kill Tony if anything went wrong with the delivery."

Bertel was silent a long time.

Finally, he spoke, his voice flat and low. "So, I'm following the guy who ordered Tony killed."

"Yeah. Reggie and Moose."

"Moose?"

"Don't worry about Moose. Remember the guy they

found in the dunes with his head bashed in? That was Moose."

"You know who did that?"

Jack shrugged. "Lots of arguing going on between the traffickers."

Not untrue. But not an answer either. Jack didn't want to answer. He'd followed Moose out to the dunes one night. Moose never returned. He'd had good reason for that but wasn't in the mood to share.

Bertel jutted his chin toward the Taurus. "And you say this guy's name is Reggie? Reggie what?"

"Don't know. We weren't exactly close."

"I'll be looking forward to sharing a little face time with Reggie." The menace in his tone was palpable. He cleared his throat. "So that's why you're following them? You think they're bringing in another load of kids?"

"That's what the word is. The auction is supposedly set for two A.M."

"How reliable is your source?"

"Very. But it could also be a trap for the gunmen who busted up their last delivery."

"The ones who made off with the girls and the money?"

Jack nodded. "Three million, I'm told."

Bertel whistled. "Yeah, I'd want that back too." He glanced at Jack. "Your being here means those two have been in contact with you."

Jack stiffened. "What makes you say that?"

"Obvious conclusion."

Sharp old buzzard.

"Yeah. They have. But don't ask me who they are or where they are. I don't know. They found me."

Reminded of the Mikulskis, Jack pulled the mobile phone out of the plastic grocery sack and plugged it into the truck's cigarette lighter receptacle. He didn't know how long the battery in these things lasted.

"They give you that?"

"Yeah. They're looking into the auction end of this scheme. Gonna be out on Long Island somewhere." He saw no reason to mention Amityville.

Bertel shook his head. "Auctioning off kids. Makes you want to puke."

"Or kill."

"Yeah. Definitely. On that subject, how come you didn't wind up dead like the others?"

"With Abe's help I managed to convince them I wasn't there willingly."

"And how about this Reggie?"

"I broke his knees."

"You should have killed him."

Now where had he heard *that* before?

"Seems to be the consensus."

"Well, he killed Tony. Maybe he didn't pull the trigger but—"

"I didn't know Tony was dead then."

Another lingering silence, then, "So what's the plan?"

"This long drive wasn't part of it. But the main idea is to get the kids safely away."

"And after that?"

"My main concern is the kids."

"And the other two? They're out for the money?"

"The kids come first for them too. They take this kind of trafficking problem personally, and they're into permanent solutions."

Bertel smiled. "From the body count of their last operation, I gathered that. But they're not averse to making a little profit on the deal, right?"

"We've all got expenses."

He gestured to Jack's grocery sack. "Your Ruger in there?"

"Switched to a Glock."

"Good for you. You gonna be able to use it should the need arise?"

"I'll be okay."

Or so he hoped. The question had been niggling at the back of Jack's mind since his ride with the Mikulskis Sunday morning. He'd never been in a firefight. He worried he might freeze up.

"I mean, I hope you won't go running around trying to break knees with the butt of your Glock. It's polymer, you know. Very poor knee breaker."

"Very funny. When we get back I think you should audition for *The Tonight Show*. I'm sure Johnny Carson will love you."

Bertel laughed.

6. Jack wondered if the trip would ever end.

The Taurus stayed on 95 all the way. The sun had set as they'd trailed it over the Delaware Memorial Bridge and down into Maryland. Jack had to admit Bertel was pretty damn good at bird-dogging. Once they got onto 95, where he had more than two lanes to play with, he'd pass the Taurus, then pull into the center lane a few cars ahead of it. After a number of miles of letting the Taurus follow him, he'd move into the right lane, slow down, and let the Taurus pass. A subtle game of leap-frog, with one frog unaware it was playing. Really, would anyone suspect they were being tailed by a truck that spent a good deal of time running *ahead* of them?

Jack filed the tactic away for future use.

They were approaching Baltimore when the mobile phone started ringing. Jack fumbled with it and found the talk button.

"*Where the hell are you?*" Blue's voice.

Crap. Jack had said he'd call in hourly.

"Approaching 695 outside Baltimore."

"Baltimore! Why didn't you tell us?"

"Ran low on gas, had to pull off, then hustle to catch up."

"But you're on them?"

"Three cars ahead. You don't think they're heading down to the Outer Banks, do you?"

"Not if they're gonna make the two A.M. auction."

Jack looked at the dashboard clock: 6:30. He had a point.

"Yeah. Probably northern Virginia, tops. How are things up there?"

"Found the auction site. It's waterfront. We've got eyes on it from a place across the street."

"You rented across the street?"

He laughed. *"We're borrowing. It's pretty much a deserted neighborhood. Summer homes and snowbirds. We can see some Mideast types rearranging furniture on the first floor. Looks like it's gonna happen."*

"What's the plan?"

"We won't have one till we know the first point of sale."

"First point of—? Oh, you mean the wholesale site."

"Right."

So sick, the idea of wholesaling kids, but that was the way it had been supposed to go last time. Reggie and Jack had driven to the Staten Island marsh where the Arabs were set to buy the two truckloads. From there the Arabs had planned to transport them to a rented house in the Hamptons and auction them off. A quick and easy operation: Take delivery and sell them off in a matter of hours, then go home and count your money . . . while the kids started journeys through hell.

Jack was glad they were all dead. Too bad the buyers waiting in the Hamptons hadn't died with them.

"But if the Mideast types are doing the shipping, maybe they're cutting out the middleman."

"Wouldn't that be nice. Much easier for us. We've discussed this. We could be wrong, but we figure they don't have the contacts on this side of the Atlantic to put together a shipment. Probably used Reggie."

"Still smells bad."

"Oh, yeah, it stinks to high heaven. But if you see them take delivery on a truck, get on that phone and let us know. Then follow it home."

"Roger. Over and out."

"Say what?"

"Will do. Bye."

He cut the connection and stared through the windshield at the taillights of the Taurus up ahead.

"What stinks?" Bertel said.

"Everything. There's no plan. This could be a fake-out."

"Pretty elaborate for a fake-out. Let's say it's not. Let's say the deal will go down. What's in this for the Arabs?"

"Money."

"I get that. How much we talking?"

"They buy the kids for a hundred apiece."

"A hundred grand? Each?"

Jack nodded. "I'm told they go at auction for at least two, sometimes three times that."

"Shit. That gives them one to two million profit to put toward blowing up America. I'm in this, Jack."

Uh-oh.

"What do you mean?"

"I want this stopped, and I'm ready to do whatever it takes to see that it is. Tell these guys I'm in."

"I don't think that's gonna fly. They've got their own thing going—a two-man show."

"They brought you in, didn't they?"

"I was sort of left on their doorstep."

"Your friends can have all the money. All I care about is keeping it out of the Mohammedans' hands."

"I don't know . . ."

Bertel looked at him. "I don't think you have a choice, Jack, seeing as how you're in my truck and your car is way back up north on the turnpike."

He had a point. A really, really good point.

Shit.

7.   Jack squeezed his Whopper wrapper into a tiny ball. He loved Whoppers but had wolfed this one down so fast he'd hardly tasted it.

They'd followed the Taurus through the Fort McHenry Tunnel under Baltimore Harbor, then on down 95 to the Capitol Beltway. Jack had been afraid Reggie and his pal were heading south to Richmond, but they soon exited onto 1 North in Alexandria and stopped at a McDonald's.

Bertel had pulled into a Shell station half a block past where they discussed their next move while filling up. They couldn't go into the McDonald's—Reggie knew Jack, and Kadir knew them both. But they needed to eat, so they stopped at a Burger King on the other side of the highway.

They'd taken turns using the restroom and buying food, never letting the Taurus go unwatched for a second, and ate in the truck.

Bertel finished off the last of his fries and started the engine.

"Let's put ourselves back on the northbound side before they get moving again."

He found a place to make a U-turn and they were just approaching the McDonald's when the Taurus pulled out.

Bertel grinned. "Talk about timing! Am I good or am I good?"

Jack figured it was a rhetorical question so he said, "Weird seeing a human-trafficking, America-hating Arab going to McDonald's for dinner."

"Mohammedans can eat beef. It's pork they can't touch."

"I know that. I'm talking about how incongruent it seems to hate America and then chow down on the most American of foods. Why'd they even stop?"

"Even pond scum's got to eat. And maybe they arrived ahead of schedule and had to kill some time. They're on the move again, that's all that matters now."

After a few miles the Taurus made a right into a Hertz lot.

"What're they gonna do?" Jack said. "Rent a truck?"

"Who can tell? That Taurus they're driving sure as hell looks rented. Maybe they're turning it in. We need to find a parking spot with a view."

As Bertel cruised past, Jack noticed a Ryder truck idling across the street.

He pointed. "The kids could be in that."

Bertel craned his neck to see through the sideview mirror. "Same model we use for the cigarette runs. How many kids did you say?"

"A dozen."

"Plenty of room. Anybody behind the wheel?"

"You passed too fast to see."

"All right. I'll swing back."

He made a left onto a side street, then used a driveway to turn around.

On their second pass, he said, "Take a gander."

Jack had already seen him: swarthy guy with a Saddam Hussein mustache. The sight filled him with a terrible urgency.

"We can take him."

Bertel pulled around a corner and eased to the curb.

"'Take him'? What are you talking about?"

"Pull him out of the cab, mess him up, and take the truck."

"We don't even know the kids are in there."

"Yeah, right." Jack felt his anger rising. "We don't *know*. But we *do* know that Reggie, a known slaver, drove all the way down here from Brooklyn with Kadiri Bumbeeri—"

"Kadir Allawi."

"—to visit this Hertz lot where Saddam Hussein's clone just happens to be sitting across the street in a truck the perfect size to haul those kids. What do *you* think he's got in there? A bunch of Persian carpets?"

Bertel held up his hands. "Hey, easy. Lower your voice. Good thing the windows are closed."

Had he been shouting?

Bertel said, "Did you see anybody else in the cab?"

Jack shook his head. "No, but it's dark in there. For all I know he's got two more crammed in beside him."

"That concerns me."

"A dozen cold, hungry, frightened kids in the back concerns me more."

"If he's got company and they're armed, we'll never take the truck without a firefight."

Jack cooled quickly. "Well, yeah, all right. Point taken."

He didn't want to risk one of the kids getting hit. Hell, the whole purpose was to save them.

Bertel set the hand brake. "Only one way to find out. I'm gonna go look."

"What?"

"I'll ask for directions somewhere. That'll let me see the inside of the cab. If he's alone, I'll come back and we'll drive around and box him in. Since he won't be able to drive away he'll probably jump out and run. He's sure as hell not going to call the cops."

Jack thought about it: simple and direct. Things could

only head south if the driver started shooting. But what would be the point in that? With the pickup blocking him, he had no place to go.

"I'll go," Jack said.

But Bertel was already out the door. "Keep the motor running. We may need to move fast."

8.   Aimal Kasi studied the rental place across the street. He'd seen a car pull in with two men in front. Were they the ones he was supposed to meet?

Everything was moving so fast. Only two weeks had passed since he'd come over from Karachi. He'd barely settled himself in Reston with his friend Zahed when he received a call to rent a truck and turn it over to a Palestinian and an American at this spot. The caller was from New York and knew that he'd entered the country with fake papers that gave his name as "Kansi" instead of Kasi. The caller had said his help would further the cause of jihad. That was all Aimal had to hear.

A second call had come this afternoon, telling him to watch for a Ford Taurus. Aimal knew little of American cars so he had gone to a dealership and studied the model. He had an excellent memory and the car that had just pulled in was a Taurus.

This was all very exciting. He had come to America with the money his father had left him; he planned to start a business near the nation's capital and blend in. But he would always be ready to strike at the Great Satan. Jihad was coming to America and he intended to be part of it. As soon as—

A rap on his window made him jump. He twisted in his seat to see an older, gray-haired man staring at him through the passenger-side window. He rapped again. Aimal sat frozen in alarm. Who was this?

The man made a rolling motion with his hand and Aimal lowered the window a few inches.

"I'm afraid I'm lost," the man said. "I'm trying to get to the Pentagon. Any idea which way I go?"

Aimal had studied English back in Pakistan. He could speak and read it fairly well but had trouble understanding the spoken form. Most Americans spoke too rapidly for him, and this one was no exception. He noticed that although the man was smiling, his gaze was darting all around the inside of the cab.

"Repeat, please?"

This time the man slowed down and Aimal understood. He had driven all around the area since his arrival. He had passed the White House, the Capitol building, the entrance to CIA headquarters in Langley, but most often the Pentagon. From that huge structure the Great Satan had dispatched the infidel troops who besmirched the Holy Land and humiliated an Arab military. How he longed to drive a truck like this filled with explosives through the front entrance and detonate it in their faces. Then *they* would know humiliation!

"Do you know Route One?" Aimal said.

"Sure," the man said, pointing. "Over that way."

"Take it north. You will see signs."

"Thank you." The man took one more hard look inside the cab, then straightened. "Thank you very much."

As he watched the man hurry away, Aimal felt his suspicions grow. He was convinced he hadn't been looking for directions but had been inspecting the truck. Why? Aimal could not imagine what he might have done to draw such scrutiny. What—?

He jumped as the driver door opened.

"Are you Aimal?"

He whirled and saw a young Arab. "Who are you?"

"I am Kadir," he said in Arabic-flavored English. "We have come to take the truck."

He saw an American with hair cut short in the front and long in the back standing behind him.

"Yes-yes!" he said. "You must take it quickly! That man—" He went to point but the man was no longer there.

"What man?" Kadir said.

Aimal jumped out of the truck. "A man was here—he was asking directions but I believe he was pretending to be lost so he could get a close look at the truck."

"Did he get a look in the back?" the American said.

"No-no. The back is locked. The key is on the seat." Aimal pushed Kadir toward the driver seat. "You must go! Now!"

Kadir hopped in and slid over. The American followed and took the wheel. The engine was already running. Without a word he slammed the door, put the truck in gear, and began moving. Aimal had gone little more than a block when a pickup truck roared around the corner and onto the street. He saw the gray-haired man behind the wheel, pounding upon it in obvious rage.

Aimal wished he could phone the truck to tell them to watch out for the pickup, but he had no way.

As it passed, the gray-haired driver turned his angry face toward Aimal. Aimal would remember that face.

9. Jack offered no comment as Bertel took out his frustration on the steering wheel. Eventually he settled down to tailing the truck. Once they were back on 95, he began playing his leap-frog game again.

In Maryland, a couple of dozen miles north of Baltimore, Bertel had his pickup in the right lane, ahead of the Ryder truck, when he said, "Uh-oh."

Without warning he tugged the wheel left, ripping

across the two other lanes as he aimed for the ramp to the Maryland House rest stop.

"What?" Jack said.

"He just put his blinker on. If he'd waited a few seconds more we'd have missed the turn-off."

Jack peeked through the rear window as the truck followed them to the top of the ramp and then pulled over. Bertel kept going.

"What do you think they're up to?" Jack said.

"Waiting to see who follows them into the rest area, maybe. It's an old trick."

Over the next five minutes, only one car—a minivan with a man, a woman, and three kids—came up the ramp. Apparently satisfied, the truck headed for the parking area.

"Now what?" Jack said.

"Their options are eat, piss, phone, gas—take your pick, or maybe all of the above, although I find it hard to believe they need a food or a pit stop so soon after McDonald's."

Bertel circled the parking area, waiting for the truck to find a spot. It did, at the far north end where it sat alone. He stopped where they could watch. After half a minute, Reggie got out and limped toward the big colonial-style brick building that housed all the fast food and services while Kadir stayed in the cab.

"Damn," Jack said. "Why the hell didn't they both go?"

"What difference does it make?"

"If they left the truck unattended, I could run up and bang on the rear doors. If someone banged back, I'd know the kids were in there."

"Well, they haven't stopped along the way to load up, so it's a good bet they've already got the kids."

"Doesn't rule out an empty truck."

Bertel looked at him. "After all this, you still think that's a possibility?"

If it was all a charade, it was pretty damn complex. But with millions of bucks possibly at stake, no charade was too complex.

Jack shrugged. "The longer we trail them, the less I think so. But I'd love to know. Because it would change everything."

And then a way to find out hit him between the eyes. A way so obvious he kicked himself for not thinking of it before.

Reggie stood at the phone bank and dropped in the required change. Why'd they have to put the phones on the goddamn second floor? His knees hated stairs.

He waited for someone to answer, and recognized al-Thani's *"Hello?"*

"Yo, it's Reg. We're north of Baltimore with the truck."

"How long till you get here?"

"Traffic's light. Brooklyn in about three hours, I'd say."

"Excellent. Your companion has the location of your final destination. You should arrive around twelve-thirty. Perfect timing. Any problems?"

"I thought I had a tail on the way down but he turned off. Your guy in Alexandria thought someone was sniffing around the truck, but we haven't seen anyone following us."

"That's too bad. Stick to the same route through New Jersey and into Staten Island that you used last time. They may be looking for you there. And remember: If you spot anyone following you, you are not to try to lose them."

What am I—stupid? I know that.

"Got it."

He hung up and headed down the steps. He was tired

of driving but didn't trust that Arab behind the wheel. He saw the signs for Bob's Big Boy, Roy Rogers, Sbarro, and TCBY, and would've liked nothing better than to take a break with a thick slice of pepperoni pizza, but he'd have to save that till later. He had many more miles to go.

When he got back to the truck he found Camel Boy Kadir standing outside, back by the cargo box. He looked worried.

"What's wrong? Someone snooping around the truck?"

He shook his head and spoke his lousy English. "I am worried about our"—his eyes darted left and right—"cargo."

Oh, yeah. Like he didn't look too guilty or nothing.

"What about our"—Reggie mimicked his look—"cargo?"

"They are very silent."

"They're good kids. They know to keep quiet or else."

"They are too quiet. I am worried. What if they are dead?"

"Not our problem."

He gasped. "But then there will be no sale, no money for—!" He cut himself off.

Reggie figured at this point it was probably best to tell him, otherwise he'd be whining for the rest of the trip.

"Okay, Camel Boy, here's the truth: I was just funnin' you. There ain't no kids in there."

His eyes damn near popped. "What?"

"It's empty, dumbass! Just like they told you it would be. This is all a trap to catch the guys who ripped off the last load."

Kadir threw his hands in the air, squawking gibberish as he wandered in a circle. Finally he returned to Reggie.

"Why did you lie to me?"

"Because I felt like it. And because I don't think they

should have told you in the first place. I don't trust you people."

"You insult me!"

"Live with it, Camel Boy! One of you gave it up last time. Because of someone on your end, all we wound up with was a pile of dead bodies and me with two fucked-up knees! For all I know it might've been you. Well, it ain't gonna happen again, Camel Boy."

The more he thought about it, the more he wanted to break this asshole's nose.

"Why do you call me this 'Camel Boy'?"

"Because you're an Arab. A camel jockey."

"I am from Palestine. I have seen pictures of camels but I have never seen a living camel."

"No shit. Really?"

"Really."

"So you don't go out and hump a camel or two when you get a little horny?"

"What is this 'hump'?"

"Forget it. We need to get rolling again."

Jack waited till the truck pulled out of the lot and started down the ramp toward 95 North before he jumped out of the pickup. Bertel exited on the driver side.

"*Now* are you gonna tell me what you're up to?"

"All in good time, my dear," Jack said. "All in good time."

Bertel followed him toward the Maryland House. "We're not gonna be able to catch them again."

"Yeah, we will."

They took the stairs up to the big house two at a time. Inside a sign pointed up to the phones. Jack ran up, dropped a quarter into the slot, and punched "O."

"*Operator,*" said a woman's voice.

"Could you connect me with the Maryland State Police, please? I want to report a crime."

When he was connected, he said, "My name is Ernest Pasquale and I'm at the Maryland House. I don't know if it's a real crime but I just saw someone open the rear of a Ryder rental truck and the cargo area was loaded—and I do mean *loaded*—with cases of Marlboros. It's got Virginia plates and I wrote down the number." He gave the truck's tag number from memory. "It just took off, headed north."

He hung up and turned to Bertel. "Let's get out of here."

Bertel was grinning as they headed back to the pickup. "I like it."

"It's so obvious, I don't know why I didn't think of it before."

"Well, we weren't following a truck until recently."

True. When the cops stopped the truck—and after that call, how could they not?—they'd find either a dozen scared kids or an empty bay. If the former, Reggie and Kadir would end up in cuffs and the kids would go to protective services.

Problem solved.

If the latter . . . well, Reggie and Kadir would simply continue on their way, very glad they had an empty truck, and Jack could call the Mikulskis and tell them this whole deal had been a big fat setup to trap them.

"What are your two friends gonna think about this?"

"Not worried about them right now."

Bertel slapped him on the back. "I always liked you, Jack. Damn, you need to come back to drive for me."

That wasn't going to happen, but he didn't want to get into that now.

"Speaking of driving, why don't I take over? You've done plenty."

Bertel gave a little salute. "The helm is yours."

Helm? Was he navy?

Jack approached the ramp back to 95 but pulled onto the shoulder where he had a good view of the north-bound traffic.

"What are you waiting for?"

"I'll know it when I see it."

"Meanwhile they're getting farther and farther ahead of us."

"I don't think catching up will be a problem."

A few minutes later a state cop roared by with his lights flashing.

Jack smiled. "That's what I'm talkin' about."

"They're gonna send more than one," Bertel said. "Count on it. Never know what you're gonna run into with smugglers. They might want to defend their cargo."

"You oughta know."

He looked at Jack. "Did I ever tell you to defend your cargo?"

"Never."

To his credit he'd always said to run if he could, or go quietly if he couldn't. He'd forbidden Jack to carry a weapon on his runs.

"But some guys are dumb. Resisting is a loser's game. Only two ways it can end: bad or worse."

"I'm gonna wait awhile longer," Jack said. "See if another goes by."

Sure enough, less than a minute later a second statie went flashing past. Jack gave it another minute, then started down the ramp. Once on the highway, he stayed in the right lane, keeping just to the limit or a little below.

Reggie's gut knotted when he saw the flashing cop lights in the sideview mirror. "Oh, shit! I hope to fucking hell that's not for us."

Kadir leaned forward and peered at the mirror on his side. "Were you going too fast?"

Asshole raghead!

"No, you dumb fuck. If you'd been paying attention to the speedometer instead of napping you'd know that!"

He hadn't been speeding. Okay, he'd gone above the limit a few times, but only briefly, only to pass some clown lollygagging ahead of him. With all the cars regularly zipping past, no way he'd be tagged for speeding.

Has to be someone else, he thought. Or he's rushing to an accident somewhere ahead.

But no. The fucker pulled right up behind him and whooped his siren twice.

"Shit-shit-shit!"

Reggie put on his blinker and eased toward the shoulder.

"What is wrong?" Kadir said, bouncing in his seat all twitchy and nervous.

"Why're you all worked up? Ain't got no ID?"

"This was not supposed to happen."

"No shit. But it is."

The big question was *why*? He had an idea but didn't want to go there.

He pulled to a stop on the shoulder with the cop behind him, lights still flashing. Reggie waited for him to get out but he didn't.

"What is he doing?" Kadir said.

"You ever been pulled over?"

"I do not have a driver's license."

"He's probably calling in to run a check on our plates, make sure it hasn't been sto—"

A second cop car zoomed up and pulled in front of him. He saw the Maryland State Police emblem on the front door.

Okay. Still no reason to panic. Cops almost always backed up each other on stops, especially at night.

When the third cop showed up he had a pretty good idea of what was going on.

He pointed Kadir toward the glove compartment. "Check for the rental papers in there and hope to fuck you find them."

As the Arab did as he was told, Reggie pulled out his wallet and loosened his license in its slot. These cops might be jumpy and he wanted everything to go smoothly.

"Are these the papers?" Kadir said.

Reggie took the rental agreement and held it ready.

Finally, both of the troopers behind him stepped out of their vehicles and approached the truck. The one ahead of them unfolded himself from his unit, but stayed by the open driver door. All three wore tan shirts, black ties, and Stetson hats.

Kadir's voice shook as he said, "What do we do?"

"You do nothing. Keep your hands in plain sight on your lap and your mouth shut. Let me do all the talking."

He rolled down his window and tried to look confused as the trooper approached.

"Something wrong, Officer?" he said in his most pleasant tone.

"Good evening, sir. License and registration, please?"

Reggie pulled out the North Carolina license and handed it over with the rental agreement. Light from the flashers reflected off the cop's badge.

"It's a rental so I don't have a registration. Can I ask why you stopped me?"

He noticed the second trooper staring at them through the passenger-door window.

"We had a report of a rented truck matching this description hauling contraband."

"What sort of contraband?"

"Sir, would you mind opening your rear doors?"

Reggie so wanted to tell him to fuck himself. Make the asshole haul him in, go through all the legal bullshit, get a court order or whatever the hell they needed to get into the truck, and finally pull open those doors to find *nothing*.

But he wasn't here to make a point or cause trouble. He was here to deliver this truck to New York.

"Not a bit. Always glad to cooperate with law enforcement."

The trooper stepped back. "Would you and your passenger step out of the cab, please?"

"Sure. Let me grab the key to the lock here."

He hopped out and headed toward the rear of the truck, hoping to hell the damn key worked. As he led the way, he tried to work through the timing of this stop. The fuzz had shown up after their visit to the Maryland House.

"Can I ask you something?" When the trooper didn't answer, Reggie went on. "Did someone call in a report about this particular truck?"

"Why do you ask, sir?"

"Well, I ain't haulin' no contraband or nothin', but I did have a bit of an altercation with someone back at the rest stop over a parking spot. I'm just wondering . . ."

The trooper said nothing, just pointed to the lock holding the doors closed. Kadir came around the far side, followed by the other trooper.

Another Ryder truck similar to theirs whizzed by. Reggie pointed to it.

"Why ain't you stopping him?"

"You might say it's a random thing."

"My lucky day, huh?"

The trooper only pointed to the lock again. He and his buddy stepped back, hands resting on their gun butts, while Reggie stuck the key in the lock and twisted.

Eventually, as he continued north at a deliberate pace, Jack spotted a cluster of flashing lights ahead and slowed even further. He eased into the middle lane as the truck came into view with two cop cars behind and one ahead. The rear doors were open. He saw Reggie and Kadir standing aside while two troopers aimed flashlights into the empty cargo bay.

"No kids," Bertel said in a breathy voice as they passed. "Dear God, that's a relief."

Jack let out a breath he hadn't realized he'd been holding.

"Yeah."

"And that white guy . . . that's Reggie?"

"You got it."

"The one who ordered Tony killed."

"One and the same. Why?"

"Might want to look him up someday."

Jack wouldn't mind if he did. But that was the future. The empty truck was the present, and as he'd said before, this changed everything. No more worrying about something going wrong and kids getting hurt.

He grabbed the mobile phone and hit the speed-dial button. "Got to call this in."

Blue answered again. *"Yeah, Jack."*

"The truck's empty."

"You're sure?"

"The cops stopped it and I got a look inside. Just bare walls."

A pause as Blue repeated the message, followed by a brief, mumbled conversation. Then: *"You wouldn't have had anything to do with that stop?"*

"Well, yeah."

Another pause. "*We made some plans, now we might have to change them.*"

"Sorry. But I had to know."

"*Don't be sorry. It's good to know. We'll just make new plans. You know, ad lib a little. We're good at that.*"

"Want me to stick with them?"

"*Not much point. Wherever that truck's aimed won't be a healthy spot for you or us. We want to stay away from it unless it's coming here. You know where Amityville is?*"

"I can find it."

"*Take the Belt past JFK and follow the signs to the Southern State and then Sunrise Highway. When you hit Massapequa, call and one of us will meet you and guide you in.*"

He ended the call.

"What's the story?" Bertel said.

"Heading home."

Bertel stared ahead at the road, drumming his fingers on his thighs.

"What?" Jack said.

"If you don't mind, I'd like to stay on them."

"Why? They've got an empty truck. All they're hauling is a bunch of air."

"Shits like them give decent smugglers a bad name."

Jack had to laugh. "You're kidding, right?"

"Not as much as you think. Slow down and let them pass us."

Jack didn't want to slow down, he wanted to move on. But he signaled for the right lane and eased up on the gas pedal.

"What's your interest? And no BS about upholding the honor of smugglers."

"Something else is going on."

"Yeah. It's a big fat trap."

"Beyond that. Don't you get a sense that there's a

bigger picture here? Something that goes beyond human trafficking and jihad?"

"Selling sex slaves to finance blowing up the country sounds plenty big to me."

"It is. But I've got a feeling there's something even bigger going on."

"Like what?"

He looked at Jack. "If I knew, I wouldn't need to stick with these pieces of human garbage."

"But why do you 'need' to?"

He checked the speedometer—the pickup was doing about fifty-two.

"Because something's happening here and I don't know what it is—"

"Sounds like a Bob Dylan song."

"—and I don't like not knowing."

"Can't know everything."

"True, but . . ."

"I'm pretty much fine with not knowing things. I'll just add your 'something bigger' to the list."

"That's it? Just add it to some list and go your merry way?"

"Pretty much."

"You're not the only one in this world, Jack."

Jack shrugged. "When I think about having to share it with guys like Reggie, I sometimes wish I were."

"Good point. But don't you feel any need to be part of something bigger than yourself?"

Uh-oh. Were they going to get all philosophical here? Okay. He'd play. He didn't like talking about himself, but right now the only other thing he had to do was drive. Maybe he could get Bertel to reveal a little about himself.

"Not really. No, let me take that back: no need at all."

"Just me, myself, and I? That's your life?"

"I didn't say that. But I don't feel the need to join a church or a theater group or the Royal Order of Raccoons to feel whole. And to tell the truth, my immediate circumstances are about all I can handle right now."

"How do you feel about your country, Jack?"

Where was this going?

"Best country in the world." Easy answer because he truly believed it. "Not that it couldn't be improved."

"How so?"

"It's a little too much in your business, don't you think? I don't mean 'your' as in you, Dane Bertel, I mean it in a more generic sense, because the government doesn't even know about your cigarette business. If it did, it'd shut you down and toss you in the clink."

"Well, I am breaking the law. I knew that going in."

"But why should there be a law that says you can't truck cigarettes from North Carolina to Jersey? Why should someone stop you? Where do they get that power?"

"It's interstate commerce."

Jack gave a prolonged shrug. "That's supposed to mean something to me?"

"It's regulated by the federal government."

"Says who?"

"The federal government. Backed up by the Supreme Court."

"The Supreme Court, huh? And who appointed them?"

"The federal gov—" Bertel paused, smiled. "Okay. I get it."

"Do you? Sounds rigged to me. How's it sound to you?"

Bertel pointed a finger Jack's way. "So you think people should just ship whatever they want wherever they like?"

"Why not? Who are you hurting?"

"The tax man, for one."

"And the tax man works for . . . ?"

"Stop right there. We could spend the night going round and round on that." He laughed. "Legalizing transport would put me out of business. I mean, I'd have no margin of profit if it wasn't illegal."

"Exactly. So if you're asking if I feel a need to be part of that circle-jerk machine, the answer is no. But if I've got to be involved in any machine, I'd prefer it be as a ghost."

Bertel sighed. "You're misconstruing what I'm saying."

"Am I?" Time to turn this around. "What about you? Do you feel a need to be part of something bigger than yourself?"

"Yeah, I do."

Jack grinned. "Like the FBI? Or the CIA? Or the NSA?"

"Will you give that a rest—please?"

"Not until you admit you're a deep-cover agent for some supersecret branch of the federal government."

Bertel just shook his head, like he was disgusted. But Jack wasn't done needling.

"Okay," he added, "let's just say you follow these guys and do find 'something bigger' going on. What do you plan to do about it?"

"I'll think of something."

"Report it to your handler, or directly to M?"

Bertel remained silent.

"Or maybe you're working for the other side. Maybe you're from SPECTRE or SMERSH or—"

A Ryder truck flew by in the left lane.

"Is that—?"

"It is," Jack said, reading the license plate. "Follow?"

Bertel nodded. "Yeah. They'll be stopping at the Chesapeake House."

"You know that?"

"They don't have a mobile phone, otherwise they wouldn't have stopped at the Maryland House to call in. They'll want to phone in about getting stopped by the cops."

Jack liked the logic in that.

"Then what?"

"While they're stopped, I'm going to see if I can tag that truck with a tracking device."

Jack almost veered onto the shoulder. "What? You just happen to have some kind of tracking device handy?"

"It's just a radio transceiver."

"And you're gonna keep tellin' me you're not a secret agent?"

"Stop talking like an idiot. I've had a few drivers I've suspected of making detours from their route so I've followed them from time to time. The tracer ensures I don't lose them along the way."

Sounded logical, but still . . . Jack couldn't help feel that Bertel was connected to something bigger than he let on.

Turned out he was right about the Chesapeake House. Just a few miles up the road, the Ryder truck exited to the rest stop.

The Maryland House had looked like a real house. The Chesapeake House looked more like a stylish warehouse. Reggie and Kadir appeared to have given up all pretense—they parked near other cars this time, and both got out and headed into the building.

"There." Bertel pointed to an empty spot a dozen or so feet away. "Pull in there."

"If they spot us . . ."

"Only take me a second." He twisted and reached behind the front seat. "I've done this before. Rented plenty of Ryders and know just where to stick it."

He came up with a duffel bag and hopped out of the

cab with it. Jack watched him hurry around to the truck and disappear as he crouched beside it. Less than a minute later he was back. He put the duffel on the floor and pulled out a little gizmo. He turned it on and soon a green light began blinking on its postage-stamp size screen.

"She's working. Let's get out of here."

Jack didn't have to hear that twice. He backed up and pulled away.

"Now what?"

"We head back to the Jersey rest stop where we left your cute little car. Then—"

"—most likely you'll go your way and I'll go mine," Jack said, unable to resist another Dylan lyric.

But he liked the idea of returning to Ralph and being back in control and on his own again. At least until he connected with the Mikulskis.

"Right."

"And which is your way?"

Bertel shrugged. "I'm assuming they're heading back to New York. After I drop you off I'll prowl the northbound turnpike till I catch their signal, then see where they take me."

Bertel and he had eased back onto better terms during the trip. But even if they hadn't, Jack didn't want to see him getting caught up in something he couldn't handle.

"It *is* a trap, you know."

"Don't worry, Jack. I won't be walking into it. I don't need to be in direct line of sight for this gadget to work. They'll never see me behind them."

"Still . . . why?"

"Just scratching a curiosity itch."

"You know how that ended for the cat."

"Won't end that way for me. But you never can tell what will happen to them."

Jack looked at him but his expression was set in stone.

"What's that mean?"

"Well, that Reggie guy did order Tony killed."

"Yeah, but—"

"Just keep driving."

"Answer, dammit," Reggie muttered. "Answer!"

While Kadir was using the men's room, Reggie had bought a coffee and plunked the change into one of the wall phones. At least this time he hadn't had to climb a bunch of goddamn stairs to reach them.

Finally al-Thani picked up. Reggie gave him a quick rundown of the cop stop.

"And you asked why he stopped you?"

"Yeah, but the guy was as talkative as a rock. Said he'd had a report of a rental truck hauling contraband and picked us at random, but I don't buy it."

"How long were the rear doors open?"

He sipped his coffee.

"Less than a minute. I got them closed ASAP."

"Did many cars pass while they were open?"

"Hell, yeah. But it don't matter how long they stayed open or if anyone who matters passed while they were. If the guys you're looking for—"

"Choose your words carefully."

"What? Oh, yeah." Mobile phone. Right. "What I'm saying is, if these guys dropped a dime on us, they didn't have to see nothin'. The fact that we're still on the road tells them all they need to know."

"Only if they made the call. Since we cannot know that, we will proceed as if it was truly a random stop."

"Seriously?"

"Seriously. Do you know your final destination?"

"Yeah, your little buddy showed me. That's like the ass end of nowhere."

"Precisely why it was chosen. When will you arrive?"

Well, they sure as shit wouldn't be hitting any traffic toward the end of the haul—not at this time of year.

"We lost about half an hour with all this. Add that to the last ETA."

"*One A.M. then. We shall be waiting.*"

Reggie hung up, with a lot more force than necessary. Shit. This was turning into one major clusterfuck.

Bertel had swung through one of those "*Official Use Only*" turnarounds to put them back on the turnpike south so he could drop Jack off at the Clara Barton Rest Stop. After feeding Ralph a full tank of gas, Jack continued the half dozen miles or so to the end, then turned around and headed north again.

He felt a pang as he saw signs for Exit 4. So easy to cruise down Route 73 into Burlington County, take 70 to 206 South to Johnson. Roll up to the driveway of his old house, pop in the door and say, "Hey, Dad, what's up?"

Home again . . .

No, he couldn't go home again. That would undo the clean break he'd made, undo the new life he was constructing for himself, the new person he was fashioning.

He put his foot in the tank and accelerated. As the exit ramp slid by on his right, he found it hard to swallow past the sudden lump in his throat.

Where had that come from?

But it got worse farther north as he approached that overpass . . . the one where the now dead Ed had dropped the cinder block that crashed through the window of the family car, crushing the life out of his mother.

Hadn't even noticed it on the way south. So intent on following Reggie and the Arab in their Taurus that he'd breezed under it without realizing.

But now, following his own course, with no focus

outside his own ragged thoughts, it hovered ahead, seeming to glow in the darkness.

He turned on the radio—AM only in this old car, but anything was better than thinking about that day, that moment, hearing again the smashing glass and his mother's final whimpering, agonized breaths. He never listened to AM so he twisted the tuning knob at random, looking for something, anything to distract him. He got a nice sampling of static, but as the overpass loomed large in his windshield, he found a clear signal playing "Surrey with the Fringe on Top," and almost lost control of the car.

He managed to guide the Corvair onto the shoulder and stop. That song. He'd always hated it. Mom had been a rabid Broadway fan. Hardly ever got to see the plays but always bought the sound tracks. The Muzak of Jack's boyhood memories was a parade of Broadway tunes. Many he came to appreciate for their melodies and lyrics—like *My Fair Lady* and *South Pacific*—but he never cared for the *Oklahoma!* tunes, and "Surrey with the Fringe on Top" least of all. A dumb, dumb, dumb song, and he'd always begged his mother to put on another Broadway LP—*any* other Broadway LP—but she loved *Ooooooklahoma!* and wouldn't hear of it.

They'd never been all that close. She was Mom and she was *there,* would *always* be there as a nurturing presence in his life. He'd always been her "miracle boy" who could do no wrong. The story behind the "miracle boy" designation, when he'd finally learned it, had left him with a feeling of vague unease, but he'd gotten over it. His father had been the central figure in his life. He'd been the one Jack had wanted to please. Mom was on his side, period. And maybe because of that he'd taken her for granted.

Damn, how he wished he'd appreciated her more while she was alive. He never got to say good-bye, never got to tell her what a nourishing, steadying influence she'd had on his life. Never intrusive, but always *there*. Someone he could count on—forever, he'd thought.

And then, that day in the car, one moment she was alive and well in the front passenger seat, the next she was gone.

He felt a pressure build in his chest and he began to sob.

Christ, what was wrong with him? Was he going crazy?

Had to remember to stay the hell out of Jersey.

WEDNESDAY

1. Nasser al-Thani let Mahmoud do the driving. After all, he operated a cab for a living. If he could navi-
gate Manhattan traffic, surely the Montauk Highway in
West Islip in the wee hours of the morning was nothing.

Besides, it gave Nasser time to think.

From the outside, everything looked perfect. Ali
Mohamed had put a minion named Saleem Haddad in
charge of setting up the auction—renting the house, no-
tifying the interested parties. To prevent an accidental slip
of the tongue, Nasser had instructed Kadir and Mahmoud to tell no one connected with Al-Kifah that the
auction was a ruse and would never take place. He had
been gratified to learn that Kadir was ahead of him—he
already had told Ali Mohamed the same.

So, word of the auction had gone out through the pederasts' clandestine and supposedly secure channels, the
same as last time. The buyers were assembled in a rented
house in a mostly empty neighborhood, the same as last
time. Reggie, a man who had run children before, was
behind the wheel of a northbound rental truck, the same
as last time. The situation was ripe for a hijacking, just
like the last time.

But from the inside, where al-Thani sat, everything
looked far from perfect.

He still didn't know how the hijackers had located
the transfer site last time. Had they followed the truck

north or had they followed the limousine Tachus had hired for the transaction? Since he couldn't know, he had gone to a lot of trouble to send Reggie and Kadir south to pick up an empty truck. He'd also rented a limo just like Tachus had done, and made it as obvious as possible that it contained only two men. The limo had come equipped with its own cellular phone and an extended-range antenna, which might come in useful, considering the remote location of their destination.

"Make a right up ahead," he said as they reached the Robert Moses Causeway.

Mahmoud nodded but said nothing as he turned onto the bridge that would take them to the barrier islands protecting Long Island's south shore.

Nasser had researched the location carefully. This causeway was stop-and-go traffic in the summer months, but the barrier islands were virtually deserted at this time of year. And why not? Strips of sand dunes and sea grass and a cold wind blowing off the endless expanse of the Atlantic Ocean. No place to be in early March, but the perfect spot for a clandestine exchange of human contraband.

And an equally perfect spot for an ambush.

To the unimaginative, only two routes led to the transfer spot: this causeway from the north and east, and lonely Ocean Parkway running the length of the thin barrier island from the west. If, by some stretch of the imagination, the hijackers had learned the location of the supposed exchange, they would be watching those two approaches. But if they were, they would see no truckload of jihadists arriving to take up positions from which they could ambush the would-be ambushers. Because the gunmen would be arriving by a third route.

Mahmoud followed the causeway across a couple of miles of Great South Bay's choppy water until they reached Captree Island, little more than marsh and scrub with a few houses on its south shore. Then over a narrow channel to Captree State Park at the easternmost tip of one of the barrier islands. If they'd kept going they would have crossed more water and then landed on Robert Moses State Park. Instead Mahmoud headed west on Ocean Parkway for three miles to the edge of Gilgo State Park, then turned south onto a sandy path with the unlikely name of Sore Thumb Beach Road. Nasser had seen it on a map and the beach did indeed stick out like a thumb, but it didn't look sore. He had never understood the English expression "stick out like a sore thumb." Really, whatever did that mean?

"Stop here," he told Mahmoud just after he made the turn.

"Are they on time?" Mahmoud said.

Nasser checked his watch: 12:22.

"They should be appearing any minute."

Drexler had arranged for two boats to ferry a dozen jihadists from a Babylon marina. Its owner had been suspicious, but Drexler had convinced him that it was a religious thing for the Muslims—that and a thick wad of cash had been enough. Nasser had the man's mobile number. He called him.

"They're not there yet?" the man said. *"Could be the chop. The wind's really picked up in the last hour. We've got a front moving through. If you don't see them in the next ten minutes, get back to me."*

And you'll do what? Nasser wondered as he hung up.

He watched through his sideview mirror and needed to wait only minutes before he saw movement atop the dune on the far side of Ocean Parkway. Mahmoud popped the trunk and the two of them stepped out of the limo to wave them forward.

When the twelve newcomers were clustered around the car, Mahmoud lifted the trunk lid and began handing out Kalashnikov AK-47s. They all knew how to use them. He directed them to positions in the dunes lining each side of the sandy road.

Nasser took as much of the icy, cutting wind as he could, then slipped back inside the limo. Growing up in Qatar had left him ill-prepared for these conditions.

When the jihadists were hidden from view, Mahmoud took the wheel again.

"Did you hammer home that we need those men alive?"

Mahmoud nodded. "They know. They will aim for the legs if it comes to that."

"Good."

They drove to the beach at the end of the road and parked. When the hijackers arrived—*if* they arrived— they would not be able to leave without passing through the jihadist gauntlet.

If . . . a big if now that the truck had been stopped and searched. If the hijackers knew it was empty, this would turn out to be a long, cold night with no return.

But no loss, either. Only some disgruntled pederasts. And that was hardly worthy of concern. A gain of sorts, in fact. With that thought nestled in his brain, Nasser al-Thani settled down to wait.

2.   Over the phone, Black had told him to turn off 27 onto County Line Road east of Massapequa and park in the visitor lot of South Oaks Hospital. Less than a minute after Jack had killed Ralph's engine, he showed up in a beat-up Chevy Suburban and drove them south through Amityville.

"Where's the Mark Seven?"

"A little too memorable."

Jack thought of Ralph. Same problem.

"Where we headed?"

"The auction house."

"What's the plan there?"

"Plan B."

"What happened to A?"

"Plan A was freeing the kids. We suspected from the git-go the Arabs might make the run with an empty truck, but just the possibility that it could contain kids narrowed our options. Forced our hand, really. We would have had to make a play—either where the truck ended up or here at the auction house. But your call changed all that."

"I hope that's a good thing."

"Oh, it is. Now that we know no kids are involved, who cares where the truck goes?"

Jack knew one person who did, but didn't mention Bertel.

"So Plan B is . . . ?"

"Hit the pervs. That's where the money will be. Whoever's waiting for that empty truck won't have any money on them. Just lots of guns in the hope of getting their money back. But *here* . . ."

Hit the pervs . . . Jack remembered all the shooting at the Staten Island marsh last year.

"Hit them how?"

"Relieve them of their assets. They come prepared to bid for kids. No checks or credit cards accepted, so they bring cash."

Jack nodded. "Hit them in the pocketbook."

"And other places."

Okay . . . but he didn't want this getting too crazy.

Black parked by the head of a lagoon.

"We walk from here."

They both had to keep their heads down against the wind coming off the bay. Blue met them halfway up the block; he had a backpack slung over his right shoulder.

"All's still quiet outside. Just one guy watching the streetside door."

"What about inside?" Black said.

Blue's expression was grim. "Trading photos while they wait."

Black pulled a machine pistol from under his coat. A long suppressor extended the barrel.

"Let's not keep them waiting any longer."

Blue shrugged off the backpack and handed it to Jack. "Here's yours."

"My what?" he said, unzipping it. Another machine pistol lay within. "Oh, crap."

"What's wrong? Your own HK."

"I've never shot one of these before."

"It's easy." He pulled it from the pack along with a long suppressor. "And you don't really have to hit anything. Just fire short bursts at the front door when someone tries to get through."

"But my Glock—"

"Fires one shot at a time." Blue began screwing the suppressor onto the muzzle as he spoke. "Not impressive. People hear a burst of automatic gunfire—even if it's only three rounds—it scares the shit out of them. Instant respect."

"Where will you guys be?"

"We'll come in from the waterfront side and get everybody facedown on the floor."

Jack was almost afraid to ask. "Then what?"

Blue reached back into the backpack and emerged with a fistful of nylon zip ties. "We immobilize them while we shear them of their assets."

"And one more thing," Black added, taking a turn reaching into the pack. He pulled out a black ski mask. "Don't want that innocent boyish face in the papers, do you?"

No, Jack did *not* want that.

3. "Where the fuck are we?"

Reggie knew he'd get no answer from Kadir.

"We are on Ocean Parkway," Kadir said. "As we should be."

Okay, check that. He'd get no *useful* information.

"Tell me something I don't know, Camel Boy."

He checked the sideview for like the millionth time but still no sign of anyone following. This whole day was turning out to be a one big fat fucking zero. The hijackers had smelled the trap, figured the truck was empty, and stayed away. A waste of everybody's time.

Yeah, but with three million smackers at stake, probably worth the effort.

He squinted ahead for a sign, anything that would give him a hint as to where he was. All he saw was sand drifting across the pavement as the wind howled around them. He'd passed a small golf course and had seen a sign telling him he was in Gilgo State Park, and now another hove into view telling him he was approaching Captree State Park and a road that would take him to Robert Moses State Park. This whole area was lousy with state parks.

The terrain looked weirdly familiar. Like he'd been here before. What did they call it? Déjà view, or something like that. Then he realized this was just like riding northbound on the Outer Banks, with a bay a few hundred feet to his left and the Atlantic an equal distance to his right.

But the Outer Banks had people. This whole stretch had nothing and no one. Great place to bury a body. Nobody'd ever find it.

And then the street sign on his right—Sore Thumb Beach Road.

He made the turn and stopped. Down the end of the road, down by the ocean, a pair of headlights blinked.

"There's your buddy Nasser."

"The man from Qatar is not my 'buddy,'" Kadir said.

"You sound scared of him."

"I am not scared. I am . . . I have respect."

"Respect?" Reggie nodded. "Yeah, probably a good idea to have respect for him and the people behind him. Maybe a little fear too."

"I fear only Allah."

He started the truck forward. "Let's not ruin a beautiful friendship by getting into that crap."

He angled down to the end of the sandy path and stopped before the limo. Al-Thani and a tall, redheaded Arab Reggie had seen before—Mahmoud, or something like that—got out. The redhead carried an AK-47 in each hand. As Reggie and Kadir got out to meet them, he tossed each of them a rifle.

"Anyone following?" al-Thani shouted above the gale.

"Not that I could see." He looked around, concerned. "This is it? I thought you were gonna have a welcoming committee."

Al-Thani smiled and nodded to the AK-47 in Reggie's hand. "You just passed through a gauntlet of a dozen of those."

Reggie turned and looked back. "Really? I didn't have a clue."

"That's the whole idea."

The wind off the water carried salt spray that stung the eyes and frosted his face.

"They must be freezing their asses off."

Al-Thani shrugged. "It's for Allah and jihad."

Reggie was pretty sure al-Thani was about as down with Allah and jihad as he was. So yeah, let the sons-a-bitches freeze.

"Well, if you don't mind, I'm going to turn the truck around and wait in the cab."

Al-Thani nodded. "I'll watch from within the limo."

Yeah, the Man from Qatar wasn't down with the cold either.

"How long we gonna wait?"

"We'll give it thirty minutes," he said over his shoulder as he hurried toward his car. "If they don't show by then, they never will."

Hell, Reggie thought. If they don't show in *ten* minutes, they never will.

4. After Jack had been properly outfitted—including latex gloves—and instructed in his duties, the three of them crept toward a brightly lit house farther along the lagoon. Its gravel front yard was crammed with cars, with more parked up and down the street. In a lighted recessed doorway near the right corner stood a beefy guy, smoking and shivering.

"Welcome to Perv-ville," Blue whispered.

Black remained bareheaded while Jack and Blue had pulled on their masks. Jack found himself shivering—and not just from the cold. The selector switch on his weapon had been set to three-shot mode, but he'd never fired an automatic weapon in any mode, and had never shot any kind of gun at another human being. What he feared most, though, was failing the Mikulskis. He didn't want his inexperience to cause one of them to get hurt.

"My move," Black said. "Wait here."

He straightened and strolled toward the house, head down, hands in his pockets, his MP5 slung out of sight behind his back.

When the guy at the doorway spotted him he tossed his butt and slid a hand inside his coat pocket.

"Who the fuck are you?"

"I'm here for the auction," Black said, not breaking stride.

"Hold up right there. What auction?"

Black took a few more steps before stopping. "You know."

"Do I? Where's your cash?"

"Oh, that. Right here."

He swung the MP5 around and fired a three-round burst into his chest. The suppressor muffled the reports but they still sounded awfully loud to Jack. As the guard or whatever he was slumped to the ground, Black pulled the ski mask down over his face while Blue pushed Jack toward the car they'd already chosen for his cover—a white Mercedes sedan with a clear view of the front door. Black disappeared around one side of the house while Blue ran around the other.

Jack had already extended the tubular stock. He set it against his right shoulder and rested his elbows on the car's hood. Checking to make doubly sure the safety was off, he stuck a shaky finger, sweaty from the latex and tension, through the trigger guard and rested it on the trigger.

Gunfire erupted from within. Seconds later the front door swung open. Jack saw a flash of a squat man in an overcoat and pulled the trigger. The MP5 jumped in his hands as it rattled off a three-round burst that tore into the wood of the door. The door slammed closed as more gunfire filtered through from inside.

And then, as quickly as the gunfire began, it stopped. But Jack held his position until he saw movement at one of the windows: Black waving him to come inside.

After a couple of deep breaths, Jack straightened and shuffled toward the house. Well, this wasn't so bad. He'd only had to fire once and had succeeded in merely messing up the front door. Not bad at all.

He glanced down at the body slumped in the entryway as he stepped over it. Wide, sightless eyes stared up at him. He pushed through the punctured door and entered the house.

"Bring him inside, will you, Jack?" said Blue.

Jack wasn't too keen on that, but he grabbed the dead guy by the back of his collar and dragged him across the threshold, leaving a wet red trail. He shut the door and turned to take in the house's large front room. Twenty or so men and maybe three women littered the floor, lying facedown—most alive and unhurt, a few bloody and very still in pools of blood.

Except for the Muslim wearing a robe and a skullcap, most looked like ordinary people to Jack. Some were pierced and tattooed, but many looked like people he'd pass on the street any day and never give a second look, never guess the highlight of their life was the sexual abuse of children.

Black nodded to Jack, then raised his voice. "Okay, everybody, we're here to lighten your load. We're gonna send you on your way with less than you came with, if you get my drift. We can do this easy or we can do it hard. A couple of you who resisted have gone to their final reward, whatever that may be. Give us a tough time, and you'll join them. Resistance is futile, so you might as well relax and enjoy it."

"Hey, isn't that what you tell the kids you buy?" Blue said, his voice tight.

Jack was staring at one of the bloody corpses when Blue sidled up to him.

"Since they're carrying heavy cash, some of them

brought bodyguards who tried to earn their pay. After they went down, the rest became real cooperative."

"Women?" Jack said, his gaze flicking between the female captives. "I thought this was mostly a guy thing."

"It is. Guys mostly have a lock on pervitudity. But some of them have wives or girlfriends who are into it too. It's not always sex. Sometimes it's just having power over someone, making them helpless, seeing how much they can degrade someone else. And who's easier to subdue than a child?"

Jack shook his head. "Rotten, lousy . . ."

"All right!" Black shouted. "You will empty your pockets of your wallets and all cash. We don't care about rings and jewelry, we just want your cash. If we see your hand come out of a pocket with anything that looks like a weapon, you will be shot dead on the spot."

Jack watched as they complied. They looked scared but none of them seemed too upset about losing the money.

Blue handed him a bunch of the zip ties. "Let's get to work."

Black stood guard while Jack and Blue laid their weapons aside and put the ties to use.

"Hands behind the back and use a figure-eight that crosses between the wrists." He demonstrated on the squat guy who'd tried to escape through the front door. "Then pull it *tight*!"

"Hey! That hurts!"

"You're kidding, right?" Blue's lips pulled back in a snarl as he rammed a fist against the back of the guy's neck. "You wanna know hurt? Make another sound and I'll give you hurt!"

Jack tied the guy's ankles in the figure-eight configuration, glad for the gloves—not just because they wouldn't leave prints, but because he didn't want to touch these people.

"Make sure you tie just above the ankles. And if they're wearing boots, yank 'em off."

They moved on and eventually Jack came to one of the women. She had a crewcut, a pair of handcuffs tattooed on her neck, half a dozen earrings on each side, above-the-knee patent leather boots.

"Let me go and I'll make it worth your while," she whispered as he tied her wrists.

He said nothing as he tugged the tie tight.

"You into B and D?" she said. "I am too. If you like tying up women, I can show you the best time you ever had."

Pathetic. He was glad he was wearing gloves as he tugged at her boots.

"Easy with those. They're my new fuck-me boots."

When he slipped off the second, she tried to kick him but he caught her foot before she could connect. She began to scream and thrash until Black stepped over and jammed his MP5 muzzle against her temple.

"I assume you've heard that expression about making my day? Go ahead."

She quieted. Jack finished tying her and moved on to the next.

5.   Dane Bertel adjusted his field glasses as he watched the scene on Sore Thumb Beach. He knew three of the players: Kadir and the redheaded Mahmoud, plus the white guy with the trailer-park haircut who'd driven the truck. Jack had explained him. But the other Arab in the thobe? Dane had never seen him before.

The new Mohammedan intrigued him. Certainly not one of the blind cleric's followers, who tended to be bearded, bedraggled, and in need of a bath as they waited for someone to tell them what to do. This

Mohammedan looked more used to giving orders than taking them.

Following the truck had been easy. He'd dawdled along the northbound turnpike till his receiver had started beeping. He'd let the truck pass him and then tailed it just as he had without the tracker—sometimes leading it, sometimes following. He'd hung even farther back across Staten Island. And when they took the Meadowbrook Parkway south toward Jones Beach, he'd stayed as far behind as he could and still keep the receiver beeping.

Out here in the middle of nowhere, he drove Ocean Parkway with his lights off. And when the tracker signal started getting stronger, he figured they'd stopped. He'd pulled into a parking lot by an undersize golf course and continued on foot to this dune.

Damn but it was cold. This wind was like to saw you in half.

Ahead had to be the spot where the supposed buy was to take place, and where they planned to ambush the guys who'd hijacked them last time. The guys who weren't going to show. He spotted men crouched along the low dune that flanked the single road to the exchange point.

Dane had to admit that whoever planned this had done a good job. Only one way in and out of the tiny peninsula, unless you had a boat. Sure as hell couldn't swim in that frigid water. No way to sneak up by land or sea unless you had a submarine. The mainland was only a couple of miles away, but even in the unlikely possibility that the sound of gunfire carried that far, who would have their windows open on a night like this?

He noticed the truck start to move. What the—? Leaving already? He started to rise to hurry back to the pickup when he realized it was only turning around.

They had to know they'd blown it. How long were they going to wait?

He hunkered down to find out.

6. Blue had backed the Suburban as close as possible to the house and opened the rear. Then the three of them had filled its cargo space with the briefcases and attaché cases and even a North Face backpack they took from the would-be bidders.

Black had all the wallets in a pillowcase. He plunked it on a car hood and handed one to Jack.

"Take the cash, leave everything else, then toss the wallet into the yard. We don't want to get caught with anything that'll tie us to them."

Jack did as he was instructed while Black did the same. The latex gloves slipped on the bills but he managed.

"That was why you didn't take their jewelry, right?"

"Right. We'd have to fence it and that's a connection. Not worth the risk."

As he tossed the last wallet across the yard, Jack started to remove his mask.

Black grabbed his arm. "Whoa. Leave that on."

"They can't see me."

Black looked around. "You never know who's watching. Cameras are getting better and better and smaller and smaller. Never know when someone might be filming you. Look what happened when those cops were beating up that black guy in L.A."

Jack tugged the mask back down. For the last couple of days all the news shows seemed to want to talk about was the beat-down the cops had laid on some guy named Rodney King Sunday night. A local guy with a camera had videotaped it and every TV set you passed seemed to be showing highlights.

"What about the Suburban?"

"Borrowed."

"As in without the owner knowing?"

"Right. Same with the plates. We'll move the cash into the Lincoln later and leave the Chevy in a safe spot."

He popped open one of the briefcases to reveal stacks of hundreds and some glossy photos. He grabbed the photos with a gloved hand and shoved them at Jack.

"This is what passes for entertainment for these douchebags."

Jack's gorge rose as he caught a glimpse of a small pale boy and a large hairy man. He tossed them to the ground.

"You didn't have to show me that!"

He controlled an urge to go back into the house, get a knife from the kitchen, and start doing amputations.

"Yeah, I did."

Black opened another, found more money and more photos. He took the photos and threw them into the air, letting the wind scatter them about the yard.

"It'll help you appreciate what comes next."

"What?"

"We've finished the roundup." He closed the rear of the Suburban. "Now it's time for cleanup."

"I don't follow."

He jerked a thumb over his shoulder at the lighted windows behind him. Jack wove his way back through the parked cars to look inside.

Everything was pretty much as he'd left it. The same men and few women facedown on the floor, bound hand and foot with the zip ties Jack had helped apply. But where most had been lying quietly before, all were moving now, writhing as if in panic.

Movement to the right caught Jack's eye. He saw Blue

emptying a can of fluid onto the struggling people on the floor. The can was red.

"Is that . . . ?"

He didn't have to finish the question as the wind carried the unmistakable odor of gasoline his way.

"Oh, jeez!"

Jack backed away from the window as he watched Blue toss the empty gas container onto the struggling forms on the floor.

"You're not . . . tell me you're not."

Black gave him a puzzled look. "Not what? Not gonna use a little antiseptic on an infection? Not gonna cut out a malignant tumor?"

"But burn them alive? I'd rather see them humiliated in court, then sent to jail where they'll be renamed 'Alice' and passed around like party favors and get hit day after day after day with the same hell they've been dishing out. Make their lives a nightmare. That's worse than death—ten times worse. They'll wish they were dead."

"Sounds great," Black said. "Too bad you can't depend on it working out that way."

"Why the hell not?"

"Lots of these folks are high up the food chain." He waved at the briefcases. "It takes *money* to buy a child and keep it around with nobody noticing and asking questions. And if they don't have influence themselves, they've got family members who do—fat cats who can insulate them from the usual legal channels. A few calls go out, investigations get dropped, deals get made, and pervs walk. Do they get scared straight? Hell no. They go right back to what they were doing."

Jack saw Blue at the front door, lighting a tube of rolled-up newspaper. Somewhere inside, a phone started ringing.

"All clear!" he yelled.

Suddenly Black had a grip on Jack's shoulder and was pulling him back, then turning him and propelling him toward the Suburban.

Jack saw Blue toss the flaming paper through the door and then pull it shut behind him as he backpedaled away from the house.

Jack ducked as the first floor of the house exploded, shattering windows and sending billows of flames roaring into the night. The sound of the explosion faded, replaced by screams of agony.

Black had both the passenger side doors open. He hopped in the front, Jack into the rear where he slammed the door shut and slumped, dazed, staring through the window at the inferno that had once been someone's summer home.

The engine was still running. Blue jumped in behind the wheel and slammed it into gear. As they roared off, Black picked up a phone and reported the fire. Then he leaned back with a contented sigh.

"Thanks for helping improve the gene pool, Jack. Even if it's just a little."

Jack leaned forward. Yeah, they'd probably done that, but still he had a queasy gut.

"Burned alive?"

"The cleansing flame," Blue said. "You sound bothered. You're not gonna go all wimpy on us, are you?"

"Those screams . . ."

"What? They'll 'haunt' you or some shit like that? You know what screams haunt me, Jack? The screams of a little boy as some guy shoves his dick up his ass. Or a seven-year-old girl as she's raped for the first time."

Jack winced. "You haven't really—"

"Heard that?" Black said. "Unfortunately we have. Lots of these pervs like to record their shit and trade it around. We need to know what they look like so's we can track them down. The only way we can find out is to watch their tapes. Can't tell you how many times I've run to the toilet to puke my guts out. Both of us."

Jack flopped back, feeling sicker than before. "Jesus Christ."

"Jesus Christ was nowhere to be found," Blue said.

They drove in silence for a while, then Black turned in his seat.

"We could have just shot them, Jack—double-tapped each to the head and had done with it. And while a massacre like that sends a message, it's not loud enough. Yeah, it decimates the perv community around here, but while it's terrifying to them, it's not *horrifying*. Burned alive is horrifying."

"You can say that again."

"Okay: Burned alive is horrifying." Then he laughed. "I can't help it. I feel *good* about tonight. I'm sorry about that owner's place, but not too much. I mean, that's what insurance is for."

Blue said, "But the big, beneficial bonus from the horrification aspect is the extra chatter on the bulletin boards and newsgroups. Fingers will point. Who leaked? Who gave them up?"

"But the last time—"

"The last time a bunch of nameless Arabs got wasted. That caused barely a ripple among the pervs. A hijacking. A robbery. It wasn't personal. We knew where they'd set up the auction that time. We could have done this then, but kids were involved. Getting them out of harm's way was the priority. The kids always come first."

"But this time," Black added, "thanks to you, we knew no kids were involved. That let us target the real scum. Last time they could tell themselves it was a money thing. This time they'll know *they* were the target. And don't underestimate the ripples that will cause. They'll spread around the globe."

"The globe? That's a bit much, don't you think?"

"Not a bit. This Internet thing is worldwide. These newsgroups are read by pervs in every country on Earth that's got any decent level of technology. You saw me toss those photos from their briefcases around the front yard. That wasn't just for the hell of it. The arson inspectors will find them and have a pretty good idea what kind of people were inside. The registrations from the cars outside will help put names to the crispy critters we left behind."

"They're gonna be scared," Blue said. "They may have suck in the halls of justice, but this is different."

Black grinned. "Right. This didn't come through the halls of justice. This came out of the blue. We aren't on anybody's radar, but now they'll know they're in someone's crosshairs, and they won't like it. And we'll be watching the bulletin boards, waiting for slip-ups."

"Slip-ups?"

"Yeah. Nobody uses their real name on those things. But every once in a while someone gives something away. We keep track."

Flashing lights were visible far north on Bayview Avenue. Blue wheeled the Suburban onto a side street and waited till the cops and fire trucks roared past.

Blue nodded approval. "Quick response."

"Let's not hope too quick," Black said. "We don't want any survivors."

"No chance. Thoroughly soaked."

Jack couldn't help a shudder.

When the fire trucks were well past, they continued on to the hospital parking lot where Jack had left Ralph.

When he got out, so did the Mikulskis. They accompanied him to the rear of the Suburban and opened one of the doors. Black made a showman wave with his arm.

"Take your pick," he said.

"What?"

"You earned it."

"That's okay."

Perv money . . . Jack was sure the briefcases would be slimy to the touch.

"Seriously. There's a good seven figures in there. You earned a share."

"Nah. You keep it and . . . do whatever it is you do with it."

"We put it to good use," Blue said. "You know that."

"Yeah," his brother added. "What's in those helps keep us from having to find day jobs."

"And that lets *this* become our day job."

"And night job."

"We're starting to be able to pay people to keep their eyes and ears open for anything that might interest us."

"Got us a growing network now."

Jack backed away. "Thanks, guys, but I'm okay. Glad to help. Maybe if I need a loan someday I'll tap you, but I'm good for now."

They looked at each other, shrugged, then Blue slammed the rear door. They all shook hands, and the brothers were already rolling before Jack reached Ralph.

He started the engine and sat there while she warmed up. In his head he could still hear the screams pouring through the shattered windows back in Amityville, but he preferred them to the screams he imagined echoing through the Mikulski brothers' heads.

7. Ernst Drexler had been pacing his apartment, waiting for word, sure that the hijackers could not pass up the opportunity he had presented them. But when the phone rang, he knew immediately from al-Thani's flat tone that he had no good news.

"Tell me."

"We've been waiting twenty minutes and they haven't shown. I think they smelled a trap."

Ernst thought about that. It didn't sit right. These hijackers weren't just thieves. They had a cause. Even if they'd known it was a trap, they would be compelled to save the children.

"The 'smell' of a trap would not keep them away."

"It would if they knew the truck was empty."

"How could they possibly know that?"

Al-Thani told him about the truck being stopped by the Maryland State Police.

This turn of events was more than a little embarrassing. They'd invested a lot of time and effort in setting this snare. To have it fail so miserably . . .

"Still, even then, knowing that those who lay in wait for them were involved in child trafficking, I believe they would have made some move against the trappers."

"I agree. However, we have to face the fact that if they haven't shown by now, it is almost certain they will not show at all."

Ernst shook his head. How could his assessment have been so wrong?

"I was sure they'd try *something.*"

"I'm going to call it off."

Ernst fought the urge to tell him to wait a little longer, but al-Thani was right: They'd baited their hook, but no one had bitten.

Even worse, tomorrow Roman Trejador would serve him a steaming platter of crow and expect him to partake.

Being an actuator for the Order was a wonderful job most of the time. But when things went wrong . . .

. . .

Nasser rolled down the limo's window as Reggie approached. He knew what he was going to say so he beat him to it.

"I think we've waited long enough."

Reggie nodded. "You read my mind."

"Help Mahmoud collect the rifles while I call for the boats."

Mahmoud must have been listening, for he stepped out and started for the dunes where his fellow jihadists were hidden. As Reggie followed, Nasser again plucked the car's mobile phone from its cradle in the center console. This time he called the marina.

When the owner answered, told him, "You can send the boats back now."

"No can do. The bay's too rough."

"It's no rougher than—"

"It's lots rougher. I ain't sending my guys out in boats that size in the dark into that chop."

"Then send bigger boats!"

"A bigger boat draws too much to make it to shore through those shallows. I'll see if I can dig up some cars and send them 'round."

Nasser's gaze settled on the rear of the truck idling thirty feet ahead of him.

"Never mind."

He ended the call and got out of the car. As the wind bit into him he realized that the marina man was probably right. He certainly wouldn't want to have to fight this gale in a little skiff.

Reggie and Mahmoud were leading the jihadists toward the limo. Nasser opened the trunk so they could return their weapons. When Mahmoud reached him he pulled him aside.

"After they've dropped off their weapons, have them get into the truck. We'll take them back in that. Find someone who can drive and knows the way back to the center."

Mahmoud pointed to Reggie. "Not him?"

Nasser turned to Reggie. "You and Kadir drive back with us. I have more questions about this police stop."

Reggie suddenly looked worried. "Hey, we did everything by the book."

Nasser wasn't in the mood to explain. "We'll see about that. You ride back with me. Fetch Kadir."

"Well, well," Dane Bertel muttered as he watched the would-be ambushers climb into the back of the truck. "What have we here?"

He forced his frozen fingers to work the wheel and focus his glasses on the suave-looking Mohammedan outside the limo. No question that he was in charge here. But who was he? Not one of Sheikh Omar's honchos, but he gave them orders and they obeyed.

Was he connected to the third player Dane sensed at work here?

He wished he had better light. He watched Mahmoud close the rear doors on the truck and then head back to the limo. The mystery Mohammedan was already inside, but he didn't see Kadir and the trailer-park white man who'd ordered Tony's death. Back in the cab of the truck, he assumed. Where else?

He pulled out his tracker as he watched the limo pull around the truck and lead it back to Ocean Parkway. Much as he'd love to follow the mystery Mohammedan and see who he reported to, he'd be kidding himself if he thought he could pull off a successful tail. At this time of night there simply was not enough traffic for adequate cover.

He saw the blinking light on his tracker. The truck's transceiver was still transmitting, but what use was that? He knew where the truck was going: It would head to the Al-Kifah center to drop its passengers, then wind up back in some Ryder lot.

Looked like here was where this journey ended.

He flipped the protective cover off a toggle switch attached to the tracker.

He'd see to it that it turned out to be the end for some other journeys as well ... especially that trailer-park trash guy. He couldn't sit by and let him ride off into the sunset.

He put his thumb on the toggle.

This is for Tony ...

Nasser turned in the front passenger seat to face Reggie and Kadir. He wanted more details on the stop by the police, but something had been niggling the back of his brain since his call to Drexler. Something the Austrian had said ...

I was sure they'd try something ...

And then it hit him: the auction attendees.

He grabbed for the car phone. "Oh, no!"

"What is wrong?" Mahmoud said in Arabic.

Nasser ignored him as he frantically tapped in Saleem Haddad's number at the auction house. As the phone rang and rang, he cursed himself for not realizing that the auction attendees might wind up targets—especially once the hijackers knew the truck was empty. Not that he cared about the bidders themselves—scum of the earth, as far as he was concerned—but they had been gathered under his aegis and if anything happened to them, it might well cost him his credibility with the jihadists.

At least he wasn't alone in his error. No one else had foreseen it either.

"Answer, damn you!" he shouted into the phone.

Then a blinding flash flooded the limo's interior through the minuscule rear window, followed by a deafening boom. A shock wave slammed the car with enough force to lift its back tires off the pavement.

Nasser stared in shock and dismay at the flying bits of flaming debris where the rental truck had been.

8.   "How could this go so astonishingly wrong?" Roman said.

Dawn lit the windows as he paced his suite's living room, staring at Drexler and al-Thani where they sat with averted eyes. He was angry, yes, but more baffled and dismayed than anything else.

When neither replied, he went on. "I didn't hold out much hope for success, but—"

Drexler's head snapped up. "Is that so? You said nothing of the sort."

"I figured that if they had even half a brain between them, the hijackers would smell a trap. But there was always the chance they wouldn't. Always a chance, as you said, that their fervor for their 'agenda' would overcome caution. So I let it proceed. Why not? The overhead was low, and the potential reward was high." He pointed to al-Thani. "You were there. How could this have happened?"

The Qatari shook his head. "I questioned Reggie and Kadir separately and they both swear they stopped only twice of their own accord, both times at public rest stops to call in. The bomb must have been placed at one of those stops. I can assure you that no one came near the truck when we were parked on the beach."

"And no one could time the explosion so perfectly," Roman said. "Someone had to be watching."

"But from—?" He stopped. "He could have been hiding behind one of the more distant dunes. Reggie and Kadir saw no one following. Was it possible he was waiting there?"

"Then he would have had to know where you were meeting."

"But only we three and Kadir and Reggie knew—and only just as they were leaving. They had no time to tell anyone."

Reggie . . . that worthless piece of subhumanity.

Roman said, "What do we know of this Reggie?"

"We know he was supposed to be behind the steering wheel when the truck blew up. The only reason he wasn't was because I wanted to question him and Kadir about their trip. If you had seen how white and shaken he was after the blast, you'd know he was as shocked as I was. More so, because he would have been blown to pieces with the others."

Too bad he wasn't, Roman thought.

"If nothing else," al-Thani added, "we know now there's more than two of them."

"Why do you say that?"

"Well, it requires more than two men to have followed the truck from Virginia or been hiding on the dune while committing the slaughter at the auction house as well."

Roman closed his eyes and fought for control.

"Yes, the auction house slaughter. We should rejoice that no one knew the Order was connected with this, because do you realize what asses these hijackers have made of us? And by extension, the Order itself?"

"But—" Drexler began.

Roman silenced him with a slash of his hand. "No *buts*! They outplayed us at every turn. I don't care about a bunch of pederasts being burned alive, but I *do* care about the painful fact that we were completely unprepared for the possibility. And I *do* care about a bunch of jihadists being blown to pieces while assisting us. They are the greatest potential source of chaos in the world today and we need communication with them to know what they're planning. We can't guide them if they suspect us of treachery or, perhaps worse, incompetence."

"I'll smooth it over," al-Thani said.

"How do you plan to do that?"

Drexler said, "They were only in it for the money. We can offer them the two hundred thousand they were to receive if we were successful."

Roman shook his head. "They lost a dozen of their faithful. Somehow I don't think that will be enough."

"It will be if we shift the blame," al-Thani said.

"To whom?"

A slight smile twisted his lips. "Whenever anything goes right, they give credit to Allah. But when things don't go their way, when they suspect treachery, they have a favorite target for blame: the CIA."

Roman nodded and saw Drexler doing the same. "Excellent. Can you sell it?"

"Of course. It feeds into their paranoia. It stokes their fervor against the Great Satan."

Roman liked it. What was the expression? When handed a lemon, make lemonade.

9. The *Post* front page said it all.

AMITYVILLE
HORROR!!!

Abe was slicing a second bagel in half. "And you're saying you were there?"

Jack had spent the better part of twenty minutes telling him just that, so he simply nodded as he skimmed the news piece. Details were scant. Not all the bodies had been identified yet, and no one was talking about those that had. He wondered if the truth about them would ever come out. Motive unknown, perpetrators unknown.

"I shouldn't doubt it. Blechedich you look."

He'd heard that word before.

"I gather that's bad?"

"Of course it's bad."

"No sleep."

Not for lack of trying. Jack had parked Ralph in the garage space he rented for an astronomical fee, then collapsed onto his bed like a felled tree. But sleep had played coy, coaxing him with false promises into believing he'd fall off, and then jolting him awake with sights and sounds from the Amityville house.

By seven thirty he gave up, dressed in his hoodie disguise, and started walking around, sipping a series of coffees from a series of food trucks. Finally he showed up at Abe's with a bag of fresh bagels and nothing else. He was too fragged to come up with anything more original.

"Well," Abe said, "I'm sure it was a horrible scene, even if they were human dreck."

"Oh, trust me, I don't feel sorry for them. And as one of the brothers said, it did improve the gene pool. But for some reason . . ."

He shook his head, not sure where he was going with this.

"What? It doesn't sit right?"

"You could say that, but I can't put my finger on what about the whole thing that doesn't feel right."

"You would have let them live?"

"I don't know. Anyway, I wasn't given a choice. I had no vote, so . . ." And then it came to him.

"Nu?"

"I think that's it: no choice, no vote. It was the Mikulski brothers' show and I was just along for the ride."

"Well, you knew that already."

"Yeah, I did. But I'd sort of lost sight of the fact that I don't play well with others—at least that's what a lot of my early grammar school reports used to say."

"But then you learned?"

Jack smiled. "Well, I learned to fake it. Anyway. I'm impressed with the way the Mikulskis get things done. The take-no-prisoners approach has its strengths, but it lacks something."

"Like?"

"I don't know." Suddenly he remembered *All About Eve*. "Symmetry?"

Abe frowned. "Symmetry? You want symmetry, draw a circle. Or a square."

"No, seriously. A symmetrical solution would have left each of them being horrendously abused for the rest of their days."

Abe shrugged. "Who's to say some of them wouldn't like that?"

"Yeah, there's that."

"And how would you arrange that?"

"No idea." He remembered what Black had said about the pervs getting off. This was further depressing him. "One thing I think I've learned from all this: I don't like tagging along."

"No *nochshlepper*, you."

"Whatever."

He was watching Abe. As he read the paper he was scooping the insides out of his bagel, leaving only the crust and piling the soft innards to the side of the counter. He'd done the same with the first, but Jack had been involved in telling his story and hadn't commented. But now . . .

"What are you doing to that bagel?"

"I'm making it low cal."

"Really."

"If I eat only the crust—which after all is the best part—by half I cut my calories. Besides, you brought no cream cheese. Already my bagel was less than happy, being eaten without a shmear"—he gave Jack a pointed look—"so I might as well gut the poor thing. My waistline rejoices already."

"What about the leavings?"

Abe glanced away from the paper at the pile of soft innards. "Not for me. You?"

"Nah. Like you said, the crust's the best part."

"A shame to throw away. I should have some sort of *chozzerish* pet to devour the leavings. A puppy maybe?"

"I don't see you with a puppy. You have to take a puppy out and walk him."

"*Gevalt!* Something else maybe?"

"A weasel?"

"Too sneaky."

"A lizard. Say, an iguana."

"A cold-blooded reptile you want for me? I'll be an alter kocker soon. I'll need warmth in my sunset years."

"You could always toss your leavings out on the sidewalk for the birds."

Abe's eyes lit. "A mitzvah for our feathered friends! I—" He stopped and stared at the paper. "Did you see this?"

Jack rotated the tabloid—the *Daily News*—and scanned the pages.

"What?"

Abe tapped a header in a lower corner. "Here."

A brief article on a truck explosion near Gilgo Beach. A dozen bodies were found scattered about the blasted remains of a Ryder truck. The dead appeared to be dressed in Muslim garb, but no further details were available at press time.

"Jeez."

"Could that have been the Ryder truck you and Bertel were following?"

"Ours was empty."

"Doesn't mean it couldn't have been filled. The brothers again?"

"They didn't know where it was. Where's this Gilgo Beach?"

"Near Babylon . . . which is near Amityville. Did they care about the truck?"

"Not once they learned it was empty." He felt a chill. "But I know someone who *did* care."

When Bertel had tagged the truck with that radio transceiver, was something else with the package? Jack never saw the contents of his duffel. Could something like C4 have gone along for the ride too?

He shook it off. Bertel a mass murderer? He couldn't see it. But then what did he really know about Dane Bertel?

"Was Bertel ever with the CIA or FBI or anything like that?"

"I should know? He shows up, he disappears, he shows up again. Otherwise his rep is a mensch. If he's a fed, I should have been raided six times already. I've never known him to be involved in anything even remotely legal, but illegal operations and government service aren't necessarily mutually exclusive."

Jack remembered Bertel's hard look when he'd told him that Reggie had been instrumental in Tony's murder. Maybe that had been his intent: revenge on Reggie for Tony, and all the rest of the damage was collateral.

As Jack mulled that, he noticed that the pile of bagel innards had disappeared. Only a few crumbs remained.

"Probably better if you don't get a pet for cleanup, Abe. It'll starve."

10. Jack bought another coffee and ambled west until he hit Riverside Drive. He found himself at loose ends, with nothing scheduled until Saturday when he took up the Zalesky trail again. A couple of empty days ahead. He could hang out with Julio and Lou and Barney at The Spot, but felt like being alone for a while. Well, he'd make an exception for Cristin, but she was busy planning her parties and events.

He crossed into the park that buffered the Upper West Side from the Henry Hudson Parkway. The late morning sun had crested the old brick apartment buildings that lined the east side of the drive. Last night's wind had died, allowing old Sol to leaven the chill in the air. Not warm by any stretch, but . . . nice.

The extra caffeine had done nothing to revive him, so he dropped onto one of the benches that lined the footpath. As his gaze came to rest on a sign wired to the low fence directly opposite—reminding him that his dog must be leashed—a middle-aged blond woman strolled by with an unleashed husky. It looked well behaved.

He pointed to the sign. "They ever fine you?"

She stopped and her dog stopped with her. Both stared at him for a second, then she spoke with a strange accent.

"No one fines me."

"Glad to hear it."

"You should not sit there," she said.

"Why not?"

"It is not a good spot. It could be dangerous."

How? Jack wondered. Muggers?

Didn't seem likely out in the open near midday. Besides, he had the Semmerling strapped to his ankle.

"I'll chance it."

Another long stare, then she strolled off with her dog.

Through the naked trees he could see the boat basin and the glittering Hudson River. With the sun warming his back and the traffic murmuring behind him, Jack stretched out his legs and closed his eyes. Maybe he could catch forty or so winks here. If so, it would be his first sleep in close to thirty hours.

He felt himself start to drift . . . he loosed the tether . . .

—jolted awake / something slamming into him / opens his eyes to darkness / something over his head, over his shoulders and arms / black plastic of some sort / "Hey! What the—!" / tries to go for the Semmerling / arms pinned at sides / can't reach it / lifted / carried / "Hey!" / voices speaking Spanish to each other / Oh, shit, not— / tossed onto a metal surface / a door slides and clangs shut / moving / floor bouncing / angry shouting in Spanish / getting kicked / can't defend / blows to his head / blows to his face / the darkness deepens / he goes away . . .

11. Jack came to coughing, his face dripping cold water. He blinked, went to wipe his face and found his arms wouldn't move. He shook his head and the move blasted pain through his skull and down his neck. His gut threatened to hurl.

Don't do that again.

He opened his eyes and as his vision cleared he realized he wasn't alone. In some sort of garage or warehouse or abandoned factory—concrete floor and walls, high windows with weak sunlight struggling through the dirty glass. Eight or nine young Hispanics surrounded him. He recognized Rico first, standing closest with an empty, dripping, plastic bucket. Then Carlos, Juan, and Ramon of Two Paisanos Landscaping came into focus, grinning like idiots. He didn't know the others. A couple of them had their shirts off, revealing a gallery of tattoos

as they strutted around. They wore fierce looks on their
faces and strings of red, white, and blue beads around
their necks. One of them was playing with the Semmerling.

DDP.

Shit.

He looked down at his arms—bungeed tightly to the
arms of a heavy, beat-up office chair. His left leg was
bungeed to a leg of the chair. He rocked the chair but it
seemed solid—way solid. His right leg, though, was
stretched out and bungeed in place on a low workbench
that looked like steel. His boot and sock were gone, as
was his ankle holster. The leg of his jeans had been
rolled up almost to the knee.

What the—?

"So, you awake now," Rico said with his heavy accent.

Jack was tempted to compliment him on his powers
of observation, but thought better of it. He was helpless
and in deep shit and couldn't see an upside to antago-
nizing this guy.

"Rico. Good to see you."

His throbbing head felt twice normal size and he must
have been kicked in the jaw at some point because it
hurt to talk.

"Good?" Rico tossed the bucket aside. "You don't
think it's good too long. Not when I finish with you."

That sounded real bad. Jack's gut made knots as he
tested his bonds. The bungees had been pulled super-
tight. He could barely feel his hands and feet. He wiggled
his fingers. They moved but were numb.

Christ, Jack thought as he watched Rico limp over to
Carlos. His knee still isn't right?

He hadn't meant to put that kind of hurt on him. He
had an awful feeling he was going to regret it even more.
The misgivings turned to terror when he saw Carlos

hand him a wicked looking machete. This wasn't one of the crude, sharpened lengths of steel these guys used in gardening and landscaping. This was one of the DDP models, polished and tapered to a nasty point.

"Aw, no, Rico."

"Yes!" He slashed it back and forth and the flashing blade whispered through the air as he approached. He touched the point to Jack's foot. "This is the foot that wreck my knee, yes?"

Jack struggled with the bungees but they held. Helpless. He began to sweat. His bladder cried out to empty.

Rico spread his legs and began to raise the machete. "Say good-bye to your foot."

The DDP guys egged him on, chanting, "¡Córtalo! ¡Córtalo!" Carlos, Juan, and Ramon didn't join in. Their grins had faded and they looked a little green around the gills.

Jack's mind raced. This couldn't be happening. Try as he might he saw no way out. Beg? That would only incite him. Reason with him? He didn't see any way either would work. Rico looked beyond the reach of mercy and reason.

Or was he? Jack saw a flicker of something in his eyes as the machete reached the high point over his head. He hesitated. Second thoughts? Amputate a foot in exchange for a bum knee—a bit over the top?

But as the "¡Córtalo!" chant rose in volume, his expression hardened.

Oh, shit!

Jack was about to shout, *Don't, Rico!* when a high-pitched scream pierced the air.

"*Rico, no! No-no-no-no-no!*"

For a second, a little girl stood silhouetted in the doorway, then she was running forward.

"*No, Rico, no!*"

Rico turned, lowering the machete. Then Jack recognized her.

"Bonita?"

Rico spun back toward him, his expression questioning how Jack knew her name. Then he turned back to the little girl racing toward him. She leaped against him, wrapping her arms around him in a desperate hug. Tears ran down her cheeks as she pointed to Jack and began speaking Spanish at blistering speed, way too fast for Jack to follow.

Rico was staring at him, his jaw gaping.

"You?" he said at last. "It was *you*?"

Bonita released him and rushed to Jack, throwing her arms around his neck. She sobbed against him.

After numerous *¿Qué pasas?* from Carlos, Juan, Ramon, and the DDP guys, Rico began explaining in Spanish. Jack followed some of it. Knowing the story ahead of time helped.

When he'd been held at the Outer Banks house last year, he'd seen the young girls offloaded from the boat offshore, and then he'd spotted an animal called Moose dragging one of them out to the dunes. Jack had followed with a tire iron and dented his skull—perhaps a bit too enthusiastically, because Moose died there in the sand. Only Jack and the girl returned. Along the way he learned that her name was Bonita.

Bonita and the rest of the girls had wound up with the Mikulskis, and now she was with Rico. The word *hermana* kept popping up in Rico's story. Sister?

Finally he turned back to Jack. "You saved my sister? You're the one?"

Jack nodded. "Yeah. She's your sister? I had no idea."

Rico was staring at Bonita. "How does this happen?"

Jack was asking himself the same question, although

in the long run he figured he could do without knowing how. He was too relieved that it *had*.

Bonita began pulling at the bungee encircling his right leg. Rico dropped the machete and began to help.

12.   It took a while for the circulation to return to Jack's hands, and even longer for the sick fury at what had almost happened to abate. He helped it along by telling himself that if he hadn't done such a number on Rico's knee, this never would have happened. Of course, another part of him had to put out a reminder that nothing would have happened in the first place if Rico hadn't sucker-punched him.

But it took the longest to put today's story together, since Bonita spoke virtually no English and Rico's command was as limited as Jack's Spanish. The three of them sat in a corner apart from the others—Rico with his leg straight out—and managed to put the story together.

Rico and Bonita's mother had died years ago. Their father had married again, and that was when Rico had left for the States. Unknown to him, his father had died within months of his departure, and their stepmother had sold Bonita to the traffickers.

Not so terribly unusual, unfortunately. Probably happened every day all over the world.

She couldn't go back to the DR, so whoever repatriated the kids for the Mikulskis learned from Bonita that she had a brother in New York City who sent them money when he could. She tracked down Rico and left Bonita with him, along with a nice chunk of change.

Okay . . . big coincidence. *Huge* coincidence. But the story of how Bonita had managed to travel from the heart of Brooklyn and end up in this empty West Side garage just in time to save Jack's foot moved way beyond coincidence into the bizarre.

Bonita had been sitting in the cramped apartment she and Rico moved into using the Mikulski money she'd been given. They hadn't figured out a way to get her into a school, so she spent most of the day watching TV and picking up what little English she could from *Scooby-Doo* reruns. Sometime before noon she'd been interrupted by a woman who rushed into the apartment and grabbed her by the arm, saying her brother was in terrible trouble and only Bonita could help him.

The woman said she came from Puerta Plata, just like Rico and Bonita, and that she'd known their mother. She even spoke with their local accent. Bonita couldn't help but believe her and they ran downstairs to her car. Along the way the lady explained that Rico was going to do a terrible thing to the very man who had saved her that night on the beach. Bonita hadn't believed it, but when the woman had dropped her off and she'd opened the door and seen her brother raising a machete over Jack, she'd realized it was all true and she'd screamed.

Jack listened in a daze. How could the woman have known? Not just about what was *going* to happen, but what *had* happened? Bonita had known the face of the man who had saved her, but never knew his name. And it was obvious Rico had had no idea it was Jack.

Who was this woman?

According to Bonita, she was slim, about the age their mother would have been—probably early forties—with dark hair and what she described as "cinnamon" skin. Apparently that meant something in the DR. She'd driven an old black Lincoln; Bonita had sat in the front while the woman's little brown dog jumped around the backseat. The last thing she'd said to Bonita as she pushed her out the car door was "*¡Prisa!*"

Hurry!

Despite pointed questioning, Bonita swore she'd never seen her before.

The three of them sat in silence for a while, then Rico said, "Jack, I do not know what to say. I would not hurt the man who saved Bonita."

That was good to hear.

"Your English is much better since I last saw you."

His expression darkened as he patted his bum knee. "I been seeing much TV."

Ouch.

"Hey, I'm sorry about your knee. I lost it when you punched me. I didn't mean to do permanent damage."

Not quite true. Jack remembered wanting to kill him at the time.

"I can't work," he said. "I am living on my little sister's money. It makes me *loco*."

"I hear you."

He felt bad. The guy had been a hard worker and he'd just let jealousy of Jack get the better of him. He had a lot of pride—maybe an excess. And that reminded Jack of Julio.

Julio . . . who wouldn't let Jack help him. But maybe Rico . . .

"Maybe I could pay for you to see a doctor."

He waved his hands back and forth. "I do not want your money."

"I'm just trying to fix what I did. All you might need is a simple operation and—"

"*¿Cirugia?* No-no-no!"

Like dealing with another Julio. Jack tried a different tack.

"Okay, so you can't work. Can you be boss?"

"Boss? Me? Who I boss?"

"Carlos, Juan, and Ramon, for starters."

"You loco."

"No, I'm not. You know landscaping, you know gar-

dening, you know how to run the machines. What's
Giovanni got that you don't?"

He laughed again. "Carlos, Juan, and Ramon!"

"Okay, true. But what else?"

"I got no machines."

"I can fix that."

His eyebrows rose. "Yeah? How you fix that?"

Jack considered that. He had a feeling Rico would
never hear of borrowing money from him, but a third
party . . . who just happened to be Latino . . .

"I know this guy named Julio who'll lend you the
money to buy what you need to get started."

"How I pay back?"

"A little at a time, whenever you can. He'll be in no
hurry. He has the soul of a saint. He lives to help people."
Don't laugh here, he told himself—do *not* laugh. "You
start with one helper. You've got Carlos, Juan, and
Ramon—one of them can leave Giovanni and come with
you. And you don't need much: an old truck, a used riding mower for you, a push mower, some rakes and shov-
els, and you're in business."

Rico wanted to work. Jack had no doubt that once he
got moving, he'd keep rolling.

Rico said, "How—?"

A gunshot, near deafening within the garage's concrete walls, made the three of them jump. One of the
DDPers had piled up a couple of empty wooden crates
and fired the Semmerling into them. He was pulling the
trigger, trying to fire a second shot, to no avail. He pulled
back on the slide but it wouldn't budge—because it slid
forward on the Semmerling.

Jack jumped up. The sudden movement gave him a
sick, dizzy feeling, intensifying the throbbing in his head.

"*Ten cuidado,*" he heard Rico say in a low voice.

Be careful . . . yeah, Jack would be careful. But he
needed his Semmerling back.

He shuffled over to the group. "¿Qué pasa?"

The shooter sneered and tossed the pistol to Jack. "¡El juguete está roto!"

El juguete? He wasn't sure about that word. Toy? Your toy is broken.

That fit. The Semmerling was small enough to be a toy—certainly not macho enough for these studs. And because it looked like a semiauto, the guy expected it to self-load like one. Jack didn't get into explaining its manual repeating double action.

He put on a sad expression. "Sí, está roto."

The DDPers laughed as he walked back toward Rico and Bonita. He spotted his ankle holster on the floor and picked it up along the way.

"How'd you get involved with these clowns?" he said when he rejoined Rico.

He shrugged. "We're all from the same country. Their attitude is, you hurt one Dominican, you hurt all Dominicans. They said they'd help me find you. They spotted you today and remembered you from last week, so when you sit in the park, they grab you." He looked at the Semmerling. "They broke it?"

Jack shook his head. "Nah. They just don't know how to use it."

Rico smiled. "You sneaky man, Jack. I think you dangerous."

Jack rubbed his aching jaw. Not dangerous enough, it seemed. Not by a long shot.

13.   Vinny smiled as he spotted the dozen high rollers waiting at the usual spot under the street light on Mott Street. Then frowned at what he saw behind them: yet another bright yellow awning with red Chinese lettering hanging over the sidewalk where an Italian bakery used to be. Damn chinks. If this kept up, no one would be able to call the place Little Italy anymore.

He pulled his van into the curb and Aldo followed directly behind.

The gamblers split their number between the two vehicles. As soon as the side door slid shut, Vinny got rolling.

"Where we going tonight?" one of the familiar faces said as Vinny made a left on Canal Street.

"Brooklyn." In response to a couple of groans, he added, "Settle back and relax. Traffic's light. This won't take long."

His passengers were a special breed of craps player. They could ride down to Atlantic City for legal action, but they liked to stay local and play the Gambino tables. The New York families had different rules for craps that these guys preferred.

Tonight the games were set up in Tony the Cannon's old social club on Avenue J. The locations were chosen randomly, never the same one twice in a row—hence the "floating crap game" moniker—and none of the players was given advance notice. The cops loved to break up the games when they could, and they took "break up" to the limit: They rounded everybody up then reduced the roulette and craps tables to splinters before they left. So secrecy was a primo concern.

Tommy, as senior soldier, helped Tony run the games when they were at his club. The rule from the bosses: keep the games honest when the regulars were involved. These regulars were valuable customers who generated a lot of action. The family made good, steady money off the games and the ponies without rigging anything, and so they wanted these high rollers back again and again.

Vinny didn't mind playing chauffeur. The family bosses

bankrolled the games and thirty percent of the take went to the operator—in this case, Tony. Some of that would go to Vinny. Easy money with no risk.

But it still didn't get Tommy Ten Thumbs out of his hair.

14. "Ooh, Jack," Lou said as Jack took a seat at the bar. "What happened to your face?"

Jack looked at himself in the bar mirror and winced. Nose swollen, a blue-black ring under his left eye. No wonder people had been staring at him on his trip here.

Julio looked up from drying a glass and smiled. "How the other guy look?"

"Perfectly fine, unfortunately."

Julio poured a Rolling Rock and set it before him. Jack stared at it, considered his persistently throbbing head, and decided to drink anyway. Beer cured just about everything.

"What the hell happened to you?" Barney said, returning from one of his frequent trips to the men's room.

"Long story. Hey, Julio. Can you do me a favor?"

"Like?"

"Help this guy I know get set up in a landscaping business."

He laughed. "You kidding, right? I don't know shit about that stuff." He pointed to the dead plants in the window. "Ain't that proof?"

Yeah, proof of willful neglect.

"That's not the point. You know how to talk business. His English isn't too good and you can help him get a good price."

"Me?"

"I hear you talking to suppliers. You know how to pinch a penny."

"Till it screams for mercy," Lou said with a grin.

"He's got the money?"

"No, I do. But he'll think *you're* lending it to him, interest free. Can't know it's me."

Julio stared at him. "What is it with you? You don't like money?"

"I love money. If I had enough I'd fill a ten-story bin with cash, install a diving board, and swim around in it."

"Then why you always trying to give it away?"

"Hey, Jack," said Barney. "If you're giving out cash—"

Julio waved him to silence. "Seriously, Jack. You got some kinda Mother Teresa thing goin' on in your head?"

"Naw. This is for me. This guy . . . we've got an unbalanced scale between us. I'll feel better if it's leveled out. You'll help?"

"He's a Rican?"

"No. From the DR."

Julio made a face. "Not one of those DDPers you were talking about."

"No. This guy's straight. Just needs a break is all."

"All right. I help. But I still don't get it."

Jack did. A guy who had wanted to put a major hurt on him would now owe him. The turnaround meant he could stop looking over his shoulder. Not only that, having a guy like Rico owing him a favor was better than money in the bank.

He changed the subject.

"You gonna be ready Saturday morning for Zalesky watching?"

Julio made a fist. "Hey, I hope we gonna do more that just watch."

"Only time will tell, my friend. Only time will tell."

THURSDAY

1. Kadir dropped into the passenger seat and left the car door open. He took slow, deep breaths to calm his quaking stomach. The car was parked behind the Suffolk County Medical Examiner's Office in Hauppauge. He'd just returned from the morgue within and had feared he might vomit as he crossed the parking lot.

Sheikh Omar had sent him and Mahmoud here to identify the fallen so they might have proper Muslim burials. Mahmoud had known most of them, having trained many in the use of the AK-47, but not all. Ghali and Ramiz had been among them—both Kadir and Mahmoud knew those two—but Mahmoud had never met Rashad and Tariq. Kadir knew them from the mosque, and so he had been sent along to identify them.

His stomach quailed at the memory of their remains—torn by the explosion, charred by the fire from the exploding gas tank, barely recognizable. All he could think of as he'd gazed at the looks of agony frozen on their scorched faces was *that could have been me.*

After identifying the four bodies he knew, he'd signed the papers and fled to the car, leaving Mahmoud behind. Mahmoud would take longer since he had more to identify. Eventually the bodies would have to be claimed. By tradition, relatives would wash the body, wrap it in a white cloth, say the funeral prayer, then bury it. But some

of the fallen had no family here. What would happen to
their remains? Sharia forbade cremation.

Kadir jumped as the driver door opened and Mahmoud slipped behind the wheel.

"You look terrible," he said in Arabic. "Don't get sick.
You are already in enough trouble."

He needed no reminder that this was the car that fer-
ried Sheikh Omar around. Nor that he was in trouble.

But it wasn't fair.

Yesterday he had had to suffer the wrath of Sheikh
Omar alone. Reggie wasn't a Muslim and hadn't been
available anyway. The man from Qatar was not a member
of the congregation. And Mahmoud . . . Mahmoud had
simply driven the man from Qatar to the ambush site.

Sheikh Omar had no one else upon whom to vent his
rage, and so Kadir had borne the brunt of it. Kadir had
had nothing to do with the renting of the truck, and had
not driven it at all, yet somehow he was at fault because
a bomb had been attached to it.

That same attitude seemed to prevail at the mosque
and the refugee center. His fellow Muslims looked at him
strangely, as if he somehow could have prevented the
deaths of their friends, or at the very least have had the
decency to be martyred along with them.

"Didn't that turn your stomach?"

Mahmoud shrugged. "I saw much worse in Afghanistan."

Mahmoud had been combat trained in Peshawar and
served among the mujahideen against the Russians during
the war. He never let anyone forget it.

"Besides," he added, "they're with their eternally vir-
ginal houris."

Sheikh Omar had declared all of those killed yesterday as martyrs to jihad, thus assuring them of a heavenly
reward. The blind cleric loved to quote the *Tafsir* of Al-

Suyuti. Kadir had heard it so many times he knew it by heart.

"*Each time we sleep with a houri we find her virgin. Besides, the penis of the Elected never softens. The erection is eternal; the sensation that you feel each time you make love is utterly delicious and out of this world and were you to experience it in this world you would faint. Each Chosen One will marry seventy houris, besides the women he married on earth, and all will have appetizing vaginas.*"

By some strange quirk of fate, Kadir had been denied such eternal pleasures. Not that he wished to have ended like those he had identified just now.

"What happened, Kadir?" Mahmoud said as he started the car. "How did that bomb get there?"

Kadir had been expecting the question, and had been surprised Mahmoud had not asked it on the drive out. He had asked himself the same a thousand times since yesterday morning.

"I do not know."

"As I see it, there are but two possibilities: Either it was already attached when you picked up the truck from Aimal Kasi, or it was attached later. I have since spoken to Kasi. He says no one knew where he was going to rent the truck because he decided at the last minute. The U-haul place he went to first did not have the right size available. He swears he never left the truck unattended."

"Neither did we," Kadir said.

But he knew that wasn't true. After the police stop, he and Reggie had gone together to the phones. It could have happened then. But how could he admit that he left the truck? Fortunately Reggie was not available to contradict him. The lapse made what had subsequently happened all Kadir's fault. Ghali, Ramiz, Rashad, Tariq, and the rest, all dead because he had not wanted to bother to stay with the truck.

"But here is something interesting," Mahmoud said. "Kasi said he told you about a suspicious man who asked directions but seemed to be looking over the truck."

"Yes. That was why we rushed off immediately."

"Well, he says he saw the same man race past on your tail right after you and the American left."

"Why didn't he tell us?"

"How?"

Yes. How? If only they had had one of those mobile phones.

"Reggie, the American, thought we were being followed on the way south but the car turned off and he never saw it again. We didn't see who was inside."

"This man was driving a pickup truck."

Kadir shook his head. "We saw so many pickup trucks along the way. Was he young with brown hair? Could it be the one at the shooting range I'd seen at Tachus's uncle's place?"

"The one we knocked off the motorcycle?" Mahmoud shook his head. "According to Kasi, this man was older with short gray hair."

"There's a man like that who still deals with Riaz Diab, the uncle. I wonder . . ."

"Could the American with you have done it?"

"Reggie? I cannot see why or how. Besides, he would have been in the truck with me had not the man from Qatar told us to ride with him."

"The man from Qatar," Mahmoud said, shaking his head. "What do we know of him—besides that he seems devoted to the cause of jihad?"

Kadir wondered too. "Yes, he seems willing to help, but only when it profits him."

"I thought so too. But he arrived early today and

donated the bounty he had promised for capture of the hijackers, even though they escaped."

Kadir blinked in surprise. That seemed out of character. "Why didn't you tell me?"

"Because I have been thinking about something else he said: He's heard rumors that the FBI and CIA are involved."

Kadir wasn't surprised, but it seemed too easy an explanation.

"Do you believe him?"

"I know the FBI is watching me ever since Sayyid killed that rabbi."

Mahmoud had been taken into custody and questioned after Sayyid shot the Arab-hater Kahane, but the FBI had let him go. The agents had been rather obvious since then in their surveillance of Mahmoud. That was why he had driven Sheikh Omar's car today instead of his cab.

"Let's face it," Mahmoud said. "You owe your life to the man from Qatar."

True. The man's whim had saved him. He had wanted to talk further about the trip from Virginia, about the stop by the Maryland police. If he had not . . .

Maybe it hadn't been a whim. Maybe Allah had whispered the thought into his ear. Maybe Allah was not yet ready to welcome him into Heaven because he had plans for Kadir Allawi.

Kadir felt suddenly humbled. Here was a sign that he was meant for greater things. Allah would not allow him to be dismembered by an infidel bomb. He was to be a sword for Allah's will.

He wondered what Allah's will might be.

2. "Oy!" said Abe when he saw Jack's face. "I know you're studying that chop-chop fighting, but maybe they should teach you to duck already."

Jack dropped a sack of still-warm bialys on the counter and gave him a rundown of what had transpired after he'd walked out the Isher Sports door yesterday.

After finishing, he said, "Can you think of any way all those pieces can possibly fit together into a sane picture?"

Abe shook his head. "No, because you're obviously missing some pieces."

"Damn right I am. The string of coincidences is mind-boggling."

"Nu?"

"I spent half the night going over it. The string stretches back to last fall when I had that fight with Rico and got fired. If that hadn't happened, I wouldn't have started driving for Bertel. If Bertel's warehouse in North Carolina hadn't been raided by the ATF, I wouldn't have wound up in that house on the Outer Banks where the girls were offloaded. Moose decides he's going to sample the merchandise and picks Bonita, who just happens to be Rico's sister. I have no idea that's the case when I stop Moose's fun before it gets started. Flash forward to yesterday. Rico's friends and their DDP buddies have been hunting me. Yesterday they catch me and deliver me to Rico for his long-awaited payback. While that's going on, this Dominican lady shows up at Rico's place and rushes Bonita to the garage just in time to prevent her brother from relieving me of my right foot."

He stopped and stared at Abe, waiting. Abe stared back.

"Well?"

Abe cleared his throat. "You're a Christian, maybe?"

"I was raised in a sort of religion-free zone. You're not going to bring God into this, are you?"

"Well, no, but I hear Christians believe in something called a guardian angel."

Jack held up his hands. "Stop right now."

"No, hear me out already. You went meshuggeneh on Rico and wrecked his knee in the fall. In the winter he catches up with you. The second event is a direct consequence of the first. Your guardian angel—who can see the future—knows this well in advance. Other than striking Rico with lightning, which I don't think is allowed in the guardian angel terms of service, what else can an angel do but manipulate your life so that Rico will have a change of heart at a propitious moment."

Jack closed his eyes. He couldn't be hearing this. Not from Abe.

"So who was the Dominican lady who delivered Bonita?"

"Your guardian angel in disguise, of course."

"Of course. In drag."

"Who says they have any gender at all?"

"Abe—"

"Nu. I've explained everything for you. *Freylech* you should be."

Yeah, right. Abe's guardian angel did indeed explain everything, but Jack had to live in the material world, and that world offered no answers, only more questions.

"You don't really believe that, do you?"

Abe gave him an are-you-kidding? look.

Jack shook his head. "You almost had me convinced. Looks like we'll have to make do with ignorance."

"For now," Abe said. "Everything has an explanation somewhere."

True. Maybe one would come along later. Right now he had a void where he wanted a *why* and a *how,* but he wasn't about to fill it with an invisible friend. The other night he'd told Bertel he was okay with not knowing things, and that was true. But this was different. He'd resign himself to not knowing for now, but by no means was he okay with it.

3. Despite his realization that Allah had plans for him, Kadir could not spend another moment at the Muslim center in Brooklyn. They did not see that he had been spared for a reason. So he returned to his empty apartment in Jersey City, but found it equally depressing. Even the Qur'an gave him no solace.

He checked his watch. Hadya should be home soon. She went to work at the bakery in the predawn hours, but that meant she was home by early afternoon. Yes, Uncle Ferran preferred to hire family, but he paid no one overtime.

When she arrived, they could discuss what she had been learning from Sheikh Omar's tapes. It would take his mind off the blackened corpses he had seen earlier. He looked around but did not see the tape player. Well, she tended to listen in her room.

The bedroom door was closed. He opened it and peeked in to find the bed neatly made and no clothing in sight. Mother had taught her well. She would make a good wife someday.

He looked around for the cassette player but didn't see it on the dresser or the nightstand. He pulled open the top drawer of the nightstand and there it lay. An excellent spot: right beside her bed, so the imam's voice would be the last sound she heard before slumber, allowing his wisdom to infuse her dreams.

Curious as to which tape she was enjoying, he picked up the player and popped it open. The label on the cassette was in Arabic but not one of Sheikh Omar's. This read *Learning English*.

Kadir stared in shock, then tore it from the player. English? What—?

He heard the apartment door open. He charged from the bedroom as Hadya was stepping into the front room and threw the cassette at her.

"What is the meaning of this?" he shouted.

She gasped and stared at him in shock and confusion, then looked at the tape on the floor.

"I-I'm learning English."

"You already know all the English you need to know!"

"No, I don't. Uncle Ferran says I can't work the counter until my English is better."

"What? You're too good for the ovens?"

"I don't want to work the ovens for the rest of my life."

He held up the tape player, resisting the urge to fling it at her face.

"You've been deceiving me! Pretending to be listening to the imam when all the while—"

"I pretended nothing! It's not my fault you made a false assumption."

"I lent you the player for one purpose and one purpose only: to enlighten yourself."

She slammed the door behind her. "Enlighten myself with hate? Why should I do that when I can spend that time bettering myself."

"By learning English?"

"Yes! That is the language of the country where I am living. I can't get ahead here speaking Arabic."

"When Sheikh Omar brings jihad to these shores, you will no longer have to worry about English. This whole land will soon be speaking Arabic!"

Her expression shifted from defiance to incredulity. "Are you living in a bubble? You need to get out among our people here and listen to them instead of your mad imam!"

"Do not dare to insult him!"

She acted as if she hadn't heard. "Do you think Uncle Ferran wants jihad? He doesn't! He is building something here. He wants to expand his business and hire more people, and someday hand it over to his children. And the men and women I work with at the bakery—do you think they want jihad? They do not!"

"That is because they don't know—"

"No! It is *you* who does not know." Her voice softened. "I see hope in their eyes, Kadir. That is something I didn't see back home. They talk of a future for themselves here. Back home talk of the future hardly ever goes beyond tomorrow."

"That is because the Americans—"

"You must stop blaming the Americans for everything, Kadir. Almost all the Palestinians expelled from Kuwait last year landed in Jordan. America had nothing to do with that. You left years before. You have no idea how horrible it is there now."

"But Israel—"

"You can blame Israel for many things, but not for what has happened in the past year. I want a *future*, Kadir! And my future is *here*, not back home." She held out her hand for the cassette player. "Now please . . . let me better myself."

Better herself by learning English and assimilating into this infidel hellhole? He'd rather see her dead.

The cassette receptacle was still popped open. He grabbed it and twisted until it broke free, then he hurled the pieces across the room.

"Buy your own player!"

He stormed out of the apartment before he found himself strangling her.

FRIDAY

1. Though he no longer had to worry about Rico and the DDP, Jack had fallen into the habit of returning from the dojo via Tenth Avenue, then turning east in the Twenties. He made a random choice of West 27th today, not realizing it would take him straight down the gullet of the Fashion Institute of Technology. As he approached the main building on Seventh Avenue where it straddled the street, he spotted Cristin stepping out of a door and striding away from him.

Well-well-well. This was a pleasant surprise: Cristin on a weekday.

She was carrying a notebook so he guessed she was coming from a class. She'd reduced her course load to three credits per semester while socking away the money she was making as an event planner. She still wanted a degree, but what was the rush?

He resisted the impulse to call out, deciding, just for kicks, to follow her. She wore a short denim jacket over tight, matching jeans, and red leather boots that stopped just below her knees. He kept his distance, but not so far that he couldn't admire the delightful curves of her swaying butt.

She raised her hand for a cab and immediately two screeched to a halt in front of her.

Yeah. If I were a cabbie, I'd fight to give her a ride too.

As she sped off in the closer of the pair, Jack rushed up and grabbed the other as he was about to cruise off.

"Follow that one," he said, pointing to Cristin's.

The driver half turned and said, "Why?"

Instead of telling him it was none of his goddamn business, Jack said, "I want to meet her."

The cabbie smiled and nodded, then shot off in pursuit.

Jack leaned back. Okay, Ms. Ott. Let's see where you go and how you spend your day.

But as the cabs headed eastward and uptown, it didn't take long for Jack to suspect she was heading home.

Yep. Her cab turned onto East 73rd and stopped in front of her place.

Well, big thrill.

"Keep going," he told his driver, then had him stop at the end of the block.

Okay, what now? he thought as he stepped onto the sidewalk.

Well, with nothing better to do for the rest of the day, why not watch her place and see if she surfaces again?

Yeah. Why not?

2.   Tommy hadn't been available so Vinny asked Aldo along on the latest body dump.

A couple of Lucchese soldiers had found themselves with a corpse they wanted disappeared—forever. They'd heard of Vinny's disposal service and contacted him around midday. Tony had no problem with Vinny dealing with the other families in his side business, just as long as he got a piece.

They dropped off the package—stowed in an old-fashioned steamer trunk—and paid in advance, in cash. Vinny asked no questions, didn't even peek in the trunk. He and Aldo stashed it in a rusted-out Fairlane where the backseat used to be, and put it in the Crusher. When it was flattened, they trucked it down to the trawler and sailed it out to sea.

Vinny was glad to have Aldo along for a number of reasons. Most of all because Aldo would be happy with twenty-five percent; Tommy would think he deserved fifty. Second, he couldn't stand being around Tommy. Might just toss him overboard for the pure hell of it. Lost at sea, sleeps with the fishes, all that crap.

After dumping the junker with the body securely crushed inside, Vinny pointed the trawler back toward the sun, sinking behind the shoreline.

3. Well, this was a bust, Jack thought as he stood in the dark looking up at the windows of Cristin's apartment across the street.

East 73rd was a lousy place for a stakeout—all bland, brick-fronted, residential high-rises with no convenient, midblock coffee shop offering a clear view of her canopied entrance. So he'd loitered on the Third Avenue end of the block, then the Second Avenue end. When he'd started feeling like he was heading for hypothermia, he'd found a movie theater on Second showing *Nothing But Trouble*. Figured he'd warm up for an hour and a half and then get back on the street. He'd have much preferred *The Silence of the Lambs*, but a film with Chevy Chase, Dan Ackroyd, and John Candy had to be, at the very least, decent—how could he go wrong?

Very wrong, it turned out. Cold as it was outside, he didn't make it to the end. What a dog.

He'd given her a call and asked if she was free tonight but she'd said she'd love to grab a bite somewhere but had to meet a couple about an anniversary party.

Stay or go? He checked his watch: almost seven. This was a dead end. Started off as a lark, but now seemed just plain dumb.

And just then Cristin pushed through the door and walked to the curb. He thought she was going to cross over to his side but she simply stood there waiting. She was wearing her fur-lined trench coat buttoned to the neck so he had no idea what she was wearing beneath.

Two minutes later a stretch limo pulled up. Cristin leaned toward the rear window and spoke to someone in the backseat. Jack couldn't hear what was said but then the door opened. The interior light went on revealing a liveried driver behind the wheel and a smiling middle-aged couple in the rear. The woman was nearer Cristin. She scooted over to let her in. The door closed but the light stayed on. Jack saw Cristin handing the woman one of her Celebrations cards as the car accelerated past him.

Another well-heeled couple looking to plan an event. Cristin liked to brag that she had CEOs and politicians as clients. Jack didn't know where these particular folks fell, but they certainly looked like they could afford to throw a hell of an anniversary party. Cristin's job was to see that it came off without a hitch.

Jack sighed and began walking toward Third Avenue. No secrets revealed. No scandals exposed. Just Cristin doing her job. As she'd said, most of her clients were available only during the week, and their parties—events—were almost always at night.

Wasted time. No, worse than that. He'd betrayed a trust in not taking her at her word. He felt a little dirty.

But seeing her during the week, even from afar, had triggered an intense longing for her. He was looking forward to Sunday more than ever.

4. Full dark was in command by the time Vinny and Aldo reached the marina. They tied down the trawler and drove back to Preston Salvage in the flatbed. But Vinny slammed on the brakes at the gate when he saw the vans parked in the lot and the light streaming from the garage windows.

"What the fuck? What now?"

Keeping his temper in check, he pulled the truck around back, then jumped out and stalked to the garage, Aldo in tow. He had a very bad feeling about this. He opened the door, expecting to find a chop shop in full swing, but instead saw crowded tables for craps, poker, and blackjack.

And standing in the center of it all, resplendent in a tuxedo, was Tommy Ten Thumbs Totaro. He whirled at the sound of Vinny's entrance.

"Yo, Vinny! Where ya been all day? Been tryin' t'reach you."

Vinny could tell he'd had a few toots.

"Doing business. What the fuck is this?"

"Business. I've been callin' all afternoon to give you a heads-up."

Vinny felt the steam rising to boil-over levels, but he kept his voice low.

"What I say about doing shit we can get busted for here?"

Tommy grinned. "Ease up. It's one night." He jerked a thumb over his shoulder at a skinny guy watching the craps table. "You know Jimmy the Blond? He called me—"

Jimmy the Blond Tonachio. Vinny had heard of him.

"He's Genovese."

"Well, yeah. Like I don't know that? We grew up to-gether. Anyways, he calls me up and says he's found some chinks who want some games but he had no place to take them on such short notice. Did I have a space that's free? I thought about that for like one second and said yeah, I got just the place."

Vinny felt Aldo's hand on his shoulder as he eyed the fire ax again.

"Easy, man."

Vinny took a deep breath. Again, no rules against working a deal with another family, as long as you cut your crew boss in on the profit. And okay, the risk was low—a few hours on a single night posed little danger. But doing this after the set-to they'd had over Tommy's chop-shop angle was like a bitch slap.

"Tried to call you, Vin," Tommy said.

Maybe he had. Vinny had been out to sea.

He took another look at the ax. No way he could use it. These were Genovese tables. That'd stir up a shitload of trouble.

Tommy stepped closer and lowered his voice. "And hey, since they're chinks, Joey brought in a couple of blackjack dealers with tap-fives."

Vinny glanced over at the two blackjack tables—five chinks at each, chain smoking and studying their cards. These guys weren't regulars. Probably tourists. That meant they'd never be back. And so, unlike regular players, these guys could be fleeced down to their yellow skins.

The tap-five was a thing of beauty—a multideck shoe that would deliver a five card when tapped in the right spot. Blackjack players loved to see a dealer pull sixteen because he was bound by the rules to draw on any hand below seventeen. Odds of the house busting skyrocketed when the dealer drew that sixteen, and so a lot of players doubled down when they saw it. After all the bets were on the table, the dealer would tap the shoe in the sweet spot and out popped a five, giving him twenty-one. House wins.

"We are taking them to the *cleaners,*" Tommy said. "Our cut is going to be sweet!"

Well, there was that. Vinny decided to let it go.

"Make sure Tony gets a piece," he said, then turned and walked out.

As the door slammed behind him, he turned to Aldo. "I'm gonna kill that fucker!"

"No, you ain't," Aldo said. "You gotta get permission first and that ain't gonna happen."

Right. Tony C would have to sanction the hit and no way he'd do that on his own. Not with Tommy's connections. And sure as hell not because he was a threat to Vinny's side business. Like who gave a shit? He had to be a traitor or a threat to the family itself, and Tommy fell into neither category.

"He could have an accident."

Aldo shook his head. "You think people don't know there's bad blood between you two? Tommy disappears and guess who they'll be tapping to put two in your skull."

Vinny knew damn well: Aldo. That was the way it was done—send a guy the target trusts, someone who can get close, and then *bang-bang*.

"I don't wanna be in that position," Aldo said.

Vinny understood. Aldo would be in a spot where he couldn't refuse.

"All right," Vinny said. "I'll think of something else."

But what?

SATURDAY

1. So far, so good.

Neil had driven the black-clad old bag to her Chase branch and let her out with the empty briefcase. Now Mrs. Filardo was walking back toward the car with—he hoped—a not-so-empty case.

"All went smoothly in there, I assume," he said as he held the door for her.

"Why wouldn't it?" she said. "It's a-*my* money."

Not for long . . .

Neil hurried around and forced a laugh as he slipped back behind the wheel. "Of *course* it's your money. But you know banks—once you deposit it, they think it's *their* money."

"Then they a-better think again."

"I'm sure withdrawing such a large sum irked them no end."

"Well, they'll be getting it all back come a-Monday."

Not if I have anything to say about it.

He drove her to the same spot in the Coffey Park lot as last week, then turned in his seat to face her.

"Now, just like last Saturday, I must ask you to open the briefcase and confirm that you were given the proper amount."

Her gnarled fingers worked the catches and she lifted the lid. Neil shifted his position for a peek inside. His heart stumbled over a beat at the sight of the five banded stacks of hundreds. Fifty Gs.

Yowza-yowza-yowza!

She lifted them one by one and inspected them.

"Everything a-seems to be as it should be."

He handed her the key.

"Okay, time to lock up."

After she'd done that, he went through the ritual of placing the sheet of legalese on the briefcase for her to sign.

"I'm a-still say this is all a-too, too complicated."

Not again.

"It's that chain-of-custody thing, remember?"

"Of course I remember. I'm a-no *stupida*. But it make a-no sense."

"I agree. But I can't explain lawyers anymore than you can."

He tossed the signed sheet on the front seat, then grabbed the briefcase. He saw her hands start to reach for it, then pull back.

You're learning, Granny.

He went through the ritual of placing the tape over the locks, then stepped out, popped the trunk lid, and placed her briefcase next to its identical twin. He hadn't bothered to hide the bogus case this time because the switch was no longer a maybe—it was definitely on.

"Now, the wait," he said as he slipped behind the steering wheel again.

"While we're a-waiting," the old lady said, "'splain again to me how this person steals a-money with the computer . . ."

Neil suppressed a groan and begged for the willpower to keep from strangling her. Thirty, forty minutes . . . that was all he needed. Survive that and he'd never see or—even better—hear her again.

2.   Jack turned down the volume on the speaker as Zalesky went into his spiel about the bank thief. He didn't need to listen to that bullshit again.

"Tell me you got a plan, meng," Julio said. "Tell me we ain't just gonna sit here and watch like we did last time."

Last fall, they'd hot-wired a car and used it to tail Zalesky and another mark to a bank—Chemical, that time—then to a different waiting spot. But that time they hadn't known what was going on inside the car. Today was different.

"We *are* gonna watch," Jack said. "But I'm gonna make a phone call first."

"To who?"

Jack pushed open the driver door. "Tell you in a minute."

Jack wasn't playing coy. He had a phone number for the guy he was going to call, and he'd verified that he had the right one earlier in the week. The problem was, he didn't know how reachable the guy was on a Saturday.

This was where Jack's whole plan could fall apart.

He walked half a block down to a public phone kiosk standing on the corner. He would have preferred an old-fashioned enclosed booth so passersby or someone waiting to make a call wouldn't overhear, but had to be satisfied with this wide-open model.

He glanced at the sky. Beautiful day, unseasonably warm for early March. Would his guy be hanging around his office on a day like today? Not likely.

Crap. After all the crummy weather they'd been having, why'd this weekend have to turn out so nice?

He plunked a quarter into the slot and began to dial.

3. Vinny was alone in the office and picked up the phone on the second ring. Tommy hadn't shown this morning—no surprise—and this was probably him calling to gloat over their take last night.

"Preston Salvage."

A guy's voice: *"Is this Mister Donato?"*

"Who wants to know?"

"A friend of Mister Donato's mother."

Vinny jolted upright in his seat. Aw, no. Aw, shit.

"Something wrong?"

"I think she's in trouble."

"What? Heart? Stroke? What?"

"Not that kinda trouble. I think somebody's ripping her off."

The relief gave way to instant suspicion. This guy sounded too young to be a friend of his mother.

"Who is this?"

"I told you—"

"Don't gimme that friend shit. You—"

"Maybe I've made a mistake. Your mother is Michelina Filardo, right?"

Hearing Mom's name on a stranger's lips chilled him.

"Yeah."

"Well, she just drew fifty thousand out of her account and is parked by Coffey Park with a man who is going to steal it from her."

The chill turned frigid. Coffey Park. He knew it—knew it real good. A stone's throw from Mom's place. He could visualize the little parking lot.

"And you know this how?"

"I've been following them. I'm watching them right now. This creep does this to naïve little old ladies. He needs to be stopped."

"Why don't you stop him?"

"That's more in your line, I believe."

Who *was* this son of a bitch?

"Let me tell you something, wiseass. Anything happens to my mother while you sat and watched, I'll find him and I'll find you too, and neither of you will be happy."

"You're wasting time, Mister Donato. While you're running your mouth, your mother's giving away fifty big ones. Look for a Dodge Dynasty."

Then he hung up.

Vinny slammed down the phone and pushed himself to his feet. The park was in Carroll fucking Gardens and he was all the way over here in Canarsie. He'd never fucking make it. Whatever was going down would be over and done by the time he got there.

Wait. Aldo lived in Red Hook. Just a hop and a skip for him. Vinny snatched up the phone again.

4.   Neil couldn't stand it anymore. He checked his watch: 3:14. Close enough. Another minute of listening to her voice and he'd run screaming from the car, leaving her with both briefcases.

He showed her the car phone. "Time to call in. Keep your fingers crossed."

As ever, he dialed his own number and spoke to his answering machine.

"Yeah, hi, it's Nate. How we do?" A surprised look. "He *did*?" Big grin. "Really?" Happy thumbs-up to the old lady. "He's nailed? All *right*! Yes, I'll tell Mrs. Filardo. Oh, I agree. She deserves it. Absolutely. See you later."

"What happened?" she said as he cut the call.

"We got him!" He laughed. "Caught him red-handed! All thanks to you. I can't thank you enough, Mrs. Filardo. Everyone down at the fraud department thanks you too.

They're talking about having the governor award you a public service certificate."

She waved a bony hand at him. "I'm a-don't need that. Just a-glad to help."

"No, you deserve it. We'll be putting out a press release later this afternoon. Is it all right if we mention your name?"

"Well, I'm a no sure. I'm a-think I better check with my son before I do that."

That took Neil by surprise. Of course he knew she had children—how else could that asshole—what the fuck was that kid's name? Lonnie, right? How else could boring Lonnie be her grandson? But this was the first he'd heard of any *son*. And he hadn't seen any pictures in her living room.

"Son?"

"Yes, my Vincent."

Okay. He'd have to play dumb here.

"I didn't know you had children."

"Just Vincent."

Wait—no daughter?

"Only one child?"

"Just a-my little Vincenzo. From my first husband."

Oh, yeah. Melinda had said she was "twice widowed."

"You . . . you never mentioned him."

"He's, um, a very private a-person. That's why I'm a-think I should check with him about mentioning my name. He might a-not—"

Suddenly the front passenger door flew open and a man slid into the seat. His dark gray porkpie hat didn't go with his half-zipped Yankees Windbreaker.

Neil stiffened in shock. "What the f—!"

"Uh-uh-uh!" the guy said, wagging his finger. "We got a lady present. Hey, Mrs. D." He waved but his hard brown eyes never left Neil. "How you doing?"

"Aldo? What a-you doing here?"

"Vinny's on his way. He asked me to stop by and see what was goin' down. Shouldn't be long till he gets here."

This guy was trying hard to be scary, but Neil wasn't buying. He leaned forward and got in his face.

"You can't come in here like this. We're on official business and—"

"Yeah? I hope for your sake that's true."

Before Neil could stop him, the guy—Aldo—reached over and yanked the key from the ignition.

"Hey! You can't do that!"

"I believe I just did."

Neil picked up his mobile phone. "I'm calling the police!"

"You do that."

He sat and stared at Neil.

The old lady reached from the back and patted the guy's shoulder, saying, "Aldo, it's okay. We just a-caught a thief at the bank."

He turned toward her. "Really, Mrs. D? I—"

"Why do you call her 'Mrs. D'? This is Mrs. Filardo."

He smiled at the old bat. "I known her since me and Vinny was kids, back when she was Mama Donato. She'll always be Mrs. D to me. Ain't that right?"

The old lady patted his arm again and smiled. "He's a-like a second son, Aldo is."

Shit!

"But let me get this straight," Aldo said. "You caught a crook at the bank? From here? From a parked car?"

"It's a-complicated."

"Oh, I'm sure it is." He turned back to Neil and pointed to the phone in Neil's hand. "It's nine-one-one, pal. What're you waiting for?"

Neil felt sweat flood his armpits. This guy had mob written all over him.

I should call his bluff and dial the cops. He'll probably take off running.

But then how to explain what he was doing parked here with this old lady? His fake bank inspector ID wouldn't pass with a cop—not for a second.

This looked like a no-win situation. Best to cut his losses and run.

"I've had enough of this," he said, reaching for the door handle.

Aldo grabbed his arm with one hand and pulled open his Windbreaker with the other, just enough to reveal the butt end of a pistol in a shoulder holster within.

"We wait for Vinny. He's gonna—"

"—wanna talk to you."

Julio was staring at Jack. "That guy that got in the car—name's Aldo or somethin'. I see him when he show up every once in a while to collect on Harry's vigorish. He's a Gambino. What they gotta do with this?"

Jack hadn't expected Aldo. But this was okay. He was holding the fort until Vinny arrived.

"You know the big guy who usually does the collections?"

"Vinny? The one with the donuts?"

"Right. Well, the old lady in that car with Zalesky is his mother."

Julio's eyes widened. "No shiiiiit! Is he crazy?"

"No, just clueless."

"How'd he get hooked up with her?"

"A little bird cheeped in his ear that she was a widow and loaded."

"You?"

Jack nodded.

"But her name's Filardo."

"She remarried after Mister Donato died. Mister Filardo died too."

"And that call you made—that was to . . ."

"Vinny."

"Jack, this is . . ." He grinned as he shook his head. *"Increíble!* How you get all this to work?"

"Guys like Zalesky make it easy. They think they're such hotshot, heavy players they can't imagine anyone playing them. I did some research, found a little old lady nobody should mess with, then dropped the bait in front of Zalesky. He jumped on it. Whatever happens after that is all on him."

"Hijo de puta—can't think of nothin' too bad."

"The real iffy part was Vinny's mama. If she told Zalesky she wasn't interested and to buzz off, the whole plan would've died aborning. But Zalesky is smooth. Once he got her on board, the only other variable was Vinny. If I couldn't reach him or he couldn't get here in time, Zalesky would get away with it—or at least think he had."

"What you mean?"

"You don't think a guy like Vinny Donuts is gonna let his mama get ripped off, do you? He'd turn the city upside down looking for Zalesky. And if somehow he couldn't find him, he'd get an anonymous call with a name and an address."

"You one sneaky bastard, Jack."

"Why, thank you. That's the nicest thing you've ever said to me."

"No, really, meng. I love it. I—"

A black Crown Vic screeched to a halt behind Zalesky's Dodge and the man himself jumped out.

Jack said, "Now things should get really interesting."

Aldo said, "Yo, Vinny!"

Neil turned in time to see his door swing open. He found himself looking up at a huge guy with a very angry face. Neil's bladder clenched. Vinny. He had Made Man written all over him.

He grabbed Neil's tie and shirtfront and yanked him half out of the car.

"Who the f—?" He ducked to look at the rear seat. "Hey, Ma. You okay?"

"I'm a-fine, but—"

"Great." Back to Neil. "Who the hell are you and what are you doing with my mother?"

"Vincent, it's all right," the lady said. "He's a-from the government."

"Yeah?" Vinny looked anything but convinced. "Let's see some ID."

Neil fumbled his ID folder from the breast pocket of his coat and handed it over.

"B-b-banking commission," he said, cursing his stutter and trembling hands. "Fraud investigation."

Vinny glanced at it, then tossed it over Neil's shoulder onto the front seat.

"What's this about fifty G's of my mother's dough?"

"Vincenzo! Let him a-go! You gonna get in trouble. We use it to catch a thief!"

He yanked Neil closer, till they were nose to nose. "Where is it?"

This was a nightmare. Neil was speechless, but not the old windbag.

"It's a-fine. It's in a-the trunk."

"Let's go see."

"I got the keys," Aldo said behind him.

Oh, no! Oh, no-no-no-no-no!

Vinny pulled him the rest of the way out of the car and hauled him around to the trunk. Aldo met them there and unlocked it. The lid sprang up to reveal the two cases.

Oh, Christ! I'm dead! I'm dead! I'm dead!

"See?" he said in a quavering voice. "Just a couple of valises."

"'Valises,' eh?" Vinny said in a menacing tone. "Aldo, ask my mother how many 'valises' she filled with cash."

Neil felt his knees turning to rubber. He needed a way out.

Aldo returned. "She says only one."

Neil looked up to find Vinny staring hard at him. "Only one, huh?" He shook Neil like a doll. "Open 'em. *Both* of 'em."

Neil's hands were trembling so bad he could barely get the little keys out of his pocket. Vinny stripped the tape from the locks, then stepped back to let Neil get to the cases. Instead, Neil spun and made a break for it. He got about two feet away before a hand grabbed the back of his collar and nearly yanked him off the ground.

"No way, asshole!" Vinny said. He turned him toward Aldo. "Convince him that was a bad idea."

Aldo smiled, and before Neil could react, he'd planted two pile-driver punches in his belly. Neil doubled over, struggling to breathe, choking back vomit. He felt the briefcase keys snatched from his fingers. Through tears of pain he saw Aldo unlocking them, flipping the lids . . .

"Well, well," Aldo said. "Looky here. Fifty G's apiece." He fanned through a stack from the old lady's case. "Looks like the real deal."

"Guy on the phone said only fifty," Vinny said.

Guy on the phone? What guy?

Aldo picked up a stack from Neil's case, started to fan, but stopped halfway through. "Uh-oh."

He showed Vinny the singles between the top and bottom C-notes.

Neil felt something warm and wet running down his left leg.

Aldo guffawed. "Aw, man! Vinny, he's pissin' himself!"

"L-look, guys. I can explain."

"No need," Vinny said in a low voice. "It's all clear as can be. Clear as crystal."

"I'm just helping out her grandson."

Vinny's face twisted. "Grandson? She ain't got no grandkids, son or otherwise."

No-no. That couldn't be.

"Sure! Name's Lonnie. Yeah, Lonnie. He wanted money to invest in some new high-tech—"

"That bullshit ain't gonna work!" Vinny said. "Ain't you listening? She ain't got no grandson named Lonnie or anything else."

Aldo was shaking his head, a disgusted look on his face. "Rippin' off a nice old lady like that? You lousy son of a bitch."

"I didn't know! I swear I didn't know!"

"Didn't know what? Didn't know she was an old lady? Or didn't know she had someone who'd find out?" Vinny shook his head. "Shit! If that guy hadn't called me, you'da got away with it!"

That *guy* again. Who was he talking about?

Before he could ask, Aldo delivered another hard shot to his gut.

As Neil doubled over in agony again, Vinny said, "Close up the cases and take 'em out."

As soon as Aldo had set them on the pavement, Vinny shoved Neil into the trunk.

"No!" he shouted. "No, you can't do this! You can't! Help! Somebody hel—!"

He heard a loud *crunch!* and an explosion of pain as Aldo's fist smashed into his nose. His vision blurred, lights danced, then the trunk slammed shut.

He kicked and screamed in the dark but knew it was no use.

. . .

Julio was bouncing around in his seat like a little kid.

"They got him! They got the hijo de puta! What you think they do to him?"

"Don't know," Jack said. "But it won't be nice."

Jack's buzz at seeing all the pieces he'd arranged fall into place was tempered by the realization that most likely no one would ever see Neil Zalesky again. Vinny Donuts probably subscribed to a philosophy similar to the Mikulskis': *Don't leave loose ends.* Then add to that, *Don't let anyone walk away from messing with your family, especially your mother.*

Zalesky played dirty tricks on his ex-wife—dirty enough to turn Julio homicidal. He made his living ripping off little old ladies, sucking off as much as he could, then disappearing. Pretty heinous. But did he deserve what Jack was pretty sure was coming?

He sighed. Not up to him. This being New York City, the good 'ol Big Apple, sooner or later Zalesky was destined to pick on the wrong little old lady. Jack had simply arranged for it to happen sooner.

Vinny couldn't decide who he was more pissed at— Mom or this two-bit asshole grifter.

He opened the Dodge's rear passenger door and helped his mother out.

"What's-a-that noise?"

The grifter's screams were muffled but his kicks against the trunk top made a real racket. Good thing she didn't hear too good.

"Something you wouldn't be hearing if you'd'a told me about this."

"How could I a-tell you? It was a-secret."

He turned to Aldo. "Do me a favor: Drive this piece of junk back to Canarsie?"

"Sure," Aldo said. "We gonna have some fun?"

"Yeah."

Fun for you, at least.

Vinny was too pissed at the moment to think of fun.

"I'll drop her off and meet you there."

As Aldo got behind the wheel of the Dodge, Vinny led Mom to his car and opened the rear door.

"I'm taking you home."

"But where's a-the bank man?"

"He's done for the day."

He slammed the door, carried the briefcases around to the other side, and put them on the backseat next to her.

"How come you got a-two?"

"I'll explain in a minute."

He moved his Vic far enough ahead so Aldo could back out the Dodge, then turned to face his mother.

"Okay, Mom. I want you to open that first briefcase, the one nearest you."

He watched her pop the locks and lift the lid.

" 'At's a-my money."

"Yeah? Check one of those stacks."

She did, and her jaw dropped. "Ones! Where's a-my money?"

"In the other case. The one you got there is the one he was going to give you back." He shook his head. Was she getting senile? "How could you fall for something like this?"

She got all teary as she rattled on how they'd done the same thing last week with twenty grand and he'd returned all the money to her, then convinced her to go for bigger stakes to catch the thief.

The oldest trick in the grifter book: Let the marks win—or at least not lose—in an early round to get them off guard, then hammer them. It worked at all levels, from three-card monte all the way up to the Big Store.

"It's okay, Mom. But just call me whenever someone you don't know wants money."

"What's a-going to happen to him?"

She wouldn't want to know, so . . .

"Aldo's gonna turn him in to the cops."

"Will I have to—?"

"We'll take care of everything. Don't worry, he won't bother you again."

That, at least, she could take to the bank.

"Ain't we gonna follow?" Julio said as Aldo drove off in Zalesky's Dodge.

Jack shook his head. "I don't think we should get any closer to Vinny and Aldo than we already have."

"Yeah." Julio leaned back. "You probably right."

He watched Julio. "Satisfied?"

He grinned. "*Muy satisfecho*. He won't be bothering Rosa no more."

And that meant that Julio would stay out of jail—no more itching to hunt down Zalesky and flatten his skull with a baseball bat. That had been Jack's whole reason for doing this.

Well, that and the pure satisfaction of working behind the scenes and playing the players. More than mere satisfaction—it left him totally buzzed.

"And he won't be buying The Spot either."

Julio's grin faded. "Yeah. But sooner or later somebody will."

"Why not you?"

"Yeah, right. We been through that."

"Let's take a drive."

"Where?"

"The Bronx, Jeeves."

"Jeeves?"

"Just drive."

5.   Despite the unseasonal warm spell, Kadir's thoughts were cold and troubled as he walked along Kennedy Boulevard toward the Ramallah Bakery.

Despite his awareness that Allah had spared him for a reason, Kadir had been avoiding the Al-Farooq Mosque and the refugee center since his trip to the morgue, preferring to stay in Jersey City. He and Hadya had barely spoken since their argument on Thursday. The tension in the apartment was almost unbearable. Even yesterday, though they had attended prayers at the Al-Salaam Mosque together, they might as well have been strangers on the walk to and from.

This had to stop. As the younger sister, her place was to come to him with apologies and make peace. Yet it was frustratingly obvious that Hadya thought she was in the right. He could almost appreciate why she would think that way. She simply had been learning another language. That was not so terrible in and of itself, but the fact that Hadya had chosen English signified a danger. He sensed an urge to assimilate. Assimilation risked being tainted by American ways, American beliefs. Americans allowed their women to dress as they pleased—nearly naked in the warm weather! American women went to college, drove cars, had careers.

He saw a group of a half dozen teenage boys and girls across the street, laughing, mingling, touching, all without supervision. Was that the way Hadya would raise her daughters?

Though both sexes were equal before the eyes of Allah, the Qur'an was very clear on a woman's place in the world: *Men have authority over women because Allah has made the one superior to the other, and because they spend their wealth to maintain them. Good women are obedient. As for those from whom you fear disobedi-*

ence, admonish them and send them to their beds apart, and beat them."

He had intended to intercept Hadya on her way home from work and talk some sense into her, but he'd seen no sign of her by the time he arrived at the Ramallah Bakery. He stopped before the window and admired the displays of *kanafeh, baklawa,* and blocks of *halawa.* Before he had come to America, his mouth would water at the sight of such delicacies. But after making them and sampling them day after day while working here, they no longer tempted him.

He stepped inside and approached the young woman behind the counter. He could have asked for Uncle Ferran but didn't want a harangue about coming back to work for him.

"I am Hadya's brother," he said in Arabic. "Is she around?"

She hesitated, then said, "Her shift ended. She is gone."

"I came from our apartment and did not pass her on the way."

"She mentioned she was going to the park to enjoy the weather."

"Lincoln Park?"

She shrugged. "She didn't say."

Kadir stepped back onto the sidewalk. She must have meant Lincoln Park—it was only a few blocks away. A few minutes later, as he crossed West Side Avenue into the park, he passed a familiar-looking young woman on the second bench. She had her head back and her eyes closed, soaking in the sun. And though she was wearing an abaya, her head was uncovered, allowing the breeze to ruffle her dark hair.

He froze. That was his sister! Hadya had her hijab loose around her neck, exposing her hair—in a public park!

As Kadir stood there, he saw a couple of young men

pass and look at her with what he could describe only as lust.

He wanted to attack them, wanted to attack her. Instead, he forced himself to turn and walk away. He could do nothing to her now, not in public, but she would be punished for the shame she had brought upon him and the rest of her family.

He would see to it that she suffered for this transgression. And soon.

6. The first place Jack checked was the bedroom closet.

"He had a briefcase full of cash in here last time."

They'd parked near Zalesky's apartment and, with Julio acting as a shield, Jack was quickly able to pick his way through the front door lock and into the building.

But no case in the closet this time.

"He no dummy," Julio said. "Last time all his money wound up in your pocket."

Though Jack doubted he'd find anything, he checked behind the bathroom molding anyway. He'd found about sixteen grand there last time, but came up empty this trip.

They moved to Zalesky's front room where Jack did a slow turn.

"Okay. You told me he used to brag to Rosa that he was pulling down six figures a year with his scams. Let's just say he inflated that real figure. Even if he doubled down on his brag, that's still fifty grand or so. Where is it?"

"Sure didn't spend it on this dump, meng."

Right. Zalesky's apartment was the opposite of lavish—like he thought of it as a place to sleep and little else.

"So he's got to keep his money somewhere. It's not legal, so he can't be banking it—banks have to report big deposits. He'll want it in a place where he won't have to explain how he got it."

Jack was in the same boat. He hid his cash in his apartment with his guns. But he'd scared Zalesky out of his previous hidey-hole. Where was the new one?

"Let's take this place apart," he said. "But softly. We don't want a neighbor to come a-knockin'."

Took them close to an hour to find no cash. But they did find a Chemical Bank checkbook and a safe deposit key.

Julio was flipping through the checkbook.

"Look like he pay his bills from here, but the hijo de puta got no balance."

"Well, if I had a checkbook I probably wouldn't keep one up to date either."

Moot point. Unlike Jack, Zalesky was a real, tax-paying citizen—one of the stubs was for the IRS—though he probably paid only a small fraction of what he'd owe if his income was legit.

The little safe deposit key, though . . . Jack assumed it belonged to a box in the same bank.

He held it up. "This has to be where he hides his stash."

"But how we get into it?"

"I could pretend to be Zalesky."

"What if they know him?"

Good question. But there had to be a way. He couldn't let whatever money Zalesky had hidden go to waste in that box.

"Well, we can't do anything before Monday anyway. Let's see what I can come up with."

7.   Neil had lost all track of time. It seemed like days since he'd been hauled out of the trunk of his car. He had no idea where he was. A garage of some kind, with car parts and tires and oil drums scattered about.

He'd feared the worst—some awful form of torture, like wiring his balls to an electric outlet or ripping off his fingernails. But none of that. The skinny guy, Aldo, he'd just stood him on his feet and faced him with raised fists.

"Come on, asshole," he'd said. "Take your best shot."

Turned out he'd really meant it. Neil tried to back off—he wasn't a fighter—but Aldo kept pushing him to take a swing. So Neil gave in. Who knew? He might land a lucky punch and be able to drive the fuck out of here.

No such luck. Aldo fought him fair and square but was too quick. Neil never laid a hand on him. Aldo, on the other hand, beat the shit out of him, to the point where he was unable to stand by the time Vinny arrived.

As they'd gagged him and tied him to a chair to keep him upright, he overheard Vinny tell one of his workers to yank the engine and transmission and gas tank from the Dodge. Neil didn't care what they did to his car as long as they let him live. Then they started to put more hurt on him and he began to wonder *when* he'd die rather than *if*.

Aldo did most of the work. He really seemed to get off on pounding someone with his fists. Vinny mostly watched and ate donuts, but every once in a while he'd pick up a crowbar and go to work. He broke Neil's knees and elbows. Neil screamed into his gag till his voice was gone, and still they kept it up.

Then one of Vinny's worker guys came in and said, "Look what we found."

A few seconds later Vinny yanked Neil's sagging head up by his hair and held something before his face.

"What the fuck is *this*?"

Neil could barely see through his swollen eyelids, but somewhere in the blur he made out a black box about the size of a cigarette pack and a wire with what looked like a microphone at the end.

"Your car was *wired*?" Vinny screamed. "You were recording my mother?"

Neil wanted to tell him no, that he knew nothing about it, but he was gagged and could only shake his head.

He couldn't say what happened after that, because everything went black.

Until now. Now he was back in his car, but not in the trunk. They'd tossed him on the floor between the front and rear seats where he lay in a pool of agony, in and out of consciousness. His pain-fogged brain could barely form a coherent thought, but he managed to wonder how many intact bones he had left. His hands didn't seem tied so he tried to remove his gag but his broken arms were useless.

He heard voices outside and then the engine started. Where were they taking him? What were their plans? Dump him in a ditch to freeze to death? That almost seemed better than what he was feeling now. No, it seemed definitely better.

Wait. That wasn't the Dodge engine—something much more heavy duty.

The car gave a violent jolt that shot a blaze of agony through every damaged cell in his body. It rose into the air, moved a few feet, then was dropped to land with another burst of agony.

Had the car stopped moving, or had he passed out and more time had passed? What now? What were they *doing*? If only he knew where he was.

Another heavy-duty engine roared to life, then another impact, gentler this time. He heard steel scream in protest. The windows shattered, showering him with glass confetti. He forced his swollen eyes open and saw the roof buckling toward him.

They were crushing the car!

He tried to scream but the gag muffled the pitiful attempt.

SUNDAY

1. Neil slowly became aware of a rocking sensation. He opened his eyes and saw nothing but darkness. He tried to move but the spikes of agony from everywhere in his body reminded him of the punishment he'd endured since this afternoon.

Since this afternoon . . . really? It seemed like an eternity. How had this happened? What had gone wrong? Better question: What had gone right?

He remembered Vinny telling him the old bat had no grandkids. If that was true, then who was the kid bitching about his cheap grandmother in The Main Event that afternoon? Neil was sure he'd said his name was Lonnie. But if he wasn't the Filardo broad's grandson, who was he?

And what was that tiny microphone Vinny had dangled in front of him? His car had been wired? How?

And something else Vinny said came back to him: *If that guy hadn't called me, you'da got away with it.*

Who'd called him? Who could have even known—?

Julio.

Shit!

Rosa knew about his scam line. She must have told her little brother. Had he put the kid in the bar up to it? No way. He wasn't smart enough. And even if he was, he was too hot-tempered to work a setup like that. It took patience, it took cool.

But how had he known the right moment to call? The wire?

Didn't matter. Had to be connected to Julio and Rosa somehow. They were the only ones who had anything to gain from all this. Julio was probably thinking he'd killed off a buyer for that crummy bar.

Wrong, motherfucker!

He'd get the money some other way. Better believe it. When he healed up, he'd be back, kicking ass and taking names.

And Rosa—did she think this would teach him some sort of lesson? Fuck no. Did she think he'd made her life miserable before? Just wait, bitch. Just wait.

And then he remembered something else—thrown in the back of his car, the roof coming down, glass shattering. They'd crushed his car with him in it!

He tried to lift his head but something held it down. Slowly he came to realize that he was hemmed in on all sides. They'd turned his car into a coffin, with him in it.

Which meant they thought he was dead. They'd probably dumped the car in a scrap yard and figured the rats and mice would dispose of his body.

And something else—the crushing had dislodged the gag from his mouth. He could yell for help.

He began doing just that, but the only sound he could manage was a faint, hoarse, high-pitched wail.

"Hey!" said a voice. "You hear that?"

Yes! Someone was out there! He was saved!

He loosed another pathetic wail.

"Holy shit! Yo, Vinny! Check this out!"

That voice sounded familiar. And he'd called to someone named Vinny—

Oh, shit! Oh, no!

"What?" said Vinny's voice.

"I heard something. I think the fucker's still alive!"

"I don't hear nothin'."

No way Neil was going to make another peep.

"I heard it. I swear."

Vinny's voice got closer. "Hey, asshole, you alive in there? If you are, I'll hand it to you: You're a class-A asshole, but you're a tough one. So if you can hear me, lemme tell you, I'm glad you're still alive. Because nothing's too bad for you, and now you're gonna drown. I hear that ain't a nice way to go."

Aldo laughed. "Yeah! You know what they say: Sleep with the fishes—and feed 'em too!"

With that the car tilted and began sliding downward. Neil heard a loud splash and then water swirled around him. It quickly engulfed him as his last breath bubbled out in a silent scream.

2. Jack and Julio maneuvered the round oak tabletop through the apartment doorway. Not terribly heavy, but its four-foot width made it awkward and unwieldy for one man. They leveled it over the paw-foot pedestal and Jack dropped to his knees to guide the holes in the underside onto the bolts jutting up from the pedestal.

"Thanks, man. I'll fasten it down later. Want a beer?"

Julio shook his head. "Nah."

"Come on. You're always buying me one."

Another head shake. "I pour the stuff all day."

"You don't mind if I . . . ?"

"Do it."

The first thing Jack had done upon moving in was to stick a six of Rolling Rock longnecks in the fridge. He grabbed one now, twisted the top, and took a pull as he returned to the front room.

"Gotta say it again, meng, this one shitty-looking table."

Jack had found it in a used furniture store down in

SoHo. The top was a scratched-up mess and someone had painted the whole thing a Chinese magenta.

"You know what this would have cost with a nice finish? Lots."

"It puts the *ugh* in ugly."

"As a kid I used to work for this guy named Mister Rosen in a store called USED."

"Used what?"

"Used anything. All secondhand stuff. I picked up a few things working for him. One of them was lock picking—because lots of times furniture would come in with locked drawers and the key was long gone. The other was an eye for quality old furniture. Not so much antiques, but good old stuff."

He dropped to one knee beside the table and motioned Julio to do the same.

"Check out the underside here. Hardly anybody ever paints that. See that wavy grain? That's golden oak. Mister Rosen showed me how to strip furniture down to the original wood. This'll clean up nicely."

He'd get to work on that soon.

"You need help?" Julio said as they rose again.

"Thanks, but I kind of like working with my hands."

"I owe you, Jack. You know, for Zalesky."

"Don't even think about it. I get off on that. But we're not done with him yet. We've got to figure a way to get into his safe deposit box."

"Too bad you can't just walk in with the key and say you're him."

Jack shook his head. "He's probably been in and out a bunch of times. Somebody might know him."

"We can get someone who looks like him."

Jack shook his head again. "I don't want a third party involved. Let's keep this just between the two of us. Besides, it would have been just his style to hit on one or more of the ladies."

Julio grinned. "Then they *really* remember him."

Just what Jack was afraid of.

"I'll think of something."

He hoped.

"I still owe you, meng."

"Well, then, if you feel that way, the best thing you can do for me is get working on helping Rico get set up in business."

Julio shook his head. "You got some kinda godfather thing going?"

"What do you mean?"

"I mean, like I owe you, this Rico guy's gonna owe you—"

"I owe Rico for his leg. I'm just evening up."

Julio gave a derisive snort. "You saved his sister! For that alone he owes you big-time. Now you set him up in business—"

"He's gonna think the money came from *you*, and he's gonna pay *you* back."

"Unless he's a real dumbass, he's gonna figure where the money's from, and so he'll owe you twice."

"Whatever. So anyway, how's that make me a godfather?"

"You keep up like this, pretty soon you have people all over town owing you favors. Like that mafia guy—what's his name? The one who talk funny."

"Don Corleone?"

"Yeah. Him."

Jack laughed. "Yeah right. Like that's gonna happen."

But he did prefer to be owed favors than owe them.

Julio had to take off for the bar, so Jack began looking for a spot in the new place to hide his cash and guns. He'd brought them uptown in a backpack he'd kept tightly strapped in place.

With the extra advance rent and security deposit on the apartment, plus the cash he'd given Julio to help

Rico, his money supply was dwindling. He was still more comfortable than he felt he had any right to be, but he needed to find an income stream. He'd have to work on that. But first he had to work on a way to get into Zalesky's safe deposit box.

He emptied his pockets and found a receipt from a one-hour photo place. He stared at it a moment, wondering where it had come from. Oh, right. Two weeks ago . . . taking shots of Zalesky's bank lady friend at that midtown pub. Well, with Zalesky out of the picture now, the bank lady didn't matter.

He crumpled the receipt and was about to toss it in the garbage when he remembered that Zalesky was in those shots too . . . from all angles . . .

He flattened out the receipt as an idea began to form.

3.   Jack noticed Cristin wince when he slung his arm over her shoulders. They were walking along Second Avenue on their way from a tapas-fest at Rioja, one of their regular feeding stations; a cold wind had risen as winter reasserted its hold on the city and Jack was trying to offer a little extra protection.

"What's wrong?"

"I'm a little sore there."

"Hurt your neck?"

"No."

She seemed hesitant—all the more reason to push.

"Well, why's it sore?"

"Just got a tattoo there."

"Tattoo? You?"

"Wasn't that the name of a Stones album when we were kids?"

"You're avoiding the question. Tattoo?"

"You've got something against them?"

"Well, I don't understand them. The stick-on kind you can wash off—fine. But permanent?" He shook his head. "I don't get it."

"What if it really means something to you?"

He shrugged. "Opinions change. Tastes change. I've seen amazingly ugly tats on people." One of the shirtless DDP guys flashed from his memory of Thursday afternoon. "Just last week I saw this guy—"

"The one who worked over your face?"

The bruises had turned a sickly yellow and were fading, but still pretty obvious. He'd given her a sketchy rundown of what had happened.

"Not sure. One of them, probably."

"You hang with strange people."

"I definitely don't hang with these guys. Anyway, he had this huge tattoo on the back of his shoulder—a black-and-white skull with Technicolor flames roaring from its eye sockets. I wouldn't want something like that on my *wall* for ten minutes, let alone on my *skin* where I'd be carrying it to my grave."

"*De gustibus* . . . right?"

"Yeah, of course. And it's his skin. But what gets me is that if he thinks that flaming skull is so cool, why place it where he can't see it? It's only where other people can see it, and only if he takes off his shirt." Jack shrugged, genuinely baffled. "I mean, what's the point?"

She smiled. "Well, if it's where he can't see it, he won't have to look at it if he decides later he hates it."

Jack laughed. "Yeah, there's that. Some of these ugly tats might have seemed like a good idea at the time—like when you were stoned or drunk—but in the light of day I'll bet there's been tons of times people have shuddered and said, *You mean I'm stuck with that the rest of my life?*"

"What if you could have van Gogh tattoo *Starry Night* across your back? Would you turn him down?"

"I'd send him to you."

"Me?"

"Yeah. If it's on *my* back, I can't see it unless I'm looking over my shoulder in a mirror. If it's on *your* back, I can sit and gaze in wonder. Might be even more wonderful across your front. Those hills could be—"

She hit him on the arm. "You're too damn practical. And how do you know I'd take my shirt off for you?"

He laughed. "That's never been much of a hurdle."

She laughed too—and hit him again.

When they reached her apartment she took off her coat, turned away from him, and lifted the back of her hair to reveal a strange symbol in black ink across her nape . . .

"Okay. What is that?"

"Ama-gi."

"Gesundheit. Really, what am I looking at? It looks like golf-tee Tinker Toys."

"It's Sumerian. I was leafing through a book in a client's apartment—"

"Making a house call?"

"He's head of an anthropology department and wanted to throw a retirement party for an old professor on the faculty. Anyway, he had this book with all these cuneiform symbols—"

"Cuneiform, eh?"

"The first writing—started out as pictograms and eventually evolved into—well, golf tees is a pretty good description. I used to reference them for dress designs."

"For your FIT assignments?"

"Right. Everyone thought they were sooo original—

like I'd come up with something totally new." She smiled. "I might have forgotten to mention that they came from the dawn of civilization."

"Why would you? I'm sure the copyright has lapsed."

"Anyway, they've fascinated me ever since. And when I saw that this means 'freed,' I had to have it."

"Why not just *'freed'*—in English, I mean?"

She dropped her hair and turned to him. "Because it's more than a word. It was the first written form of the concept of liberty. And it was originally a *tattoo*! The Sumerians tattooed it on freed slaves. The professor told me it's literally 'return to mother.' Isn't that cool?"

Jack didn't know much about slaves, but he'd heard many were abducted as children—he thought of Bonita— so it made a lot of sense.

He slipped his arms around her waist. "You want to return to your mother?"

"No. But the point is, I can if I want to, but I don't have to. I've declared myself free."

He kissed her forehead. "Of what?"

"Everything: people, conventions, society, laws."

"So you're an anarchist?"

"What's wrong with that?"

Jack shrugged. "I don't think much about politics."

All he knew about the two major parties was they talked different talk, but once in, they both seemed to walk the same walk.

"This isn't politics—this is personal."

"Okay, fine. But come on, Cristin. You've got to have *some* rules."

"I have tons of rules—for myself."

"What about everybody else?"

"Just one: Don't tread on me."

Jack nodded. "Yeah, I can go with that."

"And anarchy doesn't mean 'no rules,' by the way. It means 'no *rulers*.' Big difference, don't you think?"

"Absolutely." Sounded like Cristin had given this some real thought. He loved how she was so full of surprises. He ran his lips along the side of her throat. "Why the back of your neck?"

"Because then no one can see it."

"But neither can you. So what's the point?"

"The point is, *I* know it's there, because *I* put it there. And I didn't put it there to tell the world, I put it there to remind me to avoid all entanglements, foreign and domestic."

"You're taking George Washington personally?"

"Damn right. This is the sovereign state of Cristin."

"Correct me if I'm wrong, but I believe you've formed an alliance with the sovereign state of Jack."

"This is true. And it's an alliance that has lasted longer than any other in the history of Cristin. But that's because Jack is a like-minded state and we have no treaty."

He kissed the other side of her throat and heard her breath quicken.

"And that's important?"

"Yes, because there are no obligations."

"What about concessions?"

"Concessions are always on the table for discussion, but obligations are not. Once one sovereign state starts to think the other has obligations to it, the alliance is dissolved."

Jack felt a twinge of hurt. He understood exactly what she was saying, and mostly agreed. Yet . . . he felt obligations to her. After all the Sundays they'd spent together, didn't she feel any toward him?

She grabbed his belt buckle and began dragging him toward the bedroom.

"The alliance is about to engage in joint maneuvers."

"Joint?"

"Yours."

How could he refuse?

MONDAY

1. Since today was Hadya's day off, she was sleeping in. Kadir had held his tongue during the hours she had been home on Saturday and Sunday. That had been easier than he'd anticipated since, except for food and use of the bathroom, she'd confined herself to the bedroom. She kept her head uncovered, as was allowed at home among family members, and he found he could not take his eyes off her hair . . . the hair she had so brazenly exposed to the world.

After gathering the equipment he would use to punish her, he had set his alarm for early this morning. Now, awake and dressed, he prepared what he needed and silently entered her room. She lay on her side, her back to him, sound asleep.

Leaning on the headboard so as not to jostle the mattress, he reached across her and slapped a piece of duct tape across her mouth. As she started from sleep, he grabbed both her arms and pulled them behind her. Forcing her onto her stomach, he straddled her. As she lay kicking and screaming into the tape, he bound her wrists with more duct tape. When they were securely bound, he sat on her legs and wrapped her ankles and knees with more.

Then he turned her over and stared down at her. Her eyes were wide with terror and fury. At last he could vent his rage. But he kept his voice low so as not to disturb the neighbors.

"So . . . you wish to remove your hijab and go bareheaded? You are here less than two weeks and already you behave like an infidel? Well, remember, dear sister: There is always a price to pay for transgressions."

He plugged in the electric clippers he had bought and pressed the ON button. A buzz filled the room. She could not take her bulging eyes off it.

"I disown you, Hadya. You are no longer my sister. And after I am finished with you, you will *insist* on keeping your head covered—I guarantee it."

He grabbed a handful of her hair and began to shear it down to her scalp.

2. Jack picked up the developed photos he'd taken of Zalesky's gal pal. He smiled as he flipped through them. Though it hadn't been intentional, Zalesky was in every single one and, as he'd hoped, from varying angles.

He headed straight for the dojo and found Preston already there working out on the body-shaped standing bag. No makeup or costume today, just a simple white karategi tied with a white belt. Jack didn't know what level Preston had achieved but was sure it went way beyond white. Maybe he didn't like to advertise.

The three gym rats were absent, but the hanger-on was working out with a bo.

"Hey, Pres," Jack said, approaching. "You mentioned you knew a really good makeup guy."

He stopped beating up on the dummy, bowed to it, then turned to Jack. Close up Jack noticed he wasn't entirely without makeup. It looked like he'd penciled his eyebrows.

"Did I say 'really good'? I don't think so. I said 'genius.' Who wants to know—and shit, what happened to your face?"

Oh, yeah. The bruises. He wished to hell they'd fade completely. He was tired of explaining them.

"A disagreement."

"Not with those three—?"

"No. Different bunch."

"You should have called me."

"It was kind of a spur-of-the-moment thing. And yeah, I could've used your help, but everything's cool now. So about this makeup guy—"

"You want him to hide those bruises?"

"No. Does he hire out?"

Preston raised those eyebrows. "Really, he's not that type—"

"I didn't mean—"

"And I don't think he's *your* type. Besides, he's taken."

"I'm talking about doing a makeup job."

"On whom?"

Knowing it would launch a thousand double entendres, Jack dreaded giving the answer.

"Me."

"You look just fine—unless of course you want to go drag. Then you'll need a name. How about Dietta Pepsi?"

Jack ignored that. "I need to know if he can make me look like someone else."

Preston gave him an up-and-down. "Well, you're too thin for Boy George, and even Desiderio couldn't make you into RuPaul. I—"

Jack pulled out the photos. "This guy."

Pres took them and studied them, glancing up at Jack and then back. Finally he shook his head.

"I don't know. But if anyone can do it, Desiderio can. I'll ask him if he's game. What's your number?"

Last night had been the first Jack had spent in the new place, but he didn't have a phone yet.

"My phone won't be installed before Wednesday and this is kind of a rush thing. Give me yours and I'll call later and check."

Preston gave a seductive smile. "Jack, if this is all just an elaborate scheme to get my phone number, all you had to do was ask."

"Pres . . ."

"Okay, okay. But Desiderio doesn't work for nothing. This is his profession, his art. He'll expect to get paid."

Jack decided it was his turn, so he feigned a horrified expression. "*Laid?* Oh, no! Ain't gonna happen!"

Preston laughed. "Okay. I had that coming." He put his hands on his hips and cocked his head to the side. "Remember, I do the innuendo here. Step on my turf again and I'll put it in your endo. Got it?"

And there it was.

"Got it."

"Let me get you my card."

As he went over to his backpack, the hanger-on sidled up to Jack.

"Hey, thanks," he said.

Jack turned to him. "For what?"

"For holding me back." He nodded toward Preston. "No telling what he would have done to me."

"Yeah. That tanto would have royally pissed him off. And you shouldn't have needed anyone to hold you back from making three-against-one into four-against-one in the first place. Ever think of that?"

He looked sheepish. "I don't know what was going on in my head."

Jack knew: mob mentality. But he didn't feel like getting into that, so he opted for a cogent, "Yeah, well . . ."

"Anyway, thanks."

He hurried back to where he'd left his bo. Preston returned. A smile played about his lips as he handed Jack his card.

"I just want to make it clear: Desiderio will expect *payment*."

Jack shrugged. "I wouldn't have it any other way."

TUESDAY

1. Jack sat in the makeup chair before a light-rimmed mirror and stared at his unfamiliar reflection.

He'd called Preston last night and learned Desiderio's fee. Not unreasonable, so this morning Jack found himself in the cramped dressing room of an off-off-Broadway theater off Lafayette Street. Preston lounged somewhere in the shadows at the rear of the room while Desiderio fluttered around him, first on the left side, then on the right, then behind him looking over the top of Jack's head.

"Is Desiderio your real name?" Jack said.

"Of course not, dearie. It's a *nom de guerre*. But don't ask what my momma called me. I'll never tell."

His *S*'s were sibilant, his accent was pure upper Midwest, he wore thick eyeliner. And he was a makeover wiz.

The first thing he'd done was darken Jack's hair, then worked in some "product" and slicked it back. That done, he took a straight razor and changed Jack's hairline to match Zalesky's.

The photos Jack had taken were stuck up around the perimeter of the mirror. Desiderio touched a few in succession.

"He's swarthier than you."

"I think he might hit a tanning booth now and again."

"Easy enough to take care of." He grabbed Jack's chin and turned his head left and right. "His face is fuller too."

"Should I gobble some cheeseburgers?"

Preston's voice floated out of the shadows. "I've got something you can gobble."

"Do you mind, Pres?" Desiderio said over his shoulder. "Do you?" Turning back to Jack, "You brought one of his suits?"

"Sure did."

"We might have to pad you up a little if it needs filling out, but we definitely need to fill out your face."

From the shadows: "I've got—"

"Pres!"

And so it went . . .

2. Jack stepped through the door of The Spot and saw Julio behind the bar, cleaning glasses.

"Where's the no-good, lousy spic who runs this place?" he shouted.

Julio turned and his eyes went all goggle for a second, then he said, "Mierda! It can't be!"

Jack spread his arms to show off Zalesky's suit as he approached the bar.

"How do I look?"

"It's scary, meng. Who . . . how . . . ?"

"Long story. Think I'll pass?"

"Yeah. I do. I really do."

Jack believed him. And Julio knew Zalesky better than Jack ever would. His seal of approval gave Jack the confidence to take this to the next step.

"Then let's go."

"Where?"

"The bank. You're driving."

"I gotta open—"

"Screw opening. You'll open late today. Who're you worried about? Darren? What's he going to do—fire you? He doesn't have a buyer anymore, remember?"

"But—"

"All you have to do is stay with the car. If someone sees through this, I may need to make a hasty exit."

Julio shrugged and threw the towel into the sink. "Let's go."

3. While Julio idled across the street in Ralph, Jack entered the Chase branch on Westchester Avenue carrying one of Zalesky's briefcases. Instead of stepping up to a teller window, he went to the business area. When a redheaded woman looked up, he gave her his most confident smile.

"I'd like to enter my box," he said, handing her his key.

Oh, what Preston would do with that.

"Of course," she said. "May I see some identification?"

She didn't know him—what a relief.

Zalesky had left all his real ID in the apartment when he'd gone out in his bank inspector identity. Jack had borrowed it and he showed her that. She handed it back then went to another desk where she retrieved a set of keys. As he was following her to the rear he saw a young blonde look up from her desk and stare at him. Her lids narrowed.

Uh-oh. That look said *recognition*. He gave her a half smile and, on impulse, winked. She looked away, then back at him.

He moved on.

In the vault, the redhead used Zalesky's key and her own to open a little door in a wall of little doors, then slid out a long thin box and carried it to a tiny room where she placed it on a counter. Jack had seen this sort of thing in movies but never had participated in real life.

"Take your time," she said, handing him back his key. "Let me know when you're finished."

"Oh, can I ask a favor?" he said, pulling out Zalesky's checkbook. "Would you mind terribly looking up my balance? I'm afraid I've been a bit haphazard in my tallying."

The checkbook would give her the account number and keep her busy for a few minutes.

She smiled. "Of course."

As soon as she closed the door behind her, Jack lifted the lid on a beautiful array of stacks of bills of varying sizes and denominations, some with bank bands, some with rubber bands. He didn't bother counting—that could come later. He opened the briefcase, upended the box, and emptied it.

That done, he carried it back out to the vault area. But instead of the redhead, he saw the blonde approaching. She had one of those old-fashioned hourglass figures and walked with a natural sway. She seemed to be studying his face as she approached.

"Carol had to take a call," she said, still staring. "I'll finish up for her." She leaned closer. "Have you lost weight?"

Shit-shit-shit! She knows him.

He felt a fine layer of sweat break out all over his body.

"Well, yeah," he rasped, making his voice hoarse. "A little problem with the throat. Trouble swallowing. But I'll be fine." Had to get out of here—now-now-now. "Thanks for your help."

"I need your key," she said.

Oh, crap. Right.

He forced a smile. "Here you go."

Once the box was locked up in the wall again, he pocketed his key and turned toward the exit.

"Thanks again."

"Wait. Didn't you ask Carol for your balance?"

Yeah, he had, but he didn't care now. All he cared about was getting back into Ralph and buzzing back to Manhattan.

"That's okay. Some other time."

"But I have your checkbook at my desk."

A paranoid scenario ran through his head: Redheaded Carol was out there calling the police about someone impersonating a bank customer and the blonde had been sent in to delay him.

Following her, his heart picked up tempo as he considered his options: run, or stay and play?

As they exited the vault, the glass doors to the street beckoned. He was ready to bolt until he saw Carol, the redhead, looking perfectly relaxed as she talked to a customer at her desk.

He stuffed the paranoia back into its corner, discarded what he *supposed,* and considered what he *knew:* The only thing he knew for sure was that this blonde knew Zalesky.

Yet she hadn't said, *You're not Neil,* only that he had lost weight. That brought a little calm.

An inane *l'esprit de l'escalier* flitted through his head: Should have told her he wasn't feeling himself lately. But even if he'd thought of it then, he wouldn't have had the nerve to say it. He wasn't James Bond. He was Jack from Jersey.

Carol glanced up and gave Jack a little smile as he passed. Maybe this would turn out okay after all.

That decided it: Don't run. Keep playing the part.

He let the blonde lead him to her desk. He noticed a wood-and-brass nameplate: *Eve Stigall.* As she seated herself behind it, she indicated the free chair.

"Have a seat. No need to be tense."

He eased into the chair. Okay, he'd say it. "I'm not myself today."

She blinked, then laughed. "I'll say."

What was going on here?

"Here's your checkbook," she said, handing it to him. "The slip of paper inside indicates your balance at the moment.

Jack checked it: $1462.74.

"I assume you intend to make a withdrawal?"

Jack considered it. Fourteen hundred wasn't chicken feed, but just a fraction of what he'd emptied from the box. Still, no point in letting it rot in the account.

"Um, yes."

"How much?"

He shrugged. "All of it, I guess."

"That would close the account, which might not be a good idea."

"Why not?"

"Well, people here will wonder if you were dissatisfied with our service, if you were taking your business to another bank, and if there was anything we could do to change your mind. All sorts of questions."

Why was she telling him this?

"Well, I wouldn't want to upset anybody."

"Of course not." Her mouth took on a wry twist as she handed him a withdrawal slip. "As I'm sure you already know, this type of account requires a minimum deposit of one hundred dollars. The maximum you can withdraw today without closing it is thirteen hundred sixty-two dollars and seventy-four cents. I suggest you make it an even thirteen hundred."

Jack's mouth felt a little dry as he said, "No, let's make it thirteen hundred sixty-two dollars and seventy-four cents."

That wry smile again. "Your call."

Was this just plain, old-fashioned greed on his part?

He didn't think so—at least he didn't want to think so.

Jack didn't know if Neil Zalesky was alive or dead, but it didn't matter. He'd physically and mentally abused Julio's sister; he'd ripped off old folks by appealing to the best in them. One of the con man's shibboleths is that you can't cheat an honest man; with that in mind, the grifter uses the cupidity of ethically challenged individuals to dupe them—they get hoisted on the petard of their own greed.

Zalesky had gone the other way: he'd preyed on good folks' willingness to do the right thing, and in Jack's book that put him way down the ladder from the average swindler.

Cleaning him out was almost a matter of principle. It put an exclamation point on the end of the sentence.

Sanity insisted that he not risk the attention that would come with closing the account. Which meant Zalesky wouldn't be cleaned out, but damn close to it. Jack would have to settle for a period instead of an exclamation point.

"Just fill in the amount and sign it," she said. "I'll take care of the rest."

He complied—he'd practiced Zalesky's scrawl until he could manage a reasonable facsimile—and handed it to her, saying, "The service here is wonderful."

She smiled. "We live to serve."

He watched her rise and head for the teller area. Something way, way off about Ms. Stigall. He eyed those glass doors again. Tempting . . . he could simply walk out with his briefcase full of cash. He didn't need the thirteen hundred and change.

But he needed the closure.

She returned and handed him a legal-size envelope. Coins clinked within.

"I believe this concludes our business here today."

He rose, took the envelope, and shook her hand. "I believe it does. So nice to—" He cut himself off just before he said *meet you*. "To see you."

She stared at him. "You don't look yourself at all."

Oh, hell.

"I really must be going."

Through his tumbling thoughts he heard her mumble something about "serious."

"Pardon?"

Her eyes hardened. "I said, I hope it's serious."

They locked gazes for a second, and he knew that she knew something had happened to Zalesky—something not good—and also knew that she was glad.

He decided it best not to reply to that. He simply nodded and headed for those doors at a brisk walk. Outside he looked across the street but didn't see Ralph.

"What the—?"

At that second Julio pulled up to the curb. Jack hopped in.

"Get us moving. Go-go-go!"

As Julio eased onto Westchester Avenue, he said, "Cop came by and gave me a dirty look. Figured I better get moving. How'd it go?"

"Cleaned him out. Head for The Spot. We've got some counting to do."

As they rolled Jack thought about Eve Stigall. She'd known from the start—or very nearly—that he hadn't been Neil Zalesky. Yet not only had she kept mum, she'd steered Jack away from complications. What had happened between her and Zalesky? They had some kind of history and it obviously hadn't been happy.

Zalesky had left a tide of bad feelings and ill will in the wake of his life—exactly what Jack was trying to avoid in his own. In fact, Jack was trying to avoid any wake at all.

4. "Forty-eight thousand bucks," Julio said, staring at the pile of cash.

Jack started returning the stacks to the briefcase. "Forty-eight thousand, two hundred twenty-two and seventy-four cents, to be exact."

"What you gonna do with this?"

"No—the question is, what're *you* gonna do with it?"

"Me?"

"Yeah. It's your money."

"No, man. It's yours."

"What happened to 'meng'?"

"Seriously."

"I'm very serious."

"I can't take it."

Jack snapped the lid closed and pushed the briefcase across the table.

"I didn't do this for the money, Julio. And to tell you the truth, I didn't do it for you either. I did it for me."

Julio pushed it back.

"Right. So the money's yours."

Jack pushed back.

"I like The Spot. I like coming here. I like the way you run it. I want you to keep running it so I can keep coming here. And the only way I can see that happening is if you own it. So I didn't do this for you, I did it for me."

Julio started to push back but stopped.

"Hey, that's really twisted, meng."

He was back to *meng*—good sign.

Jack grinned. "Yeah, I know. It's my nature."

"It ain't enough."

"I got someone who'll loan you the rest."

Julio's turn to grin. "Oh, no. You not gonna pull the same game on me you pull on Rico." He shook his head. "I know you."

"And I know you know me." Jack raised his right hand. "This is legit. These guys'll lend you the dough—"

He laughed. "Who? Vinny and Aldo?"

"Speaking of which . . ." Jack tapped the case. "Vinny's due for a collection today, right?"

"Tuesday's his usual, yeah."

"Okay, today you dig into this briefcase and you hand him forty-four hundred—principal and vig—and say you're even, finished, through, *kaput*, *finis*."

"I can't—"

"Just listen for a fucking minute, will you! You've been paying Harry's vig with the first stash I lifted from Zalesky, so today—"

"Hey, wait. That never made sense to me until now."

"What?"

"Paying the Gambinos vig instead of just paying off Harry's loan. But since it was Zalesky's money, I let it go. But after Saturday I see what you were up to."

Jack shrugged. "I wanted to keep Vinny in sight till Zalesky made his move. Now we don't need him anymore."

"You one sneaky bastard, Jack."

Jack spread his hands. "I try. But listen, once the Gambinos are out of your hair, you will get an interest-free loan from my friends. They think they owe me a favor. This will make them feel less in debt."

He'd talked to Deacon Blue yesterday. They were fine with the loan—hell, they'd offered to give Jack the money, but Jack wanted everything aboveboard between Julio and him.

"How I pay them back?"

The Mikulskis did not want to be involved in collecting, didn't want to be in constant contact with any third party, so Jack had come up with a method.

"Every month you mail a money order to a PO box. They'll pick it up."

Julio looked dubious. "And if I miss or I'm late?"

"They'll kill you."

His eyes popped. "Wha—?"

"Kidding. Just send a note so they know what's going on—that you didn't forget and you're not stiffing them. They're not shylocks."

The Mikulskis wouldn't care if the loan was never repaid. As far as they were concerned, giving it to Julio was like giving it to Jack. But if Jack had learned anything in the months he'd known Julio, it was that the little man had big pride and didn't take handouts. He'd need to know he was repaying the loan.

What he wouldn't know was that Jack would be collecting the MOs and seeing to it they eventually reached the brothers.

Julio stared at him. "This is legit? This is for real?"

He raised his hand again. "Scout's honor."

"You were a Boy Scout?"

Jack snorted. "Well, no. But you get the idea."

Julio's throat worked and he blinked a couple of times. His voice was thick as he spoke. "I don't know what to say, man."

Meng had faded again.

"Best thing to say is, What're you havin'?"

Julio came around the table and stuck out his hand. "Thanks, Jack."

"No thanks necessary," he said as they shook. "And don't even think about a hug. Told you: I did it for me."

"Sure you did."

Without warning he grabbed Jack in a bear hug.

"No hug!"

"I'm a Rican! I can't help it!"

"And I'm an uptight white! Let go, goddammit!"

5.   "What's this?" Vinny said after he'd stepped into The Spot.

The little spic was out front instead of his usual place behind the bar. And three guys—two of the rummies who seemed to live here and another young guy who didn't look old enough to be in here in the first place and who Vinny didn't remember seeing before—sat at the table nearest the door.

"Witnesses," the spic said.

Vinny gave them a closer look. They seemed a bit edgy, but nobody looked like he was thinking of doing anything stupid.

Good thing too. He wasn't in the mood for any bullshit today. He was still royally pissed at that asshole—make that *dead* asshole, but Vinny was still pissed anyway—who'd tried to rip off Mom, and still ticked at her for not telling him what was going down. Add to that a pounding hangover headache and too little sleep—he and Aldo had done major damage to a bottle of grappa after bringing the trawler back—and the result was one fucking-A short fuse.

"For what?"

The spic pulled a roll of bills out of his shirt pocket and began counting C-notes onto the table into stacks of ten. When he had four piles, he looked up.

"That's four grand—that's the principal, right?"

It had been so long since anybody had mentioned principal that he had to think back to his meeting with Tony the Cannon. What had Tommy told him?

Thirty-nine ninety-three . . .

"Yeah. Right."

Four more hundreds hit the table.

"And here's the weekly vig. That closes us out, right?"

"Yeah."

Vinny didn't want to close out the loan, but what else could he say? Tony C liked to have money out there collecting vig instead of in his safe. Didn't care if the principal was ever paid off as long as the vig kept coming in. He always said, *Dough that ain't working for you ain't nothin' but fucking paper.* Vinny figured dough was dough, but he wasn't about to argue with his capo.

Tony's current rate was twelve percent a week, which meant he got his principal back in nine weeks. After that it was all gravy. Because Harry had been an old customer, he'd done him a favor by charging him only ten. Of course, nobody'd expected Harry to up and die, but he had, thanks to a little mishandling by Tommy Ten Thumbs. But things turned out okay, because even at the bargain rate, the vig had totaled many times the principal.

Vinny gathered up the bills, folded the stack in half, and shoved it all into the side pocket of his suit jacket.

"Nice doing business with you."

"What? No receipt?" the kid said.

"You a wiseass?"

The kid said, "He needs a receipt to prove he paid off the loan."

Was this guy on drugs?

"In your dreams." He looked around. "Anyone need a loan?"

The kid laughed and said, "In your dreams."

Vinny realized the wiseass punk had been pulling his chain, knowing he'd never get a receipt. He decided he didn't like him. Had half a mind to break one of his skinny arms.

That might make him feel better, but it'd only make his headache worse.

Fuck him.

He returned to the car and got behind the wheel. Aldo hadn't made it today—hungover worse than Vinny— and fucking Tommy had taken the backseat again, making Vinny look like his fucking driver. He passed the bills back over his shoulder.

"What's all this?" Tommy said.

"Paid off the loan."

"Shit. You couldn't do anything?"

Vinny felt his temper surge toward boiling. "What the fuck, Tommy, eh? What the fuck?"

"You coulda told him he couldn't pay it off until next month."

"Really? Well, why don't you fucking go back in there and tell him that? And then when Tony's business falls off because he's got this rep for making loans but not letting anyone pay them off, he ain't gonna be happy. And when word gets back to him that you're the one putting this new little twist on his game, what's he gonna do?"

Tommy sighed. "Guess you're right. Now we gotta go listen to the old fart, and you know goddamn well what he's gonna say."

Vinny started the car. "Oh, yeah."

6.   "Dough that ain't working for you ain't nothin' but fucking paper!" said Tony the Cannon Campisi as he slammed his fist on his desk.

Vinny fought to keep his eyes from rolling.

Tony added, "Might as well use it to wipe my skinny ass!"

"Ain't our fault," Tommy said.

Tony stubbed out one cigarette and lit a fresh one. "Business is off, guys. The games and ponies, they go up and down, we all know that. It's part of the flow. But loans are definitely down. Why? Don't make no sense. I mean, it's a fucking recession, ain't it? We should have people lined up out the door looking for loans, but they ain't there."

Tommy rubbed his hands together. "We hear the Genoveses have been getting busy in the loan area."

Vinny glanced at Tommy. Yeah, you'd know, wouldn't you? Who told you? Jimmy the Blond?

Tony C hadn't minded that they'd run some games for the Genoveses the other night. Or if he had, his cut had kept him from saying anything. It hadn't interfered with any Gambino operations, so no harm, no foul. But if they made a habit of it, and it affected the Gambino bottom line, things might get rough—rough as in don't count on seeing old age, or even next year.

Tony pounded his desk again. "The fucking Chin! Soon as the Chief goes inside, he starts making his moves."

Vincent "the Chin" Gigante, head of the Genovese family—Tony had a long-standing hate for the guy that went so far back everybody had forgotten why. Everybody except Tony the Cannon.

Vinny took a breath, hesitated, then decided to say something. "You think maybe twelve percent is too high?"

"Too high?" Tony shouted. This precipitated one of his ugly coughing fits. When he finally stopped, he glared at Vinny and said, "Are you outta your fucking mind?"

"I heard the Chin's people are charging ten. Don't know for sure, but—"

"And what am I supposed to do—start charging nine?"

"Just saying, boss."

Maybe just go back to ten, Vinny thought. Christ, if

the guy paid only the vig for ten weeks you had your money back and he still owed you the whole nut.

"Yeah? Well, here's what *I'm* sayin'. Ain't enough anymore you guys just go around collecting in this economic climate." He stopped and shook his head. "Hear what I just said? I said 'economic climate.' That's how bad things are. Things are so fucking bad I'm talking about the economic fucking climate. So I don't want you guys just collecting—" He looked around. "Where's Aldo?"

"He ain't feeling too good," Vinny said. "Something going 'round."

"Yeah, well, let him get sick on his own time. And when you see him, tell him what I'm telling you: You hear about someone needs money, you send him to me. Keep your ears open, beat the bushes a little, but nothin' obvious, you know? Don't want people thinking we need the business, even though we do."

"Got it," Tommy said.

Vinny had to ask. "And when they want to know the rate, we tell 'em what?"

For a second it looked like Tony was going to explode again, but instead he took a drag, exhaled a cloud, and said, "You tell 'em twelve fucking percent. I gotta preserve my price point. You hear that? I'm talking about my fucking *price point*. I coulda went to business school, coulda aced it, but I don't need no MBA to know this shit. I graduated from the school of hard knocks, and I learned that I can't look like I'm cavin' to them Genovese fucks. So you find a guy needs a loan, you say it's twelve percent, but tell him because you like him— whoever the fuck he is—you'll jew me down to ten as a special favor."

Vinny nodded in unison with Tommy. "You got it, boss."

Preserving my price point . . . What kinda bullshit is

that? Vinny thought as he was leaving. I'd go eight percent if it brought in the business.

Eight percent, even six percent—didn't Tony realize that was *per week*? Like printing money, f'Christ's sake.

This place needed an *Under New Management* sign.

THE IDES OF MARCH

FRIDAY, MARCH 15, 1991

1. When word came down from Tony the Cannon to meet at his store after midnight and come loaded for bear with tons of ammo, Vinny knew it could only mean trouble.

He arrived after Aldo and ahead of Tommy. When he saw the Colt .44 Magnum that had earned Tony Campisi his nickname sitting on his desk, he knew the trouble was going to be big.

He gave a mental shrug. It might mean more burials at sea, and that was not a bad thing.

"Okay," Tony rasped after Tommy arrived. "We're gonna make life miserable for Vinny the Chin."

"We talking hit?" Tommy said, looking nervous. His face was flushed and his eyes bright. Probably did a coupla lines before showing up.

"Yeah, but not on warm bodies. We're hittin' windows."

Tommy seemed relieved. Vinny didn't blame him. Warm bodies were known to shoot back. Windows, not so much.

"Lotta windows around. How we know which ones?"

Tony smiled, something he didn't do often, which was probably a good thing because his teeth were the same nicotine yellow as his fingertips.

"I got us a list. Soon as I heard them Genovese fucks was movin' in on the loans, I started doin' a little research.

Remember that, guys. That's what you do when you're in business: You research the competition."

For years now the feds had been cracking down on the windows racket, and probably thought they had it beat. All five families had had a hand in it to some degree. The Luccheses had grabbed the biggest share, and Junior Gotti had been up to his eyeballs in it, but they'd been mostly chased out. The Genovese family had managed to stay in, though, mainly because Benny Eggs Mangano had taken the fall for his boss, Vinny the Chin.

Vinny couldn't help admiring Gigante—and not because they shared the same first name. His crazy act of wandering around the Village in his bathrobe, looking lost and mumbling nonsense, had convinced the shrinks that he was "mentally unfit" to stand trial. Yeah, right. Plus he was smart about his family business. Unlike the Chief, who'd dressed sharp and held his meetings in the Ravenite Club for all to see, the Chin kept to the shadows, gave orders to a few close underbosses, and let them get their hands dirty.

So while all the other families were bailing out of the windows racket, the Chin stayed in. But instead of bilking the New York City Housing Authority, which was what had landed everyone in hot water, the Chin put private businesses in his sights.

He kept it simple. You find a guy with a window replacement crew who owes you or somebody money. You move in on him and take over. All of a sudden the customers on his list run into trouble with all sorts of window damage—damn kids!—and after a while it's costing them a fortune to replace them. The solution? You offer a contract that guarantees unlimited window repairs for a flat annual fee. After the contract is signed, the window damage stops. It's like a freaking miracle. You expand your customer base, and pretty soon you can fire your repair crew and just sit back and collect those annual fees.

A sweet deal, and the only thing that can mess it up is some clown coming along and busting up a ton of windows. Then you gotta deliver on your repair contract. But you ain't got no crew because you shitcanned them all so you wouldn't have to pay them for doing nothing. Now you gotta find workers and you gotta buy replacement windows and all of a sudden money's flying out the door instead of in. So you close up shop and disappear.

Yeah, you take the money and run, leaving the customers holding the bag—tough shit—but the downside for you is your sweet deal is dead, and an easy, low-maintenance income stream has dried up.

The Cannon's plan was obvious—the Genoveses were hurting his business, so he was gonna hurt theirs.

"All right, lissen up," he said. "Aldo grabbed us two cars. They're out back." He handed Tommy a sheet of paper. "You and Vinny take one and hit the places listed here. Aldo and I will go for the others."

"How thorough you want us to be?" Vinny said.

Tony hefted his Dirty Harry gun. "If you can see it from the street, I want it dead. Don't go tryin' to impress me by getting out and walking 'round the side or any shit like that. I won't be impressed at all if you get collared. In fact, I'll be royally pissed. So keep it simple, stupids: Drive up, stop, blast away, move on. Capisce?"

They nodded and let Tony lead the way out the back door. As promised, a couple of late-eighties sedans idled in the rear alley.

"Dibs on the moonroof," Tommy said, grinning like an idiot. "You drive."

He was jacked now. Shooting up storefronts was his idea of a good time. Better than plinking at the cars in the salvage lot, Vinny guessed.

Vinny didn't mind driving, though it was a tight fit behind the wheel of the Olds, even with the seat all the way back. He checked the addresses. The farthest were in Astoria—three on Steinway and two on Ditmars. Astoria was kind of a dead end, what with three sides taken up by water and LaGuardia. Probably best to start there and work their way back toward the store. That way, if anyone started chasing them, he'd have more options for escape routes.

The Van Wyck got them there in no time. Vinny ran Ditmars first, calling out the street numbers to Tommy who stood on the front seat and poked the upper half of his body through the moonroof to do his shooting: a Greek restaurant, a bagel shop, a kabob place, then two more restaurants on Steinway. Tommy laughed like a maniac the whole time.

Next was a used car dealer on Broadway in Long Island City. Tommy shattered the big showroom windows, then shot up a few cars on the way out.

"They weren't on the list," Vinny said.

"Call it my contribution to his detail guys."

And in that instant, Vinny figured a way to get Tommy out of his hair—or at least out of his salvage yard.

2.   After the *Salaat-ul-Jumma,* Kadir hurried away from the Al-Farooq Mosque with Sheikh Omar's stinging words echoing in his ears. He'd known the blind cleric couldn't see him, but Kadir could not escape the uncanny feeling that Sheikh Omar had been staring at him through those dark lenses as he'd preached about atoning for one's transgressions.

It sounded uncomfortably similar to what he had said to Hadya a few days ago as he'd shaved her bald. When he'd returned Monday night, she was gone, along with all her things. Good riddance.

But had *he* transgressed? He'd made a mistake, that was beyond doubt. He shouldn't have left the truck unattended. He had told no one, yet Sheikh Omar seemed to know. Could he hear the guilt in Kadir's voice? Of course he could. The flash of the exploding truck, the impact of the shock wave, the sight of the tattered bodies in the morgue haunted Kadir's sleep during the meager moments he found any. He was so filled with guilt, Sheikh Omar could probably *smell* it on him.

Yes, he had made a mistake, but when a mistake caused the deaths of twelve soldiers of God, it became a sin of unimaginable magnitude.

He hurried along Atlantic Avenue toward the East River. A sin of such enormity demanded atonement of equal magnitude. As he strode under the BQE overpass, with the afternoon traffic rumbling overhead, his goal came into view. Lower Manhattan rose across the river, and the two spires of evil soared above all the others, so close he felt he could reach out and knock them over with a blow from his fist.

He and Mahmoud had stood here before and dreamed of bringing down those towers and everyone in them. Now he held his palms toward Heaven and swore to Allah that he would not rest until he saw both towers lying in heaps of rubble.

3.   The tracking transmitter and remote trigger were taped to the doughy, off-white brick of C4. The detonator cap was inserted into the plastique. As a last step, Dane Bertel aligned the two wires of the cap and wrapped them in black electrician's tape. He always left them as the last step in arming a bomb; the tape prevented a random static charge or anything else from causing accidental detonation.

Yes, he knew the possibility was remote—perhaps beyond remote—but he firmly believed in Murphy's law and expended a good deal of thought and effort toward subverting it.

With the bomb ready for arming, he shoved it into the duffel he kept behind the front seat of his pickup. He would have replaced the one he'd used sooner but it had taken him longer than usual to obtain the C4.

In retrospect he regretted detonating the bomb last week for a number of reasons. Not for the loss of life—the world was better off without those dozen or so murderous, child-slaving Mohammedan crazies—but because he had not ended the life he'd intended to end. No one named Reggie—in fact, no American—had been listed among the dead.

The second reason was that the explosion tipped his hand a little more than he liked.

The Mohammedans wouldn't know. They thought of him as just another criminal in a degenerate country that didn't worship Allah. And for all intents and purposes, they were right. He broke laws left and right, and had committed mass murder last week. At least that was what the law would call it. He saw it as vermin extermination. But before the eyes of the law, he was indeed a criminal.

The country he was trying to save would put him on trial and seek a death sentence—or at the very least try to lock him away for the rest of his life.

Never happen. He'd die first.

No, the Mohammedans wouldn't suspect, but Jack would know. And that worried him some. Jack was no dummy. But then again, Jack was a criminal too. And he had as much regard for baby rapers as Dane. But just like everybody else, Jack had no appreciation of the threat posed by these wild-eyed Mohammedans, these so-called jihadists.

They preached worldwide Mohammedanism and the downfall of America. And it wasn't just rhetoric. That blind asshole, Sheikh Omar Abdel-Rahman, recorded his hate-America rants and had his trusty, sandal-licking minions sell the tapes. Dane had bought a few—he understood Arabic—and knew this guy wasn't just blowing smoke. He meant every word.

Nope, Jack was smart but he didn't see the big picture. Hell, hardly anybody saw the big picture. Most people saw a bunch of ragheaded zealots following a religion that kept them in the sixth century. And true, they produced no technology, but they didn't have to. They could afford to buy the latest and greatest, and they could adapt it to shove it up the asses of the folks who did make it, and keep shoving it until the shovee said *Allāhu Akbar*.

So Dane would have to put a little distance between Jack and himself. Too bad, because he liked the kid. But more than that, Jack showed real potential. He had a quick mind and an outlook that mixed outlaw mentality with a moral code. That kind came around only once in a blue moon. Too often the outlaws had no code, and just as often the moral types were too blindered by their code to make a distinction between the right thing and the legal thing.

Yeah, Jack had potential, but Dane had to keep his eye on the prize: Find indisputable proof that these were the most dangerous people on Earth, and then use that as a wake-up call—shove it in the face of all the assholes who thought he was crazy and make them do something about it before it was too late.

Crazy . . . He looked around the front room of his apartment with all the newspaper clippings and magazine pages and photos tacked to the wall. He'd seen his share of psycho apartments and this sure as hell looked like one. But displaying the bits and pieces at all times served an important function: He kept seeing something new and making fresh associations.

And those associations were leading him beyond jihad to something else. Something bigger, something more sinister, something so pervasive and so secret that he saw only wisps of its shadow.

He'd hinted at this to Jack, but just barely. He was already considered a paranoid nutcase in some quarters. To start talking about an ancient, ongoing überconspiracy was a one-way, nonstop ticket to a straitjacket.

So he had to keep quiet.

And vigilant.

Ever vigilant.

4. Hadya stared at herself in the mirror and ran a trembling hand over her shaven head. She still didn't quite believe it. How could he? Her own brother.

When she'd shown the other workers at the bakery, her friend Jala had offered to share her apartment. Hadya had jumped at the chance to be away from Kadir.

What had happened to her brother? He had been such a gentle soul back home. What had changed him so? It could only be his beloved Sheikh Omar and the hate he spewed. Kadir had fallen for it, every word. He was now determined to bring jihad to America.

Hadya could not allow that. She saw her future here and would not let madmen like her brother ruin it. She would keep a watchful eye on Kadir. And if she suspected that he was going to do something terrible, she would report him.

Yes. Her own brother.

But he was no longer her brother, was he? He had disowned her. And that left her free to stop him any way she could.

5. Jack stopped on the sidewalk and stared at the two new signs hanging outside The Spot—or what had formerly been called The Spot. The old sign above the windows was covered with a cloth that had been spray painted with *Julio's*. Under that hung a banner proclaiming the place *Under New Management*.

Jack had been wondering how the deal had gone this morning. No need to wonder any longer.

He stepped through the door and looked around. The place looked exactly the same. Julio stood behind the bar, Lou and Barney were in their usual places. A few of the regulars hung out at the tables. A guy Jack didn't recognize sat alone at a table against the rear wall.

"How about some truth in advertising out there?" Jack said as he approached the bar.

Julio looked up. "What you mean?"

"It's the same old management—nothing new about it in the least."

"Well, it's a new *owner*."

"Everybody's happy then?"

Julio grinned and started pouring a Rolling Rock. "When Zalesky don't show up—"

"Really?" Jack said, widening his eyes. "I wonder why not? He really seemed to want the place. Think he's okay?"

"Ain't got a clue. Maybe he had a, whatchacall, change of heart. Anyway, when I put that cash on the table, the deal was good as done."

"Congrats."

"Just some paperwork to go through, then a closing."

Julio slid the pint toward Jack, who took it and raised it high.

"To the new owner of—I almost said 'The Spot.' It's Julio's now. To Julio's. Julio's forever."

Lou said, "I'll drink to that," and he and Barney clinked glasses with Jack.

Jack took a hefty quaff and gestured toward the windows. "Now you can get rid of those damn ferns."

Julio stared at the hanging pots and their wilting inhabitants. "I think I keep them."

"Better water them, then," Barney said. "They look pretty damn thirsty."

"They look pretty damn dead," Lou said.

Jack took another sip. "I thought you hated them."

"I do, meng. Nita thought keeping them all green and shiny would bring in the yuppies. I'm figuring leaving them hanging in the windows all dead and dusty will keep 'em away."

"Might work," Jack said. "But I wouldn't count on it. People are weird."

"And yuppies are the weirdest," Lou said.

"We'll see," Julio said. "Meanwhile, I got someone I want you to meet."

"Who?"

"Friend of Rosa's."

Jack raised his hands. "Oh, no. No blind dates. Don't go trying that cupid thing. I'm doing just fine."

Julio made a face. "I look like Cupid? I'm talking 'bout a guy friend."

Lou slapped the bar. "Jack! I never would've guessed!"

"Yeah," Barney added. "Slipped right past my gaydar."

Julio ignored them and pointed toward the guy at the rear table. "He works with Rosa. She was telling me about this problem he's got."

"What kind of problem?" Jack said, suddenly wary. "You didn't tell her anything about . . ."

"No-no. The less she know about that the better."

"About what?" Barney said.

"Yeah," Lou said. "What're we missing?"

Those nosy coots had ears like bats.

Julio lowered his voice. "Something he can't go to the law about. He'll tell you about it."

"What's it got to do with me?"

"Sounds like something a sneaky guy like you might be able to fix. Who knows? You might have fun with it."

"Fun?"

"Hey, meng, I saw your face last Saturday. You was having *mucho* fun. And this guy's even willing to pay for your time."

"Fun and pay." Jack couldn't help smiling. "How can I say no?"

"He's back at your table. Come on—"

"*My* table?"

"Yeah. Your table. Nobody else sits there—unless they here to meet you. I don't care how crowded we get, if you ain't here, it stays empty." He pointed again toward the table. "Come on. I introduce you."

My own table, Jack thought as he fell in behind Julio. I knew I liked this place.

He finally had some sort of a life. He had friends. He had Cristin—well, as much as anyone could have Cristin. He had a cool apartment. With Rosa's friend here, he might be looking at a way to bring in a few bucks fixing problems, adjusting situations.

The last months had been totally crazy, but things seemed to be settling down now. He hoped they stay settled. He could do without surprises for a while.

6. Reggie shivered and turned his collar up against the wind as he limped through the Lower East Side along Allen Street. Not a great neighborhood, but Allen was a busy street and he was dressed like he belonged here, so no one paid him any mind. His knees were killing him. Some days they weren't so bad, some days they sucked. Today was a major suckage day.

But he'd had to get out of that little room. The walls were beginning to move in on him. Really, how long could you practice with your bow? And how long could you wait for some sign that the outside world knew you were still alive?

Yeah, neither the cold wind nor the pain bothered him nearly as much as not hearing from Drexler in a week. He didn't know what to make of that. His whole clinging-by-the-fingertips position with this Order was based on Drexler's hard-on for the guys who busted up the kid deal and stole the money. After last week's complicated setup to nab those guys turned out to be such a huge bust, had they given up? Were they simply gonna write off the three mil? Was that why he hadn't heard from anybody?

Or were they pissed at him? Did they think the fuckup was somehow his fault? That was all al-Thani had wanted to know as they were driving away from what was left of the truck and the Arabs it had been hauling. *How'd the bomb get there? Who could've put it there?*

Yeah, well, Reggie wanted to know too. That took planning. It had to. Unless they were dealing with a guy who just happens to ride around with a brick of C4— that was what the bomb squad had told the papers— rigged with a remote detonator on the offhand chance he might need it. What kind of nut job does that?

Had Drexler figured Reggie and Camel Boy had left

the truck unguarded? Hell, it had only been for a coupla minutes at that rest stop. How the fuck could someone rig a bomb in the time it had taken them to call in?

Whatever it was, the Order sure as hell had left him hanging. Like he was being shunned or something. At least they hadn't kicked him out of the place they'd given him. Not yet, anyway. But he was running out of money. If this kept up he'd have to get a job.

He shook his head. Me—working a fucking straight job.

That was like an insult.

He was coming up to Delancey Street, at a standstill as usual at this time, what with all the outbound traffic trying to get on the Williamsburg Bridge. Not that he cared. His plan was to reach Delancey, then turn around and walk back. He'd gotten some fresh air and exercise, got himself out of that tiny room for a while. That was all—

He froze, staring at the taxi crawling along directly in front of him. Reggie could see the passenger only in profile—the guy's attention was fixed straight ahead—but damn if he didn't look familiar. Who—?

A warning preceded recognition—*Don't let him see you.*

Reggie backed away and edged into a shadowed doorway. He peeked out for another look. Damn if that didn't look like Tony.

Impossible, of course. Tony was dead—killed in the Outer Banks house by Tim or one of his crew. Reggie still felt kinda bad about that. Tony had been a good guy but, hey, Reggie and Moose and Tim had been cooking up a gigundo omelet and Tony was one of the eggs that wound up broke. Too bad, but shit happened.

Then the guy glanced out his window and Reggie got a good look at his face full-on.

He slammed back against the shadowed door.

Tony! Holy shit! Tony's still alive!

But that couldn't be! Al-Thani had told him about Moose, who'd been found in the dunes with his head bashed in, and another guy done execution style. Reggie had figured Tim had done both of them—Moose because Tim had been pissed at him, and Tony because Reggie had neglected to call in once the shooting began up north.

While Reggie had been recovering from his knee surgery, he'd read everything he could find on the Duck murders, as they were called at the time. The guy killed execution style had been identified as Tony Zahler. Reggie had never known his last name, but the first names matched. And that's the way Tim would do it: two quick ones to the head.

So what was the dead guy doing alive and well in a New York City cab?

Had to tell Drexler. This could change everything. This could put Reggie's name back in the "Needed" column. Because this could mean Tony was behind the hijacking.

Tony . . . alive! This changed *everything*.

www.repairmanjack.com

Coming soon . . .

All debts will be paid, all accounts settled in

FEAR CITY

the final volume of The Early Years Trilogy

THE SECRET HISTORY OF THE WORLD

The preponderance of my work deals with a history of the world that remains undiscovered, unexplored, and unknown to most of humanity. Some of this secret history has been revealed in the Adversary Cycle, some in the Repairman Jack novels, and bits and pieces in other, seemingly unconnected works. Taken together, even these millions of words barely scratch the surface of what has been transpiring behind the scenes, hidden from the workaday world. I've listed them below in chronological order.

Note: "Year Zero" is the end of civilization as we know it; "Year Zero Minus One" is the year preceding it, etc.

The Past
   "Demonsong" (prehistory)
   "Aryans and Absinthe"** (1923–1924)
   Black Wind (1926–1945)
   The Keep (1941)
   Reborn (February–March 1968)
   "Dat-tay-vao"*** (March 1968)
   Jack: Secret Histories (1983)
   Jack: Secret Circles (1983)
   Jack: Secret Vengeance (1983)
   "Faces"* (1988)
   Cold City (1990)
   Dark City (1991)

Year Zero Minus Three
   Sibs (February)
   The Tomb (summer)
   "The Barrens"* (ends in September)

"A Day in the Life"* (October)
"The Long Way Home"****
Legacies (December)

Year Zero Minus Two
"Interlude at Duane's"** (April)
Conspiracies (April) (includes "Home Repairs")
All the Rage (May) (includes "The Last Rakosh")
Hosts (June)
The Haunted Air (August)
Gateways (September)
Crisscross (November)
Infernal (December)

Year Zero Minus One
Harbingers (January)
Bloodline (April)
By the Sword (May)
Ground Zero (July)
The Touch (ends in August)
The Peabody-Ozymandias Traveling Circus & Oddity Emporium (ends in September)
"Tenants"*

Year Zero
"Pelts"*
Reprisal (ends in February)
Fatal Error (February) (includes "The Wringer")
The Dark at the End (March)
Nightworld (May)

---

* available in *The Barrens and Others*
** available in *Aftershock & Others*
*** available in the 2009 reissue of *The Touch*
**** available in *Quick Fixes*

Turn the page for a preview of

FEAR CITY

F. PAUL WILSON

Available in November 2014 from
Tom Doherty Associates

TOR® A TOR BOOK

Copyright © 2014 by F. Paul Wilson

TUESDAY

FEBRUARY 16, 1993

1. "Is this the Shadow?" Jack said, holding up the cellophane envelope. "I mean, *the* Shadow?"

The sixtyish guy behind the counter—lank hair, three-day stubble, ratty brown cardigan—looked annoyed as he brought it close to his smeared glasses and squinted at the label. Jack wondered how he saw anything through them.

"If it says 'genuine glow in the dark Shadow ring,' which it does, then that's what it is."

Attracted by the BACK-DATE MAGAZINES sign, Jack had wandered into this narrow, coffin-sized store off Times Square. The place seemed to specialize in *Life* magazine and had moldy issues piled to the ceiling. Jack had been curious to see if the place stocked any old pulps. It did, but only a few, and those had disconcerting titles like *Ranch Romances* and *Fifteen Love Stories*. None of the *Black Mask* types he was hunting for. But tucked in among the yellowed, flaking issues he'd found the ring.

The white plastic body was shaped like the Shadow on each side—Jack could even make out a .45 Colt semi-auto in one hand—but the stone set in the top was bright blue and shaped like Gibraltar.

"But this looks nothing like the Shadow's girasol ring."

The guy stared at him. "Do you even know what a girasol is?"

"Fire opal."

This seemed to take him by surprise. "Okay. Point for you. What are you—eighteen?"

Jack didn't react. He got this all the time. "You're half a dozen short."

"Coulda fooled me. But still a kid. How does a twenty-four-year old like you know about the Shadow's girasol ring?"

"Read a few old issues."

"That's the pulp Shadow. The character started on radio, sponsored by a company called Blue Coal. That blue plastic 'stone' there is supposed to be a chunk of blue coal."

Jack was thinking it was just about the neatest thing he'd seen in a long time.

"And it glows in the dark too?"

"That's what it says. Never tested it."

"How much?"

"Twenty bucks."

"What?"

"That'll be a bargain next year after the movie comes out."

"What movie?"

"*The Shadow.* Gonna star Alec Baldwin, I hear."

Jack remembered him from *The Hunt for Red October.* Yeah, he had the look for the Lamont Cranston part.

"So if I'm tired of it next year you'll buy it back for more?"

"Can't promise that. Can't even promise I'll be here, what with Disney moving in."

News to Jack.

"Disney? Here?"

"Word is they're negotiating a ninety-nine-year lease on the Amsterdam."

"Donald Duck on the Deuce? No way."

"Everybody's scared shitless because it'll be proof that the Times Square cleanup every mayor since La-Guardia's been talking about is gonna happen, and you know what that means."

Jack pushed aside a vision of Minnie Mouse in hot pants saying "Hiya, sailor."

"What?"

"Rents through the roof. Guys like me forced out, moving over to Hell's Kitchen or farther downtown or just closing up and walking away."

"Oh, no! Where will people go for their copies of *Ranch Romances*?"

His eyes narrowed behind the grimy lenses. "You a wise ass?"

Jack could see the guy was genuinely worried. He thought about boxing up and moving all those copies of *Life* and regretted the remark.

"Sometimes the mouth runs ahead of the brain."

"People get in trouble that way."

"Tell me about it."

He forked over a Jackson. The guy slipped it into his pocket and didn't ask for sales tax. Fine.

Jack walked out with his treasure and slipped it onto his pinky finger. He ambled east toward Times Square, thinking not of the Shadow but of Disney instead.

What he remembered most about Disney World from the couple of times his folks had taken him there during the seventies was how clean it had been. Could that happen here? Times Square was anything but clean, and 42nd Street even less so. But grime and kitsch and porn and fringe people were part of the ambiance. Take that away and replace it with a bunch of high-end chain stores and what did you have? You had a freaking mall. Might as well move back to Jersey.

As he crossed Duffy Square and headed up Seventh Avenue, he realized the writing had been on the wall for a couple of years now, ever since the state started buying up properties along the Deuce, especially the old theaters.

Plus ça change . . . ?

Jack doubted it.

If the magazine guy was right about the Amsterdam, then change was sure as hell coming and, as far as Jack was concerned, not for the better. Well, better if you were a landlord, but no way for a small businessman. Things would not, as the saying went, stay the same. All the quirky little stores and all the quirky people who frequented them and all the quirky people who ran them were going to go the way of the Neanderthals.

His growing dark mood about the end of an era was blown away by the sight of a familiar face trying to hail a cab across the street from the Winter Garden. She was talking on a cellular phone as she waved her arm.

"Cristin?"

She turned and, for an instant, looked not-so-pleasantly surprised. Then she smiled. "Jack! How nice to see you!"

They shared a quick, slightly awkward hug.

He pointed to her phone—one of the new smaller versions. Unlike the older brick-size models with the big antenna, these could fit in a pocket. He noticed NOKIA under the oblong screen.

"Up with the latest technology, I see."

"I looove this thing! It's made my life so easy. No more looking for a pay phone."

He gave her a lopsided grin and cocked his head toward the Winter Garden marquee. "Going to see *Cats*?"

"Not likely."

Their fling thing had lasted two years and during that whole period the only times they'd been to a theater was to see Penn & Teller. Cristin had ended it. She hadn't called it quits, per se, more like weaned them off each other. They used to get together every Sunday—every single Sunday—but last fall she'd started begging off with increasingly lame excuses until Jack got the message.

She may have engineered the actual parting, but Jack had been the reason. They'd gone into the relationship with the understanding that they'd get together one day a week and be friends with benefits, nothing more. Cristin had been very strict about not wanting strings and Jack had been all for it. At least at first. Along the way he became attached and started wanting more. But Cristin wasn't looking for more. She liked things just the way they were and wouldn't bend.

Jack had suffered through the process of attenuation, but after clearing the air at an official breakup lunch between Christmas and New Year's, they'd parted friends.

Seeing Cristin again for the first time in weeks made him realize he was still carrying a torch for her.

"You've let your hair grow," he said.

"A little."

She had a roundish face, dark hair, blue eyes, and a bright smile that always made him want to smile too. She wore her fur-lined raincoat.

"Can I see?"

"What?"

"The *ama-gi.*"

"You still getting off on that?"

"I don't know about getting off . . ."

She rolled her eyes, did a quick turn, and lifted her hair. She had one tattoo and it decorated her nape: a Sumerian symbol known as *ama-gi.*

He caught the briefest glimpse, and then she dropped her hair.

"I was heading for a late lunch . . ." he began.

"Oh, I'd love to, Jack, but I've got to get down to FIT. I have a class."

Years ago she'd dropped out of the Fashion Institute to work full time for an event planning operation called Celebrations. The job kept her hopping all over the city, but she still wanted her degree and took one course a semester to keep herself moving toward it.

"Tomorrow then? Or Thursday?"

He hoped he didn't sound desperate. He didn't *feel* desperate . . . he simply wanted to spend a little time with her.

She gave him a long look. "Just lunch?"

"Two old friends from high school sharing food and small talk."

She smiled. "That sounds great. Dutch, right?"

"Of course."

She'd always insisted on paying her share and, since Jack wasn't exactly flush these days, that was a good thing. Cristin, on the other hand, made excellent money planning events.

But where to eat?

Apparently she already had an idea. "I found a cool little French place on East Sixty-first called Le Pistou."

Jack made a face. "Really? What's choice number two?"

"But you like French."

"I do." He could eat just about anything, even snails. "But I don't know if I could eat at a place called Piss Stew."

"It's vegetable soup."

He held up his hands. "Stop. You're only making it worse."

"You'll never change," she said through a laugh. "Thursday's good. Meet there noonish?"

"Deal."

He hailed her a cab and one pulled over right away.

"But just for lunch," she said as he held the door for her.

"Of course. We broke up, remember?"

"I do. But you don't know why."

That took him by surprise. "I thought it was because I was getting too attached."

"No. I was."

She gave him a quick kiss on the cheek then slipped into the cab. He shook his head as he watched it weave down Seventh.

Cristin, Cristin, Cristin . . .

Despite her paranoia about strings, she seemed happy with where she was in her life. He didn't know anybody else like that. That didn't mean she was going to stay put. He knew she was three years into a five-year plan that involved socking away every extra cent for now and eventually opening her own boutique to sell her original designs.

She was also happy with *who* she was. Jack wondered what that felt like.

He'd read something from Wilde last year and his brain had attached it to Cristin: *Most people are other people. Their thoughts are someone else's opinions, their lives a mimicry, their passions a quotation.* Not because Wilde had been describing Cristin, but because it was so *not* Cristin. He didn't know anyone who thought like Cristin. She danced to her own tune and to hell with what everyone else was playing.

He missed her.

When her cab disappeared into the traffic crush he turned and continued his uptown ramble.

Okay, the week was looking better, even if it involved a French restaurant in the East Sixties. How bad could lunch be? Twenty bucks apiece? Thirty?

Yeah, his resources had dwindled. Perhaps he'd been too generous in his flush days. He didn't regret it, though. He lived a simple life. His two major expenses were rents: on his apartment and on the garage space for Ralph. Other than that, he lived on junk food and beer.

His fix-it business hadn't exactly taken off. He collected a fee now and again, but the jobs were sporadic. Nothing he could count on. So he'd been supplementing his income as a waiter in a hole-in-the-wall West Village trattoria that paid him under the table. Perhaps "paid" was a euphemism—a teeny fraction of minimum wage—but the tips were good. Everybody had heard Dylan's "Positively 4th Street" and all the tourists flocked to West 4th when they visited the Village. Trattoria Villagio waited there to provide drinks and light fare when they took a break from prowling the specialty shops.

He checked his watch. Lots of time to kill before meeting a prospective customer at Julio's. Maybe he'd grab a Whopper and train over to Brooklyn to check on an investment.

F. PAUL WILSON

TOR

Award-winning authors
Compelling stories

Please join us at the website
below for more information
about this author and other great
Tor selections, and to sign up for
our monthly newsletter!

www.tor-forge.com